YOUTH

E.S. Higgins

For mum.

In playful oceans where waves roam,
Forests full of trees on beds made of stone.
Over sea and under sky
The purpose of life is to live and die.
By and by we come and go
Towards the edge of night and morning glow.
All things rise just to set again;
Most things in life are just pretend.
What's real can't be seen until it's too late,
And that's why in death we celebrate.
What life was, now it's gone,
In laughter, tears and in song.
Of who was who and what it was to be;
The losses in life are what make it poetry.

youth.

Prologue

The universe is made of waves. Light, heat and sound. All of them come in waves. Life moves in waves that roll by as little moments that come and go. And in their wake, all that's left are memories that ripple faintly across the ocean of our minds. There are waves of swell that ripple through the ocean too. They form lines when they come close to shore before they crash against the sand. There aren't many things more beautiful in life than a breaking wave. The feeling, the sound, and the pull and push of water. But above all that is the feeling of catching and riding a wave. It's like you're dancing with the universe.

There are no words to properly describe the feeling, and all the descriptions in this story are just vain attempts to capture a shadow of its beauty.

There's freedom in the ocean. There's light, and dark. There's a great stillness too, but one that contradicts itself in its perpetual motion. It's where the sun rises and where it falls, depending on where you're looking from. It's where life started and, ultimately, where it ends. It's in this push and pull that the universe finds balance, and we are all somehow, by some miracle, standing at the edge of it all.

1

It was early in the morning and the sun was just about to rise from the depths of the ocean. The birds were up and singing and the air had that fresh chill to it that smelled of dew and wet grass. The trees were of the dry, rugged variety spread across the east coast of Australia: bottlebrush and gum trees, and spinifex grass. Waves crashed and exploded at the base of a steep cliff, and the beach behind it had almost been swallowed whole by the rising sea.

Three boys wearing black neoprene wetsuits were running through the darkness with their surfboards. They were running partly because they were cold, but also because they could hear the rumble of waves, like thunder in the early morning stillness. All three had checked the forecast the night before, and every website they looked at predicted the same thing – the swell of the decade.

They were running as fast as they could. Above anything else, surfing a swell like this could only mean one thing: respect. All three of them were eager to prove themselves to the older surfers in the area. But when they got a glimpse of the ocean, they stopped.

It was like nothing they'd ever seen before. In the darkness of the morning it looked as though there were mountains rising and falling on the horizon, and all they could hear over the birds was the deep, rolling drum of tumbling giants.

All of them were thinking the same thing, but none of them said anything. There was no way anyone, not even fully grown adults would have a chance surfing a wave like that. It was too steep, too heavy, too fast. It wasn't a wave so much as a giant mess of swell and a current that looked like guaranteed death.

Jenno was 14 years old and the youngest of the three. After a long moment of silence, he dropped his shoulders. "Fuck that, I'm not gonna go and kill myself…"

Jimmy, the second eldest at 15 nodded in agreement. "Yeah, fuck that…"

Ratty was 16, and the eldest of the three. He shook his head; he didn't like the look of it either, but out of the three of them, he was the most desperate to prove himself to the older boys who surfed the wave. "As if, you pussies! There's a couple makeable ones on the shoulder, for sure…"

"Fuck off… if I paddle out there I'm never coming back in again!" said Jenno.

"Fuck it, even if you two don't come I'm still gonna go it…" said Ratty, determined.

Jimmy and Jenno looked at one another; they knew there was no talking Ratty out of it.

"Alright, well, I'm gonna watch from the shore," said Jenno. He hated himself for not paddling out, but he couldn't bring himself to do it.

He was scared for Ratty as well. Normally even the older boys would be out surfing by now, but no one was in the water. A few cars had pulled up in the carpark to check it out, but all of them ended up pulling off again in search of a wave that was a little more hospitable.

Ratty pulled his wetsuit up over his head and zipped it.

"Wish me luck, pussies!" he said to Jimmy and Jenno, before picking up his board and running down towards the sand.

"That kid's an absolute nutcase," said Jenno.

Jimmy nodded. "Yeah, I just hope he doesn't get himself killed…"

Although Ratty, Jimmy and Jenno were spread apart by a few years, they were inseparable. They'd surfed together almost every day since they could remember, and all of them lived within walking distance from one another. They went to the same school, surfed the same beach and all of them had the same dream every kid growing up surfing does – to be a professional surfer. Ratty was the best surfer out of all of them. He had an understanding of the ocean far beyond his years. The way he surfed was calculated and stylish. It was an unmistakeable style, one that looked simple and effortless. He found himself in positions no one else his age could. He was bold, confident, agile and knew how to flow on a wave, so much so that even the older surfers started to take notice, and his name was starting to be mentioned at the local board-shapers' places as a prospect for the next sponsored surfer from the area.

It was looking likely that he would do it too. The following week there was a qualifying competition for the local circuit. Ratty had signed himself up and had been training hard for the last couple of months. There was talk of him being good enough to compete professionally one day.

Jimmy and Jenno followed Ratty down to the beach. They found him standing in silence, peering out to sea intently. It was still too dark to paddle out, but as Ratty watched the outline of the waves and heard them detonating on the sandbar ahead, he began to lose confidence in himself. The sea had reclaimed much of the beach; all that was left of it were the dunes that they stood on. Enormous lines of swell exploded at the base of the northern headland, sending an avalanche of spray and white wash that looked and sounded powerful enough to swallow whole anything that stood in its way.

"Are you sure you wanna surf?" Jenno asked Ratty; there was a note of concern in his voice.

"Yeah, it'll be sweet," said Ratty, trying his best to keep his tone steady.

A set of headlights floated through the carpark in the early morning light. They belonged to an older lifeguard called Pat. The boys didn't know him well; he kept to himself mostly and performed his duties with an almost ceremonial seriousness. He was quiet and humourless, and spent most of his days atop the lifeguard tower in solitude. The other, younger lifeguards left him alone, mostly, too busy checking out every girl who walked by to be bothered anyways. Trailing behind his car Pat towed a sleek-looking jet ski, a lifesaving tool that was only deployed in the most serious of circumstances. He peered out into the violent sea and *hmph*ed to himself. This would be an easy day.

When there was enough light to see well enough, Ratty took a deep breath and grabbed his board. He looked back at Jimmy and Jenno and smiled. "Fark, one of you grab a camera! I want a new profile picture at least…"

With that, he turned and sprinted toward the water. He dove in on his board and with the momentum started paddling as hard as he could. He knew he had a small window in between the set waves where he could make it out the back without copping a big one on the head.

The conditions were even worse than they looked from the beach. The lagoon that flowed through all the industrial estates ended at this beach, and it had overflowed during the storm in the night. Putrid brown water rushed and swirled all over the place, creating clouds of strange-looking yellow foam, and bits of rubbish and water bottles floated past.

It was for good reason no one else was out.

Ratty thought to turn back. He knew in his heart he had no chance surfing these waves, but the thought of going back without catching anything in front of Jenno and Jimmy was too much for his pride.

His heart was pounding, and every time he looked out towards the horizon his stomach dropped; he knew there were some big ones coming any moment.

Just as he made it out back, a set of three waves appeared on the horizon. They were some of the smallest ones they had seen so far, but still much larger than any wave that he had ever surfed before. He paddled over the first two, but before the third one passed him he turned around and paddled for it as hard as he could.

Jenno and Jimmy grabbed hold of each other in disbelief.

"Fuck off… No way he's gonna make that!" said Jenno, with bated breath.

Ratty paddled furiously, and at the last moment before the wave picked him up he stood up on his board and airdropped down the face of the wave. He closed his eyes in anticipation, and as he dropped he felt butterflies in his stomach. But he landed perfectly at the bottom and somehow managed to stay on his board. He felt fear at first as he dropped, then surprise when he made it to the bottom and steadied himself, and finally joy as he raced across the wave. Wind whistled past his ears and through his hair, and in that moment, he felt alive with adrenaline.

The wave finished and he hopped off his board and paddled back out. It was the biggest wave of his life.

Jimmy and Jenno watched in amazement from the shore.

"That was crazy… I don't reckon even any of the older boys could have made that," said Jenno.

"Nah, no way. That was nuts," said Jimmy.

Ratty felt more confident now.

The red light of a waking sky glowed across the horizon as the sun rose quickly from the depths of the sea.

Ratty covered his eyes with the palm of his hand, trying to block out the light.

His heart was racing; all he could hear was the blood pumping past his ears. He looked back at the shore towards Jimmy and Jenno, two small figures sitting amongst a mass of sand dunes and beach bush. He raised his arm and stuck his middle finger up towards them, then laughed to himself boyishly.

The period between waves was by no means calm, and he found himself constantly paddling to keep his position. The water was choppy and volatile, and he struggled to keep the nose of his board above the water as he paddled. The current was gaining on him, and he felt himself losing more and more stamina as the minutes went by.

Three more waves formed on the horizon. They were twice the size of the ones before, and the biggest waves he'd ever seen in his life. He turned his board and scrambled frantically to get over them.

He just got over the first one, feeling it pulling him back as it exploded like a bomb behind him.

The second one was even further out; he watched the tip of it feather over and topple, but he just managed to dive under it before it broke properly.

The third wave was the biggest of them all. He looked up at its peak, eyes wide with fear, but then steadied himself and forced himself to turn his board around and paddle for it. But something felt off. His newfound confidence was gone, and as the water sucked up beneath him he looked down at the bottom of the wave; it was steely and solid looking.

"Don't do it!" screamed Jenno. He and Jimmy couldn't believe what they were seeing. It was suicide.

Ratty paddled as hard as he could to get onto it, but the mass of water was too much. Instead of standing up and airdropping like he did on the last wave, he was flipped upside down and fell head first. It was like falling from a two-storey building, and the air was knocked out of him on impact.

The lip of the wave landed on him like an explosion. With an eruption of force, it drove him deep underwater, spinning him around, upside down, rattling his head and his spine as it devoured him. He tried to pull his arms and legs into himself but gave up after a moment's struggle. It was better to let go and allow himself to be taken. He felt a sudden tug at his ankle, then a release. His leash had snapped.

His ears popped from the pressure, he was deep by the time the wave had finally let go of him and his lungs were wrenching for air in his chest.

He swam upwards as fast as he could.

Air rushed into his lungs when he finally breached the surface. He almost felt like crying.

His board was nowhere to be seen, and he was far out from shore. He cried out towards the beach, but his voice was drowned out by the waves that still exploded at the shoreline.

He tried swimming back towards the sand, but there was too much water moving around; he could barely stroke or get a full breath of air in without swallowing and spluttering water.

Eventually he gave up and lay on his back so he could breathe.

He looked up at the sky. The clouds were pink and fluffy from the sunrise. They looked calm and peaceful, and as he bobbed up and down for a time, he lost himself in their stillness.

…

Jimmy and Jenno were on the shore trying desperately to help any way they could, but it was early in the morning and not many people were around besides a few beach joggers and a fisherman.

Up at the lifeguard tower, Pat noticed Jimmy and Jenno jumping around frantically on the beach.

"Surely not, boys…" he said to himself, grabbing his binoculars. He put them to his eyes and followed their line of view, then to his disbelief he saw Ratty floating boardless far out from shore.

"You fucking idiots!" he roared, jumping out of his chair and racing down to the sand so he could launch the jet ski.

…

"Fuck! He's gonna fucking drown out there!" yelled Jenno desperately.

"I'm gonna run and get help! Just keep watching him and don't lose him!" said Jimmy before sprinting up the beach towards the carpark.

No one would have seen Ratty from the beach. All you could see of him was his head bobbing in the water. He was so far out that Jenno wasn't even sure if he was really looking at him. The morning sun bounced off the chops in the water and thousands of glimmers of light flashed, like a clear night sky full of stars. A beautiful scene for a tragedy. Jenno strained his eyes, putting all of his effort into following Ratty's movements.

...

Ratty was thinking of a few things. In the face of death, it suddenly dawned on him that he was alive, and that at any moment it was going to be taken from him and there was nothing he could do about it. He thought about his mum and all the people at his school, and how he would have liked to say goodbye to them all properly. And then he thought about the newspaper article that would be written about him the following day – '16-year-old Boy Dies Surfing' or something like that.

He thought all those things in just a few moments, fleeting thoughts that were everything and nothing at all. On the horizon, another set of waves was forming. They were bigger even than the ones before. They were rough and bold looking, beautiful and mesmerising, but cold and as remorseless as ice and steel.

Jenno watched them build in size, until the first wave pitched up to its full height right above Ratty.

"Ratty! RATTY!" he tried calling out, but it was no use.

The first wave broke and Ratty disappeared under an avalanche of white wash. Jenno grabbed his board and dove in, but as hard as he paddled he couldn't make it out past the shoreline. He screamed in frustration as he was pushed effortlessly back to the sand.

Ratty's board washed up on the beach 10 metres up from where Jenno was standing. He picked it up in disbelief.

Not long after Jimmy returned with a small crowd of people, who were mostly in excerise clothes. All of them were scanning everywhere in the water for a sign of Rattty. It was a sickening feeling. A part of them was still expecting him to pop his head out of the water just near shore and clamber back onto the beach, and walk out like nothing happened.

. . .

Finally on the jet ski, Pat flew across the horizon in search of Ratty. The water was choppy and he clung on desperately as he raced, squinting and spluttering from the sea spray. In between the surges of waves, he dipped in and out of the impact zone searching for any sign of a body.

He was turning around to ride back out when suddenly he stopped and swung around. Ratty was there, floating, face down and lifeless. He leaned over the handles and pulled him onto the ski.

Back at the beach, the growing crowd of onlookers gasped when they saw Ratty being hoisted onto the jet ski. Pat rode full throttle towards the shore, desperately clinging on to Ratty's limp and heavy body. He rode the jet ski onto the sand and leapt off, holding Ratty in his arms.

"Get out of the way! Where's the ambulance?" he shouted.

"They're on their way!" an older woman in running clothes yelled; she had tears in her eyes.

Jimmy and Jenno stood frozen as Pat placed Ratty down and started CPR.

Jimmy looked at Ratty's face. It was purple and lifeless. His eyes were wide open and glassy, peering off somewhere between spaces.

More people gathered at the carpark, wondering what all the commotion was about. Suddenly it seemed like there were people everywhere, watching as though it were all some kind of soap opera. Jimmy was transfixed. He looked into Ratty's eyes, but they were empty. His cheeks shook as Pat pumped his chest desperately. He was dead.

When the ambulance came, they placed his body on a stretcher and covered it in a sheet. One by one, the crowd dispersed. The boys said nothing. Their parents were called. Their cars screeched as they pulled up to the carpark and they ran desperately towards their children. Ratty's mother collapsed on the sand next to his covered body before the paramedics carried him away, crying noiselessly in a crumpled heap. They stood around for a moment, unable to take their eyes off such a horrific sight, before they moved in around her and comforted her.

The next day the swell disappeared, and the ocean was still once again.

It looked too calm, too inviting and peaceful. People dove into it on their morning swims and returned to the surface, smiling and grateful for everything in their lives. They had no idea that just a day before a boy had died there.

A week later, a hundred people gathered on the shore, holding flowered wreaths and boards. They paddled out and sat in a circle and one by one they tossed their wreaths into the middle and splashed water and cheered in memory of Ratty, that crazy kid who loved to surf. That was one of the more beautiful traditions of surfing.

It was a quiet funeral. The collective grief in the place fell about them like a thick blanket, and one by one they all dropped their heads under the weight. It was a sight that no one had ever expected to see. A coffin of a boy, carried upon the shoulders of people who should have passed long before him. It was a twist in reality, one that destroys the nature of things. The effect was silence. A tragic silence. And a grief that changed them forever.

Ratty's grave was towards the edge of a little cemetery. There was a tree growing above it.

For years after kids would climb that tree, unaware that a boy not much older than them was underneath it.

They made a bench with his name engraved on it. It overlooked the beach from the carpark.

The boys would sit on it on sunny days, and think about it when it was raining.

Jimmy and Jenno were quiet for a long time after that. They still surfed, but it wasn't the same. After seeing what they had seen, and after all the grief, the confusion, the anger and disbelief, it was hard for them to open themselves back up. It troubled them a lot, and eventually Jimmy just about gave up surfing because of it.

Jenno often had nightmares about it. He'd wake up screaming in the middle of night. It was always the same dream, where he watched Ratty get swallowed by the ocean, and as soon as he was gone the water grew still again, and all was at peace.

2

Life went on in the town after Ratty's passing. After a year, it seemed like the wound had healed for most people, and that his story was slowly coming to an end.

This was an ocean town, and much of its way of life depended on the moods of the sea. There was a great stillness there, too, that was disturbed every now and then in different ways. It was a place under constant erosion. Resistant to change but worn down over the years by the weight of time and shifting sands, its fate was tied up with the sea, which ceaselessly licked at the face of the headlands, rubbing them slowly away.

Two old boys sat against the wall by the beach carpark under the noon sunlight like baked potatoes and watched the world go by. Their skin was tan and leathery, and the wrinkles on their faces were long and deep from years of exposure to the harsh Australian sun. A row of empty beer bottles lined the edge of the wall next to them, and sat between the two of them rested another six pack of beers that would undoubtably join the line of empties soon.

"Fuck me, look at this bloke runnin' 'past" said the one on the left, rubbing his hairy belly.

The man in question ran by and smiled at them politely. He was wearing tights and running singlet.

"I don't get why they all gotta wear them tights. Back in the day you woulda got bashed for that, no questions asked," said the one on the right, shaking his head.

"The world's gone crazy. I remember when this place used to be just workin'-class blokes. Now look at it.

When all them CEOs moved in, the place went to shit. You remember the old video stores and that?"

"Yep," the one on the right nodded. He put his beer to his mouth and tilted his head back.

"I remember when all the houses here used to be cheap as piss. Used to be just single-storey shacks back then – now look at the fuckin 'place. Mansions everywhere. If I hadn't bought my place all those years ago, I dunno where I could live now – not here. How any of them young people afford to live here beats me."

"Rich parents, I reckon, they must have. There's only a few shitholes left now, and they're gettin ' bulldozed daily."

"Yeah, like that grommet Jenno. You seen his house? Shit all over the front lawn. His old man doesn't work at all, I heard. Never see him around much, anyways. Wouldn't be surprised if they packed up and left soon as well."

It was true that not long ago the only houses built there were holiday houses. After that, it became the place for blue-collar workers and surfers. Land was cheap. But seemingly overnight, it became a place for the wealthy. Local chip shops turned into cafés; the video stores, CD shops and all the businesses that belonged to the old world were closed down and reopened as gyms, yoga studios and designer clothes stores. Only a few remnants of the old world still remained, like faded shadows on the street, their customers like phantoms and spectres that slipped through the cracks in the walls. The chicken shop operated by three generations of a Chinese family still stood, while the old bakery and a single news agents stood like eyesores in what had become an influencers' paradise.

This town wasn't so far out of the city itself. You could see the tallest buildings far off on the horizon if you stood at the top of the right hill. There was a magic in the air that was carried through the town by salty early morning mists and sea breeze. There was a feeling and an energy that was beyond anything that could be put into words. It was a place of accidental spiritualism, where the practices of mindfulness, quietness and observation were upheld and practiced daily, but blatantly ignored and abhorred at the same time.

At night, when all the traffic stopped and the world went to sleep, there wasn't a place where you couldn't hear the sound of crashing waves in the distance. The noise seemed to vibrate through the air and get carried along with the wind.

It was as much a place of beauty, love and peace as it was a place of ignorance, racism, selfishness and vanity.

But above all things, this place was home to Jimmy and Jenno, and that was all that mattered to them.

...

Both Jimmy and Jenno were starting to get their first proper taste of teendom. Jimmy was 16 now. After he quit surfing he learned guitar, and not long after his 16th birthday he joined a local band called The Pegs. They mostly played at people's parties.

All in all, they were a putrid-sounding band, but all the kids from the area got around them. Their hit song was called 'Sixteen and Taking Pills'. The chorus went something like, "Sixteen and taking pills, eat 'em up, yeah, we're never gonna come down!"

The dancefloors erupted with long-haired little shits head-banging and doing shoeys while their mums looked on in horror and their dads feigned anger, but were proud deep down.

MDMA was so common around the area that if you hadn't tried it at least once by the time you were 16, you were the odd one out. Jimmy was one of the odd ones. He still felt like a kid inside, and the thought of doing drugs filled him with a sense of dread and moral uncertainty. He felt like his toes were pressed against a line he had no intention of crossing, but the world around him was trying to pull him over.

Most kids took it every weekend. It would get passed around at parties and things would go from there. Drinking was light stuff. Kids in the town started drinking at 13, and by the time they reached 16, they were able to handle eight to 10 beers easily, so it was only natural for them to move on to MDMA. Twenty bucks was all it took to have the night of your life. At the start, all it took was one. Kids would take one and then fall in love with everything. They had no idea how to control themselves. Their faces would twist and contort and they'd disappear into the night in search of other parties and friends' places far off. They'd cause havoc on every public bus they hopped on to, and every fast-food place they stepped into after midnight. That's what was expected of a person at that age – it was a cool and respectable thing to do.

A lot of names started popping up to describe the effects of MDMA. The most popular ones at the time were: cooked, fried, peaking, spangled, chokkas and gurning. The action of going to a friend's place and taking MDMA until the sun came up was called a whip.

These were all things that Jenno and Jimmy learned year by year. Jimmy was a little older than Jenno; he'd already started drinking, but he'd never touched anything else. Jenno had tried beer before, but he'd never been drunk. They were about as standard as teenagers got. They looked up to the older boys in their neighbourhood, although, to the average adult, the older boys looked nothing more than kids themselves. They were all in their late teens to very early twenties. Most of them were good-for-nothings, and some of them were lifeguards. All of them spent every day at the beach. But to Jenno and Jimmy, they were heroes, living legends to be admired and emulated in everything they did.

Jenno would often watch them ride around on the lifeguard quadbikes and he'd daydream up scenarios where he'd get the biggest wave of the day in front of them or something like that.

It wasn't often that they had to save anyone. And if anyone had known what they were up to on their time off-duty they would never have trusted them to save anyone's life.

Dizz was the main lifeguard. He was as dumb as dogshit, but his word was law. Twenty years old and full of confidence, he was the best surfer on the beach and the most feared and respected. He loved being the centre of attention and prided himself on being a ladies' man. There was a local legend that said that one day on one of his shifts, Dizz took two girls around the rocks at the same time and had a threesome while he was meant to be on duty.

Nobody had trouble believing it. Dizz and the boys were always surrounded by girls up at the lifeguard tower.

"Fuck, dude… Look at him! He's going out with Jess Lacy…" said Jenno outside school one day, as they watched Dizz pull off in his ute with an older girl from their school in the front seat.

Jimmy nodded at him. "Yeah… My band got asked to play at his younger sister's 16th in a couple weeks."

Jenno looked at him. "Fuck, are you serious? Why didn't you tell me?"

"I dunno, just didn't wanna jinx it, I guess…"

"We gotta make a pact. Every party we get invited to we gotta bring each other. That means no one's gonna get left behind," said Jenno.

Jimmy nodded. "Yeah, sounds good."

It was March and the air had that soft warmth in it. The sun was still shining and everything felt at ease. It was one of those times of the year when everything seems to fall into place. The light, the sounds and the smells were in perfect balance, and there was an air of romance that made you feel grateful of everything.

"You wanna come to mine?" asked Jenno as they rounded the corner to his street. They both lived relatively close to school and walked home together every day.

"Yeah, alright. Your dad's not home, is he?"

"Nah, I don't think so, I dunno where he is at the minute."

"Yeah, sweet, I'll come."

Jimmy had reason to ask if Jenno's dad was home. He was gone most of the time, and when he was home he was mostly distant and distracted. He was covered in tattoos and scars. He loved drinking beer, watching rugby league and also surfing, but above everything he loved art. Jenno would often come home from school to find his dad sitting at the living room table, drawing. The last few times Jimmy had come over he'd tried to convince Jimmy to sell weed for him.

He'd talk to him all nice and say things like, "C'mon, mate! It's only a bit of weed, it's basically legal now anyways. Think of how cool you'll be at school. Look, I'll even give you a good deal. We'll split the profits 80 to 20, 80 my way, 20 yours..." He'd hold out his enormous tattooed hand and say, "Deal?"

Jimmy always felt pressured to shake his hand and say deal, even though he never wanted to, and he was worried that if he bumped into Jenno's dad again he'd actually have the weed for Jimmy to sell.

Jenno had always been oblivious to it all. He was young, but recently even he had started to have questions. His dad wasn't a bad man, he was a middle man. An opportunist and a lost soul. He knew dangerous people, but under all his scars and tattoos he was really just a boy himself.

Every time Jenno went over to Jimmy's house, he noticed the stark differences in the way they lived.

Jimmy lived in a four-storey house that overlooked the beach. They had a pool and a spa. But what stuck out most to Jenno was that Jimmy's family had dinner together around a table every night.

He never forgot the first time he and Ratty had gone over to Jimmy's place to stay the night. Neither he nor Ratty had ever really eaten dinner like that. It felt so unnatural and formal to them both. Both of them were leaning on their elbows, and Jimmy's mum shot them dirty glances before finally asking them to take their elbows off the table. They felt like they were at some fancy restaurant, even though it was just Jimmy's living room.

All the artwork on the walls was of naked women painted in abstract shapes and colours, and there were expensive ornaments everywhere.

Both of Jimmy's parents were lawyers, and very strict. For a long while, Ratty was banned from coming over for dinner because of his manners. Not lack of – he was always very polite – but he was just very rough around the edges. The first time he and Jenno went around for dinner, Jimmy's mum made enchiladas. Ratty couldn't believe his eyes; he dug in greedily before anyone else had started, and through his full mouth he exclaimed to Jimmy's mother enthusiastically, "Fuckin' hell, Mary, this is good!"

Jimmy also saw stark contrasts whenever he used to go to Ratty's or Jenno's places. Their homes were both old and rundown-looking. The carpets were covered in ancient stains and mould. The paint on the ceilings was peeling and there was random junk everywhere. Jenno's family seemed to collect random stuff and leave it in heaps on the front yard or the porch. Most of it was useless, like old rusted bikes that other people had thrown away, left out in the garden to rust further.

But the state of their houses made him feel strangely at ease and welcomed, like he could sink into the couch and become a part of it. So he enjoyed going over to their houses, just when Jenno's dad wasn't home.

The midday news was playing on the TV when they got to Jenno's place, even though no one had been home to watch it.

"Record high rainfall expected this year, so keep your raincoats on and your umbrellas handy!" said the weatherman, who was standing in front of a greenscreen that showed dark masses of clouds swirling across the whole country. It was due to a four-year weather cycle they called El Niño and La Niña, wet and dry periods. The only problem was that the wet period had lasted twice as long as it was meant to. It seemed like every other day was torrential rain, and for a country that had been historically plagued by drought, people had no idea how to handle the constant rainfall.

It meant more than that to Jimmy and Jenno. It seemed to them as if it had all happened after Ratty's death, like some dark cloud of grief was following them everywhere, raining down the tears that they had been holding in.

"Oi, how good's this!" said Jenno half an hour later in his bedroom. They sat on the floor in the only spot where there weren't any dirty clothes. Jenno's room was halfway through a state of change. It was as though he'd woken up one morning and suddenly realised he was a teenager. The old computer game and TV show posters that had once covered his walls had been ripped down and mostly replaced by pictures of chicks with big titties and surfing magazine ripouts. The only exception was a little photo of he and Ratty together. It was taken on the headland where they all lived. They had their arms over one another's shoulders. Behind them was an endless expanse of ocean, lit white in the glare of the sun. It was stuck on the wall just above Jenno's bedside table. He looked at it often. He'd sit there and almost press his cheek against the wall so that he could study Ratty's face. The photo was one of his most prized possessions.

Jenno looked round his bedroom door for a moment before bending low and pulling out an old porno magazine from atop the slats of his bed.

Jimmy looked at the front cover and laughed. "What do you have that for?"

Jimmy had never even seen a porn magazine before; they were a thing from the past, an ancient relic of a time when the parts of the human body were still secret and taboo. He looked at the woman on the front, posing with her breasts out but her nipples covered, and then flicked through the raunchy, but relatively tame in comparison pictures within the cover. It seemed weird to him that this was what porn used to be.

Jenno looked down, almost embarrassed. "I accidentally left a tab open on the family computer and Mum saw it. Now she's banned me from it for a month."

"Faark! That's heavy, man…" laughed Jimmy, before a moment of realisation came over him and he dropped the magazine in disgust.

"Yuck, you fucking grub! Why did you let me hold it?" he said.

Jenno grinned. He talked about porn a lot for a 14-year-old, and that was saying something.

When he wasn't banned from the computer, he'd spend hours every night watching it. He didn't even masturbate. The first time he ever watched porn had been by accident when he was 11 years old. He'd been browsing the web when one of those old virus popups flashed onto the screen with a group of naked women. He bent his head so close to the computer screen that he almost blinded himself. He sat there in the darkness, his face illuminated by the sterile computer light. His heart was racing and his adrenaline was through the roof. Seeing a pair of breasts was not only a life-changing moment for him, but perhaps one of the most pivotal points in his life thus far. After this first exposure, he had no idea where to find that sort of content. He knew his mum monitored his search history, so he started out by typing in every word that rhymed with 'porn' in the image search bar in hopes that something would come up. He'd search 'love', or 'corn', or 'man and woman' but he never saw anything remotely close. After these failed attempts his phrases got a little more daring. He would search things like 'double Ds' or 'hot'. But when those didn't work he just purposely clicked on every shady website he saw in hopes that porn would come. It cost his mum a fortune on virus protection software. She had no idea why the family computer kept getting hacked, and was almost on the verge of a breakdown when she finally caught Jenno redhanded.

By the time all the other boys his age had got around to watching porn he was already a veteran. Nothing excited him anymore, and so his taste became exceedingly deplorable. It was lucky that the tab his mother found open was relatively tame compared to his usual search.

Jenno would go on and on about what his favourite positions were and he'd act out exactly how he'd do them. Jimmy was more reserved, and although he was always entertained by Jenno's putrid imagination, he never shared any himself.

Jimmy hung around for a little while longer before he eventually had to go. His parents made him sit down with a tutor a few afternoons a week to get help with his math homework. Jenno had to surf.

. . .

The surf was good that afternoon. Jenno grabbed his board and rode his skateboard down to the beach. A couple of the older boys were out there when he paddled out.

Slowy, one of the friendlier older boys, was up and riding on one of the better waves of the day. He raced and swerved effortlessly. His style was lanky and noodly, but he made it look beautiful. Just as the lip of the wave began to throw over, he slashed it apart with an enormous top turn. A few people who were sitting and watching hollered. After the top turn the wave got steeper as it rolled over a shallower bank. Slowy pumped as fast as he could and then at the last moment before the wave crashed, he launched himself into an enormous frontside air and landed right in front of Jenno. Jenno was in awe of what he'd just seen. Slowy's surfing seemed godlike to him, and akin to the pros he watched on the internet. Slowy noticed him there and smiled, "Aye, grommet, there's a couple fun ones out here!"

Jenno grew very serious. Slowy was someone he desperately wanted to impress. It was the only thing on his mind the whole surf.

He got a couple of good ones. On his first wave he got a few decent little turns in, and even tried to do an air like Slowy had done, but he didn't get close. Slowy gave him a little "Yew!" when he rode past him on a wave. Jenno felt a swell of pride when he paddled back and sat on his board, trying to look as calm and collected as possible.

He could still remember the first time he started surfing. He was just seven years old when his dad found an old fibreglass board on the side of the road during council cleanup. He brought it home, grinning as he carried it under his arm, before waving it above his head for Jenno to see. Jenno danced and stomped in excitement when his dad handed him the board. He promised that he'd use it every day, and he did. But in all the pure joy and beauty that is surfing, he witnessed almost an equal amount of confrontation and aggression from surfers.

As a young child he watched nervously as older men would yell at one another for being in the way, and every now and then their arguments would come to blows. Jenno watched in horror first, but then, after noticing that everyone else was laughing, he laughed too. His opinion of a surfer wasn't in how much fun they were having, but in how skilled and how well known they were.

As he got older, he began to notice that when it got crowded, it was as if all at once people abandoned common decency, common sense and spatial awareness. Suddenly, big crowds became one big feeding frenzy, and only the best or most aggressive surfers got any waves. Surfing alone was meditation, but surfing against other surfers was war. At every beach, reef and pointbreak across the world, there is a pecking order in the lineup, and 'grommets' fall somewhere at the very bottom.

It was for good reason that Jenno was eager to prove himself. The higher you got in the pecking order, the better waves you rode.

Dizz, the main lifeguard at the beach, paddled past him and greeted him with the standard, "Aye, grommet, you gettin' a couple?"

Jenno smiled at him with a mixture of fear and respect. "Yeah, it's pumpin'," he said.

"That's the way…" said Dizz over his shoulder. He skipped the queue of people waiting for the next wave to come, and sat at the best takeoff spot without acknowledging anyone else except for Slowy.

Jenno watched him curiously. Dizz took every good wave that came, and dropped in on everyone he didn't recognise.

Dizz dropped in on a burly man who looked to be in his late forties, and as he fell he roared in frustration as Dizz glided away from him effortlessly.

"Are you fuckin' serious, cunt?" the man spat at Dizz as he paddled towards the front of the queue again.

Dizz smiled at him almost pleasantly. "Fuck off, you ugly cunt!"

Jenno looked on in fascination. The man paddled over to Dizz and splashed water in his face, but, before he had a chance to do anything else, he was surrounded by the rest of the older boys.

"Fuck off! Get back to shore you fuckin' kook…" said Dizz. He was standing on his board, towering above the man and pointing towards the shore.

"Fuckin' little cunts…" the man muttered to himself, before waving his hand and taking the next wave of white wash to the beach.

Jenno watched the man get out of the water, shaking his head and muttering to himself, and then looked to Dizz and the older boys, who were laughing uncontrollably.

"See, that's what you gotta do whenever any kooks come out here, Jenno!" Dizz called back at him. "And that goes for the rest of you, if anyone else wants to get chirpy."

Dizz turned to look at the rest of the non-locals sitting in the water. All of them looked the other way, pretending they hadn't heard.

'Dropping in' is the act of cutting someone off from a wave that was theirs, and is the cause of the majority of fights in the water. It's something that you don't do as a surfer. Your initial reaction hearing that people get into fights over waves might be to scoff. To someone who has never surfed, surfing and fighting are two things that they never would have put together. Fighting over a wave might seem moronic and immature. Your confusion would be justified if you saw two people paddle back to the beach and start throwing hands at one another. For someone who has never surfed, and can't seem to wrap their heads around people getting into fights over a wave, just imagine trying to find a spot in one of those tight, busy underground carparks. After a few laps in your shitty but respectable rustbox of a car that you worked hard for and bought with your own money, you finally see someone reversing out of a spot. You look around and realise you're the first in line. and you lick your lips gleefully as you get ready to pull in, but just as you lower your foot on the gas pedal, some ballbag drifts around the corner in the wrong direction and at the last minute squeezes between you and the space and snatches it straight from your sweaty little fingers. They get out of the car, they're younger and far more attractive than you. The car is way too expensive for someone their age to have bought alone, and you can guess that it was bought for them as a birthday present by their dad. You're just about to wind the window down and let loose an entire lifetime of pentup anger and frustration, when the parking space thief locks eyes with you and smiles. They walk away without a care in the world, swinging their empty shopping bag up and down happily as they go, and now everyone in the line behind you is beeping, and you have no choice but to swallow defeat and keep searching for another space. That's what it feels like to be dropped in on.

Jenno and Jimmy respected Dizz, but it was mostly out of fear. They always felt on edge when he was around. Ratty was family friends with Dizz's family, but Ratty's mum forbade him from hanging around Dizz after Dizz convinced him to smoke weed for the first time at 12 years old.

No one caught any good waves for the half hour following. Dizz caught every single one. No one could do anything to stop him, he was too good and too confident in himself. He sprayed anyone that got in the way, and he never made a mistake on any of his manoeuvres. He was a surfing prodigy. He sat back on his board, calm and composed, and chatted with Slowy while they waited for waves to come. Jenno peered out into the horizon, trying to act like he wasn't listening to everything they said.

A perfect wave formed on the horizon and Dizz, who was halfway through telling Slowy about his night with one of the girls from the area, was in the perfect spot as usual. He paddled as hard as he could for it, and as he stood he scooped in under the lip and tucked into a barrel. It was beautiful to watch, and even though most people in the water disliked Dizz, they couldn't help but watch him as he passed through. He disappeared for a moment behind a curtain of water, but just as the wave was about to close out, he popped out of the barrel in a cloud of spray.

Everyone looked back at Dizz, in awe at what they'd just seen, but a few moments later the best wave of the day formed on the horizon, and by luck none of the older boys were in the right position. Jenno was in the right spot. Everyone called him onto it as he paddled determinedly. He knew that this was his time to prove himself. Dizz was watching, and the wave was going to barrel, it was clear to everyone; Jenno had no doubt in his mind that he was going to pull into it and make it out. A lot of things went through his mind as he paddled. He watched the water suck up underneath him, he watched the wave curl into that perfect little wall just before it folded over, and he watched, in confusion at first, and then in horror, as the nose of his board dipped under the water and he was flung head first into the flats. For a split second as he fell, he saw the glory of the barrel, and the small view of the outside world through the tunnel, and then it was only darkness, and the sensation of being thrown in a washing machine.

Once the wave had let him go, Jenno swam up to the surface and gasped for air. Dizz paddled past him. "Fuck sakes, Jenno… If you knew you were gonna kook it you should have let someone else get it. That's the last good wave you're getting out here for a while, grom."

Jenno's stomach sank.

"Sorry, Dizz! I thought I had it…"

Dizz shook his head and paddled off.

"Fuckin' kook…" he said over his shoulder.

The other boys glared back at Jenno; if Dizz was angry then so were they.

Suddenly, Jenno felt the urge to turn and leave. He trudged up the beach with his head down, not daring to look back up towards the pack. On the way home, he imagined the scenario happening in different ways over and over in his head. In one vision, he imagined himself standing up on the wave and getting barrelled in front of Dizz, and then all the older boys cheering him on. But it didn't happen, and there was nothing he could do to undo it. He felt like he'd made a fool of himself, and that he had no right surfing out there with the others.

When he got home he looked at himself in the mirror. He was the opposite of what he saw in the older boys. And knowing he'd just fucked up the chance up to impress them made him despise himself.

It helped light the fire of a desperate kind of insecurity in him, one that made him driven to do whatever it took to prove himself. And it gave him a craving for self-worth that could only be fulfilled by the approval of the older boys.

...

He woke up from a nightmare early the next morning. It was one of his recurring nightmares about Ratty. In the dream, he watched Ratty swim out into the ocean. He tried to call him back, but it was as though Ratty couldn't hear him. All of a sudden, the sky turned dark and stormy, and the seas became rough and choppy. He was back on that morning when Ratty drowned. He had to save him this time, but there was an invisible barrier stopping him from getting in the water. He pushed against it, but it was no use. He watched Ratty run into the ocean and paddle out, only to drown all over again. The sea swallowed him completely, and then grew calm and still once again.

Jenno tossed and turned for an hour afterwards, trying to get back to sleep, before he sat up defeated and skated down to the beach.

She was there, exactly where she was every day. Ratty's mum, Fleetwood.

Fleetwood was beautiful. Her family was from the Caribbean, but she was born and raised in London. Ever since Ratty's passing she had closed in on herself. After the accident people tried their best to see her and comfort her, but she mostly turned them away. She didn't have the energy, and for the longest time since it had felt like she was constantly in survival mode. She never returned anyone's calls or read their messages, and eventually most people gave up. She became almost wraithlike. Every morning at sunrise, she could be seen sitting on her knees in the sand with her hands in her lap, staring silently out into the horizon. Whoever she had been before to the world was soon lost, and most people around town saw her only as a grieving mother. They'd pass her on the street and give her warm smiles when they could, and when she'd pass them by they'd look at one another and shake their heads regretfully.

"Miss Augustus?" Jenno said as gently as he could, so as to not frighten her.

She opened her eyes slowly and turned her head to look at him.

She smiled when she saw him. Her face radiated natural beauty, and in the glow of the rising sunlight it almost seemed to Jenno that he was looking at an angel.

"Jenno, what a surprise! How are you?" Her voice was gentle, yet every word was audible, even over the sound of crashing waves.

"I'm good—" Jenno started; like most kids his age he'd memorised a few lines of dialogue for adult encounters and was about to repeat them by habit, but he remembered why he had come.

"Actually, I'm not that good. I miss Ratty every day, and I dunno how I can get through it. It's been a year and the pain still feels the same. Jimmy feels it too."

Fleetwood Augustus put her hand on his shoulder and smiled at him. It was the kind of loving smile that was born from pain. Sweet and sad. She sighed, as if trying to expel some great weight from within her chest.

"I know. He was my boy," she began, softly. "I miss him every day. I miss his laugh and his face. I even miss him when he was grumpy and tried to struggle out of my cuddles."

"Yeah. He was like my brother," said Jenno. He sat down next to her and put his skateboard face down on the sand next to him. It felt strange to be talking this way to an adult, but at this moment they were no longer adult and teenager, but equals in grief. He stared out across the horizon. The sky was a soft peach colour.

"I've realised something over time," said Fleetwood. "As long as there is an ocean, you'll be close to Ratty. That's why I come here every day."

Jenno looked at her, one of his eyes closed, squinting in the sunlight, the other meeting her gaze.

"Did you know that? We give parts of ourselves to the people and the places we love, and when we pass on we live on through them. My son's heart beats with yours, as long as you remember him, and I'm sure you always will."

"Yeah… but that won't ever bring him back."

"No, it won't," she began, her voice suddenly heavy and firm, "and nothing ever will. That's something you'll have to learn to understand the same as me, but you're far too young for all of this and I'm so sorry. That's just the way life goes. He will never exist physically again. He'll never surf, he'll never hug or kiss me, or even be grumpy with me. I'll never see him grow into the man I was watching him become, and that's a pain I have to deal with every day. It's my duty as a mother to love my son, and send that love to wherever he is. His spirit rests in the sea, and that's where it always belonged. I come here every day and speak to him, and tell him that he's loved and missed. And you can speak to him too whenever you surf. He can hear you, he's listening. I can hear him. His voice and his laughter is in the waves and its carried on the breeze. And I've come to realise that's all life is. It's feeling, it's listening, it's a connectedness. Can't you feel it?"

"Feel what?"

"The waves. You understand waves more than anyone, I'm sure. That's what the universe is created out of. Waves. Light, heat, sound, electricity, they all come in waves. So, when you're riding a wave, you're dancing with the universe. Toby's energy is in the universe. He exists in those waves. I want you to go out there and feel it next time, and come back and tell me you don't feel alive…"

"I will."

"I'm sure."

Jenno sat next to her for a time in silence and watched the lines of swell roll towards the shore. The sun was on them now and they had that morning wobble to them, when there wasn't any wind about to give them shape.

"Are you lonely, Miss Augustus?" he asked suddenly. It was something that both he and Jimmy talked about from time to time. He even overheard his mum talking to one of her friends about it on the phone one morning. Besides a few flings, Fleetwood hadn't dated anyone since Ratty's father walked out 17 years before.

"You can call me Fleetwood, you know, I'm not your teacher," said Fleetwood.

"Sorry," said Jenno.

Fleetwood paused for a moment, thinking over her response.

She thought about her empty house, and the ticking of the kitchen clock. About her quiet mornings and evenings, the empty spaces, and, worst of all, the constant, deafening pain and the heavy blanket of silence that seemed to smother her everywhere she went.

"No, I don't feel lonely," she said, smiling softly to Jenno after a few quiet moments.

Jenno smiled. "Thanks, I reckon that made me feel a lot better."

Fleetwood Augustus smiled too. "I'm glad to hear it."

Jenno said goodbye to her and went home to go and get ready for school.

Fleetwood sat there for longer than usual after Jenno left, rewatching distant memories in silence.

3

We are born crying. The journey of life is learning how to laugh. There are tears of laughter and tears of pain, but they are one and the same. It just depends on how you look at them.

The sun rose and rested softly on the cliff face by the sea. The birds had already sensed its arrival, and were up and ready by the time it showed its light. The world came to life wherever the light fell. Flowers lifted their bent heads to be caressed by its warmth, insects stretched themselves out again and burst into life, trees shook dew from their leaves, and all the things that lived within them began the routine of their day. Lastly, Tahiti awoke with a groan from his hammock in his cave. He'd lived in a cave at the base of the headland for years, but had still never got used to waking up early.

"Fuck sakes…" he groaned, wiping the sleep from his eyes.

"Gonna take me fuckin' ages to get used to this again…"

He rolled out of his hammock and reached around for the bottle of rum he'd been drinking the night before, but found to his dismay that it was empty.

"Fuckin' dog…" He looked at the empty bottle angrily.

He sat for a while and just watched the sun rise over the sea, squinting as he peered out into the glowing redness. It was too early to start his day. The only people about were fitness types, and to him they were the most insufferable of all. Their 'go getter, life's what you make it!' attitude made him sick to his stomach, and the last thing he needed to be reminded of was other people's jolly happiness.

When the bottle-o finally opened, he scraped together the little money he had and bought a couple of longnecks to sink on the curb by the lifeguard club. When the day got going and his spirits lifted a little, he'd talk to everyone who walked by, but never asked for anything.

When Jenno was little he'd skate by Tahiti to check the surf, and Tahiti would always call out tricks for him to do.

"Oi, grommet! Do a fuckin' ollie!" he'd say.

Every time Jenno landed a trick Tahiti would clap his hands and laugh loudly. "Fuck yeah, grom! Now fuck off!"

Jenno had always been enchanted by Tahiti. There was something admirable he found in him that no other adults seemed to have – a freedom from responsibility and a refusal to do anything productive. Jimmy feared him, and often tried to avoid walking past him whenever he could. He had his reasons. When he was a little boy, his skateboard slipped from under him and rocketed towards a sleeping Tahiti. It collided with his face with a sickening crunch and Tahiti, now standing, bewildered and angry, picked up the skateboard and launched it high into the bushes. He looked down at a trembling Jimmy, nostrils flared with fury, but Jimmy ran before Tahiti had a chance to say anything. He'd been terrified of him ever since.

No one knew exactly how Tahiti had become homeless, or when he showed up to the beach for the first time. It seemed like he had always been there. Jenno couldn't remember a time in his life when Tahiti wasn't sitting on the curb drinking beers. He often wondered how Tahiti had found himself there, and in his childlike wonder he created elaborate stories in his head that always seemed to draw the conclusion that Tahiti was some kind of spy. It wasn't until Jenno, Jimmy and Ratty accidentally stumbled upon Tahiti's hideout that Jenno realised that he really was living at the beach.

It was all by accident. They were climbing around the rocks around the back of the headland when they found a cave with a hammock in it. But what interested them more was the old chest underneath it.

"No way!" said Ratty, his eyes glinting.

He picked the chest up and opened it expecting to find treasure, but it was filled with letters written on crinkled line paper.

"What's all this shit?" said Ratty disappointedly.

Jenno took one of the letters.

It read:

I have and will always love you,
Under moon and under stars.
I look towards them and wonder where you are,
Do you miss me, like I miss you?
A thousand days and nights pass so blue,
And if I could take it all back I would,
If only I ever could
Feel the warmth of you...

The boys read it in silence.

"You reckon this is Tahiti's s place?" asked Ratty.

The other two shrugged, but their question was answered a moment later.

"What the fuck are you little cunts doing!" Tahiti's nasally voice came from atop one of the rocks.

"Fuck, run!" said Ratty, and all three of them scrambled out of the cave and clambered over the rocks to run away.

Tahiti didn't chase them. He picked up his letter from the ground and read it in silence. When he was finished he folded it carefully and placed it back in the chest.

When the boys came back the next day, the chest was gone.

A few days later Tahiti disappeared. The boys were never sure where he went.

Jenno wondered where he was sometimes. He liked to imagine he cleaned himself up and found the love of his life again, he was never sure that he'd ever see Tahiti again.

But Tahiti had returned. He didn't know what brought him back, only a gut feeling that he'd followed for the majority of his life. He hadn't always lived in the cave around the headland, but after so many years, his life had become a blur of movement, always coming and going, never staying anywhere for long.

4

The world is a flame that attracts our souls like moths to witness and experience the beauty of life. Beauty is an equal mix of both happiness and pain. Jenno grew to distinguish the beauty of his own life as the balance between surfing and family. The ocean was the place where he felt himself. It was a place where he could observe his movements, and listen to everything that went on inside of him so that he could pick it all apart in his own way. It was peace and order, a place where everything seemed to fit together and make sense, where he could channel all of his energy and put it into something beautiful and raw.

For him, family was pain. It was something that he couldn't understand. The very mention of it filled him with uncertainty, and a desperate hope that he couldn't define. It meant misunderstandings and arguments, grudges and unresolved pain that had long since turned to bitterness.

Jenno's dad wasn't often on the scene, but Jenno thought about him every day when he was gone, wondering where he was and what he was doing. He'd disappear for weeks on end and then come home like nothing had happened. Jenno'd often come home from school to find him back, sitting in the living room drawing or drinking beers, or both.

…

Jenno was walking home from school when the heavens opened and rain poured down and soaked him. He ran for cover and flagged a bus down. He hopped on and looked out of the window at the world passing by.

Droplets fell against the glass like soft piano notes; he watched them slide slowly down and disappear into the window frame. The bus engine was groaning as it struggled up the hill not far away from his place. There was an elderly woman sitting at the front of the bus with one hand on her knee and the other holding her walking stick. Jenno had seen many elderly women and all of them seemed to look and act the same. He wondered if that was what she thought about teenage boys.

He hopped off the bus and raced home. When he rushed through the door, shaking the raindrops from his hair, his dad was there, sitting at the dining table and drawing. He looked up when he heard the door open and smiled at Jenno.

"Jenno!" he said.

Jenno didn't say anything. It was the first time they'd seen each other in weeks. It was always the same story. His dad would find a job and work for a little bit. He'd do well for the first few weeks, but then the stress of everyday life would get to him and he'd start drinking heavier and heavier. Once he'd got to that stage, he'd close into himself and block everyone out. Then it was like no one else existed. There'd be times where Jenno would stand over the dining room table and just watch him draw. He'd be so wrapped up in himself he rarely noticed Jenno there. And then finally, when it all became too much for him, he would leave unexpectedly. It would be more accurate to say he vanished into thin air. One moment Jenno would see him at the table drawing, then he'd go into his room and come back out a minute later to find the seat empty and his dad's car gone.

But today he was back, which meant the cycle had started again. He stood up from the table and pulled Jenno over to him, wrapping him in a big hug.

"You sad or somethin'?" he said, looking down at Jenno.

"Nah, just tired from school," said Jenno, not knowing how he felt.

His dad let go and Jenno walked into his room to put his bag down.

"How's Benny?" his dad called after him.

"Benny?" said Jenno. "You mean Jimmy?"

"Fark! Sorry, mate – Jimmy. How's Jimmy doin'? You boys been surfing?"

"Nah, Jimmy doesn't surf anymore, but he's doin' alright. His dad's been working him pretty hard. Makes him stay home most nights and do tutoring and that."

"Fair dinkum? Fuck, if I had the coin that's what I'd make you do too…"

"Yeah?" started Jenno.

"Yeah… 'Bout time you started pickin' your marks up. Mum's been tellin' me you've been fuckin' around too much at school."

"Where've you been, Dad?" asked Jenno. The question had been weighing him down and he needed an answer. It threw his dad off guard. His absence was always a thing that Jenno had accepted when he was a young boy, but it was changing with his age. He needed a father figure now more than ever. He needed guidance desperately, but sometimes it seemed like his dad was just a boy himself.

"Just been out workin' out of town. I'm sorry I didn't get a chance to see you before I went. Was just a last-minute call-up. But I got you something, though," he said.

Jenno raised an eyebrow, then smiled when his dad lifted a white baker's paper bag from under the table. Jenno looked inside and saw a chocolate croissant, his favourite treat. It was something that his dad had figured out he could win him over with.

"Got this job, startin' tomorrow... Your old man's gonna be a leaf-blower at the zoo!" he said.

"A leaf-blower?" asked Jenno.

"No shame in leaf-blowin', mate. Know a lot of blokes who'd cut their left nut off to get that gig. I can picture it now – I'll be walking in the sunshine just blowin' leaves this way and that while I look at the animals."

"Yeah, that does sound pretty sick," said Jenno.

"Bloody oath it does. Means I can get you and your mum tickets to the zoo whenever you want."

"Fuck off! I'm not a kid anymore, I don't wanna go to the zoo." Jenno laughed.

"Yeah, I guess I forget that sometimes. All you kids grow too fuckin' fast. You used to beg me to take you to the zoo when you were younger."

"Why don't you just do a plumbing job again?" asked Jenno.

His dad sighed. "You know why I can't get another plumbing job..."

Jenno knew.

His dad had been drinking on the job for almost two years when the health and safety patrol caught him two times over the legal drink-driving limit. He was fired on the spot and his licence was revoked. It was a touchy subject that he hadn't got over yet.

"How'd they expect you to work in those conditions without a bit of piss to get you through it?" he'd say. "You reckon you could dig holes all day, crawl under houses and through roofs, inhaling dust and grime and dirt and touching shit all day? You reckon you could do that day in day out, year after year, completely sober? You'd be a better man then me, but I don't believe it one bit. That profession's made for pissheads. If only the politicians would see that this country was built on piss. It was built on sunburn and fuckin' meat pies. They wanna act all disgusted, like drinkin' on the job's somethin' they can't begin to comprehend, all while they're goin' on pissy lunches every day and drinkin' every evening with clients. They wanna act like they're not the biggest criminals around. You seen what they did to this town? They sold its soul for a bit of profit; you can see it in their pearly white smiles. All these smug faced CEOs and politicians, they don't fool me one bit, but I don't have the power to show 'em. They wouldn't listen to a bloke like me anyways, so what's the use?"

"But I heard you tell Mum that you were gonna stop drinking so you could get your licence back," said Jenno.

"Here's a lesson for you, Jenno. Don't trust people's word. I don't operate on words, mate, I operate on action. I could say anything with a straight face; it doesn't mean that I'm serious. You gotta judge people on what they do, not on what they say they're gonna do."

There was something Jenno felt like he needed to say, but he didn't have the words yet, so he remained silent.

"Look, Jenno," his dad started, "when all this is over, and I've got a more stable job, things are gonna change for us. I'll take us on holidays, get you a new surfboard so you don't have to pick them off of the side of the road anymore. You just gotta give me some time."

"Yeah, nah, I get it, Dad. I'm fine the way things are, so don't worry about me," said Jenno, before he turned and left the room. His dad watched him go. Jenno's dad had never believed in much. He viewed the world as just a place where rich people made money, and poor people made it for them. It all felt like an illusion to him, some trick to keep everyone in their place.

After he lost his plumbing licence he came to the conclusion that there was nothing in his life that was real or tangible besides Jenno and the feelings he experienced when he made art.

He sat back down, opened another beer and continued drawing.

...

That evening, Jenno was tired of sitting in his room. He was bored. The hour or so of attempting to do homework had turned into aimless scrolling on his phone. The vortex he felt from scrolling made him feel sick and, with effort, he tossed his phone on the bed behind him and stood up quickly from his chair. He shook his head and rubbed his eyes, wondering for a moment what he could do. His train of thought landed on skateboarding, so he left his room and grabbed his skateboard from by the front door, but before he had a chance to leave his dad stopped him.

"Where you off to, Jenno?" he said, without looking up. The number of empty beer bottles had grown around him as he sat and drew throughout the afternoon and evening. Jenno counted 10 – the 11th was in his dad's hand.

"Nowhere, Dad, just gonna skate for a bit," Jenno replied.

"What? You got no homework to do or nothin'?"

"Yeah, nah, I do, I'm just takin 'a bit of a break is all," said Jenno.

"Bullshit," his dad snorted, "you've never done a sheet of homework in your fuckin 'life. How'd you ever expect to be shit if you don't study?"

Jenno was quiet, he knew what was coming. When his dad was in one of his moods, he'd drill Jenno about the misery and unfairness of life until Jenno felt as though he could shatter from the weight.

And Jenno, who wanted nothing else in life but to feel close to his dad emotionally as well as physically, listened to everything he had to say, no matter how many times he said it. Most of the time he blamed himself for his dad's sudden mood swings, as if it were something he'd said, or something he did or didn't do.

"Look at me," said Jenno's dad. Jenno met his gaze. His dad's eyes were watery and out of focus.

"I never did shit at school but fuck around. I got my plumbers' licence, but look where that got me. Nah, I never wanted any of this. I'm an artist, Jenno! Look at all these drawings. I should have been fuckin' great! Hundreds and hundreds of them all piled up over themselves. All of them meaningless to everybody except me."

He said this most evenings he was home, each time as though it were a sudden and new realisation. For as long as Jenno could remember, it was always the same. It was a performance he'd grown used to playing a part in, like a warm prop in a monologue to no one.

"I like them, Dad," said Jenno, on cue.

"Yeah, but you're not everyone..." his dad replied.

"But I'm someone."

"Yeah, you're someone, you're my boy," his dad agreed, shaking his head. "I dunno, Jenno. I think you're old enough to hear this now... When I was younger I planned my life to play out differently. I never wanted any kids. I had a dream and passion and something to fulfil, and having a child was never part of that."

Jenno was expecting him to come to the roundabout conclusion that having a child was a blessing in disguise, but his dad kept going.

"But I pissed it all up the wall. It was like one day I woke up in a relationship I didn't wanna be in, with a kid I didn't even want in the first place. Next thing I know, all I do is work to put food on the table and a roof over your head and all my dreams were out the window. I should have been great, Jenno. You understand that? I *was* great. I was a fuckin' prodigy! No art school, no guidance, no nothin'... and look at all of this!" He motioned to the piles of detailed drawings on the table, each of them just as beautiful as the next.

"I love you Jenno, don't get me wrong. But you took everything away from me," he said. He sat back in his seat and reflected for a moment, before he waved the thought away. "Gah!"

Jenno watched him quietly. He knew that the performance was over now. There was nothing else for his dad to say.

A moment later, as if nothing had happened, Jenno's dad put his head back down and continued drawing.

Jenno watched him for a few moments longer, his stomach twisted in knots, feeling an emotion that he couldn't quite identify.

The word greatness, in the sense of using it for your own accomplishments, is nothing but a verbal lubricant that people use before they fuck themselves over with unrealistic expectations.

The journey of self isn't about being great, it's about being grateful. It comes in the understanding of self, of learning how to love and most of all how to be loved.

The depths of Jenno's mum's understanding and love knew no bounds, but she was tired. She was physically and emotionally drained, and had just enough energy to get meals on the table each night. She often worked 60 hours a week while juggling everything else, and the carelessness with which Jenno treated her haunted him for many years when he was older.

When he wasn't drinking, Jenno's dad was a beautiful, loving and intelligent man who had a twinkle in his eye and saw things differently. In the rare times when he was home he'd pick Jenno up from school and they'd both blast out music in the car and sing the wrong lyrics to songs together. That was what was most conflicting to Jenno. The relationship with his dad was bittersweet. Bitter in the hurt and the confusion, but sweet because he loved him with all his heart just the same.

The biggest mistakes we make in life are lived out by our children. In them we see ourselves for the glorious and ugly creatures that we are, and the loving, colourful child we have inside ourselves that is shown from time to time.

...

Jenno left his dad behind and skated down towards the beach. It had just turned night, and the sky was a dark blue that was quickly dissolving into blackness. As he skated, he dodged the headlights of cars coming the opposite way and zigzagged across the road to gain speed. This kind of skating was an emulation of surfing; he used all the same movements and the same flow and style. The only difference was that when he fell, he slid across gravel and concrete.

He sat under the light of a streetlamp on Ratty's bench and watched the faint outlines of waves crashing in the darkness. Jenno peered out at the sea, the same place that had taken the life of a child, and he wondered at how cruel life could be. It was cruel that he would grow old and Ratty never would. That he might have kids one day and raise them, and watch them pass Ratty in age and have children of their own. He realised that there was nothing that he had that couldn't be taken away in an instant. Beautiful things and horrible things weren't so different. They led to the same place, people just stumbled over the line from time to time on the way there.

The waves sounded like distant rumbles of thunder in the night. Jenno could smell the salt in the air. He got up from the bench and walked towards the sand. He threw his skateboard down and ran into the water.

It was icy and made his heart skip a beat. He felt alive, floating in darkness, suspended in space and time in what was the fabric of his universe.

He lay on his back for a while and looked up at the moon and the stars. His body bobbed up and down over the passing waves that looked like black masses on the horizon. He could feel the push and pull of it all, and the great balance that comes in the midst of deafening silence.

A few minutes later, he was forced to swim back in. He was freezing cold, and shivered profusely on his walk home.

He tried to slip into his room without being seen, but his mum was in the living room and caught a glimpse of his soaking wet clothes and hair.

"Where have you been? And what happened to you?" she said.

"I'm sweet, Mum, I just went for a swim…"

"A swim! Are you crazy?" she replied.

"It's fine, Mum, trust me," said Jenno defensively.

Jenno's dad had been in the kitchen when Jenno walked in; now he hobbled into the living room to see what the commotion was. He looked at Jenno.

"What happened to you?"

"Nothing, Dad, I just went for a swim…"

His dad grew angry. "What the fuck have I told you about going out at night?"

"It's fine, Dad, seriously…" said Jenno, less defensively this time.

His dad moved across the room and stopped face to face with Jenno. Jenno could smell the beer on his breath, but he didn't look away.

"Don't ever, *ever* disrespect me and your mum like that. What if somethin' happened to you? Where's Jimmy?"

Jenno didn't say anything; he was looking down at his feet.

"Huh?" his dad prompted him.

Jenno remained silent.

"You're a fuckin' dumb cunt sometimes, Jenno. Have I ever told you that?" he said, before sitting back in his spot on the sofa where he watched the news by himself and complained whenever a bad story was covered.

Jenno dried himself off in his room and sat in the dim light for a while listening to music with his headphones on.

He lay down and thought about floating in the ocean at night and how dark everything was, then drifted slowly to sleep.

...

If there was one consistency that was stalwart in Jenno's life, it was his love of surfing. He surfed every afternoon and most mornings before school. He'd improved so much over the last year that the older boys started to take notice of him. They started chatting to him in the water and calling him onto waves, and they'd invite him up to the surf club from time to time. All of them except Dizz, who was neither here nor there. Jenno had mastered small waves. He could surf them just as well as anyone else, but what he hadn't proven was his ability in big swell. When the surf got to a certain size, Jenno grew hesitant. It made him think of Ratty, and that morning when he was swallowed whole by the sea.

A big wave is a big wave, and a place called Hospital Rock had the biggest. Hospital Rock was a rock shelf at the base of a cliff that faced right out into the open sea. Swell would come from deep water and suddenly stand atop the rock shelf like an avalanche. It was the ugliest and most beautiful wave at the same time. It was unpredictable, violent, dark and heavy, but from time to time it produced waves so immaculate it'd make anyone's mouth water. Surfing Hospital Rock was as much a testament of skill as it was dumb luck. But above anything else, it was the greatest test of bravery, or stupidity, whichever opinion you favoured.

Surfing in big swells is one of the most unnatural and natural feelings at the same time. It should never have come to be. Humans were never designed to be out in stormy seas floating on bits of foam and fibreglass, but there's something out there that drew a certain kind of person to it.

Feeling the raw power of a big wave is the ultimate experience as a surfer. To feel the wind screaming past your ears and the sea spray against your face, blinding you to everything but a few glimpses of light, spray and the dark chasm of water that's exploding at your heels. It's the experience of feeling alive and simultaneously at the edge of death, only to just scrape through unscathed.

Jenno knew that all it would take for him to prove himself to the older boys was one *big* swell at Hospital Rock, and one night his prayer was answered.

It was eight o'clock on a week night when Jenno saw the forecast. It was one of the biggest swells he'd ever seen on chart.

It took more than just a big swell to make a good wave. For the perfect wave to form, every aspect of nature must be in perfect harmony. The wind must be light and blowing in the right direction, the swell must have long periods and the tides need to line up too. Days like that were few and far between, but it looked as though this would be one of them.

The swell was coming down from a cyclone that was out to sea near the coast of Southern Queensland, which not only meant that the swell was going to be large, but that it was coming *quick.*

Jenno felt his stomach sink with a mixture of excitement and fear as he studied the charts. The swell was expected to hit two days from then, and when it did he would surf Hospital Rock.

Two days later, he woke up before sunrise and rolled out of bed. He stretched silently in the darkness, trying his best to ready himself for what was to come. In the stillness of the morning he could hear the distant rumbling of waves in the distance. He wasn't sure if he was imagining things, but the rumbling sounded deeper than usual. There was an energy in the air he hadn't felt in a long time, as if everything was waiting in anticipation.

He pulled his wetsuit off the line, which bounced behind him as he walked away, sending droplets of morning dew this way and that.

The sunrise was bleak and without colour. It was as though the clouds were so dense that the light couldn't penetrate through them. He ran to the carpark atop the cliff above Hospital Rock to find a crowd of spectators had already formed, pink-cheeked and snugged in jumpers and beanies that were only half effective against the ice in the wind that whipped around them. Jenno felt like a celebrity when he slipped through the crowd holding his board. He felt their eyes on him, and wondered what they were all thinking about him as he climbed over the protective fence and started his slow descent down the cliff to Hospital Rock.

The wave there didn't break often, but when it did it was monstrous. Waves triple the size of anyone riding them would gurgle over a rock shelf that sucked up dry above the water on the takeoff. In the beginning, it was mostly a wave for bodyboarders. It was so heavy and so close to the cliff face you'd have to be an absolute maniac to want to surf it. But nowadays anyone who was anyone surfed it. He reached the base of the cliff and breathed a sigh of relief, only to hold it when he saw the first set of waves form in the distance. They looked as heavy as the ocean itself. He watched the surfers in the water paddling frantically to get over them.

Jenno looked up at the tops of the cliff at the spectators. He could see their forms lined across the edge of cliff above him. It felt almost like a colosseum.

Waves crashed against the cliff and exploded into pillars of sea spray. Jenno put his leg rope on and got closer in position, ready to time the rock-off into the water. This was not a wave you wanted to get caught by. With just a moment's wrong timing you could find yourself washed up against the rocks and cheese-grated across the barnacles. Jenno waited patiently, trying his best to stop his right leg from trembling with anticipation. He saw his moment and jumped. When he landed in the water he wasted no time and paddled as hard as he could out the back. It was lucky he did, because a moment later a set of three more waves exploded over the rock where he had just been standing.

There were only a few people out. Dizz and Slowy were the only people Jenno knew. He nodded at them when he paddled past.

"Fark... Bit hairy for you out here, Jenno. No one wants to watch you kill yourself," said Dizz.

"Fuck off, cunt..." muttered Jenno under his breath.

He'd watched this wave break his whole life. He knew where to sit and where to take off. It had looked so easy from the headland when he used to watch it.

Now that he was there, he understood just how crazy the wave was.

The few waves that had rolled past in the time Jenno had been sitting there looked near enough vertical. He had no idea how anyone was able to get to their feet quick enough to surf them. But that wasn't the only thing that put him on edge. The area around Hospital Rock was a known breeding ground for bull sharks. He tried not to think about it, but couldn't help but feel vulnerable every time he tried to peer through the grey water.

A few spectators atop the cliff whistled, which meant another set of waves was forming way out on the horizon.

Everyone scrambled as fast as they could towards the wave.

Jenno just made it over the top of the first one before it collapsed behind him. He could feel it trying to suck him down with it, but he managed to paddle through.

The second wave was even bigger. Dizz was in the right spot for it and turned around to catch it. Everyone on the cliff started cheering as he paddled desperately.

He stood up at the last minute and airdropped from the top of the wave. Jenno was watching as though it was all in slow motion. It looked as though Dizz wasn't going to land it, but somehow he did and kept riding. The rock shelf sucked up beneath him as he rode, but he wasn't concentrating on it. He crouched down and stuck his arms out for balance as the whole wave barrelled over him. A cloud of spray erupted from the depths of the wave and a moment later Dizz emerged, standing proud and tall. Cheers erupted from all around as though he was a gladiator who'd just defeated an opponent.

"You nervous, Jenno?" smiled Slowy.

"Nah, no way!" said Jenno, but Slowy could see right through him.

"Nothing wrong with being nervous. I'm a little nervous. Listen to me, keep in line with that big rock and when a set comes, paddle as fast as you can to the shoulder if you wanna make it."

He pointed to a giant whitish boulder that rested in the rock pile beneath the cliff face. Jenno nodded and positioned himself.

"And Jenno?" said Slowy.

"Yeah?"

"If someone says go it, you better fuckin' go…"

There was an unspoken rule at a spot like that. If a wave came, and someone told you to go it, you had to no matter what, and if you didn't you'd be deemed a pussy and you'd never get a wave there again.

A half-hour passed and Jenno had witnessed the rawness of Hospital Rock. Some people made it, but others wiped out so badly it made him feel sick. Whatever the outcome was, the crowd of onlookers atop the headland roared just the same.

Dizz was easily the best surfer out there. He was so confident that he made it look easy. No wave seemed too dangerous or too big for him, and after every wave he paddled back past everyone and skipped the queue, but no one said anything.

"Come on, Jenno, you gotta get one…" Jenno muttered to himself.

He could picture it. The paddle in, the airdrop, the crowd erupting above him. He wanted the glory.

He looked back over his shoulder at the white boulder Slowy had pointed out earlier. He was in position.

Three waves formed on the horizon; they were the biggest waves of the day. Jenno's heart sank at the sight of them, and he paddled desperately to get over them. He could hear the crowd roaring behind him, and the beating of his heart in his chest thudded into his brain, like a steady drum.

He got over the first one, and just over the second, but just as he was about to paddle over the third he heard Dizz yell, "GO IT, JENNO!"

Without thinking, Jenno turned his board around and paddled as hard as he could towards the shoulder of the wave, just like Slowy had told him to.

Beneath him, the rock shelf gurgled up above the water – he couldn't take his eyes off it – and before he knew it he was falling upside down before he'd even had the chance to stand up.

He just managed to gulp in a lungful of air before his body skipped and skimmed down the face of the wave.

When he hit the bottom he tumbled again and was sucked back over as the wave broke properly. It was brutal. It felt like his head was concussed and his body was torn in two. He got held down for so long he had no idea how far away he was from the surface.

When the wave let go of him he opened his eyes and saw a figure floating a short way away from him.

It was Ratty. He was still wearing the same wetsuit he was in on the day he died.

Jenno screamed underwater. Ratty's eyes were closed. He was floating peacefully. Jenno swam as hard as he could towards the surface. When he breached, he sucked in air and then screamed in horror.

Everyone in the water and all the people on the cliffs stopped what they were doing and raced into action. Although Jenno didn't know it, the emergency services were called, and a few of the surfers tried to paddle over to him before the next set of waves came.

Jenno was panicking. He clung to his board for life as he was washed around the violent surges of water that crisscrossed in all directions, making it almost impossible for him to steady himself.

People on the cliffs started yelling as another wave formed on the horizon. Jenno was in the worst spot possible.

There was nothing anyone could do for him now. Even the people who were paddling to help him were now paddling for their own lives.

Jenno watched it and didn't move. He couldn't move. He was still thinking about what he'd seen underwater. He knew it wasn't real, but it didn't matter.

The wave broke and he heard screams, and then nothing at all.

Somehow, he wasn't sucked under the rock shelf, and instead ended up washed up in the rock pile at the base of the cliff.

He collided with rock after rock until by instinct he wrapped his arms around one and pulled himself from the water. He crawled blindly to safety, stumbling over himself and scraping his arms and legs against the oysters. When he was a safe enough distance away, he rolled onto his side and gasped.

He was half conscious when he felt a pair of hands clasp him on the shoulders and pull him further away from the water.

A little way up the cliff and away from the waves, Jenno coughed up water and vomited.

He lay on his side and let the water dribble from his mouth.

"Are you ok?" asked the stranger who had pulled him up.

Jenno looked up at the face through his blurred vision. It looked vaguely familiar. A moment later he realised that it was Tahiti.

"*Tahiti?*" said Jenno.

Tahiti looked at him with a puzzled expression, unsure how Jenno knew his name.

"You're lucky, grommet... I thought you were gonna die for sure."

"I thought you were gone..." said Jenno, half deliriously.

"Yeah, nah, not anymore. Lucky for you..." said Tahiti breathlessly as he pulled Jenno further away from the water, and pulled Jenno's half dangling board from his ankle. In Jenno's delirious state, Tahiti looked like an angel that had swooped down from heaven to save him. He looked down at his arms and legs to find his wetsuit torn up and bloodied, and when the adrenaline had subsided a little he began to feel the sharp sting of saltwater when it touched open wounds.

By that time, more people had climbed down the cliff to help. As a group, they carried Jenno up to the top where an ambulance came to pick him up.

He was fully conscious in the ambulance. When they closed the ambulance doors and drove off, Jenno caught a glimpse of Tahiti's stooped figure climbing back down towards his cave.

It was the worst wipeout anyone had seen to date, and everyone felt a mixture of pity and respect for Jenno.

He was released from the hospital that afternoon. His mum showered him with kisses until he yanked his face away from her desperately, horrorstruck by her blatant display of public affection, but he was grateful to be alive another day to be subjected to it.

He replayed the entire event in his mind, and was troubled by what he had seen in the water.

An hour later Jimmy pulled up on his bike.

"Jenno! Are you ok? Everyone's been talking about what happened…"

He saw the bandages on Jenno's head, arms and legs, and climbed through the window.

"They're all saying you were charging!"

Jimmy looked at Jenno's face.

"What's wrong?"

Jenno shook his head. "I saw him underwater…"

"Who?"

"Ratty."

"Ratty?"

"Yeah…"

"But I don't understand—" began Jimmy, but Jenno cut him off.

"I know he's dead. It's just what I saw."

Jimmy sat down on the edge of the bed.

"I'm sorry."

"Don't worry about it…" said Jenno.

"What happened?"

"I dunno, I paddled for the wave but I froze when I saw the rock shelf. It's fucked, I dunno how they do it."

"Who was out?"

"Dizz and Slowy, and a couple others."

"What'd they say when you ate it?"

"Nothing. I saw Ratty after I fell. I dunno, it just looked like he was floating there."

Jimmy sat back and exhaled loudly, the vivid scene painted in his mind.

Jenno winced as he raised his bandaged arm and rested it gently on his pillow.

"You think you'll ever get back in the water?" he asked Jimmy.

Jimmy shrugged. "I dunno. I want to, but I don't know if I can yet. Every time I'm out there I think of him."

Jenno nodded, understanding.

Jimmy stood up from the bed and walked over to the table in Jenno's room. It was covered in heaps of crinkled looseleaf sheets of paper from the various weeks of homework and assignments Jenno had missed or forgot.

He looked over at the photo of Jenno and Ratty that was stuck to the wall and a forlorn expression overtook him.

"You'll never guess who saved me…" said Jenno.

"Not Dizz, surely?" Jimmy replied.

"Nah, fuck no. It was Tahiti."

"Tahiti?" said Jimmy. "I thought he was dead…"

"Yeah, same. I dunno where he went, but he's back. He grabbed me from the rocks and pulled me out of the way. I dunno if I would have survived it if it weren't for him."

"What did he say?"

"Not much. I asked him where he'd been, but he didn't really say. Mum reckons I should go down there with something to say thanks."

"You reckon he still lives in that cave?"

"Yeah, I think so. Dunno where else he would go."

"When are you going to see him?" asked Jimmy.

"Tomorrow morning, I guess. I reckon he wakes up with the sun. I could probably get him early before he starts wandering."

Jimmy stayed a while longer before he had to go home for dinner. After he left, Jenno lay down and stared up at the ceiling, thinking of everything that had happened that day.

5

The next morning, Jenno woke up early and walked down to the headland to watch the sunrise. In the darkness, his silhouette clambered carefully over rocks and between bushes until he stopped at the cliff's edge. His arms and legs were still bandaged, and although his wounds were superficial he still winced every now and then if he bumped them or brushed them too hard against the overgrowth. The world was waking up around him. The sun was rising, and with it a soft breeze from the sea that pushed Jenno's hair from his forehead. In his hands, he held a little bottle of water and an orange and poppyseed muffin he'd stolen from the petrol station the other day after school.

He ripped open the packaging and ate the muffin quietly, trying to act as casual as possible. The real reason he was here at this time, at this place, was because of what Fleetwood had said. She told him to speak to Ratty, and see if he didn't feel any different. After what he'd seen the day before, he figured there was no better time to do so than now.

He took a big bite out of his muffin and then looked over both of his shoulders to make sure no one was around. It seemed too quiet. He felt nervous. He sighed, and then spoke.

"Hey, dude. Hope you're doing well. We miss you."

It was a strange feeling; the sound of his own voice made him cringe, so he sat quietly and reflected, waiting, as though something were meant to happen.

But there was only silence. Only the world stared back at him, and it seemed as though his words were swallowed by the horizon. In a way, he was just talking to himself, his inner self, the part of him that was always observing but never saying anything.

"I've been feeling lost ever since you left. It's just not the same without you," he said.

A row of ants trickled over and across the back of his hand; he lifted it up from the ground and shook them off.

Everything seemed as though it were alive in the glory of the sunrise. The wind, the cliffs and the ocean, all of them moving. Lines of swell rolled across the sea towards the shore like the pulses of a beating heart, while the breeze sifted through the trees and across the water.

The cliffs were moving too, but too slowly for Jenno to see. With every breath of wind and every lick of water, the cliff faces were slowly crumbling away.

He waited a few more minutes before he shrugged and continued, "Anyways, I just wanted to tell you that I miss you, and I hope you're doing well wherever you are."

He stood up, picked up his bag and made his way towards Tahiti's cave.

In his bag Jenno had 50 dollars and a bottle of wine he'd stolen out of the cupboard to give Tahiti.

He could see the hammock when he got closer, and Tahiti's body wrapped within it like a cocoon.

Jenno had expected Tahiti to be awake by now. The sun had fully risen, and the morning light was golden and warm, but Tahiti was still fast asleep. He looked comfortable and content, like there was nothing in the world that could have woken him. Jenno contemplated waking him for a moment – he wanted to talk to him – but thought better of it. His dad reckoned it was bad luck to wake a sleeping man up. He placed the bottle of wine down next to the other bottles that were strewn about the cave, and then he tried to tuck the 50-dollar note as gently as he could into the slot between Tahiti's shoulder and the hammock.

Tahiti must have sensed his presence, because the moment Jenno leaned over him with the money his eyes shot wide open.

"What the fuck?!" he said, rolling out of the hammock suddenly and leaping to his feet.

A sudden look of recognition flittered across his face as he stared, bewildered, at Jenno.

He looked at the bandages on Jenno's arms and legs and his expression softened.

"You're that kid from yesterday," he said, in a matter-of-fact way.

Jenno nodded.

"What's that for?" said Tahiti, looking down at the 50-dollar note in Jenno's hand.

"Fark, sorry for waking you. I was just trying to say thanks is all."

"Nah, you're alright, grommet. I don't want your money," Tahiti said, before knocking over the wine bottle with his foot. It rolled but didn't break. He looked down at it and smiled. "But I will take this!" He threw up the bottle and caught it in the air.

"2009? You've got a sophisticated taste, grommet," he said, squinting as he read the back label.

"Cheers," said Jenno.

"How're you feelin', anyways?" asked Tahiti, sitting on the ground and placing the bottle safely behind him.

Jenno remained standing.

"Yeah, I'm good. Pretty lucky."

"Pretty lucky? A fuckin' miracle, more like it!" said Tahiti. He looked over his shoulder and rifled through a small pile of dirty-looking clothes. There were a few black t-shirts, a pair of jeans and an old, beat-up looking suit. A relic from the man he was before Tahiti. Jenno had seen him wearing it one night a few years back. He was standing in the telephone box next to the lifeguard club with the phone in his hand, but he wasn't talking to anyone. The image had never left him. The phone box had been the only source of light in the darkness of night. It looked like a little beacon in a sea of blackness, and Tahiti clung to it, drawn into it like a moth.

Tahiti stuck his hand into the suit jacket pocket and rummaged around. He pulled out a crumpled box of cigarettes, drew one out by the brown tip and balanced it in between his cracked lips.

"You got a lighter?" he asked Jenno hopefully.

Jenno shook his head. "Fark, nah, sorry…"

"Fuck sakes," Tahiti muttered to himself. "And come sit down, you're makin' me nervous."

Jenno took a seat next to him silently. Tahiti squinted as he looked over the ocean; the lines on his face looked more pronounced than ever in the morning light. He looked as though he'd once been a handsome man in another life. His hair was long and golden brown with sun-bleached streaks of blond running through. His skin was tan and he was in surprisingly good shape for a man who ran on liquor and pastries. The only thing that gave him away were his teeth. They were as brown as his skin and cracked along the front row. He knew it, too. Over the years he'd developed a habit of talking without showing them.

"That wave should have killed you. What the fuck were you even thinking going out there?" he said, putting the cigarette gently back into the box.

"I dunno. It was all good at the start. I reckoned I was ready to surf it. I ate it, yeah, but everyone eats it out there on their first wave. It's just, I saw something underwater after I fell."

"What, like a shark or somethin'?"

"Nah, I saw my friend," said Jenno.

"What was your friend doing down there?" laughed Tahiti, until he saw the look on Jenno's face. He fell quiet for a moment.

"You were friends with that boy who drowned," he said.

Jenno nodded. "His name was Ratty."

"Yeah… I remember you now. You boys used to ride your skateboards past me when you were younger."

"Yeah, we did," said Jenno.

"I'm sorry for what happened to your mate. I wasn't here when it happened, but I heard about it," said Tahiti, pulling the wine bottle from behind him and unscrewing the cap. He offered it to Jenno. Jenno took a swig but then spat it out.

"That's fucked…" he said.

"You get used to it, mate," said Tahiti, before taking a swig himself.

"We were the ones you caught reading your letter," said Jenno, remembering the time he, Jimmy and Ratty found a chest full of letters to someone in Tahiti's cave. He'd always had a suspicion that that was why Tahiti left in the first place.

Jenno saw something flash in his eyes.

"Sorry. We didn't realise they were yours. Ratty reckoned there was a treasure map or something in there."

Tahiti scoffed. "That's alright. I got nothin' to hide anyways."

He took another sip from the wine bottle and winced a bit. Jenno looked at his teeth. They looked even browner than usual in the sunlight.

"Who were you writing to?" asked Jenno.

"Someone who thinks I'm dead," Tahiti replied.

Jenno didn't understand what he meant, but the tone was the kind that adults used when they didn't want to discuss something further, so Jenno let it be. "Why did you leave?" he asked him instead.

Tahiti's eyebrows furrowed in concentration. "I dunno," he said. "Just woke up one day and figured, fuck it. I reckoned I'd been here long enough. It gets borin' when you're in the same place doing the same thing every day. That's why they started calling me Tahiti, I reckon."

"Why'd you reckon that?"

"Cos they reckon I live my life like a holiday. I don't reckon so. This isn't a holiday, this is a fuckin' sentence. I done some bad things in my life. I guess this is just my way of paying for them."

"Paying for what?"

"Doesn't matter, grommet. Just how my life unfolded, is all."

"Yeah, but didn't you ever wanna change it? You could work if you wanted to."

"I guess I probably could. But why the fuck would I go work for some corporate cunt who'd stab me in the back just as easy as buyin' me a coffee? You're too young to get it, grommet. Life's not that simple. Everything you have can be taken away from you in an instant. It makes a man question what the point of it all was anyways. You reckon people can change? The problem is that most people don't want to."

"But why not? If you're in that much pain, why not just change? I don't get it," said Jenno.

"Cus they're fuckin' scared to, that's why," said Tahiti. He spat a golly off the edge of the rock; it arced down perfectly and splattered a few metres below. Light danced off the water's surface. Jenno looked out into the ocean and followed the light blue pathway created by the current that swerved out towards the horizon.

"It's scary to change. Means you gotta risk losing it all in the hopes of gaining something. You'll get it one day, grommet. You'll realise that everybody's too fuckin' concerned about life that they completely forget to live it. You spend it gathering all your shit and makin' something of yourself, but what does it matter in the end? If there's one thing I know about life, it's that there's not a single thing that can't get taken away from you in an instant. All that shit we collect and hold onto just gets heavier and heavier. Until one day it gets so fuckin' heavy that you can't even smile cus your lips can't lift the weight. But one day we all end up floatin' somehow."

"What do you mean?" asked Jenno.

Tahiti was silent for a time. He covered his eyes from the morning sun and squinted into the horizon, recollecting all his thoughts.

"I dunno. Maybe I've been living alone on this headland for too long. I get to thinking about things. Sometimes I reckon I could just fall into the horizon, I get that close to touching it. You wouldn't believe the things I seen and heard. I seen everything from sharks to whales, dolphins, fuck, even penguins coming through here. I wonder where they're goin' and what they're doin' and if they're anything like me. I get jealous of 'em sometimes on a sunny day, but when it's rainin' and stormy I'm happy to be me."

Jenno thought back to the evening he'd seen Tahiti wearing his suit in the phone box. He lived a life of isolation, so separate that he had become a witness to everything. An observer, a listener and a thinker.

"Sometimes I reckon we're all already floatin', we're just tethered to our bodies for some reason. It's like the universe is tryna teach us something about life before it's all over. Fuck knows why, with all the pain its brought me. I dunno what lesson there is in all this, and I guess all I can do is hope that it reveals itself at the end of it all. A moment's clarity just before my story fades to black. Wouldn't that be a fuckin' kick in the nuts – one final moment where you see how you went wrong in life. If I ever meet God I'm gonna ask him what the fuck he was thinking when he made me, and why the fuck did he let me suffer for so long. What's it all worth? All that happiness, all that pain and anger at everything and everyone, but mostly myself. All that fuckin' bitterness… But you know what? When I'm feelin' heavy, I just try and remember that there's a part of me somewhere that's sooooaarin' through the air and he doesn't feel a fuckin' thing!"

Jenno watched him curiously.

"You'll get it one day, grommet…" Tahiti said.

"Are you scared?" asked Jenno.

Tahiti paused for a moment, scratching his head thoughtfully.

"Yeah, I'm scared. I always planned on livin' my life beautifully. But I came to the realisation that life's not beautiful, it's a fuckin' pain in the ass and it only gets worse. I dunno how to change, this is just who I am. And that scares me. That's why I came back. I left cus I thought I needed a change. Went up the coast, but funnily enough after a little while I started to feel the same thing. So, I figured, fuck it, and came back here again. It's nicer here. I got this cave and this hammock, the baker down the road gives me bread every mornin' and I can scrape up enough dough by midday to get some beers."

"Seems alright," said Jenno.

"As good as it could be, I reckon. No one expects anything from me and I don't expect anything from anyone else. My life was normal once. I had a job, an apartment, everything you could ever want," he explained. "I dunno what happened. Well, I do know what happened, but sometimes I look around and think to myself, 'What the fuck's goin 'on? 'You ever do that? Maybe you're too young yet, grommet, but when you get older, the more it happens. It's like you come to all of a sudden, and realise you're not where you're meant to be."

"What do you mean?" Jenno asked.

Tahiti paused for a moment and considered. "You ever look at yourself in the mirror, and it feels like you're lookin 'at a stranger? That's how I was feelin', that's what got me here," he said, finally.

"Yeah, I know what you mean, but I still don't understand," said Jenno.

"Yeah, nah, I wouldn't have expected you to," Tahiti replied, smiling.

"But how'd you actually get here?" asked Jenno.

"I dunno, it seemed like one day, I realised that I was in the exact same spot doing the exact same thing as the day before, and the one before that and the next. Like I'd just been on fuckin 'autopilot my whole adult life. I dunno, it drove me crazy. I was married, had a kid, good job, but yeah, nah, I threw it all away. And now I'm here."

It felt like Tahiti wasn't saying everything, again, and Jenno knew not to press any further. He knew that he was holding something back, because a moment later, Tahiti groaned and got up.

"Anyways, grommet, I gotta go get my day started. I got a reputation to uphold," said Tahiti.

He shook his legs out and tried to stretch his back.

"Cheers for the piss," he said, holding up the bottle of wine Jenno had brought him.

"No worries. Cheers for saving my life," said Jenno.

"No worries," said Tahiti.

Jenno got up and left Tahiti, who stayed a little while longer. When Jenno was far enough away, he peered back over his shoulder and watched for a moment as Tahiti finished the bottle he'd brought for him, while he peered out into the horizon in silence.

. . .

"What do you reckon he did?" Jimmy asked Jenno later that day, after Jenno had told him everything that had happened. They were sitting at the edge of Jimmy's pool, baking in the sunlight. It was the first time Jimmy's mother had let Jenno near it in more than two years, after he and Ratty had backflipped off the balcony into it. It didn't matter anyway – with Jenno's bandages, all he could do was dangle one leg into the water, and occasionally lean over and dunk his head in.

"I dunno. I don't reckon anything against the law, I mean, it doesn't look like he's on the run or anything," said Jenno.

"You don't think so? Why else would he be in that situation? He said it himself, he had a good job, an apartment, everything... How would he just all of a sudden become homeless?"

"I dunno, it felt like he was holding something back," said Jenno, considering.

"I wonder if we should tell the police," said Jimmy.

Jenno screwed his face up in disgust." The police? For what, he hasn't done shit…"

"Yeah, but what if they've been looking for him?" said Jimmy.

"Fuck that, I'm not going to the police," said Jenno, shaking his head. He looked at Jimmy, almost disappointed." You sound like your dad, dude."

"Nah, it's not like that. It's just, what if he killed someone, what about his wife?" said Jimmy, bowing his head in shame.

"Nah, he's not a killer. I just reckon he didn't want me knowing his business, and fair enough, I guess," said Jenno.

"Yeah, well, just be careful around him, Jenno. He doesn't give me a good feeling," said Jimmy.

"Shut up, Jimmy. You're just scared of him cus of that time he threw your skateboard into the bush when we were younger," laughed Jenno. He leaned over the edge of the pool and dunked his head in the water. But a seed of doubt had been planted in his mind, and as much as he tried to ignore it, it began to grow.

6

Every second Saturday morning of the month, Jimmy had maths tutoring in the next town over. He didn't mind it so much, the bus ride was half an hour on a good day, and an hour on a bad, but it gave him some time to himself where he could look out the window and think about things as the world crawled slowly by.

He left early in the mornings, and usually got home around midday. When he finally made it back, he found Jenno waiting for him at the edge of the driveway.

"What's doin?" asked Jenno.

"I just had tutoring. How long have you been waiting for?" asked Jimmy.

"Not long. Was just skating past and figured you'd be home soon. You ready for tonight?"

"Tonight?" asked Jimmy.

"Yeah, it's Letty's party, dude!" said Jenno, excitedly.

"Ah shit, yeah, I forgot," said Jimmy.

"Fark, what do you mean? You can still come, can't you?" asked Jenno.

"I don't reckon my dad would want me going to a party."

"Just tell him you're staying at mine tonight!" said Jenno.

Jimmy thought it over for a moment before nodding. "Alright, I reckon he'd be ok with that – just let me go ask him," said Jimmy.

He disappeared up the driveway, lugging a bag full of textbooks on his back. He came back smiling five minutes later.

Jenno looked at him expectantly.

"We're on," laughed Jimmy.

"Fuck yeah!" exclaimed Jenno. He put his arm around Jimmy's shoulder and shook him. "Wanna skate down to the shops?"

"Yeah, alright," said Jimmy.

They grabbed their boards and took the long way, swerving back and forth down the backstreets, over pavement and across grass. Jenno skated so erratically that Jimmy could never tell what he was going to do next. One second he was cruising, and the next he was low to the ground, both hands planted to the concrete, sliding his board out beneath him. It felt like a lifetime to Jimmy since he skated last. He laughed as wind whistled past his ears and down into his clothes, the feeling and sound of smooth road beneath his wheels that gripped so well to the rubber. It felt so similar to surfing that he could picture himself flying across a wave, and in that thought he yearned to be in the ocean again.

Newspaper covered the front windows of a dark and empty store. Jenno scraped to a halt in front of it and kicked his skateboard up into his hands.

"Farrkkk, you're joking!" he said.

"What?" asked Jimmy, pulling up behind him.

"The milk bar shut down!" said Jenno, pointing towards the store. It stood like a corpse amongst roses, an empty husk neighboured by bustling shops.

"Yeah, I know. Mum says they're putting a new yoga studio there," said Jimmy.

Jenno's face twisted with anger. "Who the fuck's gonna use that?"

"Loads of people," said Jimmy. "When's the last time you even went to the milk bar, anyways?"

"Nah, not for ages, but I still liked it," said Jenno.

"Yeah, everyone liked it, but nobody's bought anything from them for years, that's the problem. It happened to the video shop, it happened to the CD store, now the milk bar, and it's gonna keep happening. How were they meant to stay open if they weren't making any money?" said Jimmy.

"Fuck off, Jimmy," Jenno rebutted, shaking his head. He looked away from the empty shop and jumped back on his skateboard. Jimmy followed him, laughing to himself.

...

Later that night, Jimmy and Jenno made their way to Letty's party. Letty's parents were away again and so he took advantage of the opportunity and told as many people as he could to show up. Girls and boys from all around the area were going to be there and it was an opportunity that they were not going to miss.

Having such a large and open party was a mistake Letty would learn the hard way. Every party from the age of 16 upwards was guaranteed to get crashed by dozens of kids. The worst of the worst would show up, and often the bad kids would end up smashing the house up or getting in fights out front. It got so bad that proper security guards would be hired for a 16th birthday party with a door list. They'd have two guards at the front and one patrolling around the back of the house, and all of them would be communicating with walkie-talkies the whole night.

Both boys had told their parents they were staying at each other's houses, and so their nights were completely free from constraint of curfews and overly worried text messages from their mothers.

They hopped on the bus with reusable supermarket bags full of warm beers, stuffed between socks so they wouldn't jingle. A few hours before, Jenno had begged Slowy to buy him and Jenno some beers, and he finally cracked and bought them two six-packs of the cheapest stuff he could find.

The bus was full of kids going to the same party, yelling and screaming, talking over each other and throwing stuff. A few older passengers got fed up and asked them to be quiet, but every time they did the kids only got louder and rowdier.

The army of kids hopped off the bus and wandered through quiet suburban streets in search of Letty's house. Soon they could hear the thumping of speakers in the distance.

Before they rounded the corner to Letty's house, Jenno put his arm in front of Jimmy.

"We should sink a few of these first before we get in there…"

"Yeah, definitely…" said Jimmy.

The two of them unslung the shopping bags from their shoulders and took two beers out each.

"Let's just pump 'em both quick," said Jenno, and he and Jimmy tried to skull both beers as fast as they could.

Both of them started spluttering after half of just one, but through persistence they managed to get the rest down.

"Alright, let's go," said Jenno, excitedly.

"I'm kinda nervous," said Jimmy.

"Huh, what could you possibly be nervous about?" Jenno replied, with a look of disgust on his face.

"Well, what if it turns out like Skeelsy's party?" said Jimmy, defensively.

"Skeelsy?"

"Ratty told me about it," started Jimmy." He said there was this kid called Skeelsy in his class who just moved here from the UK. He said Skeelsy was the cockiest kid he'd ever met. Anyway, in his first couple weeks at school he told everyone that he was gonna have the biggest party the town had ever seen, and that everyone in the year was invited."

"What a legend," laughed Jenno.

"Yeah, until 500 kids rocked up at his door and smashed his house apart," said Jimmy." They had to call the riot police and everything. Apparently Dizz was the one who broke all the windows in his house, but they never caught him for it."

"Faark, what a dog," said Jenno.

"Yeah," said Jimmy." So what happens if 500 kids rock up to Letty's?"

"It'll be sweet, dude! Besides, Letty got security guards."

"Really?" asked Jimmy, surprised.

The security guards turned out to be none other than Dizz, Slowy and a few of the other older boys. They were sitting around the front door drinking beers, holding a clipboard with a few scribbled names on it for a guest list.

"Well, well, well," said Dizz as they approached.

"Doin', Dizz?" said Jenno, before dapping him up.

Dizz crossed Jenno's name off the list. He and Jimmy went to walk through the door, but Dizz stood in Jimmy's way before he got a chance to get through.

"Don't think I saw your name on the list, grom," he said.

Jimmy looked down at the clipboard and saw his name right under Jenno's.

"I see it right there." He pointed at it, trying to keep his composure.

"Ah yeah, you're right!" said Dizz, but he didn't move.

"Fuck off, Dizz," said Jenno from the doorway. "Just let him through."

Dizz looked back over his shoulder at Jenno, and then to Jimmy.

"Alright, grommet, you can go in. But it'll cost you," he said. He looked down at Jimmy's shopping bag and smiled.

Jimmy joined Jenno inside a few moments later, and Jenno looked down at his empty hands in dismay.

"Fark, what happened to your beers?" he said.

Jimmy didn't reply.

"Fuck that, I'm gonna go say something to him," said Jenno, turning around angrily.

"Nah, dude, don't! It's not worth it," said Jimmy, pulling Jenno back.

Jenno readjusted his shirt and looked at Jimmy seriously.

"You gotta learn how to stand up for yourself. What would Ratty have said if he was here? He would have swung, for sure..." said Jenno. But he pulled one of his beers out of his bag, and held it out to Jimmy. "Take one of mine."

Jimmy shook his head. "Nah, dude, thank you, but it's fine."

Jenno put the beer back in his bag, almost offended.

"I reckon Letty will have some drinks anyways," said Jenno.

"Yeah, I reckon so," said Jimmy.

They walked through the front hallway and entered the party.

It was carnage inside. Youths were everywhere. They'd pushed all the furniture to one side to make a dancefloor, and in the back garden there was a fire going with some camp chairs around it and one of those shitty stained-glass tables with an umbrella hole in the middle that anyone growing up in Australia would have found themselves sitting around at some point in their lives.

Letty was in the kitchen pouring some goon into a cup for himself.

Goon was just casket wine. It was awful, but it cost eight dollars for four litres and did the job. Most people carried it around in the sack it came in. They'd hang it on clothes lines or pass it around parties, and every now and then someone would finish one, blow the sack back up with air and use it as a pillow to sleep on.

"Aye, boys!" Letty laughed when he saw them. He was hammered already.

He saw Jimmy without a drink and poured a cup of goon for him. Jimmy took it and smiled, feeling better already.

"I invited heaps of those rigs from Renona High, they're over in the living room, I think!" said Letty, excitedly.

Jenno's ears perked up and he raced to the kitchen door to get a peek at the girls.

"One of them is so hot. Her name's Skye, I'm pretty sure – she's the blonde chick," Letty told them.

Jimmy leaned over to take a look and saw her there. She was beautiful, he thought to himself.

"Fark, yeah, they're all pretty hot!" said Jenno.

"Go talk to them then, you pussy..." laughed Letty.

Jenno suddenly grew nervous. For all his talk about girls, the idea of suddenly confronting a pack of them seemed terrifying.

Jimmy could tell he was nervous, so he and Letty both grabbed Jenno and pushed him into the living room towards the girls.

He collided with one and they both toppled over.

"Fark, sorry!" said Jenno, scowling at Jimmy and Letty, who were both bent over with laughter.

The girl looked at him, then at Jimmy and Letty, and put two and two together.

"It's ok, I'm alright," she said.

Jenno stood up and helped her up.

"Are you sure?" he said.

She nodded and smiled, and for a moment they locked eyes.

In all the porn he watched, this was the moment when the actors kissed and then had sex shortly after. Never in his universe had Jenno imagined there were things that led to that, and certain ways of approaching things in a respectful and genuine matter.

"Do you wanna hook up?" he asked, looking into her eyes.

She looked at him, somewhat taken aback. "Um... no?"

"Ah damn, really...? Well, see ya later." He turned around and walked straight back into the kitchen.

"Did you talk to her?" asked Jimmy.

"Yeah, but she was frigid, so I figured, fuck that..."

The boys laughed and took a swig of their drinks.

It was the first time Jenno had ever been properly drunk. He felt like he could do anything. He walked around the party almost in a dream. The house was full of kids and there wasn't a free space to stand or walk, so he had to wriggle through the crowd.

He passed kids laughing, arguing, kissing and vomiting all under one roof. He'd never experienced anything like it. It felt like he'd stepped into a new chapter in his life.

...

Jimmy was looking for Jenno. He'd disappeared and left Jimmy all alone. He was drunk too. The world was spinning around him as he walked. He stumbled over and sat on the sofa in the corner of the living room. His body sunk into the cushions, and his head lolled over to the side. There was a girl sitting next to him on her phone. It was the girl Letty had pointed out to them in the kitchen.

"Jimmy," he blurted out, trying to introduce himself without sounding too drunk.

She looked at him and assessed him for a moment before replying, "Skye."

Jimmy's palms all of a sudden went clammy. "Where you from?" he asked, trying his best to sound cooler than he was.

"Just down the road… What about you?"

"Yeah, same," he said, realising at the same time he'd run out of questions to ask.

"Do you want to dance?" he asked her.

"Yeah, sure," she nodded.

The two of them got up and stumbled over to the centre of the living room where everyone else was dancing.

"I love music," said Jimmy; he was hoping to tell her that he played in a band, but she didn't hear him.

They danced with the crowd for a bit, but then Jimmy made his move. With one fluid motion, he put his arm around her waist. It was a leap of faith. But his heart dropped when he felt her hand gently pull his arm away.

"Sorry," he said.

"No, it's ok. I just feel like I don't know you well enough for that."

"I understand. Do you wanna find somewhere better to talk?" he asked her.

"Alright, but only to talk," she said.

They went upstairs to where it was quieter and found a room.

"I'm sorry about before. I don't really dance with girls that much, I just thought that's what you were meant to do..." said Jimmy once they'd sat down inside the room. By the looks of it, it was Letty's parents' room. There was a walk-in wardrobe filled with expensive-looking coats and suits, a bathroom and also a little balcony.

"It's ok, I think it is what you're meant to do. I guess I don't really dance with that many boys either," she said.

Jimmy was surprised. By the sounds of it most of the boys knew her; he would have thought all of them would have tried.

"Sometimes I think I'm not meant to party. I don't know, I just don't feel like it's for me. I see everyone having fun and losing themselves, but I just don't feel the same."

"Yeah…" said Jimmy, "I know how you feel. I've never really felt a part of that kind of stuff either. I feel so isolated a lot of the time, like there's something wrong with me."

"I don't think there's anything wrong with you." She smiled.

Jimmy felt his stomach flutter.

"I don't wanna come off as forward or anything, but could I have your number?" he asked.

She paused for a moment that felt like an eternity to Jimmy, before nodding.

"Yeah, of course. I think it'd be nice to see you again," she said.

"You too," said Jimmy.

They pulled out their phones and exchanged numbers.

...

Ten minutes later Jenno was walking up the stairs in a state, but before he made it to the top an arm stopped him. It was a boy a year or two older than him.
"I wouldn't go up there, bro, all the rooms are full of people rooting…"

"Rooting? Really?" said Jenno. "Fark, who is it?"

"Why do you care?" replied the other boy.

"Nah, I don't, I was just curious…"

"I dunno, a bunch of people… I just saw that Skye chick go up there with someone…"

...

It didn't take long before the party got out of hand. More and more people showed up, and every bunch seemed to be rowdier and rowdier. There was a fight in the back garden, the sounds of breaking glass and terrified shrieks from some girls. The neighbours called the cops and within 10 minutes they were at the front door.

As soon as people saw their uniforms and torches everyone scrambled to get out of the house.

Jimmy was upstairs with Skye when they heard the commotion. The two of them ran downstairs to find Letty being questioned by the police. Next to the cops were a man and a woman in dress robes, who Jimmy assumed to be neighbours; both of them looked annoyed.

Jimmy looked around the room and saw Jenno pouring himself a shot.

He ran over to him. "Jenno, dude, what the fuck are you doing? Let's go!"

He said goodbye to Skye, grabbed Jenno by the shoulder and the two of them ran out and hopped over the back fence.

Jenno was blind drunk and stumbled this way and that as they ran into the darkness.

"Where'd you go, bro, I was looking for you for ages…?" said Jenno when they finally slowed into a walk.

"I was with Skye," Jimmy replied casually.

Jenno remembered what that older boy had said to him and suddenly the pieces of the puzzle came together.

"No way!" said Jenno, clasping his hands on Jimmy's shoulders.

Jimmy laughed.

"Yeah… I got her number."

"Oh… so you didn't fuck her?" asked Jenno.

"Huh?" said Jimmy.

"Some guy told me you were rooting, is all. I thought you lost your virginity for a second."

"No, Jenno, what the fuck… We just talked," Jimmy said defensively.

"Fark, alright… Dunno what you're so excited about – I got loads of girls' numbers tonight."

"Yeah, but she gave me her number because she wanted to, not because she was terrified like the girls who gave you theirs."

"Fuck off… They were all over me tonight."

"Yeah, yeah!" laughed Jimmy. "She's really beautiful though, I hope I'll get to see her again," he added, his heart swelling at the thought.

…

It took a long while for them to walk back to Jenno's house. Both his mum and his dad were fast asleep and the two boys snuck around the back.

Jimmy pulled a bit of tin foil out of his pocket and opened it. There was a nugget of weed inside.

Jenno's eyes lit up at the sight of it. He'd only smoked it once before, the time he, Jimmy and Ratty smoked after the movies. He studied it intently. It looked completely harmless, almost like a tuft of grass that'd been plucked off of a soccer field, and in all honesty it could have been for all they knew. Jimmy let him smell it a bit.

It was a distinct odour, almost sweet and fruity.

"You want some?" asked Jimmy.

Jenno nodded.

They snuck into the kitchen and grabbed a bowl as quietly as they could, and then Jimmy sat down and chopped the weed up.

"How are we gonna smoke it?" asked Jenno.

"I'll show you," said Jimmy.

He stood up and opened the plastic recycling bin against the wall behind them. He leaned in and rummaged for a bit before pulling out a used drink bottle.

"Perfect!" he whispered.

"Now what?" Jenno asked, confused.

"Do you have a hose?" asked Jimmy.

"Yeah, why?"

"Show me where it is; I gotta chop some off."

"What! No way, my dad will kill me…"

"Relax, he won't notice, I'm only gonna chop off a bit."

Jenno showed him and he chopped off a tiny length.

"See… there's no way he can tell."

Jenno watched him work at the drink bottle.

He took out a lighter and melted a hole in the plastic near the bottom of the bottle, just big enough to squeeze the hose piece into it. He pulled a small metal cone piece that looked just like a thimble with a hole in it. He filled the bottom of the bottle up with water, then placed the cone filled with weed onto the tip of the hose piece.

It was a makeshift bong, of the type used by countless Australian teenagers. It had almost become a rite of passage.

Jimmy lit the cone and pulled a hit.

Jenno watched silently as Jimmy pulled. Smoke gathered inside the bottle. Then in one swift motion, Jimmy pulled the cone piece away and inhaled.

He held it in his chest for a few seconds and then exhaled a thick cloud of smoke. He spluttered and tried his best not to cough too loudly.

"You want some?" said Jimmy, his eyes tearing up as he handed the bottle and the lighter over. "Here, I'll pack your first cone piece."

Jenno watched as Jimmy filled the little cone piece until the weed was a little above level.

"I won't pack a Christmas tree for you just yet…" Jimmy said, passing the bong over to Jenno. Jenno held it carefully and brought it to his mouth. When he was ready, he lit the cone piece and pulled just as Jimmy had done.

"Keep pulling… yep, yep, alright… now take your finger off the shotty and pull the cone piece out…" instructed Jimmy as Jenno pulled his hit.

Jenno gulped it all in. He held it in his chest for a few seconds before he exhaled like Jimmy had done, but it burned his throat and he started coughing.

Jimmy put his hands up. "Be quiet, you're gonna wake your parents up!"

Jenno was shaking his head as he spluttered loudly, unable to stop.

The back light flicked on, and before either of them had a chance to do anything Jenno's dad opened the door and stuck his head out.

"The fuck are you boys making so much noise for?"

"Sorry, Dad…" Jenno tried to say through his coughing fit.

Jimmy panicked and tried to hide the bong and the weed, but Jenno's dad had already seen them.

"I don't give a fuck that you're smoking weed, just shut the fuck up and be quiet about it, it's two o'clock in the fuckin' mornin'!"

He closed the door behind him and turned the light off.

It was a strange experience for Jimmy; he wondered what would have happened if it were *his* dad who stuck his head out.

Jenno was high as a kite. He was staring off into the darkness, miles away from where they were.

Jimmy was high too, and in a minute his train of thought had taken him far away from Jenno's dad popping his head out.

The two of them sat in silence for a long time.

Jenno had never been this high before. It was if he suddenly saw everything for what it was, and he appreciated it all. He appreciated the darkness, the stars and the moon. The moon was full that night; he looked up at it, in awe of its craters.

He looked over at Jimmy and the thought came to him that if he ever died he would live on through him, just as Ratty lived on through them.

The thought made him smile.

"I wish Ratty was here…" said Jimmy.

"Yeah…" said Jenno.

"His mum told me she said she speaks to him every day. You've gotta start surfing again, dude…" said Jenno.

Jimmy nodded. "Yeah, I know."

"I got barrelled for the first time the other day," said Jenno, all of a sudden remembering. "I couldn't believe it… I saw it coming and everything. The vision was just like how they film it, but the feeling was like nothing else. It felt like I was falling and climbing at the same time, everything just went so steep, and the noise was like I was in some collapsing tunnel crashing down all around me."

"Did you make it?"

"Nah… I ended up flipping upside down like two seconds after I got in. But it felt like slow motion. You know what I mean?"

Jimmy laughed. "Yeah, I know what you mean."

They both smoked a little more.

"Do you reckon you'll see that chick again?" asked Jenno.

"Yeah, I hope so…" said Jimmy. It had been in the back of his head all night. The thought of Skye filled him with excitement and also a strange sense of fear.

They sat there for a little while longer before they both fell asleep. Jimmy woke up at before sunrise, and shook Jenno awake, so he could get ready for his morning shift at work. Jenno skated home, gliding quietly through the empty streets. He passed the main intersection, which was deserted now. The only noise he could hear was the traffic light colour change, which clicked routinely, but for no one in particular on the empty street. When he got home he climbed the stairs to his room quietly and got straight into bed. He lay on his back and looked up at shadows of the bedroom windows on the ceiling, thinking of all that had happened.

Until the sun rose and orange bars of light slipped through his blinds and onto his floor.

7

It was a morning just like all the others she'd had after Ratty's passing. Fleetwood woke in darkness, got changed and walked towards the beach just as the sun was rising. She knelt in the sand and watched as it floated up slowly from the horizon. She listened to the waves crashing and the birds waking. She felt the morning breeze drift past her and play with her hair. In all these things, she found Ratty.

After sunrise, Fleetwood left to get a coffee before work.

As she walked back through the beach carpark, she watched a group of young boys with bright, bleached blond hair skate past her holding surfboards under their arms.

She always expected Ratty to feel different. He was the only mixed-race child in the area, which separated him in a way from the get-go. Her mind drifted to the first time she visited Trinidad. It was like a breath of fresh air. She had fallen in love with the food and the music and the accents she grew up around at home in Brixton. Walking down St. James strip she had bought some doubles from the doubles man, a small, chickpea curry nestled between two slices of fried flat bread, and a roti from a roti tower just down the road. These were street foods of Indian origin that had become breakfast staples in the Trinidadian diet. She walked up towards the Savannah park and sat in the grass for some time while she ate.

She'd never been there before, but she had heard so much about it while growing up that she almost felt a sense of inherited memories. Her grandfather always talked of the Savannah. Fleetwood smiled as she sat and watched the world moving around her.

There was a haze in the air; as the southernmost island in the Caribbean, Trinidad is so close to the coast of South America that, far off in the distance, you can just make out the mountains of Venezuela.

It was humid and the sun was harsh, but the jungle thrived. There were mango trees, zaboca, banana and breadfruit. It was a place that was rich in different foods. Down at Marracas Bay, there was shark and bake, a local food that had earned fame around the island. Her mother and grandmother cooked stew chicken often, and at parties there was always pilau.

She was staying at her grandmother's house. It was a beautiful place with a colourful garden. Her grandmother would play calypso and soca music; it seemed to follow her everywhere, and when she wasn't listening to it she was humming it to herself softly, or singing notes while she caught her breath. Around Christmas time, she'd buy a new set of clothes and then give the house a lick of paint to the sound of parang.

She'd cook something big every day. The portions were always way too big for the amount of people who ate, but somehow, they'd always manage to get it down. Her grandmother's defence was always, "Better yuh belly buss than good food waste."

It was a different way of living, but one that made Fleetwood feel free. Every day there was music and singing, and most people were extroverted and friendly.

Trinidad had its troubles too. It was the first place that she'd ever felt unsafe. There was crime in London, but the councils did their best to hide it. But in Trinidad she stared poverty and desperation right in the face. And amongst all the beauty, the friendly people and the fruit trees, people went missing often, and there was murder every day.

But despite the comparative danger, she felt at home, as well as a sense of ease that the majority of people who lived there were Black. Even though Brixton had a large Caribbean population, sometimes it felt like she was tightroping over two very different cultures.

The biggest shock for her when she arrived at the town in Australia was that there were very few Black people at all. Most people were friendly, but it took a while for her to adjust. She found it strange that she'd seen very few Indigenous people there either, and she asked her partner why. He shook his head. No one was taught anything about Indigenous cultures at school, no one was taught any of the languages and most people seemed as though they were completely oblivious to their existence.

She always had mixed emotions on Australia Day. As much as she wanted to assimilate into the country, it felt wrong to be celebrating. While Indigenous people mourned and protested, most non-Indigenous Australians sank beers and had barbeques. The disconnect between non-Indigenous Australians and Indigenous Australians was in plain sight, but to what extent it ran, Fleetwood didn't know.

As Ratty grew older, the tradition still continued. Kids looked at their parents getting pissed and having barbeques, and as soon as they could, they did the same thing. On Australia Day kids as early as 13 and 14 covered themselves in Australian flags, got blind drunk and caused a ruckus. It was one of the uglier sides of Australia she witnessed, and something she tried hard to get Ratty to understand when she raised him. To respect, to listen and to accept, and, most importantly, acknowledge the peoples who had held the land they were on.

…

"Morning, Fleetwood, small cap?" said the barista.

Fleetwood smiled and nodded. She came to this café every morning before work. She liked the music they played and all of the plants around the place. She worked as a teacher's aide at a primary school just down the road. It was the same primary school that Ratty, Jenno and Jimmy had gone to.

Before Ratty's passing, she worked there part-time while studying to become a psychiatrist. She'd always been drawn to helping people. She had a healing soul and people felt comfortable around her.

In the wake of Ratty's death she dropped out. She couldn't focus on it anymore. She had only just enough will to roll out of bed each morning, let alone study and work.

It was hard for her when she returned to work at the school. She didn't think she could do it. Seeing all those kids going home with their parents at the end of each day. All the hugs and kisses, the laughter and the crying that comes all at once with children. But it felt right to her, that she could help and support kids, and mother them in her own little way. It was beautiful to her, seeing them grow up all the way from kindergarten to year six.

And sending them off to high school each year was always just as bittersweet as the year before. The first time she watched the kids graduate from primary school after Ratty passed away she had to run to the bathroom to cry. They were sweet tears. The kind that fall out of joy for what is, and grief for what isn't anymore.

She'd grown used to being alone. She rarely had visitors. Most days she came home and put the TV on for some background noise while she cooked and ate. They were always the same shows, but they provided a routine for her and it made her comfortable.

After dinner was when it was the quietest.

Ratty used to beg her to let him play video games every night. It was a constant battle between them. He was only ever allowed to play them once he'd done all his homework. He'd never do it, but he'd be just as outraged every time she wouldn't let him play.

For a while it seemed like he'd turned a new leaf. Every afternoon after he surfed, he'd come home and do his homework straight away on the kitchen table. She'd check on him from time to time, see all his worksheets filled up and then let him play. It wasn't till her parent-teachers meeting, when Ratty's teacher told her he needed to go to learning support because none of his homework was ever correct that she realised what he'd been doing. It turned out that he'd just been writing random answers on the paper so it'd look like he'd done his homework and he could play.

She laughed to herself. She'd been fooled.

But now it was quiet.

The barista handed her the coffee and she sat down out in front of the café in a patch of morning sunlight while she drank it.

She was just about to pull out her book from her bag when a Labrador came and sniffed at her leg.

"Hello," she whispered, and scratched the dog under the chin.

"Sorry about that! She slipped away," she heard a man say.

"No, that's fine, I love dogs," she said as she looked up at him. Their eyes met and she felt something rush through her. It felt like a bolt of electricity. She'd never seen this man before. He had an interesting look to him. His hair was jet black and wavy, his face was kind and soft, but his eyes had an intenseness to them that she'd not seen in anyone before. They were a light grey-blue colour that seemed to catch and hold the light of the sun within them.

"Yeah, me too before I met this one…" he laughed.

"What's her name? She's beautiful!" said Fleetwood.

"You'll hate me for this, but she's called Scrunch," he said.

"Scrunch! How could you call her that?" she said in feigned horror.

"I know, I'm sorry, I tried…" he said.

"It doesn't sound like you tried all that hard," she commented.

"My daughter named her. I tried to get her to see reason, but you know how kids are…"

"Well, I hope you picked a better name for your daughter."

He smiled. "I tried my best. Her name is Milly."

Fleetwood paused for a second, wondering if she knew any kids at her school called Milly.

"Milly…" It suddenly clicked. "You're not Milly Claret's dad, are you?"

He looked surprised. It wasn't a large school, and Fleetwood made it a point to remember the names of all the kids. Milly was a sweet but shy little girl who'd only recently started at the school.

"I work at the primary school as a teacher's aide," she said before he could open his mouth. "You've just moved down from Queensland?"

It explained why she'd never seen him around before.

He nodded. "Yeah, we have! Work moved us down here a few months ago, so we're still getting settled in. I'm Adriaan, by the way."

"Fleetwood," she smiled. "I bet, it must be a big change for Milly."

"It is, but she and I are loving it. It's hard sometimes, when she's missing her friends... Do you have any children?"

Fleetwood was silent for a second. "It's just me, unfortunately."

It was clear from his face that Adriaan felt that there was something more to her response, but he didn't ask any more questions. His coffee order was called.

"I've got to get running," he said. He knelt down and put the lead on Scrunch's collar. "Hopefully the rest of your morning is dog free..."

She smiled at him and he ran off. She watched him round the corner and disappear, then she finished her coffee and went to work, hoping that she would see him again.

Later that day, Fleetwood was on duty during morning tea at school.

School had always felt much bigger to her as a kid. It was one of the only worlds you knew as a child. The grass area, the lockers, the basketball hoops and soccer pitches all seemed as though they were as far away and dissimilar to one another that they felt like they may as well have been on separate continents.

She looked across the patch of grass next to the playground. Milly was there by herself, bent low over a patch of flowers.

Her light brown hair had a little bang over her forehead, and as she leaned over the flower, her hair covered her face from Fleetwood. It shone gold in the yellow sunlight.

"Good morning, Milly!" said Fleetwood.

Milly looked up and smiled at her. "Good morning, Miss Augustus!"

Fleetwood paused for a second. "Milly, could you please put your hat back on your head while you're outside? I'd hate for you to get burned."

Milly grabbed her hat and stuck it on her head hastily. It was one of those wide-brimmed hats with the chin strings.

"Sorry, Miss Augustus!" she said, innocently.

"That's ok, there's no need to be sorry. You don't want to play with any of your classmates?" asked Fleetwood.

"I don't think they want to play with me…"

"I'm sure that's not true! Why don't you go over and ask them?"

"That's ok, I just want to look at these flowers," she said.

Fleetwood smiled. "Suit yourself, but come see me if you ever want someone to talk to…"

She left Milly with the flowers, and made her way across the playground.

She had lunchtime off, so she sat in the staffroom with Miss Painter and Mrs White while she ate.

"I saw the new girl, Milly, sitting by herself at teatime this morning. She's very sweet," said Fleetwood.

Mrs White made an 'aawwww' sound. She loved kids, especially the cute ones. She was a short, stout woman with a wide smile and crinkled eyes. Her hair was curly and wiry, and her arms were freckled. All of the kids loved her.

"Isn't she just gorgeous!" said Mrs White enthusiastically.

"She is, but I worry about her. I wonder why the other kids don't play with her," said Fleetwood.

"I worry too," began Miss Painter. She was an older woman who always wore her hair in a bun.

"She and her father moved here not so long ago; it's the middle of the year, I suppose all the other children have already formed their friend groups."

"What about her mother?" asked Fleetwood.

"I'm not sure. I assume her parents are no longer together, but I'm yet to hear anything about that," said Miss Painter.

Fleetwood's heart skipped a beat.

...

The next morning, she walked to the café from the beach to find Adriaan there again with Scrunch. They locked eyes and she smiled at him as she walked through the front door.

"Hello again," he said, smiling.

"Good morning," said Fleetwood.

"I talked to your daughter yesterday. I saw her playing with some flowers by herself at morning tea."

"Ah, yeah, she told me she doesn't have many friends," said Adriaan. "I don't really know what to do about it. I was thinking of signing her up to a soccer team or something."

"Football," Fleetwood corrected.

"You would say football, wouldn't you?" Adriaan laughed.

"Well, I am English. What about karate lessons?"

"Karate lessons?" said Adriaan, thinking it over. "Yeah, maybe I'll check it out… Do you know any good ones?"

"I can have a think of a few for you. What's your number? I'll send some ideas to you." She said it matter-of-factly, but her heart was racing. It was a jarring attempt at asking for his number, but she was relieved at Adriaan's reaction. He almost blushed.

They exchanged numbers.

Fleetwood went to pay for her coffee, but Adriaan got there first and paid.

"I'll get this one, thanks for the idea," he said before she had a chance to say anything. "I'll be in touch!" He smiled and left.

"He's got the biggest crush on you, I can tell!" laughed Aimee, the girl on the till.

Fleetwood almost blushed, "Oh, shut up, you!"

. . .

Fleetwood was on playground duty again that day.

She was walking around the playground past the handball courts when she spotted Milly sitting by herself among the flowers again.

"By yourself again? Are you sure you don't want to play with your friends?" asked Fleetwood, smiling down at her warmly.

"I'm ok, Miss Augustus," said Milly sweetly. She was watching a little bee swivel around one of the flowers.

"Alright, as long as you're ok…" said Fleetwood, sitting down on a playground bench behind her. "So, you and your dad moved down here – did your mum stay up in Queensland?"

Milly stopped watching the bee and was quiet for a moment. "My mum isn't here anymore. She died last year," she finally said, looking down at her feet.

"I'm so sorry, Milly, I had no idea…" said Fleetwood. She crouched down to Milly's level and looked her in the eyes.

"It's ok, that's why I talk to the flowers. My daddy told me I can talk to her anytime I like. He said she's in the trees and in the sun, and in the flowers too, and she's always watching over me, but I keep looking and I can't find her anywhere…"

Fleetwood put her hand on Milly's little shoulder and smiled. "I understand. I lost my little boy last year too."

"Have you found him?" asked Milly.

"No, but I still talk to him every day. Your dad's right – when we lose our loved ones we can find them wherever we look, you just have to look without your eyes."

"I tell my mum that I love her and miss her a lot."

"I say the same to my boy."

A small accident happened across the other side of the oval. Two boys had run into one another playing cricket and both were crying.

Fleetwood could hear the sobs growing louder. She said goodbye to Milly and raced over. She held both of the boys' hands and brought them to the sick bay, then the bell rang and all the kids went back to class. She looked out across the oval to where Milly had been, but she was gone.

Fleetwood had mixed emotions after talking to Milly. It was awful to know that Milly was going through such a loss at her age. It almost brought her to tears thinking about it.

After Ratty's dad had left, she was broken. It felt like she had lost a part of herself, and the responsibility of raising Ratty alone weighed on her heavily. She couldn't imagine what it would be like to grow up without a mother.

For the longest time, even before Ratty's passing, she had felt alone. Her heart yearned for love, but she was too scared to put herself out there. She'd gone on a few dates over the years. Each of them different in their own ways, but all of them ended up the same.

She felt as though she couldn't connect with anyone. The realisation that Adriaan was widowed played on her mind. It made her feel a strange excitement, one that was mixed with guilt. But she couldn't seem to get him out of her mind either way.

...

The school bell rang at a quarter past three, and all across the city every kid rushed out of their school gates.

Jimmy and Jenno were on their way home when they spotted Fleetwood walking home from school. She had her earphones in, but when she saw them she smiled at them, sadly. They could only guess it was because they had always walked home with Ratty too.

Every afternoon all three of them used to rush home from school to surf. In summer, they'd surf until 8:30PM, and in winter they'd surf until they were sitting under the moon and stars. They never worried about sharks, the only reason they stopped was because they couldn't see. The boys had seen sharks before, but usually they were just cruising further out. They grew accustomed to seeing sea life surfing every day. Dolphins, penguins, stingrays, jellyfish and sharks were all things encountered by everyday surfers.

On flat days when there were no waves they'd find things to do around the headlands.

Jenno had a disgusting habit of taking shits off the top of big rocks around the base of the cliff. He never told anyone where he did them, in hopes that someone would stumble across one by accident, but he never heard anything.

They'd spear fish on clear days. Ratty bought a hand spear with his pocket money one day and he, Jenno and Jimmy went out. None of them had any idea what they were doing. They swam out around the shallowest part of the headland. The swell was dead calm and there wasn't a breath of wind. It was a beautiful day, one of those days where the sea and the sky were as blue as each other and the line between the two was hard to distinguish.

"Fark, I don't see anything big enough anywhere!" said Ratty, pulling his goggles and snorkel off his eyes as they bobbed in the water.

"We gotta go deeper, I reckon!" said Jenno.

"Fuck that, I'm not going past the ledge; it's pitch black down there…" said Jimmy.

Ten metres or so off of the headland there was a ledge where the bottom dropped from five metres deep to 20. It was a beautiful and terrifying sight. The deep ocean stood like a wall of impenetrable darkness against the bright and clear waters closer to the shore.

They'd swum down to the edge before and stuck their heads over the gap. It was enough to send shivers down their spines.

"Don't be a pussy, Jimmy. Yeah, let's go, there'll be bigger fish down there for sure…" said Ratty.

The three of them swam to the edge of the ledge and then dove down.

They swum down together through pillars of sunlight, and one by one disappeared into the darkness.

Ratty was the first to descend, holding his spear close to him. His heart was racing. It was quiet. He could hear the sound of boat engines far off in the distance, and even what sounded like a lonely whale song, like an elk whining in the woods.

There was nothing but darkness under the shadow of the ledge. Ratty was about to give up and swim back to the surface when something caught his eye.

Nestled atop a rock was an octopus. Its body was a reddish white and it was covered in horns. Ratty pointed. Jimmy and Jenno looked at it. It was beautiful.

A moment later it leaped and glided up towards the top of the ledge like a ghost.

They followed it, transfixed. It hung in the water like a spectre, a silent church organ; one of its catlike eyes was on Jimmy.

Ratty pulled the spear back, ready to shoot.

All eight of its tentacles were outstretched. It looked like a silk wedding dress caught in an updraft. Jimmy locked eyes with it and it raised a tentacle. It felt like the octopus was trying to communicate something to him, like an acknowledgement that they were both alive and that the same energy that flowed through the universe flowed through the both of them too. He realised that they were not so different, and that the bond of life tied them together in more ways than just physical presence.

A moment later Ratty released the spear. It pierced the octopus right in the middle of its head.

Its tentacles reached for the spear, coiling up and down it desperately, trying to pull itself free and cling to life.

Blood and ink erupted from it in thick clouds.

Jimmy snapped back to the moment, as if out of a daydream. The octopus was dead now, and its eyes were nothing but two bottomless holes.

They swam to the surface and gasped for air.

Ratty laughed. "Fuckin' oath!"

"Fark, dude, you got it right in the face!" said Jenno.

Jimmy didn't say anything.

They swam back to shore.

All the old men that hung about the lifeguard club gathered around the trio when they walked by.

"Fuck me dead! He's caught a fuckin' octopus!" one of them said, and all the others nodded approvingly.

Ratty held it up in front of them, still on his spear. He felt like a man.

Its tentacles flopped about like a lifeless puppet whenever he moved the spear around.

"Fuckin' good size too! Your mum's gonna love you for that, grommet!"

Ratty was grinning from ear to ear.

He took it home and he and Fleetwood had it for dinner.

It was the natural order of things. But it felt cruel to Jimmy. That life could only live by taking other life.

He and his family had a roast chicken for dinner, and by that time he had forgotten the octopus, and the cruelty, and that single moment it had tried to communicate something to him.

His stomach was full, and he went to bed.

8

Jimmy and Jenno were slowly making their way to school on the Monday a few days after Letty's party.

As they walked, Jenno kicked every stick and rock in his way.

"So, when are you gonna see Skye again?" he asked.

"I'm seeing her after school today, actually," Jimmy replied. He was walking with his thumbs pressed against the straps of his backpack.

"Ah, what! Actually? What are you gonna do with her?"

"I dunno, maybe go to the movies or something…"

Jenno burst out laughing.

Jimmy looked at him, annoyed. "What?"

Jenno stopped laughing and wiped his eyes. "The movies? What are you, twelve, dude? Fuckin'… maybe you two can hold hands or some shit while you watch it."

"What would you do, then?" said Jimmy.

Jenno paused for a second. "Fark, I dunno… Go to the lookout or something?"

"Fuck that, so many people are gonna be sitting there…"

"Yeah… I dunno, that's where you go to root, isn't it?" asked Jenno.

"Nah, no way!" said Jimmy. "And I dunno, man, I don't really want to root in the car… I want to get to know her."

"Where would you do it, then? On your single mattress at home? Your room smells like wet socks and cum rags." Jenno laughed.

"Fuck off…"

"Nah, but seriously – there's no way you can take her back to yours; what are your parents gonna say when you walk in with her behind you? No way that's happening."

Jimmy considered for a second. "Yeah, you're right. There's no way that's happening."

They'd arrived at the front gate of school. It was near enough 8:30AM and they both had to get to class.

They split up and went to their lessons. Jimmy was in year 11 and Jenno in year 10 at Oceanside High School, a local co-ed school. It had made a name for itself for producing the most dropkicks. Most of the kids were surfers. From ages 14 and up, the majority of them smoked weed. Every now and then a bong would be found in the toilets and the whole school would get called into an assembly. But nothing changed. Next to the school there was a small forest. All the smokers would disappear there at lunchtime, and every now and then a teacher would walk in, and a few moments later dozens of kids would run out.

But overall it wasn't the worst school; the education was good if you wanted it to be. The teachers treated the students like adults, and in return most of the students were pretty mature in class.

That day Jenno had health class with a substitute teacher called Champo. They called him Champo because he called everyone champion, or champo. He was one of those old boys from the Australia of long ago, the era of *Crocodile Dundee* and a few blues down at the local. He was nice enough, but he was way in over his head teaching at a high school.

Champo genuinely wanted to teach, but he couldn't seem to get any of the students to respect him. Jenno liked to rile the class up and take the piss all the time. One time Jenno was so poorly behaved that Champo threw his hands up and begged him, saying, "C'mon champion, I'm gonna lose my job here…"

Jenno seemed to feed off the weakness. He loved making teachers crumble, but when he applied himself, he was capable of being a good student.

After Ratty's passing, both Jenno and Jimmy had struggled to concentrate in class.

Neither of their parents had taken them to psychiatrists, and so a lot of the turmoil they felt inside just sat there and stewed.

Jenno would find himself drifting away in class, and if he wasn't being a ballache he was usually sleeping. Most of the teachers gave up trying to get him to engage.

Jimmy was different. He tried his best to concentrate, but everything went in and out.

…

When school finished that day, Jimmy raced home to get ready for his date.

He put on his favourite clothes and deodorant, and rushed out the door before his parents saw him. He got to their meeting place at the mall half an hour early, so he sat in the food court just outside the cinema for a while and waited.

Half an hour later his phone buzzed; it was Skye, she was standing by the escalators. He went over and hugged her.

"So, what do you wanna watch?" he asked her.

She considered for a moment. "I don't mind! Just nothing scary, please…"

He panicked a little on the inside; he didn't want to bore her on the first date. He'd seen this very scene in television shows.

He scanned the title board quickly and picked the first name that stuck out to him, a fantasy-looking movie called *Return of the Zeg*. He bought the tickets and food, and swelled his chest up proudly as he handed Skye hers.

"Thanks so much, Jimmy. This is really nice." She smiled at him.

Jimmy felt his stomach flutter.

He had it all planned out. They'd go to the very back row in the corner, and then that way he could kiss her without feeling embarrassed. All he had to do was pick the right moment in the movie to put his arm over her shoulder and then it was a done deal.

When they walked into the theatre Jimmy almost groaned. The movie had started already and the theatre was full. It looked like the only seats that were free were right up the front.

Fuck sakes, Jimmy thought to himself.

They made their way to the front and sat down.

Return of the Zeg turned out to be a boy's movie. Jimmy could tell Skye had no interest in it and as he watched it he pretended not to like it, even though deep down it was everything he liked in a movie. It wouldn't have mattered to him what movie it was anyway; all of his focus was on the fact that there was a girl sitting next to him. He saw his cue and without thinking lifted his arm up and pretended to yawn, then placed it around her shoulder. His heart was racing; the first move had been made. He held his breath, his arm lying awkwardly across her shoulders. It was her move. A wave of relief washed over him when she shuffled about so that his arm could sit there properly.

Adrenaline rushed through him and he had to steady himself. He was waiting for the right moment to kiss her.

There was an action scene. The main character was fighting in some space-age colosseum, and the crowd in the movie was roaring. It seemed like a good time.

Jimmy looked at her, trying to get her attention. She noticed his gaze and returned it. For a moment he was still, teetering over the edge, about to leap. He leaned in and kissed her, and she kissed him back.

It was an awkward kiss. He kind of had to lean over the armrest, and his face levelled with hers at an odd angle. But they were kissing. And that was all that mattered to him. He opened his eyes for a moment, and at that exact point he linked eyes with someone sitting behind them through the gap in the cinema chairs. The person, who now found themselves victim of an awkward moment, shifted their gaze towards the movie again and did their best to seem like they hadn't noticed.

Jimmy pulled away. He and Skye didn't speak for the rest of the movie.

It was raining outside when they left, so they sat under a shelter in the carpark for a while.

A chill breeze swept past them both, and Jimmy put his arm around Skye. She leaned into him. It felt better than he had ever imagined, holding a girl in his arms.

When it was time for her to go, she gave him a kiss on the cheek and left.

He walked home with a spring in his step. It was a half-hour walk, and halfway back it started pissing down with rain again, but he didn't care.

"You're soaking wet!" said his mum when he walked through the door.

"Yeah, no shit, Mum…" he said.

"Don't talk to me like that! How dare you…" she breathed angrily.

Jimmy ignored her and climbed the stairs to his bedroom.

He jumped onto his bed and sent Skye a message that said, *Had a really good time at the movies, we should chill again soon :)*

Five minutes later she messaged back saying, *Yeah, for sure! :)) x*

His heart raced, and he wondered if the double bracket smiley face meant more than the single.

He felt warm inside, and he couldn't stop himself from smiling. He thought about her the whole afternoon, and about how lucky he felt to be with her.

…

"So, did you fuck her?" asked Simmo, the chef at the café Jimmy worked at, when he told him about the date.

"Nah, I didn't," Jimmy started, but after he noticed the look on Simmo's face he added quickly, "but I will."

"Good lad!" laughed Simmo.

Jimmy washed dishes every Saturday at the café, just down the road from his house. It was tough work, but he didn't mind it all that much.

"If I could give you one piece of advice for your youth it would be to fuck as many girls as you can. Trust me, you'll regret it otherwise," said Simmo. He was always saying stuff like that.

Every time an attractive woman walked into the café, he'd whip Jimmy with his tea towel and go, "Look at that!"

Jimmy always looked, but only did so because Simmo was there.

Simmo was in his late twenties. He had a girlfriend, but their relationship was turbulent. He was constantly at war with himself. He hated and loved himself equally, and was permanently exhausted because of it. He never planned on being a chef for long, but somehow, he'd found himself feeling like he had nowhere to go and nothing to offer except stories and advice to the younger guys he found himself with.

He couldn't go half a day without snorting coke in the work toilets to pick himself up, and often Jimmy would have no idea what kind of Simmo he'd walk into at the beginning of a shift. For the most part he was a funny, good-at-heart guy. But he was also one of the biggest cunts in the world.

From eight in the morning until one in the afternoon they were getting pumped by customers.

Jimmy would either be frantically washing dishes or running in and out of the cool room grabbing ingredients for Simmo while he screamed shit like, "Hurry up, you little cunt!"

It was never meant to be taken personally. The kitchen was a stressful place, and chefs are as temperamental as the dishes they're cooking.

Jimmy had never seen someone work under such brutal conditions. Simmo was constantly under stress. He had to manage the fryers, the stove, the grills and then at the end of it all he had to plate up all the food and do most of the prep work too.

One time he threw a bucket full of onions and a tray at Jimmy's feet and said, "Here, grommet, cut up these onions for me, quick as you can."

Jimmy picked up a knife and started cutting them earnestly.

Twenty minutes later, Simmo rushed past, but stopped dead in his tracks at the edge of Jimmy's workbench.

"What the fuck are you doing?" he said. "I meant cut enough onions for the tray, not cut the whole fuckin' lot, you dumb fuck!"

Jimmy looked down at the full tray and the mountain of chopped onions next to it, mouth agape.

Simmo shook his head and grabbed the tray. "Fuck sakes! Last time I'm letting you touch anything besides the dishwasher."

Jimmy was devastated, but by the end of the shift Simmo had already forgotten. He was back to laughing and making jokes.

"I really like this girl," said Jimmy while he was mopping the floor on the shift after his date with Skye.

Simmo was cleaning down the grills and replacing the oil in the fryers. He stopped what he was doing and looked at Jimmy.

"Look, best advice I can give to you is to get a few rides in with this chick until you're confident with what you're doing, and then get out of there. Don't get strapped down with this chick, whatever you do, or you're fucked, grommet. You'll get her pregnant, she'll keep the baby or some shit and then you're gonna be trapped for life! Trust me, I've seen it happen too many times before."

"You reckon?" Jimmy replied.

"Reckon? Mate, I know so. Happened to too many of my friends. I got this one friend who was with his high-school girlfriend for almost 10 years. They buy a house together, get a dog and all that. One day he comes home from the gym and she's giving some random bloke a blowjob on the sofa while he's watching the footy."

"Really? That's crazy!" said Jimmy, shocked.

"Yeah, mate. Women are fucked. Look, don't get me wrong, there's some lovely women out there, and they should all be respected, but just be careful."

Simmo stopped wiping again, as if something had just flown into his brain. "Ah yeah, and whatever you do, don't fuckin' fall in love at your age. One day you'll tell her you love her, and it's all gonna be sweet, but then she's gonna get bored. Woman are like cats. You gotta be like a ball of string. Keep yourself just dangling out of reach and she'll be all over you. Soon as you let her get her claws into you, she'll stop being interested and she'll move on. Happens nine times out of 10."

"Yeah, I guess so…" said Jimmy.

"Trust me," said Simmo.

He slid a plate with a bacon-and-egg roll across the bench towards Jimmy.

"Eat that, big dog. Why do you always look sad? You're 16, for fuck's sake!"

Jimmy laughed. "Nah, I'm not sad, I just can't stop thinking about her."

Simmo gave him an uncharacteristically warm smile. "You'll learn, grommet. Just take everything as a lesson and have fun, yeah?"

Jimmy checked the surf after work. He was carrying a little bag full of leftover food from the café. There was a sandwich, a raspberry and white chocolate muffin and a croissant. His shirt smelled of dirty dishes, food scraps and water, and as he skated a trail of foul air wafted in his wake.

There were a few small waves about, but the water looked beautiful. He sat on Ratty's bench for a while and watched the ocean.

There were a few people surfing the main peak.

He looked for Jenno in the water, and saw that he was walking on the beach with Dizz and Letty. They were all laughing about something.

He stood up from Ratty's bench, grabbed his skateboard and skated off to go and hang out with Skye.

She was waiting by the pathway that went up to the headland.

"Heyy," she said when he pulled up next to her.

They hugged, but after a second she pulled away, laughing.

"You stink!"

Jimmy face turned red. "Ah yeah, sorry. I just finished work."

He lifted up the bag with the food in it, smiling innocently. Skye peeped inside.

"I guess I can forgive you then," she said. She took the bag and walked towards a patch of grass on the side of the headland.

They set up a picnic blanket and ate the food together.

Jimmy always loved the muffins. He took pride in the fact that he was the one who made them. It was the first responsible task the café had ever given him. It wasn't often that the café had any leftover food to give to the staff, but Jimmy always made sure to make a few dud muffins in every batch that he could take home with him.

Skye lay down and rested her head on his lap. He met her gaze as she looked up at him and smiled.

"What?" he asked.

"Nothing…" She paused for a moment before finally adding, "I'm just happier when I'm with you. You're not like the other guys I've been on dates with."

"Uhh, thanks," said Jimmy, focusing more on the idea that she'd been on other dates before him.

His heart was racing. He wanted to tell her right then and there that he loved her. He was taken by the excitement of it all. The warmth of having someone next to him, and the idea that they could grow together.

But then he thought about what Simmo had said about being like a ball of string, and realised he didn't want to come off too eager.

For some reason, he felt like he was being watched by all the men in his life that he wanted to be respected by. He made a move for a piece of muffin, and Skye lifted her head up again. He saw his chance and shuffled just a touch away from her. He hated himself for it, but it eased the pressure he was feeling.

Skye noticed his sudden change of mood.

"Are you ok?" she asked him.

"Yeah…" he said. "I'm sorry, I'm just tired from work."

"It's ok. I should probably get going back to my place. Having dinner soon."

Jimmy was torn between doing what he wanted to do, and doing what he thought was expected of him. He did nothing in the end, which was even worse.

They stood up and rolled the picnic blanket up, and walked down the headland together.

"I'd love to see you again. Before work next time…" she said when they were standing down at the beach carpark.

"Yeah, for sure!" said Jimmy.

He looked around. They were standing in the middle of the carpark. Dizz and some of the older boys were sitting on the back wall of the lifeguard club, looking over at them.

"Well, I'll see you soon then," said Skye. She leaned in for a kiss. Jimmy noticed one of the boys tapped Dizz on the arm, and pointed at Jimmy. Jimmy leaned in and kissed Skye back, but pulled away almost instantly.

Skye opened her eyes; her lips were still puckered momentarily, before a look of confusion and embarrassment flashed across her face.

"I'll see you later!" said Jimmy. He was dying on the inside, but before Skye could say anything else he walked back home.

9

Since she'd exchanged numbers with Adriaan, Fleetwood couldn't help but keep checking her phone. She felt foolish in a way. She hardly knew him, but there was something about him that excited her.

She was walking home from school three days later when she felt her phone vibrate in her pocket.

She checked her phone and smiled. The text read, *Hello, it's Adriaan. Any luck with the karate masters? I was wondering as well, and forgive me if I'm a little forward, but are you free Thursday night? Cheers.*

She laughed to herself. *"Cheers?"*

She thought it was lucky they'd met in person, because he came off like an absolute dork in text message format.

Hello Adriaan, she began, *Yes I'd love to do something Thursday night. Regards.*

. . .

Adriaan's phone buzzed on the other side. He pulled it out of his pocket and laughed to himself. *"Regards?"*

He thought it was lucky they'd met in person, because she came off like an absolute ironing board in text message format.

He thought for a moment before he replied. *Great. Meet in town for a hot chocolate?*

Sounds good. What time? she replied.

7pm?

...

At quarter to seven on Thursday evening, Fleetwood walked through town towards the chocolatiers.

It was a calm night. There was no wind, and all the trees were still and birds of all kinds swooped from branch to branch above her, singing to one another in the dying rays of sun.

Adriaan was waiting out front when she got there. He looked up and smiled when he saw her, and she smiled back.

"Hello," he said.

"No dog today?" asked Fleetwood.

Adriaan laughed. "No, fortunately. I left the neighbour's daughter in charge of everything tonight, with strict instructions to not burn the house down."

"I hope you're paying her good money, then."

"Big-time money for a teenager to sit and watch TV, that's for sure."

They ordered two hot chocolates from the place. Adriaan paid, however Fleetwood put up a protest and almost demanded that the next time they get coffee she would pay for them.

They walked down the esplanade towards the beach.

"So, when did you come to Australia?" Adriaan asked her.

"When I was pregnant with my son. We figured it'd be easier for my ex to work here than back in London – he never did like it there, really."

"Yeah, I don't blame him. I've been to London once, but never again."

"Never again?"

Adriaan side-eyed her. "So cold and so dark!"

"Oh, grow up!" said Fleetwood. "London's a great place. It's full of music, good food, good pubs—"

"Yeah, but it's full of English people..." said Adriaan. He saw the look on her face. "I'm just kidding. I love London. I think I went there at the wrong time. I was too young and had too little money. It was actually the place where I fell in love for the first time."

"Oh god, not with an English girl, surely..." Fleetwood joked.

"She was Spanish, actually. An artist – we worked at the same café together."

"Oh really? And what happened?"

"She went back to Spain, and I came back here broken-hearted... It wasn't meant to be anyways. But I would like to go back one day and see it again."

"I fell in love for the first time in London too..." laughed Fleetwood.

"Really? Wow, I never would have guessed!"

"Yeah, he was a boy who went to my school in Clapham. He ended up cheating on me, actually."

"Oh, really? What an asshole..."

"Yeah, total twat."

"What happened to him?"

"I'm not sure. It was such a long time ago..."

"Mmm, he'd be kicking himself now," said Adriaan.

"Oh, shut up!" laughed Fleetwood.

They sat down at the beachfront and talked some more. The date was going well. Both of them felt comfortable with each other. Adriaan was taken aback by how beautiful she looked. He had never glanced at her long when she was at the café, but now when they spoke their gazes locked, and neither of them could seem to pull away.

"Do you get in the ocean much?" Adriaan asked her. The waves were calm and the water was smooth. The sun had set and the full moon took its place. It looked beautiful in the last blue light of day.

"No, not at all," said Fleetwood.

Adriaan saw a look of pain shoot across her face momentarily before she caught herself, and he decided not to push the topic any further.

They said nothing else, but the silence spoke for them. They felt themselves drawing closer together until Fleetwood rested her head on his shoulder.

He offered her a lift home afterwards; she only lived down the road from him.

When they pulled up outside of her place neither of them were ready for the date to end. She invited him in for a glass of wine. He parked up and they went in together.

Adriaan took a seat on the sofa while Fleetwood went to the bathroom. She looked at herself in the mirror, straightened up her hair and smelled her breath.

"What do you drink?" she asked Adriaan when she walked back into the living room.

"I'll have whatever you're having," he said, looking back around from the sofa.

Fleetwood sat down on the sofa with two glasses and a bottle of wine a moment later. Suddenly she felt nervous; it'd been a long time since she'd kissed someone.

Adriaan was calm and relaxed.

He opened the bottle and poured them both a glass of wine; they cheers'd one another and held each other's gaze before they drank.

"You've got a lovely place," said Adriaan.

"Thanks, it's been a while since I've had any visitors over to see it," she said.

"Who was the artist that did your paintings? I like the one with the boy," he said.

"I painted them," said Fleetwood.

The painting was of Ratty sitting on a headland, watching the sun rise. There were splashes and streaks of colour thrown about it, while Ratty appeared golden and almost ethereal in the light.

"You painted them?" said Adriaan, "They're beautiful…"

Fleetwood smiled, but she wasn't one for sitting and taking compliments, especially when it was about her art.

"Let's see… What kind of music are you into?" asked Fleetwood, changing the subject and getting her phone ready to queue some songs.

"Oh, come on! What kind of question's that?" Adriaan laughed.

"Boy!" she said.

"Ok, how about this? You choose a song and then I'll tell you if I like it…"

"Fine, but only if you play the song after."

"Deal," said Adriaan.

Fleetwood thought for a moment before she played "Sunrise" by Norah Jones.

Adriaan raised his eyebrow.

"You know what, this is a great song…" he said.

"You were getting ready to say something bad about it; I can see it on your face!" Fleetwood laughed.

Adriaan laughed. "Yeah, I was. But Norah Jones is pretty good."

They listened to the rest of the song, getting closer and closer.

Adriaan put his arm around her, and she tapped her hand against his chest to the beat.

She passed him the phone just before the song ended and he queued the next one. Adriaan looked at the phone screen, and then laughed to himself.

The next song that played was "Lovin' You," by Minnie Riperton.

"Boy, give me a break!" Fleetwood laughed.

"Ok, ok. Maybe that was a little too much. I'll pick something else…" said Adriaan.

The next song he played was "White Flag" by Dido.

"Wow, now I wasn't expecting this…"

"Great song," nodded Adriaan.

They smiled at one another, and then kissed. It was a soft, tender kiss. They pulled away slowly, looked at one another and then laughed.

It was a laugh that Fleetwood hadn't heard from herself in a long time. She leaned in and kissed him again.

They wrapped their arms around one another and fell to the floor.

…

Sometime later they were lying in Fleetwood's bed in the darkness. Her head was resting on Adriaan's shoulder. Their hands were outstretched about them and their fingers were intertwined.

"How long has it been since your wife passed?" she asked.

Adriaan was looking at their hands twisting and turning in the darkness above them.

"Two years," he said, after a few moments.

"I'm sorry," said Fleetwood. "I lost my boy last year."

Adriaan rolled over and kissed her on the forehead.

"I'm still in shock; even after two years it still doesn't seem real. I couldn't imagine losing Milly," he said.

"I still don't believe it. I don't want to believe it," she said. "He was surfing."

"My wife died of lung cancer. The sad irony in it all was that she'd never smoked a cigarette her whole life. She was staunchly against smoking, and drinking too. She felt a pain in her chest one day, and when the doctor had a look he found a tumour…"

Fleetwood gently pulled him closer, so that both of their faces were level.

Adriaan was staring up at the ceiling, piecing together broken thoughts that floated through the darkness above him.

"You know, the most painful part of it all isn't her passing, it's watching Milly grow up without a mother…"

"She's lucky she has such a good father."

"I'm the lucky one," said Adriaan. "I don't know where I would be without her."

Both of them were quiet for a time. They held one another, and appreciated each other's presence.

After a while the mood lifted, and both of them were smiling again.

"I should get going, I only paid the babysitter to stay until 10," said Adriaan.

He picked up his phone and checked the time; it was midnight.

He got dressed, kissed her, then left.

Fleetwood was smiling to herself in the darkness. She fell asleep not long after he had gone, and dreamed that she was back in Trinidad with her grandmother, listening to her humming old calypso tunes and drinking sorrel.

"How's it going with that girl, man?" asked Simmo one day when Jimmy had clocked on for his shift at the café. It was a quiet morning. Jimmy had had a feeling that it would be. The sky was darkened by thick black clouds, and just as he walked through the café door the heavens opened with torrential rainfall.

It was one of those work days that he had always dreamed of. One where he got to help Simmo cook instead of having his head down in the sink all day.

Simmo was in a noticeably good mood also. He was swearing significantly less, and laughing more. It was a perfect pace. Every 20 minutes or so, a dripping wet patron who'd dashed from their car would order a meal, but at such a slow pace it made the work almost seem pleasurable. Jimmy learned how to crack the eggs properly with one hand, and also how to taste for salt, pepper and garlic. He learned to cook quinoa, how to cook chicken without killing himself and how to manage the grill.

"Yeah, it's going good. I dunno, I've never really dated anyone before, so it's hard to tell," said Jimmy.

"For sure, grommet. It's all a learning curve, and there's loads of different types of chicks out there too. Trust me, I've been with loads of them."

"Really?" asked Jimmy.

"Yeah, man. There's some good chicks and some bad ones. But they're all the same in ways," he said.

There were no customers in the café now. Simmo took it as an opportunity to do a deep clean. He removed

the extractor fan grills from the ceiling and passed them
to Jimmy, who looked down at them in disgust. They were
caked with grease and grime.

To Simmo's credit, he hopped atop the kitchen
bench, stuck his head into the empty cavity where the fans
were and began scrubbing.

Jimmy looked at Simmo. Simmo wasn't a terribly
attractive man. He had long, thinning, greasy blond hair,
and his left eye was lazy so that you never really knew
where he was looking. But his features were interesting,
and they suited his character. He had an almost self-
destructive sense of humour, and a general charisma about
him that made his opinions valid and trustable. He was
full of funny stories from his past. Travel stories, stories
from his teenage years and young adulthood. The majority
of them seemed to end with sex. His romantic resume was
almost as bad as his temper. He could never be with a girl
long enough before he either cheated on them or they
dumped him.

He knew what kind of person he was, and was
honest about himself at least.

The rain grew heavier outside. They could hear it
on the roof, like a deafening blanket that swallowed all
other noises. Outside, cars pulled to the side of the road
with their hazard lights on for safety. The gutters became
like rivers that were like great floods to the small creatures
that called them home. Leaves and rubbish alike were
caught in the widening flow. Deep puddles formed and
were made shiny by petrol and oil that had leaked onto the
road from passing cars.

"How do you mean they're all the same in ways?"
asked Jimmy.

Simmo stopped scrubbing and pulled his head out
of the cavity. "How do I mean? You'll see... Don't trust

women. They'll say anything. They'll bring your guard down, spin the scenario so they don't feel like they're being a slut, but they're all the same. Look, mate, I'm not saying there's not some really good, honest women out there. All I'm saying is there's a sea of lying whores you gotta swim through before you find one. And you gotta be damn sure they're the right one before you even think about taking that rubber off and fuckin' them raw. Don't EVER cum inside of a girl. Even if she begs you for it, even if she tells you she's on the pill. It's not worth it. I know too many people who've found themselves in some fucked situation where they're in some loveless marriage where both them and their partners fuckin' hate each other, but the only reason they're together is because they got some kid who's probably gonna turn out to be a little shit anyways because they've grown up in a loveless household watchin' their mum and dad argue every day over meaningless bullshit. They're gonna grow up thinking that's what a relationship is like, and then they're gonna go out into the world and continue that cycle. You know how many people grew up in loveless households? Fuckin' too many. So be careful out there. Most people are fucked in the head. She might tell you she loves you, she might look you in the eyes and promise you the world, she'll tear all your walls down, she might make you skip home and smile to yourself on the bus when you're lookin' out the window and watching the world go by, she might have you buying her chocolates and flowers, thinking about her when you go to sleep at night, dreaming about a future where the two of you are gonna be in love and buy a house and have a baby and all that bullshit. But in the end, she's gonna leave. And you'll be fucked. Happens nine times out of 10.

"That's just my experience anyways. You're gonna have to find the rest out for yourself. All I'm saying is, be careful. You don't know who else she's talking to. Unluckily for you, you're a guy. Most guys don't get any attention from girls, so you gotta take what you can get. But girls? Even the ugliest-lookin' chick has a line of keen guys who look better than you, have better jobs, better jokes, are more confident and way slimier. You gotta defend your right at all costs. Don't ever look like a pussy. All those romcoms are lying. Chicks don't want that little sensitive nice guy, chicks want a good-looking asshole who can sometimes be nice!" He pointed at himself as an example.

"But here are some rules that go without saying. Don't be too nice – chicks say they want a nice guy, but they'll leave him for the asshole nine times out of 10. You know why? Because nice guys are boring cunts! What? You really think some chick wants you to act all flowery all the time? Get a bit of edge to you, for fuck's sakes! You got little noodle arms and chicken legs – at least get an aggressive haircut or something.

"Women want you to be assertive. They say they don't, but they do. You just gotta find the balance between leading the way and being too controlling, because if you get too controlling you'll fuck the whole operation up and you'll look like a scumbag. Be a gentleman, but don't ever be a pushover. Some chicks can sense it in you and they'll take you for everything you got. You said you're getting your licence soon, yeah? I bet you that bird will be calling you every day to give her and her friends lifts all about the place. Don't be that guy, trust me. Don't show yourself all at once. You gotta keep a wall up to these chicks; it's for your own good, and girls seem to love a guy who's emotionally unavailable."

He ranted like that for the rest of Jimmy's shift. Jimmy didn't say anything. Simmo was someone he respected, and he listened to everything he said without caution.

All of Simmo's stories made his mind race. What if Skye was just using him? He thought about when he got his driver's licence. She'd already asked him about picking her up and dropping her off from school. She went to a girls' school just down the road from the one he and Jenno went to.

He suddenly felt like a fool. Simmo noticed the expression on his face.

"Fark. Look mate, I'm not trying to break your relationship off, all I'm saying is be cautious. She could be the one for all I know – I dunno, I've never met her."

"Yeah, nah. Thanks for the advice, man," said Jimmy. He took his apron off and clocked off for the day, then raced home in the rain. He was soaked to the bones by the time he made it, and his mum made him stand by the front door so she could towel him off before he came in and ruined the floors.

...

Skye had also been listening to almost the same advice from the older girls at her work. She worked at a local jewellery store. It was one of those minimalistic places where everyone wore linen clothes. The manager there was a woman called Gemma who was reluctantly in her mid-thirties with two little boys. Her husband had cheated on her just before the birth of their second son. From that day on, she made two promises to herself. One was to never trust men, and the other was to raise her boys right so they never dreamed of doing what their father had done.

When Skye came into the store one afternoon after hanging out with Jimmy she couldn't stop herself from smiling.

Gemma asked her why, and frowned when Skye told her it was because of Jimmy.

"Just be careful, Skye. There's only a few things in this world boys enjoy, and none of them are good for women. Just keep an eye on him. Boys will tell you they love you as easy as them asking you for a glass of water. You've got to focus on his actions more than his words. How do his actions make you feel? Do you feel important? Loved? Cared for? Do you think he'd leave everything for you if he had to? Do you think he'd choose you over his friends? If he doesn't at least do those things, then he's not worth your time, trust me. You've got to set standards for yourself, otherwise you'll end up with some good-for-nothing slob who only uses you for sex and never makes you cum anyway. Trust me, I've been there, I've got the kids to show for it, too, and I don't want that for you. Just be careful."

Skye listened, and a seed of doubt about Jimmy was planted in her heart.

...

The two of them met up at their usual spot atop the headland the next day. Jimmy was waiting for her with half a block of chocolate. The rain had come and gone the day before, and the remainder of wispy light-grey clouds had been burned away by the sun.

The block of chocolate had melted by the time Skye got there. It looked more like goo than anything else.

"Sorry, it started melting, so I ate my half super quick," said Jimmy, holding the half-eaten, melted clump of goo and aluminium wrapping out to her.

She looked down at the melted chocolate in his hands and laughed. "Why am I not surprised!"

Jimmy laughed sheepishly. "You wanna go for a swim?" he asked her.

"Yeah, but you have to promise me you'll hold my hand on the walk down."

"Of course," said Jimmy.

They walked down the headland towards the beach. They were holding hands, fingers interlocked.

Jimmy had to stop himself from groaning when they rounded the corner and saw Dizz and the older boys sitting on the wall that overlooked the surf.

He put his head down in the hopes that they wouldn't spot him holding hands, but he was too late.

Dizz laughed loudly and pointed. "Awwwww!"

Jimmy didn't look back, but Skye saw him wince.

"He's such a fuckin' gay cunt! Look at him!" Dizz's voice bit at his heels as he walked.

"Were those the older boys you're scared about?" asked Skye once they had made it to the beach. It was a beautiful day. The ocean was calm and smooth, but every now and then a small ripple of swell would form and break its glassy surface.

"I'm not scared of them," said Jimmy, but the tone of his voice wasn't convincing in the slightest.

"It's ok if you are. I'm not judging you," said Skye.

Jimmy thought about what Simmo had said in the kitchen about not looking like a pussy, and suddenly he grew tense.

"Forget about it. I'm not scared, I just didn't wanna get in a fight in front of you," he said.

"You would have fought them if I wasn't there?" she asked him.

"Yeah, for sure," said Jimmy. "I've been in loads of fights."

"Why?" asked Skye.

It was a simple question, but one that Jimmy wasn't prepared for.

"I dunno. It's just what men do."

"Well, I think it's stupid. What's the point of fighting?" said Skye.

Jimmy's stomach sank. He hated fighting too. In fact, he'd never so much as been in a shove-off, let alone a fistfight.

He felt stuck on how to recover himself.

"Nah, like… it's not that I like to fight. You just have to sometimes in order to protect people," he said.

"Right… or in your case, your ego," said Skye. "I didn't take you as a fighter, Jimmy. I thought you were different than the other boys."

He looked at the disappointed look on her face and panicked.

"I am! Trust me, I am!" he said. He realised that he needed to change the topic, and fast. A sudden idea came into his head. It was terrible, but the only one he had.

"Can the other boys do this?"

He ran towards the water and bellyflopped.

Skye couldn't help but laugh; she followed him in. "You're an idiot. But no, I guess maybe none of them would think to bellyflop in front of their girlfriend."

Jimmy laughed his sheepish laugh again, relieved to have finally changed the subject.

"Hold my hand," she said, looking into his eyes.

Jimmy reached his hand out and took hold of hers. He was always reminded of how beautiful she really was whenever he looked into her eyes. He realised he must have been smiling, because she smiled back at him.

"Do you like me?" she asked him.

The question took him aback. "Yeah, of course. Why?"

"Because I like you, a lot. Just don't break my heart, is all I'm saying."

"I wouldn't dream of it!" said Jimmy. He took her other hand and brought her close.

"Ok. I trust you," she said.

"Good." said Jimmy.

She put her hands against his chest; he could feel the warmth from her face radiating softly over his skin. It made his hair prickle.

He had no idea what she saw in him. In the face of her beauty he was suddenly aware of all of his insecurities. He felt like a scrawny bag of bones. He had acne, he was awkward and sheepish, and he wasn't confident in himself at all. But she looked at him as if he were something completely different. He saw himself in her eyes, and what he saw made him feel something he'd never felt before. Something he didn't feel at home, or around his friends, or even when he was alone.

Skye went home after the swim, but Jimmy stayed on the beach for a while and watched the water. After a little while it got too hot to sit any longer, so he dove back in. He thought of Ratty, and remembered that morning when the sea was dark and violent. It seemed almost unbelievable when he compared it now. It was so soothing, so calm and welcoming. Every time he put his head underwater it felt as though all the worry, the sweat and grime he carried around was washed away. It was such a source of healing, he wondered how it could just as easily take life away. He got out and took one last look at the water before he walked back up to the carpark.

Dizz and the boys were still there when he walked through.

"Fuck, she's pretty hot, good work, big dog!" said Dizz from the wall behind Jimmy's back.

Jimmy ignored him and kept walking without looking back.

"Oi, you reckon you could give me her number? I reckon she'd go alright…" he said.

"Fuck off," said Jimmy.

"Aye?" said Dizz. He hopped off of the wall. "Jimmy's finally sticking up for himself! I'd slap the fuck out of you right now if your dad wasn't a lawyer, you snivelling little wretch."

Jimmy turned around. "I said, fuck off!"

Dizz burst out laughing. Jimmy clenched his fists.

Dizz looked down at his balled-up fists. "You gonna hit me? Then hit me, cunt! Come on, hit me, big dog!"

He dangled his face just inside of Jimmy's reach.

Jimmy looked at his outstretched jaw, and relished for a moment in the thought of swinging at it. But when the moment passed, he remembered himself and where he was. He looked behind Dizz at the other boys. All of them were watching. Dizz smiled arrogantly when he noticed the look of hesitation on Jimmy's face.

"Pussy," he said.

He stood back up to his full height and walked back to the wall.

"Seeya around, Jimmy, hopefully see your missus again soon, too!"

Jimmy turned and walked away.

When he got home, he slammed his bedroom door behind him and looked at himself in the mirror. He wondered why he hadn't just hit Dizz. He looked at himself in disgust. He looked like a scared little boy.

He threw himself onto his bed and looked up at the ceiling, replaying the scene over and over again in his head. He wished he had hit him. He could imagine the feeling of standing over Dizz, crumpled and cowering, and all the older boys looking on in astonishment. He imagined himself feeling like a man among boys, with his fists clenched and his word as law. A darkness that came from fear stirred in him and took over for a time.

But then he thought of what Skye would think. Simmo told him girls didn't want a soft boy. He was confused now, torn between what Skye had said and what Simmo told him she was actually thinking.

"Don't ever look like a pussy. All those romcoms are lying. Chicks don't want that little sensitive nice guy, chicks want a good-looking asshole who can sometimes be nice!" Simmo's words rang in his head. He certainly felt like a pussy, whatever that meant.

He swore to himself that the next time he saw Dizz and Dizz said something, he'd hit him, no matter what. He promised himself, as though he were promising Simmo, his father and all of the men that he looked up to.

...

The next afternoon he and Skye went for a walk after school. The clouds were thick and ominous above them, but they ignored the warning signs.

They walked through the park holding hands. There was no one around and the air was still. But then the heavens opened and a flood of heavy rain and bits of hail fell like thick curtains.

They ran screaming and laughing through the rain towards Skye's place and burst through the front door and up into her room. They jumped on her bed and lay there for some time, just staring into each other's eyes. Then Jimmy kissed her. She was smiling when he pulled away.

Rain and wind hammered against the window, and thunder rumbled in the distance. Her room was simple but well laid out. There was a peace lily with a single flower in the corner near the window, and a few photographs and drawings that were stuck to the wall. She slept with a teddy bear every night; it was old but well looked after.

"I really like you," she said.

"I really like you too," said Jimmy as he gently sifted his hands through her hair.

"There's something I've been meaning to ask you," she began. "Have you ever been with someone before?" She looked at him almost hesitantly.

"What do you mean?" said Jimmy.

"Like, have you ever had sex?"

Jimmy's heart raced. This was the last thing he had been expecting her to ask and he had to put all of his willpower into stopping his leg from shaking nervously.

"No, I haven't... Have you?" he asked her, trying his best to sound casual.

"It's something that I've been saving for the right person. I could have done it so many times by now, but I don't trust anyone else like I trust you. I think you're really special, Jimmy. You're in touch with your emotions, but most of all you're a good person, and I know that this must sound weird, but I think you're the person I'd like to experience it with for the first time."

"I feel the same way about you," he began. "You make me feel so excited about life, and that's something I haven't felt in what feels like the longest time. I think you're beautiful, Skye, in more ways than just physical."

He held her close to him, and then she kissed him and it went from there. It was a strange and awkward experience. He thought about it afterwards – it was nothing like what he expected it to be. They made it look so good in the movies.

They lay together for a while afterwards, holding hands and staring at the ceiling in silence, both of them letting the gravity of it all sink in.

Later on, once the rain had died down, Jimmy made a dash to get home. He tried his best to stay mature, but his excitement got the better of him. He phoned Jenno as soon as he walked through his bedroom door.

"S'doin'?" answered Jenno on the other end. From the sound coming through the line, Jimmy knew he was lying in his bedroom throwing a tennis ball at the wall.

"Nothing," said Jimmy casually, "I was just hanging out with Skye."

"Ah yeah, what did you do?"

"Nothing much… Except one thing."

"Huh?" said Jenno.

"You know…" said Jimmy.

"No, I don't know… Spit it out, you weird cunt!" said Jenno.

"We had sex!" said Jimmy.

Jenno was silent for a second. Jimmy checked to make sure the call was still connected.

"Fuck off!" Jenno said, finally.

Jimmy laughed boyishly. "Yeah!"

"Damn... I always figured I'd have sex first. I didn't think you had it in you," said Jenno.

"Yeah... It wasn't really anything planned. She kind of did everything. I don't know, I think I really love her," said Jimmy. His head was in the clouds, high on love and young romance that made him feel giddy.

He came back to earth when he heard Jenno laughing on the other end. "Shut up, Jimmy!"

Jimmy laughed and hung up. It felt as though everything in his life was finally starting to look up.

11

It was a clear Friday evening when Jimmy called Jenno. He was sitting in his room with his feet up on the table, breathing the fresh breeze that wafted through his bedroom window.

"What's doin'?" answered Jenno, on the other end of the line.

"I was just thinking," Jimmy began, "you keen to smoke a joint tonight?"

"Faarkk," said Jenno. "I would, but Mum's making me go to Nan and Pops' tonight to keep them company; Pop just had a big surgery."

"Ah damn, is he ok?" Jimmy asked.

"Yeah, nah, he'll be right," said Jenno. "I'm spewing I gotta go but, it's so boring around their place."

"You'll be right," said Jimmy.

"You still gonna smoke?" asked Jenno.

"Yeah, I think so. I don't know, it feels right tonight."

"What, just by yourself?" asked Jenno.

Suddenly it dawned on Jimmy that if Jenno was busy, he had no one else besides Skye, and he didn't want to smoke in front of her just yet.

"Yeah, I guess so," he said.

"Alright, well, don't do any dumb shit," said Jenno.

"Fuck off, I'll be fine." Jimmy laughed.

They hung up and for a few moments Jimmy wondered who else he could call. He looked down at his phone and scrolled down his contact list, but stopped when he saw Ratty's number. His thumb hovered over it for a moment, before he pressed down and put the phone to his ear. His heart was racing, but he didn't know why. The call went straight to answer phone. He exhaled, and hung up.

Sometime later, when night had fallen, Jimmy skated down to the beach carpark alone. The carpark was empty, save for a few campervans that were parked together in the back corner. Jimmy sat down on Ratty's bench and pulled out a little joint from his pocket. It was rolled terribly. The filter was loose and the paper was already peeling back from itself. Ratty was the one who had had a gift for rolling. Jimmy put the joint to his lips, lit it and pulled a drag. He leaned his head back and exhaled. The smoke cloud was picked up by the soft sea breeze and carried away gently. Jimmy thought about the first time he and Jenno ever smoked a joint.

It had been a few weeks before Ratty's death. They smoked in a little forest behind the cinema in the next town up and watched some horror movie about a house haunted by a spirit. A young family moved into the house and got possessed in their dreams and killed one another. What had initially seemed like a funny idea to the boys had suddenly become something of a nightmare in itself. It was dark and windy when they left the cinema, and all three of them started wigging out.

"Fuck that shit, dude. If I ever got caught in a haunted house I'd just pencil dive straight onto my neck!" Ratty shivered.

"What? As if that'd work, you'd just end up fuckin 'yourself even more before you got killed," Jenno laughed.

Jimmy was quiet; he was still thinking about the movie.

They walked to the bus stop just as the bus pulled up and rushed in before the driver had a chance to shut the doors on them.

The bus was empty, save for an old man who sat up the front. He looked up quickly at the boys as they passed, and each one of them were wondering the same thing – *Does he know we're high?*

They sat down on the back seats and tried to act as normal as possible.

"Boys, I dunno, I just have this gut feeling that something awful is about to happen…" said Jimmy, with a pained look on his face.

Jenno and Ratty looked at one another briefly before erupting with laughter.

"Shut up, Jimmy! You're just wigging out, dude, it'll be sweet," said Ratty.

"But what about that old man? Did you see the way he looked at us?" said Jimmy

"Yeah, but what's he gonna do? He's just old. I reckon he looks at everyone that walks past him. That's just what old people do."

"Yeah, I guess so," said Jimmy, unconvinced. He tried to look out of the window but was faced by his own reflection instead. His lips were dry and his eyes were red.

"We're only a few stops away from my place, anyways," said Ratty. As he spoke, the bus pulled over and a group of rowdy 20-somethings got on. They stumbled along the aisle and collapsed into the first few rows. The old man was surrounded. He eyed each one of them curiously.

The loudest of the group was a man with long, matted hair and one leg. He leaned back on his seat and held a bloodied white shirt to his nose. "If I ever catch that cunt again, I'm gonna kill him!" he roared drunkenly from his seat. His head was lolling back and forth as the bus drove. His friend sat next to him, nursing what looked like the beginnings of a black eye.

"Fuck that, bra! Next dog I sees getting king hit, straight up…" he said, angrily. He looked at the old man and raised his fist. The old man stared back at him, expressionless. Suddenly, the man smiled and slapped the old man on the shoulder. "I'm just playin' with you, old boy! I'm not gonna king hit ya… maybe someone else…"

Jenno, Jimmy and Ratty were sitting up the back of the bus, on the left. They were trying their best to pretend like they hadn't noticed the one-legged man and all his friends. But Jimmy couldn't help but look. He turned his head slowly, carefully, until he could just get a glimpse at the man. His heart dropped as the one-legged man caught him before he had a chance to look away. He stared out of the window again, hoping that nothing would come of it.

"What the fuck's this little gronk looking at?" said the man with one leg, looking up at Jimmy. Jimmy's stomach sank.

The one-legged man's friend stood up from his seat and walked up to the back of the bus where the boys were sitting. He grabbed the swinging triangles as he walked, pulling himself closer despite the bumpiness of the ride. He sat next to Jimmy, smiling pleasantly. Jimmy looked at him wide-eyed, and noticed a tattoo of a panther clawing through skin on his neck. As he put his arm around Jimmy, all Jimmy could smell was rum and sweat.

"What's happening, boys? You having a good night?" he asked.

"Yeah…" said Jimmy quietly. "How about you?

"That's good, buddy," said the man. "And nah, I haven't had as good a night as you. As you can probably tell by my eye, I've been in a scrap tonight."

"I'm sorry to hear that," said Jimmy, uncertain of what was coming.

"Sorry? You should have seen the other cunt. I nearly collapsed his face in!" He threw his head back and laughed.

Jimmy laughed too, nervously.

"Nah, nah, but, that's not why I came up here to talk to you," he said, calmly.

"What did you want to talk about?" Jimmy asked, uncertainly.

"I just wanted to ask you a favour, is all. You reckon I could borrow your phones? Mine's out of battery, and so are all my friends, so we might need a couple to share between us!" He looked over at Ratty and Jenno, who both put their phones in their pockets, but Jimmy was frozen. The smell of the man's breath and the weight of his arm on Jimmy's shoulder was too much for him to bear. He nodded his head and took his phone out.

"Cheers, big dog!" The man laughed as he took the phone. He walked down the bus and sat back down next to his friend with one leg.

Jimmy looked at Jenno and Ratty and mouthed, "What the fuck!"

"Fark, he just took your phone!" whispered Ratty.

"Dude, why'd you let him take it?" whispered Jenno.

"Why'd I let him take it? What do you mean? It's pretty fuckin' obvious... It's not like you two did anything to help, you just sat there!"

"Fuck off... no way he's getting my phone! Dude, you gotta get that back, what's your mum gonna say? She thinks we're all having a sleep over at Jenno's…" said Ratty.

"Are you fuckin' crazy? Did you see the same guy I did? He just told us he beat someone's face in! Plus, look at his friend… he's got one leg and he's covered in blood!" whispered Jimmy, frantically.

Jimmy looked at Jenno, who looked like his mind was racing. Jimmy had remembered the instructions Jenno's dad had given to them both when they were younger. Always retaliate whenever something is done to you. He thought about it, and what Jenno's dad would say if he found out that Jenno had let someone steal his friend's phone, even if they were older and larger. Jimmy's eyes widened when Jenno stood up suddenly, and yelled, "OI! FUCK YOU!"

The one-legged man and his friend looked even more surprised than Jimmy did, who was looking at Jenno with his mouth agape.

Jenno's face screwed up, his chest moved in and out violently as he breathed heavily.

"Aye?" said the man with Jimmy's phone.

"Give him his phone back you fuckin' cunt!" said Ratty, standing up to join Jenno.

"No, boys. it's sweet!" said Jimmy, shrinking into his seat.

"Tell him come get it himself," said the man with his phone.

Jimmy had to make a move, but he didn't have it in him to get his phone back. But before Jimmy had a chance to do anything, the old man erupted.

"Shut the fuck up, you FUCKING CUNTS!" he roared.

The entire bus was silent for a moment, before everyone on the bus besides Jenno, Jimmy and Ratty burst into laughter.

"Relax, matey, we're all friends here!" said the man with Jimmy's phone.

"Just fuck off and give 'im 'is phone back, for fuck's sakes!" said the old man.

They laughed again.

"Alright, alright," said the man with Jimmy's phone, "just for you…"

He pulled Jimmy's phone out of his pocket and launched it towards the back of the bus where Jimmy was sitting. Jimmy ducked just in time for it to smash against the wall where his head had been a moment before.

The one-legged man and his friends got off at the next stop. Before the bus had a chance to pull away, they came to Jimmy's window and started punching it in. Jimmy was facing forward, pretending not to notice as their fists collided with the window, bending it and shaking the perspex glass as they struck.

He picked up his phone once the bus pulled away. The screen was cracked, but besides that everything worked fine. When they reached their stop not long after, Jimmy stopped next to the old man to say thanks.

"Thank you," he said, "I really appreciate you getting my phone back."

"Get fucked," said the old man.

Jimmy shrugged and walked off.

"That was crazy!" laughed Ratty, as they walked away from the bus stop. He put his hands on Jenno's shoulders and shook Jenno back and forth excitedly.

Jimmy looked down at his cracked phone, feeling relieved to be finally off the bus and breathing fresh air.

"Fark, Jimmy! Why didn't you say anything?" said Jenno. "Me and Ratty were about to cop a belting for you…"

"Sorry…" said Jimmy, "I just wigged out."

A car full of boys not much older than them drove by. Jimmy shrunk into himself as they yelled at them from the window.

"You gotta learn how to stick up for yourself, Jimmy. Me and Jenno aren't always gonna be there to back you up," said Ratty, looking over his shoulder at the car as it drove away.

"Yeah," said Jenno, "you just gotta hit them. My old man reckons all you gotta do is hit them once, and then they'll know you mean business and they won't fuck with you."

"Yeah!" agreed Ratty. "You always gotta fight back, Jimmy. You can't just let people walk over you, otherwise they will."

They reached Ratty's place and climbed through his bedroom window quietly. Ratty and Jimmy slipped through first, but, as Jenno climbed clumsily over the window frame, he caught his back foot and dropped loudly to the floor.

Jimmy winced, and Ratty threw his hands up in the air.

"Fuck sakes, Jenno! You may as well have woken up the neighbours too…" he whispered.

Jenno rubbed the spot on his head that had collided with the floor regretfully. "Fark, sorry…" he said.

Ratty stared at his bedroom door, waiting for Fleetwood to burst through at any moment. But, by some miracle, Jenno's fall hadn't woken her up. Ratty sat back on his wall and breathed a sigh of relief.

"We were that close..." he said, holding his fingers up.

He tiptoed over to his bedside table and pulled out a joint from the drawer. "What do you reckon... one more before bed?" he said, grinning.

The boys lit the joint and took turns smoking it with their heads out of the window. When they were finished, they sat on the floor with their backs against the wall. Ratty was lost in thought, studying the surf posters that he had stuck up around the room.

"I reckon I'm gonna make it one day," he said, suddenly.

"Huh?" said Jenno. His eyes were bloodshot and every few seconds he opened his eyelids fully, as if shifting some great weight.

"Make it pro..." said Ratty. "Midget showed his dad that video of me surfing the other day, and he said his dad wants to set up a meeting with me."

"Farrk! No way, that's hectic!" said Jenno, awestruck at the idea.

"You reckon pro surfers get much money?" Jimmy asked, curiously.

"I reckon the good ones do, a couple million a year probably," said Ratty.

"Imagine having that much cash," said Jenno, his eyes suddenly gleaming at the idea.

"Yeah. If I had a couple million, I'd buy my mum a house," Ratty began, "and then I'd bring my granny over to Australia, I reckon she'd like it here. It's not as fun as Trinidad, but it's nice, and she wouldn't have to worry about anything anymore."

"What about school?" asked Jimmy.

Ratty considered for a few moments. "I reckon I'd still study. Maybe I could do a course online while I'm on the tour; there's a few pros who do that."

"Damn..." said Jenno. He looked at Ratty with respect. "You reckon Midget's dad would like my surf clips?"

"I dunno," said Ratty. "Send them to him and see what he says."

The heaviness of the hour and the weight of the joint seemed to press down on them all at once, and one by one they drifted off to sleep.

Jimmy was woken up by the early morning sun. He covered his eyes against the red light and breathed heavily. In the blurriness of his vision, he saw Ratty standing by the window, looking out at the world beyond.

"You're up early," said Jimmy, rubbing his eyes.

Ratty looked back over his shoulder. "Yeah, apparently the surf's meant to be pumping this morning. You wanna go?"

"Alright," said Jimmy.

Ratty threw a shoe at Jenno, who groaned. "Fuck off, cunt!" he muttered into his pillow.

"C'mon, Jenno, let's surf!" said Ratty. He threw the other shoe at Jenno, which finally had the desired effect. Jenno sat up regretfully, still half asleep.

The world had come to life by the time they made it to the water. The sand was still cold from the night, but the water was warm. The waves were almost perfect. The water was glassy and still, until about every five minutes three or four set waves climbed from the depths of the horizon. They were head-high runners, which peeled across the sandbank and raced towards the shore in perfect formation.

Ratty was the first to make it out the back, and as Jimmy and Jenno trailed sluggishly behind, Ratty was already paddling for his first wave.

They watched as he put his head down and scratched to get in position, and then as he stood and stuck his hand into the face of the wave. It was a peach of a wave, juicy and beautiful, and it looked like it was going to barrel. Ratty instinctively crouched just in time to scoop into it, and a moment later he disappeared behind a curtain of water, lit green and white by the rising sun, only to reappear again from the midst of a thick cloud of spray, roaring with delight.

Jenno called after him excitedly, sitting up on his board and clapping loudly. "You fuckin' sick cunt!"

Jimmy smiled to himself quietly, saving the vision in his memory.

"Fark! You'll be on the tour in no time if you keep making it out of barrels like that…" said Jenno, as Ratty paddled past him, still grinning.

"That was sick!" he said. In the light of the morning sun his eyes were the colour of the sea.

The three of them sat next to one another, laughing together and taking turns catching every good wave that passed.

…

Jimmy looked at the half-smoked joint in his hand, before he put it out in the grass. He sat back down and watched the waves pass by unridden in the moonlight, before he finally got cold and went home.

12

Fleetwood was halfway through helping a little girl in Year Three do her maths equations when she felt her phone buzzing in her pocket. She pulled it out curiously and then smiled to herself. It was Adriaan. She stepped out of class and answered.

"I'm in school! What's up?" she said, quietly.

She heard Adriaan laugh on the other side. "I'm sorry! I was thinking about you this morning, so I figured I'd call and ask if you'd want to join Scrunch and I for a walk this afternoon?"

"A text wouldn't have done?" Fleetwood laughed.

"It could have, but then we wouldn't be here talking right now," said Adriaan.

"I guess you're right," admitted Fleetwood. "Well, I'd be delighted."

When school ended, Fleetwood met Adriaan at the dog park. She found him waiting on a bench near a bubbler, Scrunch lapping up water from an old plastic container beneath it.

"No Milly today?" she asked, as she sat down.

"She's sick today, I dropped her off at my mum's house this morning," said Adriaan." She loves it there, plus it means I can catch up on some stuff at home while she's gone. How was school?"

"Just like any other school day. Although a boy in Year Five got called into the principal's office for going number two in the urinals."

Adriaan leaned his head back and laughed loudly. Fleetwood laughed also, but more at the joy that it seemed to bring him.

"A bright future ahead, I imagine," said Adriaan. "You know, I heard somewhere that Einstein used to do the same thing."

Fleetwood whacked him on the shoulder playfully.

They got up and followed the windy pathway through the dog park. It wasn't just a dog park – kids played soccer in the same field, cyclists used the pathway as a shortcut, people kayaked in the lagoon that paralleled the path. There were people everywhere in high spirits. Fleetwood looked down at Scrunch, who was wagging her tail excitedly, and then to Adriaan, who was throwing a mangled-looking tennis ball up and down in his hand. She suddenly felt glad to be there with them.

"So, what made you move down here in the first place?" asked Fleetwood.

At that moment, Scrunch squatted and relieved herself. She looked up at Adriaan almost guiltily. He stooped down and picked it up with a plastic bag.

"Comes with the job…" he laughed, then considered Fleetwood's question.

"It was a number of reasons. After my wife passed, everything there reminded me of her. I needed a change. My parents still live here, and I figured it'd do Milly good to have them around, and, to be honest with you, I thought it'd do me good as well. When I talked to work about it, they said I could work down here remotely for as long as I wanted. I couldn't be in that office anymore; it was where we met."

"I'm sorry," said Fleetwood.

"It's ok," said Adriaan." Most of my memories in that office are good ones – I just couldn't face going back without her. We were together for 10 years before anyone found out."

Fleetwood laughed." How did you manage that?"

"Not without difficulty. It was only when we fell pregnant with Milly the jig was up. I couldn't blame it on the office snack bar anymore." He laughed. "But what about you – you said you moved here with your ex?" he added, a moment later. Scrunch sniffed at the ball in his hand, and began to lick his bent knuckles impatiently. He looked down at her and smiled, and then threw the ball as far as he could across the field.

"Yes, I came here with him, but that was over 15 years ago now," she said.

Adriaan glanced at her and smiled softly, before Scrunch came bounding back.

"I'm guessing he was an Australian you met over there?" he asked.

"He was. We met at the bar I used to work at while I was studying art at university in London," began Fleetwood. "It's funny, men would try something on me every shift. At best, they'd ask for my number, at worst, they'd try and slap me on the ass when I walked by."

"What a bunch of assholes," said Adriaan.

"I hated that job, and I was on the verge of quitting when I met him. I was crying to my mum about it on the phone the morning before he came in for the first time. I don't know what it was, I just felt compelled to talk to him. He was in construction clothes, covered in dust, but he only ordered a Diet Coke. We talked for hours, until the manager got annoyed and sent me to the back. I found him so fascinating. He came in most days after work, and when we weren't talking, he was sitting alone by the window reading."

Scrunch rushed back, holding the ball in her mouth. She stood up on her two hind legs and padded Adriaan's waist with her front, before dropping the ball at his feet.

Adriaan picked it up and threw it again, and Scrunch was off. "What did he read?"

"Loads of things. Dickens, Kipling, Jack London. But I'm not convinced he ever had any real interested in reading them. After we got together, I never saw him read again. Our first date was at Clapham Common. It was freezing, but he was wearing board shorts and a thick jacket. He looked about the most Australian guy I'd ever met."

"Sounds like it," said Adriaan.

Fleetwood noticed that he was looking at his feet. "I'm sorry, I'm boring you…"

"No, no, you're not boring me at all, it's a nice story," smiled Adriaan." So then what?"

"We starting dating, and not long after we moved in together. It was more out of necessity than anything else. I wasn't earning much at the bar, and he'd only recently finished his carpentry apprenticeship. I fell pregnant not long after we moved in together. That's when we decided to move here. He figured he could get better work back here, and he wanted Toby to be a surfer. It's funny, never in my wildest dreams would I have imagined myself to wake up one morning pregnant in Australia!"

"What happened between you two, if you don't mind me asking?"

A few moments passed and Fleetwood didn't speak, trying to find the right words.

"Not that long after we moved, I woke up to a letter on my bedside table. He left Toby and me for Queensland. He said he wasn't ready to be a father, and that was it."

"I'm sorry," said Adriaan.

"It's ok," she said." There was something off about him for a long time, I was just too caught up in everything to see it for what it was. And I'm glad he left when he did, and not when Toby was old enough to realise. It was hard on Toby, though, growing up without a dad." Something caught in her throat, and she stopped. Tears began to surface, but she managed to hold them back. She sniffed a little and wiped her eyes with the cuffs of her jumper. Adriaan held his hand out and placed the chewed-out ball in hers.

She took it and then looked down to Scrunch, who was now sniffing at her knees excitedly.

Fleetwood laughed when she threw the ball and it landed only half the distance of Adriaan's throw. Scrunch turned back to her, looking cheated. When Scrunch finally got the ball, she ignored Fleetwood and went straight back to Adriaan.

"Looks like we know who the better ball thrower is," Fleetwood laughed.

"Years of practice…" said Adriaan.

"I'm sorry, I feel like I've been doing all the talking," said Fleetwood, suddenly.

"I like listening to your stories," said Adriaan. "They make things in my own life make sense."

"How do you mean?" asked Fleetwood.

"When my wife passed away, she left this huge, gaping hole in my heart. I was destroyed, but deeper than that, I was angry for some reason. Angry at the world, angry at myself and angry at her for leaving us. But beyond all of that was this sense of inescapable loneliness." He threw the ball again, harder than he had all the times before. "I know that sounds awful, it's just how I felt at the time."

"I understand," said Fleetwood.

"I know you do." He smiled at her softly." You're the only person I know who does."

…

That same afternoon, Jimmy and Skye met after school and went for a walk around the headland. The headland wasn't a great place for a walk, it was more of a climb and a scamper, but it offered them privacy. It looped around for almost two kilometres before it tapered off into the next beach up the coast. For a long time, Jimmy, Jenno and Ratty were banned from playing at the edge of the cliffs above the headland after Ratty had thrown a rock off and nearly killed a fisherman below.

Before he'd passed away it had become his go-to spot to take girls on a date. The headland went out to sea far enough that no buildings or lights could be seen in the periphery, so when you looked out towards the horizon there was nothing but an endless expanse of ocean that felt as though you were standing at the edge of the world.

Boulders, rock pools and caves were scattered along the base of cliff for most of the way around, until suddenly the rock platform fell into the sea and it was no longer possible to walk or climb. When the tide was high and the sea was violent, water rushed and swallowed the base of the headland in white wash and spray. Afterwards, the rock pools were filled with sea life that'd been unfortunate enough to get stuck. Fish, octopus and starfish could all be seen beneath the crystal waters of the pools, which had become almost worlds in themselves. Sometimes, when Jimmy needed to think, he'd go and sit by the pools and just watch in silence as the little fish circled and darted around his feet.

"Me, Ratty and Jenno used to come around here all the time when we were younger," said Jimmy as he and Skye clambered over one of the large boulders that were scattered around the base of the cliff.

"This is kind of scary, Jimmy!" Skye called out hesitantly as she followed him.

"Nah, it's sweet, trust me! Look, the waves are barely making a splash when they hit the rocks."

"Ok, I trust you," said Skye.

"It can be dangerous, though. We used to hide under the boulders when the waves were big enough to wash over. It was kind of like being in a barrel. But one time the swell was massive, and when the wave came it blew us out from behind the rock and we got washed over the edge."

"Oh my god!" Skye gasped.

Jimmy laughed, pleased with her reaction.

"Yeah, it was pretty scary, but we were ok in the end. Ratty got cut up pretty bad, though. I remember seeing him starfished on the top of that big rock in the water. I thought he was a goner for sure, I dunno how he didn't get dragged out to sea. He was always lucky like that…" He trailed off. It was only when Skye put her hand gently on his shoulder that he came back. He smiled at her. His eyes were watery, but no tears fell.

"That was the last time we ever tried it. I don't know if I ever would again. It was pretty crazy. There's a cave here that you can hide in, and when a big wave comes it fills the cave almost to the brim with water."

"You're nuts," said Skye, with a concerned look on her face. "Promise me you won't do anything like that again."

Jimmy took her hand.

"I promise," he said, before kissing her on the cheek softly. She bent her head and rested it on his shoulder, closing her eyes for a moment.

Jimmy led Skye further around the headland, past Tahiti's cave and even past the rockpools. Finally, he stopped at the edge of the rock platform. He sat down and let his legs hang over, the soft swell licking at the tips of his toes every time it rushed gently up the cliff face. He put his hand into one of the small divots of the rock and scraped the dry sea salt from the bottom.

Black crabs scuttled across the half-submerged boulders, their shells shiny and glinting in the sunlight. A flock of seagulls circled above a ball of baitfish not far out from where Jimmy and Skye sat. One by one, they dove beneath the surface and reappeared again a moment later clutching a small, wriggling fish between their beaks.

"Have you chosen what you want to study at uni yet?" Jimmy asked Skye.

"I think so. But I'm still not sure," she started, "I think I want to go into teaching."

"Really?" said Jimmy.

"Yeah. I don't know, I love school and I love learning. I think it would be an amazing experience being able to teach kids. I want to watch them grow and figure out what they like and who they want to be. I think teaching's an important job."

"Yeah, you're right. I guess I never really thought of it that way," said Jimmy.

"I like how I feel in class as well," Skye added.

"Like what?" Jimmy asked.

"Like I'm safe. I feel like there's nothing in the world that could go wrong when I'm in class. It feels like a protective bubble."

"I can tell you don't go to school with boys..." Jimmy laughed. "Class at my school is like a jungle. Kids throw chairs at the ceiling fans in my class."

"You mean, your friend Jenno throws ceiling fans in class..."

Jimmy laughed." Yeah, he does too. Lucky we're not in the same year. Ratty was worse."

"What about you? Do you know what you want to study?" asked Skye.

Jimmy thought for a moment.

"Nah, I haven't put much thought into it. But I feel like it's been decided for me... My dad wants me to go into finance."

"Finance? You don't strike me as someone who's into money."

"Yeah, I'm not. I dunno, I'm good at maths, and I like to learn, but I don't really know what I want to study. I dunno where I want to go or who I want to be, it all seems like a dense fog at the minute, and all I can do is just make one decision after the next and hope that I end up somewhere good."

"Well, what do you like to do?" asked Skye.

"Surf," he said simply." I like music as well."

"What about studying music?"

A crab scuttled just beneath the surface near Jimmy's toes. He watched it, contemplating.

"Sometimes I feel like he's got such high expectations for me that he's never even bothered to get to know me for who I am. He looks at me like I'm another person, and when I do things my way, he gets angry, like

I've done something wrong, but it's more than that, it's like *I'm* wrong. It's like I'm the wrong person."

"You're not the wrong person," said Skye, "you're yourself, and that's all that matters."

She put her hand on Jimmy's shoulder. He looked at the warm smile on her face and felt a tremble inside himself.

"I don't think I can pretend to understand what you're going through," she began, "but I like who you are now. Even if you don't feel the same about yourself."

"I like you too," said Jimmy, softly.

They kissed, until a large lap of swell splashed against the rocks and sprayed them.

"You're drenched!" Jimmy laughed.

Skye wiped the water from her face and pushed her wet hair back from her forehead. For a moment it looked like she was upset, but to Jimmy's relief she grinned.

"I was getting hot in the sun anyway; I think I needed that."

She grabbed Jimmy and pulled him close to her, and before he had a chance to pull himself away she rubbed her wet face all over his shirt.

"Hey! Get off me, you crazy lady!" Jimmy laughed.

When she stopped wrestling against him, she burrowed herself in his arms.

They held each other in silence for what felt like an eternity. Water slapped against rock, birds cried as they passed over, and a gentle breeze wafted past Jimmy's ears.

...

"I've got something else to ask you," said Jimmy on their way back from the ledge a little while later.

"What is it?" she said, looking back over her shoulder.

"What did you mean, before, when you said that you felt safe in class?"

The question had been playing on his mind ever since she'd mentioned it.

"I don't know how to put it. Sometimes it feels like it's the only place in the world where everything is under control. It's somewhere I feel like I belong."

"What about at home?" said Jimmy.

"You said it yourself. Sometimes it feels like my parents have no idea who I really am. They get angry at me all the time, and I feel like I've done nothing wrong except be me."

"I'm sorry," said Jimmy.

"It's ok, I know who I am. And I know who I want to become, and my parents will just have to accept that."

"I wish I could say the same," said Jimmy.

"I know you'll figure it out," she said." You're already who you are. You just have to appreciate yourself."

"Yeah, thanks," said Jimmy.

"And I know whoever you choose to become will be someone nice, and caring, and sweet." She smiled.

Those were three words Jimmy didn't want to hear. They were the opposite of what Simmo had told him girls wanted, and his stomach twisted itself in knots.

"I'm not that nice…" he said, uncaringly.

"Maybe not," said Skye, then, from atop a boulder, "Take my hand."

Jimmy took it and climbed up level with her, then put his arm around her shoulder. They stood and looked out into the horizon together, a soft breeze playing with their hair.

"When's school's finally finished, I want to take a gap year. I'm going to see the world!" said Skye, gazing out into the horizon. "Would you come with me?" she said softly, a moment later.

"Travelling?" replied Jimmy. Skye nodded. "Yeah, of course. But where?"

"Anywhere! I need to get lost somewhere. I want to experience cultures, and foods, and music!"

"I've always wanted to go to Indonesia…" said Jimmy.

"I've heard it's beautiful there," said Skye.

She breathed in deeply, then exhaled. The sunlight filled her eyes, and they sparkled like sapphires.

Jimmy peered into the horizon and tried to see it how Skye did. To him all the horizon had meant was just the edge of his world, an impenetrable wall of sky and water. But now, there was something beyond, something that was waiting for him, calling to him. All of a sudden it was as if the breeze was carrying smells and sounds from far away, drawing them closer and closer.

"I'd love to travel with you," said Jimmy," one day…"

"One day…" said Skye. She leaned over and kissed him on the cheek.

13

The following week was one of the biggest in Jimmy's life so far. It was his driver's test. If he passed it, his life would never be the same. Most of his focus went into practicing. He felt confident. His mum had finally started to relax in the passenger seat. She no longer inhaled and tensed every time he passed another car, and for the most part his parking and three-point turns were up to scratch. The only thing that he had to focus on now were head checks and signalling.

Jenno was almost more excited than he was.

"Just think about all the trips we could do! All we gotta do is wake up early one morning and blast it three hours up the coast and next thing you know we'll be surfing uncrowded waves," he said. "And also, think about all the girls. You're gonna be the sickest cunt in the year!"

"Chill, dude," said Jimmy, trying to stifle his own excitement. He had always felt it was bad luck to want something too much. "I still have to pass the test. Until then we can't plan too much. And besides, I don't even have my own car. I'll have to ask my mum to borrow the car every time I wanna use it."

"Yeah..." said Jenno, "but still..."

Jimmy was nervous. The local driving instructor was a man everyone called Kill Bill. The name was more interesting than the man. He was the most depressing person in the world, and over the years it had seemed like the only joy he got in life was from failing hopeful learner drivers. They called him Kill Bill because he killed any hopes of getting your driver's licence, but he also killed the mood of anywhere he walked into. His greatest pleasure in life came from the misery of others. He had cold grey eyes that sat deep within puffy, overtired sockets and thinning grey hair, which he slicked over his shiny bald head in a diabolical combover. His neck and head crooned over like an old vulture, and his gullet flapped around like a pelican's.

He'd fail people for the smallest offences. One time he failed someone because the bottom right-hand corner of their windshield was a little foggy. That was the only time his crusty little lips would resemble a faint smile. He'd puff his chest up in importance when someone would complain about his lack of tolerance, and shake his head. "Well, I'm sorry, but I absolutely cannot pass you. It would be unfair and dangerous to everyone else on the road."

He'd inhale their desperation, and exhale it as though it refreshed him and gave him life.

There are bad people in the world who are simply misunderstood, or victims of a greater evil. If you peeled back a layer or two you'd find that most people are just trying to make the best out of their situation. But Kill Bill wasn't one of those people.

There was Kill Bill, and an older woman called Joan who was a local treasure. Joan was nice, too nice, and passed anyone who smiled at her. She was probably responsible for half of the crashes in the area. There were a few people who'd crashed on the way home after she'd passed them.

In Jimmy's eyes, he had a 50-50 chance of passing, all dependent on which examiner he got.

On the morning of his exam, he woke up and stared at his ceiling. His stomach and legs felt heavy and he tried his best to exhale all of the nerves out.

His mum pep-talked him on the way there. "Just remember to check your blind spots always, and stop for at least three seconds at every stop sign. They can never fail you for being too careful."

"Yes, Mum, I know. Fuck sakes, could you just let me drive…?" said Jimmy. He was nervous, and lucky for him his mum understood. She pursed her lips and exhaled furiously, but managed to stay calm.

They pulled into the carpark of the driving centre. Jimmy turned the key and exhaled. "I'm sorry for getting mad at you before," he said to his mum. He looked at her; there was fear in his eyes.

"It's ok. Good luck," she said.

He walked in and waited in line.

It was one of those dull, grey government buildings that sucked the life out of you. The walls were a sanitary white that somehow seemed to absorb all of the light in the place. There were desks everywhere adorned with random paper forms, all of them just as pointless as the last. There were forms to do in order to do other forms, and lines that people waited in just to get into other lines. It made absolutely no sense. It was a place beyond hell, where souls went to be tortured by a pitiless and merciless bureaucracy. Jimmy filled out the form to allow him to take the test, and then he took a seat and awaited his fate.

If there is a God, Jimmy was praying to Him.

Please, God, Jimmy prayed, *please don't give me Kill Bill!*

A voice called his name. He looked over at the counter. It was Kill Bill.

Jimmy groaned to himself. *I'm fucked…*

Kill Bill eyed him almost hungrily.

"Good morning, James," he said, reading Jimmy's name off the sheet of paper he had on his clipboard. Jimmy watched his gullet swing back and forth.

"Good morning," said Jimmy, smiling as politely as he could. He still had hope that maybe Kill Bill was in a good mood.

"Are you ready to go?"

Jimmy nodded his head.

They got in the car. Jimmy exhaled nervously.

"Don't worry, there's nothing to be nervous about," said Kill Bill. He smiled in what he might have thought was a reassuring manner. It was a wretched smile and it made Jimmy feel even worse.

Jimmy started the car, and the test commenced.

He did well. Much better than he expected. He remembered all of his head checks, indicated correctly and even managed a perfect reverse parallel park. Somehow, against all odds, he passed. Jimmy almost bowed to Kill Bill when he signed off his form.

That afternoon his mum let him borrow the car, and for the first time in his life he got behind the wheel and pulled onto the road completely alone.

He looked at himself in the rearview mirror and whooped with excitement. He felt free. He pulled up to the beach carpark in the late afternoon and looked out for Jenno.

He spotted him on his way home holding his surfboard. He pulled up next to him and drove at the same pace. Jenno looked over momentarily, aware of the car, but he didn't recognise it was Jimmy at first.

Jimmy was laughing to himself as he watched Jenno, who looked as though he was getting more and more annoyed by the second. Finally, he snapped.

"What the fuck do you want, cunt!?" he yelled at the car.

Jimmy wound down the window and burst out laughing at the look of surprise on Jenno's face.

"You're joking!" he said in disbelief.

"Did you get Kill Bill?"

Jimmy nodded.

"Fuuuck! You sick cunt! Alright, let me hop in so I can get a lift home!"

Jenno reached for the handle but Jimmy locked it just in time.

"Sorry, dude, you're soaking wet and this is my mum's car..."

"Fark, you would say that, wouldn't you..." said Jenno.

"Sorry, bro." Jimmy peeled off and left Jenno in the rearview mirror, watching as he drove down the road.

Jenno shook his head and laughed to himself.

...

Getting his driving licence was one of the greatest things to ever happen to Jimmy. Every second behind the wheel alone was a second spent in pure bliss. He begged his mum to let him use the car to drive to school the next day, and after a while she gave in. He called Skye that evening and told her to be out front of her place early next morning.

The next morning he pulled up to Skye's house. She was standing out front waiting for him. She sat down in the car, leaned over and kissed him on the cheek.

"Congratulations!" she said.

Jimmy beamed. He turned up the music and pulled off onto the road. It was a feeling unlike any other, driving around with Skye by his side. Every now and then he would steal a glimpse of her. She had the window rolled down and her hair was blowing in the wind. Her left foot was resting on the dashboard. If Jenno had put his feet up on the dashboard, Jimmy would have pulled the car over and told him to get out. It was his mum's car, and she had given him strict rules to abide by, and an immediate takeback of the car if he broke them. But seeing Skye enjoying herself so much was irresistible; she could have poured coffee all over the seat and he wouldn't have said anything.

They reached the front of her school and he pulled over.

"Thanks so much for the lift!" she said. "Do you think you could pick me up this afternoon?"

"Yeah, of course!" said Jimmy.

He kissed her goodbye and watched her walk through the front gate.

School passed just as it did most days for Jimmy. He sat at the front of the class and did his best to concentrate, but his mind was elsewhere. He was picturing himself driving with Skye by his side. They were flying down the highway. The wind was in her hair again and her foot was up on the dash.

The next thing he knew the bell was ringing for the end of the school day.

He packed his bag as quickly as he could and rushed to the front gate so that he could be there in time to pick Skye up. He slipped out of the gate and speedwalked up the street towards his car, but groaned when he saw Jenno sitting on the bonnet.

"YEEEEEWWW!" screamed Jenno. "Finally, we don't have to walk home anymore!"

"Get off the bonnet, dude, this isn't my car!" Jimmy pleaded.

Jenno hopped off.

"And sorry, dude, I already promised Skye I'd give her a lift home…" said Jimmy.

"Yeah?" said Jenno. He looked over his shoulder at the inside of the car. "I count five seats in there…"

"Yeah, I know there's five seats in there… I just mean I just want some alone time with her."

"Fuck, dude, if you two had any more alone time you'd merge into one another… It'll be sweet – trust me, you won't even know I'm back here."

"Fine," said Jimmy.

He jumped into the driver's seat and Jenno jumped into the back. As they drove back past the school gates Jenno wound the window down and screamed, "WAAAOOOOOO" out towards the headteacher Mr. Pollard, who stood in front of the gate scowling at him.

Jimmy ducked. "Jenno, what the fuck!"

"What?" said Jenno, laughing.

"We're gonna be in trouble now, thanks… Mr. Pollard already hates us enough."

"It'll be sweet, dude, relax!"

They pulled up in front of Skye's school. She was standing there with two of her other friends.

Jenno perked up like an excited dog that was about to go for a walk. "Fuck yeah, dude, she's bringing friends! They're rigs too…"

He near enough pressed his face against the glass to get a better look at them.

Jimmy felt deflated at the sight. He had imagined a nice afternoon where he and Skye drove around together and listened to music and maybe kissed, but now it looked as though he may as well have been a taxi driver.

He pulled to the curb in front of the girls. Skye leaned down to the window and smiled at him. "Is it ok if you give Hannah and Siana a lift too? They live on my street."

"Yeah, no worries," said Jimmy, flatly.

The girls hopped in. Jenno wasted no time in introducing himself.

"What's doin', I'm Jenno," he said, trying his best to make his voice deeper than it was naturally.

The girls smiled at him awkwardly. They could feel his desperate presence beating down on them and both of them looked uncomfortable.

"You girls surf?" asked Jenno.

They shook their heads.

"Ah yeah, true. You should do it one time, I can take you, I surf," he said.

"Thanks…" the friend called Hannah replied.

Jimmy turned up the volume on the radio in hopes that he would drown out Jenno's embarrassing attempt at flirting.

He looked over at Skye. "How was your day?"

"Good! Nothing exciting. We got given our roles today for the play, though," she said.

"Oh really!" said Jimmy. "Who did you get?"

"Not the lead… But I have some good lines. The girls and I are going back to mine this afternoon to practice," she said.

"Ah true…" said Jimmy, cutting himself short.

Skye looked at his crestfallen expression. "What's wrong?"

"I just figured we could go to the headland this afternoon and listen to some music…" he said.

She took his free hand in hers and squeezed it. "We definitely will. I just can't today!"

"Nah, that's ok," said Jimmy. He dropped the girls off not long after. Jenno climbed into the front from the backseat head first, kicking the chairs and the windows as he struggled.

"Fuck sakes, dude, be careful, this is my mum's car!" Jimmy pleaded again.

"Sorry, dude!" said Jenno. "Fark, Skye's friends were pretty hot. You reckon you could set up a double date one time?"

"Fuck no," said Jimmy. He looked at the expression on Jenno's face. "Alright, fine, I'll see if one of her friends is keen."

Jenno's spirits lifted. They pulled over outside of his house. There was another pile of random trash on the front lawn. A few wooden pallets, a couple bricks, a half-used bag of cement mix and some old-looking bits of timber. New piles of trash were normally a sign that Jenno's dad was back home. He'd often hoard things with the hope of reselling them or making something out of them, but nine times out of 10 they'd sit there and end up getting destroyed by the elements.

"What's all that for?" asked Jimmy.

Jenno shrugged. "Dad reckons he's gonna build a new fence or something. I'll believe it when I see it."

They said goodbye and Jimmy drove home.

...

Later that afternoon, Jimmy was sitting in his room trying to do his homework when his phone buzzed. It was a text message from Skye. He opened it excitedly, but grimaced when he read the message.

Five minutes later he was in the car, driving towards her place.

"Hey!" she said, when she hopped in. "Thanks for picking me up. I'm sorry it's so late notice, I just completely forgot about it!" She was holding a bag that had her netball jersey in it. She had training twice a week, but she'd been so wrapped up in learning her lines she'd completely forgotten that training was on that afternoon.

"No worries," said Jimmy, smiling.

They drove 10 more minutes before Jimmy pulled over to let Skye out.

"Thanks so much!" she said, and kissed him on the cheek, but before she hopped out she stopped and looked contemplative for a moment.

"Do you think you could maybe give me a lift home later?" she asked.

"Yeah, of course," said Jimmy.

"You are the best," she said, smiling. She blew him a kiss goodbye and then ran off towards the courts.

Jimmy was working the closing shift at the café the next afternoon. It was a relaxing shift that mainly entailed packing up the kitchen and mopping the floors. Simmo was usually in a good enough mood by then to joke and talk.

"I got my licence a few days ago," said Jimmy.

"You're kidding! Good work, grommet," said Simmo. He was wiping down the grill and his bench.

"Yeah. It's been awesome. Only thing is, it kind of feels like what you warned me about is already happening."

Simmo looked confused for a moment, trying to remember what on earth he could have warned him about. He said a lot of things in the heat of the moment.

"Ah yeah, what's happened?"

"Nothing. It's just I feel like I spend half my life picking up my girlfriend and dropping her off," said Jimmy.

A look of recollection fluttered across Simmo's face, as he suddenly remembered the conversation they'd had not too long before. "Ah yeah, man, you gotta be careful. Women will use you till you're an empty dried-out husk of a man. Do you wanna drive her around?"

"Yeah, and no."

"Then tell her, man! Don't let her use you like that," said Simmo.

"Yeah, for sure. But how do I know if she's using me…"

Simmo stopped wiping and contemplated. "Does she use you to take her friends around as well?"

"She has one time, yeah…" said Jimmy.

Simmo raised his eyebrows. "How do you know she's not talking to a bunch of other guys right now, getting them to do her dirty work for her as well? I had this one mate who was with his girlfriend for seven years. She somehow convinced him to pay for her to go to university and not work for a year – all the while she's taking out credit cards in his name and he's signing the forms not even knowing what they're for. She's maxin' them all out buyin' dumb shit like clothes and that, all the while she's banging some guy in her class that she does group assignments with, and then, to top it off, when he finally finds out that she's been cheating on him she tells him to get fucked, takes all her belongings and he never sees her again! Coldhearted. He's never been the same since. Used to be a good-looking, confident man. Now he's a nervous fuckin' wreck. Doesn't trust anything or anyone, and can't even look at himself in the mirror."

"That's awful..." said Jimmy, his stomach sinking at the thought of Skye with someone else. He pictured her with Dizz, and he began to feel a sick pang of panic in the pit of his stomach.

"Yeah, man," said Simmo, "you just never know..."

After a short, contemplative pause, he went back to work, and the topic wasn't discussed for the remainder of Jimmy's shift.

Jimmy's mind was racing. He and Skye hadn't been together all that long, what if she was seeing other guys? They had never had the conversation about being exclusive with one another, Jimmy had just assumed it was a given. She was beautiful, the most beautiful girl he knew. There was no doubt in his mind that other guys would be going for her too. Guys like *Dizz*. A wave of helplessness washed over him, which crashed and turned to anger and resentment towards Dizz and any other guys like him, and also towards Skye, for her beauty that made him feel scared and insecure, but behind all of that and greatest of all, a resentment towards himself because in the face of it all he felt cowardly and unworthy.

There is a problem in the idealisation of the perfect man. And simply put it's because the perfect man doesn't exist. And the misunderstanding of the principles of this perfect man leads to young men thinking real men are the ones who are quick to anger and face things with aggression. They think real men are the only ones who make shit happen, who can drink the most, who love to fight, who never back down from confrontation and face it head on with both fists closed. Real men bottle it all up, they go to the gym and burn it away, they get so big in the hopes that they'll look too scary for anyone to even bother being confrontational, because deep down they are scared that they don't feel like men at all. They're scared to look inside and find what makes them truly feel like a man, what their passions are and who they really want to be, so they focus entirely on their external image. They try their best to fool everyone, but they can never fool themselves. It breeds a sort of man; a man whose whole persona is based on being a man. An insufferable kind of man who is hellbent on showing up other men just to prove how much of a man he really is. Who uses force and aggression to achieve, who seeks to dominate but never understand. And even after they have won every fight, even after they've shouted down every opponent, after they've fucked all the girls, after they've done every manly thing imaginable, they still feel like boys, and at the end of it all they cry like a little boy does. Helpless, and sweetly, and then they drink to forget it all.

Not all of these men cry. The ones who don't let other people cry for them, the people who love them and know them for who they really are. More than a man, if a man is a thing worth measuring.

There are too many little boys in the world who look like men, and Jimmy, who was above all things scared, knew that his greatest desire was to feel like a man. Once he did, his dad would respect him, he wouldn't be scared of people like Dizz and, most of all, he would feel worthy to love a girl like Skye.

"Do you know what it means to be a man, Jimmy?" his dad would always say to him. "To be a man is to have an unwavering will. A domination, a ferocity, but also a softness and compassion when need be. A man is to follow your word, and never pull back on a promise."

He'd go on these lectures that turned into monologues; they were always the same in the way that

they always seemed to circle back to the point that Jimmy
wasn't half of these things.

"A man is unbreakable, but he is wise enough to
know when he should assert himself and when he should
step back. Read more, listen more, learn more and fight
more. You're too nice, people will take advantage of you
– don't let them."

Afterwards, he'd walk to the kitchen and pour
himself a glass of wine before dinner. After dinner he'd
disappear into his room to read, holding another bottle in
his hand. Jimmy was forced to consider what being a man
was all about most days, and it left him wondering if
anyone could actually call themselves a man. He
wondered how many men looked at themselves in the
mirror and saw the man their fathers told them they
needed to be, and if any reasonable man really felt like he
was all those things.

...

The next morning, he picked Skye up from her house
before school. She kissed him on the cheek and then put
her feet up on the dashboard as she did every morning.

"Take your feet off the dash, this is my mum's
car," said Jimmy.

Skye took her feet off and looked at him with a
puzzled look on her face. "Is everything ok?"

"Yeah," he said, smiling. "What are you doing
after school today?"

"The girls and I are going back to mine this
afternoon to go over some lines again," she said.

"When's the play?" he asked.

"In two weeks," she said. He could hear a nervous
tone in her voice.

"That's awesome, I'm sure you'll do fine," he said, smiling.

"And then I think we're going out afterwards to hang out with some other friends," she said.

"Oh really, from school?" he asked.

"Not from my school, from Mount View."

Mount View was a boys' school not far away from Jenno and Jimmy's school. It was renowned for being the school where most of the bullies went. Jimmy used to hate getting on the school bus whenever those boys were on it. It was half the reason he and Jenno started walking home. He would walk on and take a seat right at the front and not look back, because the Mount View boys would sit up there and cause havoc. Around halfway through every journey, whichever bus driver had been unlucky enough to get the school pickup and drop-off roster that day would end up pulling over and shouting the whole bus down. The Mount View boys would throw food, pull kids up and beat them at the back of the bus. They would call people names, rip people's shirts and carve things into the bus windows. It was Dizz's old school.

A sudden pang jolted through Jimmy's stomach at the mention of Mount View.

"Boys?" he said.

"Yeah, boys…" she said, casually.

She looked at the expression on his face and smiled. "Relax, Jimmy. Hannah has a crush on one of them so we're just going to back her up. You've got nothing to worry about."

But Jimmy was worried.

"I was wondering," began Skye, "could you give us a lift?"

Jimmy's heart pounded in his chest. "No," he said.

"That's ok!" said Skye, reassuringly.

"Because you're not going," said Jimmy, sternly.

"Excuse me?" said Skye.

"I said you're not going," said Jimmy. "What? Am I supposed to just sit at home by myself while you're off with boys doing who knows what…"

"I can hang out with whoever I want," she said.

"Yeah, that's true," said Jimmy, "but not when I'm driving you there." He pulled over. "Get out," he said.

"What?" said Skye.

"Get out," said Jimmy, gripping the wheel.

"Fine!" said Skye. "I don't know when you became so insecure, Jimmy. All you had to say is that you couldn't give me a lift."

She hopped out of the car and slammed the door as hard as she could.

"This is my mum's car!" he yelled at her, but she couldn't hear him; she was already 10 metres away, walking as fast as she could, holding her books up to her chest.

He drove off, confused by the emotions he felt. The deepest part of him felt wrong. He knew that Skye was right. She could see anyone she wanted. But Simmo's warning was at the forefront of his vision. It made him feel like his manhood was at stake. He wondered what Simmo would say once he told him what had happened that afternoon.

…

"What, she reckons she can go hang out with other boys? You know what that means… Good on you man, fuck that chick," said Simmo after Jimmy told him what had happened. Jimmy had a closing shift that afternoon. Once the final customers left and he and Simmo were cleaning the kitchen, Jimmy told him everything that had happened that morning.

The feeling of guilt that Jimmy had been harbouring in his stomach all day somewhat eased after Simmo's reaction. Maybe he was right, maybe Skye was just using him. He still felt uncertain about it all, but after the praise he'd received from Simmo it felt worth it. He pictured Skye hanging out with guys like Dizz and the older boys that very moment, and then he felt justified, even righteous.

But what Jimmy didn't know was that Skye didn't end up going out with her friends at all. She left school early that day in tears.

"What you gotta do now is act cool. Act like you don't care at all. Trust me, man, she'll come crawling back to you. She probably thought she had you wrapped around her finger this whole time. This morning would have been jarring for her, she's probably confused now because she feels like the power's shifted. Chicks want a good-looking asshole who can sometimes be nice. Be that asshole, but be nice also. You got the power now, you get what I'm saying?" said Simmo.

"Yeah," said Jimmy. He thought of Skye laughing and flirting with the other boys. He had to be an asshole. *She wanted an asshole.*

...

Skye was in her room. She pulled the last tissue from the box and dried her face with it. She was confused, upset and embarrassed, but she was also frightened. Frightened because she was in love for the first time in her life, and what had once felt like a fairytale had all of a sudden been thrown into jeopardy and she had no idea why.

She couldn't help but put blame on herself. She thought about all of the lifts that Jimmy had given her. In her mind, she'd thought of them as just another excuse for them to hang out and be with each other, and she'd thought Jimmy enjoyed it too. But now she felt foolish. She wondered what he was up to. Her hand hovered over her phone, but then she thought better.

...

The next day, Jimmy pulled up outside of her place. She was waiting for him on the grass. She smiled when she saw him. She was nervous, unsure of how everything would pan out. They still hadn't talked since their argument.

She pulled open the door and sat down.

"Hey," she said, smiling softly.

"Hey," said Jimmy. He glanced at her and smiled quickly.

The engine started and the car hummed to life. Jimmy was quiet.

"I'm sorry, Jimmy," Skye began, although what she was sorry about she had no idea. "I didn't mean to make you drive me around everywhere. In my head, I just thought you enjoyed spending the extra time together."

Jimmy was looking forward, trying to keep composure. He wanted to apologise, he wanted to kiss her on the cheek and laugh about it, but he remembered what Simmo had told him. He had to be an asshole, it was the only way he would get her back. "It's ok," he said.

Skye looked at him almost expectantly, waiting for him to apologise as well, but it never came.

"What?" said Jimmy bluntly, noticing her gaze.

"You're not going to apologise?" she said.

"For what?" said Jimmy.

She almost gasped in shock, taken aback by a sudden fury. "For what?... For screaming at me and kicking me out of your car!" she said angrily.

"Yeah, well, you disrespected me. Was it worth it? Hanging out with those other guys? Was it fun?" said Jimmy.

A look of disgust flashed across her face.

She was about to tell him that she spent the whole day crying instead, but she stopped herself. She was in pain, and she wanted to hurt him as well.

"Yeah, it was. All those boys were gentlemen, unlike you. And... one of them asked for my number and I gave it to him."

Jimmy was cut deep; he'd fucked it all and he knew it. He was scrambling to keep composure.

He remembered Simmo's words. *Just act cool. Act like you don't care at all. Trust me, she'll come right back to you.*

"Yeah... whatever," he said.

"Pull over," said Skye, breathing through her nostrils.

Jimmy pulled over, suddenly scared, it wasn't going at all how Simmo said it would.

"You were so sweet and kind when we met, Jimmy," she said. "What's going on with you? You used to be so respectful, and caring and loving." She felt her throat catch.

Tears welled up in her eyes. Jimmy's face dropped. He had never wanted to hurt her, and now he was more confused than ever. He had no idea what to say, he just looked at her helplessly, trying to grasp the words. He wanted to say sorry, he wanted to hold her and kiss her and tell her that he was like that, that he hated confrontation and drama. That he was just trying to be a man, so that he could feel worthy to be with her, so that he wouldn't feel insecure around guys like Dizz, so that he could make her happy, because that's what he thought she wanted. But he couldn't find the words. Instead he stuttered over himself.

"I don't want to be with someone who treats me like this. I deserve more," she said.

"No…" said Jimmy quietly.

"Goodbye, Jimmy."

She got out of the car and walked away with her head down so that no one could see her crying.

Jimmy watched her walk away in disbelief. *What had he done?*

She'll come back. Just play it cool, he said to himself. But he wasn't convinced.

…

"Fuck, what happened to you?" asked Jenno on the way home from school after seeing the crestfallen expression on Jimmy's face.

Jimmy sighed, "I think Skye and I are finished."

"Faark, really, what happened?" Jenno asked.

"I dunno, dude. I fucked it."

"Ah fuck, dude, that's heavy…" said Jenno.

Jimmy nodded. "Yeah…"

"Well… you got to root her, at least."

Jimmy looked as though he were about to slap Jenno over the head.

"What was it like, anyway?" asked Jenno.

"What was what like?" asked Jimmy, confused.

"Sex!"

"Oh… yeah," started Jimmy. He felt uncomfortable talking about those kinds of things to other people. It felt like a sacred topic, and one that wasn't meant to be talked about so lightly.

But he felt put on the spot. "Good, I guess. I dunno, it didn't go on for that long…"

"Yeah, nice… Did she squirt?"

"What?"

"You know… squirt?"

"I don't know… why are you asking me this shit?"

"Cos, dude, I wanna know what to do!"

"I dunno, man, I'm sure you'll figure it out…"

"Yeah, I reckon I will, but, like, what'd you do to get it to that point?"

"I don't know! She did most of it…"

"Why are you getting all weird about it? Stop being a pussy!" said Jenno.

"What do you mean? I'm not being weird, I just don't wanna talk about it…"

"Why not? If it was me I'd be telling everyone! You should be stoked, you lost your virginity…"

"Yeah, well, it wasn't worth it," said Jimmy.

"As if, man, so what if she dumped you…"

"So what? I loved her!"

"Ah well, what can you do about it? There's plenty more chicks out there. Isn't Jess Brown having a party next week? Just get a new chick there…"

"You don't get it. You don't have feelings."

"I've got feelings…" said Jenno, taken aback and a little hurt.

"Yeah, well, you haven't had them crushed…"

There was a silence between them.

They got to Jenno's house. Jenno's dad was in the living room, drawing. The subjects of his drawings were always bittersweet things. It was strange, because at first glance you would have thought he had a complete ineptitude for empathy. He was covered in tattoos, he stank of beer and his hair was hanging on for dear life. But somewhere deep down there was a glimmer of softness in him. It was in the slight twinkle of his eye, or on the edge of his grin. It was what drew people to him, for better or worse.

He looked up at the boys when they walked in. "Aye, Jimmy! How ya been, mate?"

He stood up from his chair and clasped Jimmy on the shoulder. Jimmy could smell the beer on his breath, that rank, stale smell of beer that's not been followed with water.

Jimmy looked down at the drawing on the table. It was of a mother walking her son to school in the rain. There was a longing in the drawing.

"Yeah, I've been alright…" said Jimmy.

"Jimmy's all sad cos he got dumped by some girl," said Jenno.

"Ah no, mate! That sucks… Did you root her at least?" he said, half sympathetically and half jokingly.

Jimmy didn't reply.

"Yeah, he did!" said Jenno.

"Ah well, that's alright then…" He laughed, then saw the look on Jimmy's face and smiled. "You liked her?"

"Yeah, I loved her…" stated Jimmy matter-of-factly.

Jenno's dad laughed. "It's like looking at myself when I was your age. You loved her, aye? It happens, Jimmy. All you can do is learn from it. Come on, mate, you're gonna go through a lot more than that... Just get out there..."

"Yeah, I will," said Jimmy, and then he and Jenno went into Jenno's room.

Jenno's dad opened another beer and went back to drawing.

Jimmy slid down the wall and sat on the floor in Jenno's room. Jenno sat on a stool.

"What am I gonna do when I see her out?" said Jimmy.

"Just act like you don't care, girls hate that shit," Jenno replied.

"How would you know what girls hate?"

"What do you mean? Everyone knows what girls hate..."

"I don't..."

Jenno laughed. "What? Maybe that's why you got dumped..."

"What are they, then?" asked Jimmy, angry, but half curious.

"I dunno, I can't just say them all willy-nilly like that..." said Jenno.

"What? But you just told me everyone knows what girls hate... How could you say that then have nothing to say?"

"Because you just have to know... you know what I mean?"

"No, for fuck's sake! Just name a couple then..."

"Alright, fine... Well, they hate you not paying attention to them, I can tell you that much..." began Jenno.

"Yeah..." said Jimmy.

"And... they hate it when you smell bad too."

"You've got no clue what you're talking about! Of course they hate those things, everyone hates those things…"

"Yeah, exactly…" said Jenno defensively.

"Ah whatever, I'm sorry, I'm just upset."

"Nah, you're alright…" said Jenno. "I dunno, I just reckon acting like you don't care is better than moping around whenever you see her. No one wants to be around a fuckin' crybaby."

"Yeah, thanks. That made me feel loads better," said Jimmy.

They stayed in Jenno's room for a little while before they got bored and Jimmy went home.

He wasn't in the mood to be around people anyway. When he got home he lay on his bed awhile and listened to some music, before he fell asleep. He dreamed of Skye.

14

Jimmy and Jenno skated through the streets the next day. The surf was flat and neither of them felt like swimming.

Skating was what they did when there were no waves. In a way, it was just another extension of surfing. The boards they rode emulated surfboards, and as they rolled across the pavement they swerved back and forth, up, down and across just as they would have done on a wave. Neither of them wore shirts or shoes. Jenno had a large scrape on his back from falling off and sliding across the gravel. There were still bits of road stuck to his skin, but that was all part of the fun.

"Oh shit, dude, isn't that Fleetwood?" said Jimmy, tapping Jenno on the shoulder. Jenno looked over at Fleetwood and Adriaan walking across the street holding coffees.

Jenno smiled. "Yeah…"

He and Jimmy were sitting on the brick wall next to the chip shop down the road from the beach. They'd ordered a couple milkshakes, and Jenno got a deep-fried Mars bar. He bit into it in front of Jimmy, who made a face when Jenno got all the goo on his chin.

"That's fucked…" he said.

"Tastes pretty good but," said Jenno.

"You think that's her new boyfriend?" asked Jimmy.

"Yeah, probably. I hope so."

When Fleetwood was closer she noticed them sitting there.

"Boys! How are you?"

"Good, Miss Augustus," they replied.

The pair of them looked at Adriaan expectantly, eyeing him up and down. His clothes were clean and basic: a plain navy-blue t-shirt and jeans that were almost the same colour, and white trainers that made him look like one of those inner-city dorks that get super into craft beer in their mid-thirties. He was clean-shaven and in shape. His eyes were dark and kind, and when he spoke the wrinkles at the corner of his eyes deepened. He looked like a good-tempered, well-meaning, respectful man. The kind of guy that Jenno's dad would scoff at whenever they drove past one walking home or waiting at the bus stop.

"Look at this cunt! How many dicks you reckon he takes to walk like that?" he'd say to Jenno.

Jenno had been taught to slander any man who was like that. And he strove to never be one himself, although he had no idea why. But now that he was face to face with one of these men, he was surprised at how at ease he felt.

"This is Adriaan," said Fleetwood.

Adriaan smiled at them. "What's happening, boys?"

"Not much..." they replied in unison.

"That's good. What happened to your back, mate?" asked Adriaan, pointing at the graze that started on Jenno's shoulder and finished at his lower back.

"Fell off my board..." said Jenno.

"Damn! Looks painful, you all good?"

"Yeah, I'm sweet..."

"I used to skate back in the day. My friends and I would find motorbike helmets in the council cleanups and bomb hills with them. I remember eating it once or twice too. Alright, well, stay safe on those boards..." said Adriaan, before he and Fleetwood said goodbye and kept walking.

Jimmy and Jenno turned and watched them walk away; they were holding hands as they walked, and then Adriaan said something to her and she laughed and kissed him on the cheek.

"She looks happy…" said Jimmy.

"Yeah, that guy seems like a bit of a dork but…" Jenno replied.

"Yeah, but I reckon that's what she'd like. Not everyone has to be an alpha male."

At that moment Jenno's dad strolled out of the bottl-o with a case of beers on his shoulder. He spotted the boys on the way to his car and walked over. "Ah yeah! What are you two pooftas up to?"

"I'm aboutta go check the surf, Dad," said Jenno.

Jenno's dad grabbed Jenno's milkshake out of his hands and took a sip.

"Fuckin' hell, how do you boys drink that shit?" he joked. "You not surfin', Jimmy?"

Jimmy shook his head. "Nah, I haven't surfed in a while…"

"Come on, mate, you gotta get back out there. Don't end up like me, aye. I wish every day that I never stopped surfing. It's too late for me, my body's all fucked now."

He looked down at his beergut and patted it almost lovingly.

"Yeah, you're right," said Jimmy, polite but short.

"Yeah, mate, as usual. Anyways, boys I got a barbecue to get to and a couple of beers to sink," Jenno's dad replied.

He grabbed Jenno's milkshake again and took one last sip before he left.

"Does your dad drink a whole case a week?" asked Jimmy as they watched him walk off to his car with the beer.

"Yeah, easily. Probably drinks two, I reckon."

"Damn," said Jimmy. His dad wasn't a beer drinker. He'd have a few every now and then at parties, but that was about it. He probably drank just as much, but it was disguised by the sophistication of his wine glass and business suit.

Even in Jenno's earliest memories his dad had a beer in his hand. And from the time he could walk his dad would say stuff like, "Go grab ya dad a beer, mate!" and Jenno would race off to the fridge as quickly as he could.

When he was around 13 he started to realise that his dad's drinking wasn't a normal thing. He was older and more observant, and his mum struggled to hide it from from anymore. He'd catch them having arguments about it, and overhear his mum venting about it on the phone.

One day he overheard her in the kitchen on the phone to her friend, crying. It was school holidays and he was meant to be cleaning his room. But the sound of her shaky voice made him stop what he was doing almost instinctively and listen.

"I don't know what to do anymore," she said. "One day they'll just ring me up and say he's fallen over in a ditch somewhere and died. God. He refuses to get his liver checked, it makes me feel sick just thinking about it. I'll be surprised if it doesn't shrivel up in a few years. Nothing I say or do will change his mind. I've tried everything."

Jenno peeped through the crack of his bedroom door. His mum was standing over the kitchen sink; her hair was down and he couldn't see her face.

He looked at his dad differently that evening when he saw him drink. He wanted to say something but he didn't.

That night he had a nightmare, the first of many of the same to come.

He dreamed that he was standing over his father's body. It was lying on an autopsy table, stomach was cut open with a scalpel. The room was dark except for the light that shone on the body, and no one else was in the room besides Jenno.

Something was beating. Jenno put his hand to his dad's chest and felt for his heart, but it was dead still and icy cold. The beating was coming from somewhere else inside his body.

Jenno peered down at the hole in his dad's stomach. His intestines were sticking out. He pulled out the intestines and reached his arm into the dark and seemingly endless cavity that remained. His hand felt for the beating, until he found it. It was small, about the same size as his hand. He closed his palm and tried to pull, but it was stuck. The beating was getting louder and more rapid. Panicking, Jenno reached his other arm in and pulled with all his strength. Finally, he felt whatever it was give, and from the dark pit he pulled out his dad's liver. It was black and shrivelled, almost dried out to a crisp. Jenno stared at it in his cupped and bloodied hands. It beat softly now, growing fainter and fainter until it stopped completely. There was rasping noise. Jenno stared down at his dad's face. His eyes were now wide open and they were staring back at him.

He woke up screaming.

Over the years he had the same dream over and over again. Always the same.

There was something in his dad's eyes when he drank that Jenno began to notice as he grew older. He noticed it in other older people too. Teenagers drunk to get lost in the moment, adults drunk to get away from it.

It was the glassiness in their eyes that gave them away. If Jenno looked too closely he saw emptiness in them. And when their faces crinkled into laughter he could see their eyes unchanged, cold and emotionless in their sockets, the only betrayer in an otherwise perfect performance. It was a thin film of sorrow that shone in Jenno's dad's eyes when he drank, and one that Jenno could scarcely come to understand in the midst of his seemingly endless youth.

...

That afternoon, Jenno got changed into his board shorts and grabbed his surfboard. His dad had come home early from the barbecue and was sitting on the sofa about to crack into another six-pack.

"Where you going?" he asked Jenno as he was opening the front door.

"I'm gonna go surf," said Jenno, looking over his shoulder, wondering if he'd done something wrong.

"Ah yeah? I'll come watch ya!"

Jenno looked almost confused for a moment, but then he smiled excitedly. "Yeah, alright."

They walked down to the beach. It was a strange feeling for Jenno – he realised he hadn't walked more than 15 metres side by side with his dad in years. He only ever saw him at home, and even then that was a sometime thing. The novelty of the situation clearly felt apparent to his dad too. The first few minutes of the walk were spent in silence while they tried desperately to find a topic to discuss.

"Fuckin' beautiful day," Jenno's dad said, finally.

"Yeah, it's nice," said Jenno.

Another awkward silence.

"So, ah, you got a missus or anything?" he asked.

"Nah, not yet. There's a couple girls that I'm interested in, but I dunno if I want a girlfriend," said Jenno.

"Yeah, I know what you mean, mate, but you say that now. Next thing you know, all those girls are gonna have boyfriends before you woulda had the sense to realise you liked one of 'em, and you'll be left with nothing."

"Yeah, I guess so…" said Jenno.

"I'm not tellin' you that you need a girlfriend, all I'm sayin' is that if you like a girl, fuckin' tell her before someone else does."

"Did that ever happen to you?" Jenno asked.

"Fuckin' oath it happened to me…" He laughed.

They walked through the carpark and Dizz and the boys saw them from a distance. They laughed at Jenno's dad. He was wearing a filthy grey shirt and was carrying a six-pack in his right hand. But he didn't seem to notice, he was too busy either looking up at the clouds, or earnestly at the sea. It was almost like there was a new spring in his step, and Jenno had no idea where it had come from.

The waves were head-high and fun-looking. Jenno's dad found a spot up on the dunes and sat down with a couple of beers while Jenno ran towards the shore.

He felt giddy and excited – neither of his parents had ever seen him surf before.

He paddled out and sat on his board while he waited for a wave to come. He looked back over his shoulder and saw the figure of his dad sitting up on a sand dune on the shore in the distance. Every now and then he would look over his shoulder again, just to check that he was still there.

The first wave formed on the horizon. Jenno paddled for it eagerly, but was too earnest on the takeoff and ended up falling off of his board.

He shouted in frustration underwater. Suddenly, the excitement of having his dad watch him surf had turned to pressure, and a dark determination came over him.

When the next wave came he set himself up more patiently. He made the takeoff and bottom turned, but as he flew back up the wave, he made a jerking motion he'd never done before in the hopes of doing something big, but he slipped off his board and skipped down the wave on his back.

"FUCK!" he yelled underwater.

He paddled back out and looked over his shoulder to see if his dad was still watching. A part of him expected the spot where he was to be empty, terrified that his bad surfing had bored his dad so much that he'd left. But he was still sitting there.

Jenno turned back towards the horizon, took a deep breath and tried to calm himself.

Another wave formed on the horizon. This time he took only what it could give him. He paddled and stood up, and instead of trying a manoeuvre he glided down the wave as fast as he could. Wind rushed through his ears as he gained speed. He saw the end of the wave coming, it was starting to fold over into white wash, but instead of straightening out he launched himself from the top of the wave and grabbed his board. It felt as though he'd launched a few feet in the air above the wave. He landed back on his feet and kept riding until the wave died out completely.

He looked back to see if his dad was still watching.

Jenno caught a few more waves after that one and was happy. He rode his last one in and walked up the beach to see his dad.

"Mate, you surfed amazin'!" his dad said when he saw him. "You're a fuckin' ripper, that's for sure; no wonder you been down here every day of the fuckin' week!"

Jenno couldn't help but grin.

They walked back home together, and then his dad went out for a beer with his friends.

Jenno went to bed that night and thought about the day, and he felt a little swell in his chest when he remembered how happy his dad was about his surfing.

The next day the spring in his dad's step had already come and gone, and he seemed to be his usual self again. He'd been out drinking all night, and judging by the absence of Jenno's mother, the two had obviously had a fight during the night.

When Jenno passed his dad in the living room he was bent over the table drawing something. It was a red dragonfly over crystal blue water. The dragonfly's wings were detailed and transparent, and the colours blended into one another beautifully.

...

When Jenno walked past, his dad didn't even look up. It was only when the front door closed behind Jenno that he stopped.

He sat there for a while in silence, reliving some distant memory, and then continued drawing.

There was a row of empty beers on the table, the bottle caps strewn across in different places.

It seemed to him to be the never-ending cycle of his life. A consistent rising and falling as quickly as the beat of a heart, and after every moment of bliss and serenity, there were four more moments of bitterness and torture. It was what he'd become used to, to the point where he was frightened to be happy, because he knew the drop that came after, so he stayed low. In his mind, he suffered for his art, and for his family also. He hadn't worked in months, and the only money streams he had were the dole and the occasional shipment of weed he'd take as a middleman and drive across the border.

His depression was a state that he both hated and yearned for, and one that he ultimately couldn't live without. And, in the depths of it all, it was made worse because of the loneliness he'd felt his entire life. Alcohol had become like a trusted companion to him; it felt like the only thing that could make this loneliness tolerable.

The loneliest people are the ones surrounded by the wrong company. For his whole life, Jenno's dad had always felt like he'd never found the right people. He was an alcoholic, a lowlife, a scumbag, a ruffian, a drug-dealer and an average father, but above all of that he was an artist. And in all the glory he felt in his creations, he felt in equal parts mourning too, in the thought that none of them would ever matter to anyone but himself.

He'd always planned his life going differently than this. He'd never imagined himself being rich, or successful, but he had imagined something bigger. He had always dreamed of freedom. A romantic freedom where the only thing in front of him were long and windy roads going this way and that, and the wind on his back and the sun on his neck. He dreamed of hopping on trains and getting lost in different countries, of meeting different people and making love to different women all across the world. A life that was dirty, challenging, scary and full of unknowns, but ultimately free and with endless possibility.

He looked around at the table covered in beers, the messy kitchen and the papers flung about the place and then back to himself. He could feel the bottom of his gut resting on the tops of his thighs. It seemed as if this had all just happened all of a sudden. Like he'd suddenly snapped out of a long daydream and found himself somewhere completely different to where he was expecting.

He felt sorry for himself, and then angry. It was always the same. He both despised and loved himself to the point of agony, and the only thing that could remedy such excruciation was substance.

He put his pencil down and stood up, the wooden legs of the chair scraping back behind him. He grabbed his jacket, keys, phone and a deck of cigarettes, and walked out of the door.

...

It was almost a month before Jenno saw his dad again. He walked in from school one day to find him sitting at the table drawing as if nothing had happened. He never offered any excuses or apologies. It was something Jenno had grown up with and felt to be normal. He gave Jenno a brief hug when he walked by before he put his head back down. Jenno went into his room, got changed and then went for a surf.

When he came home, his dad was asleep at the table and his mum was making dinner in the kitchen in silence.

"Why don't you leave him, Mum?" Jenno asked his mum one day while his dad was out.

She was in the middle of making a pumpkin risotto, a meal Jenno loved to hate.

Thud, thud, thud went the knife hitting the chopping board, and then sudden silence.

She looked out the kitchen window for a moment. "Because I love him."

"But how? All you guys do is argue all the time. He never does anything around the house and he's gone most of the time."

"You don't understand who he was when I met him. He was so full of life and energy."

"Yeah. But he's not that anymore. I just want you to be happy, Mum."

"I am happy. I have you, and you are all I need."

Jenno wasn't convinced, but he didn't press any further. He went to his room and left his mum to make dinner.

The chopping noises resumed. Jenno jumped onto his bed and buried his face into his pillow.

His mum was lost in thought as she prepared dinner. She really did love his dad. But over the years it had become a sad love. A yearning kind of love as if she was waiting for someone to return. Every now and then she saw glimmers of who he was come to the surface, but they disappeared just as quickly, and beyond all hope she waited for him to come back. There was so much anger in him.

It was as though he lived behind a thick pane of glass – there, but separate somehow, and to Jenno, it had felt like he'd lived his whole life with his face pressed against the glass, trying to get in.

15

The next morning the sun was red and pink in the horizon, setting the clouds ablaze. It was like watching a flower blossom. Jenno was the first one out in the water. The waves came one after another, almost as if they were in slow motion, and broke like glass against the shore.

In the blazing red light, Jenno's silhouette paddled for a wave and stood up. His hair flew back as he raced down the wave. He could feel it all. The water beneath him and the wind rushing over his face. He looked up at the corner of the wave and saw it starting to hollow out. Almost instinctively, he crouched and tucked in. The wave barrelled over him, and for a small moment he saw glory, the vision every surfer dreams of seeing. Being inside of a barrel is a feeling unlike any other. It's as if everything is moving in slow motion and high speed all at once. All you can hear is the echoing crash from behind you, and all you can see through the tunnel of water is a small glimpse of the outside world.

It's one of the few experiences we can get in life that just is. There is no purpose to it, there's no reason to go out and do it, it just is. The modern world is full of excuses to exist, and things to keep us entertained. There are things to marvel at like mobile phones and laptops, but the essence of them brings us no meaning or joy. If a caveman were to be transported into the future, he would be confused at the state of things. Nothing would make sense to him. But if that caveman walked to a beach and saw someone getting barrelled he'd lose his mind.

For just a small moment, Jenno witnessed that glory. The pure feeling of being. For one moment only before he was flipped upside down and drilled underwater.

He came up spluttering and out of breath.

"WOOOOOOOO!" he screamed.

He hopped on his board with a grin on his face and scrambled to get back out behind the waves. He got out the back and sat on his board and just watched the sunrise for a while. The glare hurt his eyes and he had to look at the beach. The world had come back to life. Birds flew over the headland and across the water. Some of them glided just above Jenno's head, and he looked up at their undersides as they passed over. Wave after wave came, but none of them barrelled again. It was the first time he'd ever properly been inside a barrel, even just for a short moment. He would never forget it. He was disappointed that no one was there to see it, but then he remembered what Ratty's mum had told him and he smiled at the thought that Ratty was with him.

He looked over his shoulder at the beach. He could see her there, a little dot on the north side. He wondered if she could see him too. The sight of her kneeling there alone in the sand stirred a strange feeling of empathy inside of him that he had never felt before.

She made him think about his own mother, and how she would feel if he were to die. He imagined her kneeling on the beach every morning like Ratty's mum, staring out into the horizon and listening out for him.

Thick clouds were gathering in the sky, and the air drew still and quiet, a warning sign of the storm that would come.

Jenno ran home before the rain came.

He was in his room when the first droplets fell. They fell one by one, and then all together. All he could hear was the sound of rain, then thunder.

He wondered what Jimmy was doing.

…

Jimmy was in his room, thinking about Skye. He couldn't believe that it was over between them. He thought back to all the times they had had. And as he lay there, scene after scene rushed through his head. He started dreaming up scenarios where they got back together, and a little balloon of hopefulness was slowly being inflated. He hoped that maybe in a few days she would realise what a big mistake this all was and come back to him. He imagined holding her in his arms again, and all the new adventures that they'd go on.

But those were daydreams on a rainy day and deep down he knew it.

He felt like an idiot for listening to everyone, and for a while he twisted scenarios in his head where he put the blame on Simmo, on Jenno, on Dizz and the boys. But he knew that he only had himself to blame.

He put in his earphones and listened to some music. Sad songs that matched his mood and the weather. He didn't really listen to the lyrics; he mostly liked the overall energy and flow of it all. He loved piano music. It was something he never spoke to his friends about but something he listened to avidly. There was something about it that made the pieces fall into place around him.

Over the rainfall he could hear the soft sounds of piano music playing in the background. He lay back and listened, and wondered why everything happened the way it did. How some people can come together for a short time, leave one another, and then pretend like nothing happened. And how painful it was when that happened. He had to block her off of everything. He kept telling himself that it was all just a learning experience, but it was hard to feel positive.

Suddenly, his phone rang. His stomach dropped, but he sighed when he realised it was just Jenno.

"Hey dude, what's doing?" he said.

"Nothing, I just got out of the water. It's pumping – I got fully barrelled before!" said Jenno.

"No way, that's awesome."

"Yeah... but I didn't make it out. You sound sad, man?" Jenno asked.

"Nah, I'm sweet. I was just thinking about Skye, is all."

"Fuck sake, still? That was like two weeks ago…"

"Huh? There's not a time limit on heartbreak…"

"Brrtt! What!" laughed Jenno. "Listen to yourself! You gotta get back out there and shake your dick around! Trust me. You're a good-looking kid, you'd probably have loads of chicks secretly frothing over you."

Jimmy smiled." Thanks, that actually helped a bit."

Jenno hung up not long after that; the only real reason he had called Jimmy was to tell him that he'd got barrelled. Jimmy felt a little better after talking, but it wasn't long before he plummeted back into sadness.

...

Have you ever wondered what you would be like if you had never met the people around you? Jimmy thought about it while he walked. If he had never met Simmo, or listened to his father, if he had never listened to the older boys, or watched how they interacted with girls, then maybe he and Skye would still be together. He wondered what Ratty would have said about it all. He'd always had a strange depth to him for someone his age. Ratty would have given him good advice, or at least listened to him. That was all he really felt he needed – to be listened to without judgement or opinion. Most of the time we figure things out ourselves, we just need to watch our words bounce off of someone else for us to make sense of them and see what might be in plain sight. Jenno didn't listen. Or maybe he did and just didn't understand. His father didn't listen, he only talked.

Even Jimmy didn't listen to himself. He had known how he acted was wrong the whole time, but he chose to ignore it.

He walked faster, trying to distract himself from the pain he was feeling, but it was no use. Everything he looked at seemed to remind him of her.

He walked past the hillside where they used to have picnics, and by the netball courts where she would practice.

He changed course and headed towards Skye's house. He had to tell her that he loved her. Maybe that would change her mind. His heart raced as he rounded the corner onto her street, and then all of a sudden his legs felt like lead. He was looking at her bedroom window when he pulled his phone from his pocket and called her. She didn't answer. He tried again, but still nothing.

He knew that she was ignoring his calls; she was always on the phone. Defeated, he walked towards the beach with his head down.

He walked towards the carpark in hopes of catching Jenno coming out of the surf, but groaned when he saw Dizz and the older boys instead.

He put his head down and tried to slip past them, but Dizz spotted him.

"Big dog!" he called out to Jimmy. He was still in his lifeguard uniform, but he had a beer in his hand.

Jimmy didn't say anything, but his heart raced. Here was Dizz. The cause of so much of his internal grief. He remembered the promise he had made to himself after the last time he saw him. He wasn't going to let Dizz make him feel like a boy any longer. He clenched his fists.

Dizz stood in his way, even more confident and obnoxious than usual. Jimmy looked at the beer bottle, and then to the row of empty ones on the wall behind him.

"Heard your missus dumped you, big dog! Fark, you must be guttered…"

He watched Dizz's mouth move, inaudibly at first over the sound of his blood beating past his ears.

"Might hit her up," he started, " she was pretty hot. You should be stoked you made it that far."

He could feel his pulse rising and all the blood in his body rushing to his head.

"Say something, cunt…" said Dizz, laughing cruelly. "Come on, cunt!" he repeated, pushing Jimmy.

Jimmy didn't move.

"You're such a pussy!" he said." Even when I push you around you don't do shit. No wonder she dumped you…" He leaned his face closer. "Come on, Jimmy, first shot's free…"

The rest of the older boys circled them like vultures. Jimmy could feel that all the eyes were on him. Jenno spotted the commotion on his way back from the beach. He could see the circle and knew that something was up, although he had no idea that Jimmy was at the centre of it. He started to run towards the group.

Jimmy was staring at Dizz with his fists clenched. He'd been in this spot before. This was his chance to redeem himself. But he couldn't do it. The collective presence of the circle was too much for him, and he buckled under the weight of it all.

He turned around and tried to walk away, but the circle wouldn't open.

Dizz had his phone out when Jimmy turned to face him once again. His stomach sank when he realised he was being filmed.

"Do something, cunt!" said Dizz, laughing.

The boys behind Jimmy shoved him back into the centre of the circle. Some of them poured their drinks on him. All round him he could see the recording light from the phones.

A rage began to bubble up in Jimmy's stomach. It was a primal rage; he was a rat backed into a corner and he needed an escape. Without any warning, he launched himself at Dizz and swung at his jaw. His fist collided and he felt a shockwave of pain jolt up his arm from his knuckles as it gave way. Dizz's eyes rolled to the back of his head. He fell backwards and his head collided with the curb with a sickening thud.

Jimmy stood triumphantly over him for second, clutching his hand. He felt disbelief, relief and a strange swell of pride wash over him all at once.

But something was wrong. Dizz didn't get up. He lay there, lifeless. A trickle of blood ran slowly down the pavement from a deep gash in the back of his head where it had hit the edge of the curb.

For a moment, the older boys just stood there, trying to process what had just happened, before they rushed to help Dizz.

"What the fuck have you done to him!" one of them said. A few of them raced to the lifeguard club to get medical supplies.

They swarmed all about him in a panic.

"Dizz! Dizz! Wake up!" they said, trying to rouse him to consciousness.

"Fuck, fuck, fuck! You've fucking killed him!" one of them said, his voice breaking.

Jimmy stood wide-eyed, unable to comprehend what had just happened.

He heard someone on the phone to the ambulance. All of a sudden people emerged from all around, trying to figure out what was going on. They looked at the scene, and then at Jimmy in disgust.

Jenno arrived, gasping and out of breath. He looked down at Dizz and then up at Jimmy, his eyes wide in disbelief.

"What the fuck happened!" he said, looking at Jimmy.

"I don't know... I... I didn't mean to," spluttered Jimmy as chaos erupted all around him.

Two sets of sirens grew nearer and nearer. The ambulance, and the police.

Jimmy watch as the paramedics rolled Dizz onto a board and lifted him into the back of the van. They closed the doors and then rushed away, sirens blaring, until the sound disappeared completely.

The two police officers who had arrived pulled Jimmy around to the front of their car for questioning. He tried to tell them everything, but the words weren't coming out. They put him in handcuffs and sat him down in the back seat to take him back to the station.

Jenno watched in disbelief. Jimmy was in the back of the car staring forward at the front headrest, a vacant and distant look on his face.

The car turned and drove away, and all was quiet again. If you had arrived at the scene that moment you would have had no idea what had taken place just minutes before. Save for a little patch of blood that had soaked into the pavement and dried.

...

They brought Jimmy to the station and left him alone in the questioning room. He sat in silent disbelief, staring off between spaces. He didn't know how to feel, but he was praying that Dizz survived. He shivered when he thought of Dizz's lifeless body being lifted into the ambulance, and the pool of dark blood left behind, dripping slowly and thickly down the storm drain.

The room was white and sterile. There was nothing on the walls and no windows, just the door, which was thick and oak-coloured, with a slender plastic window in it. He had no idea what would happen next. The officers hadn't said much to him, but he felt as though his life was about to change.

As he sat in silence, he pictured how everything would play out from that point. He saw the two officers coming back with handcuffs and informing him that Dizz was dead. He pictured them taking him to jail and throwing him into a cold, dark, concrete cell all alone. Worst of all, he imagined talking to his mum through a phone behind glass, like they did in the movies. His stomach sank at the thought of her crying with her hand pressed up against the cold pane, phone in her other hand, hoping that even just a little warmth would seep through so that they could feel each other physically. He shivered, realising that all his visions could be a reality. No more hugs and kisses, no more school, surfing, hanging out with Jenno, and no more Skye. He wondered what they were all thinking of him right now. Were they disgusted?

He thought about Dizz, too. As much as he hated him, he never wished death on him. It was surreal, that just a split-second decision could change his life forever. He felt sick thinking about it.

It was an hour before the police officers returned. A man and a woman. Both of them held takeaway coffee cups in their hands. Jimmy's mouth dried up and his legs went heavy at the sight of them.

They sat down in front of him, and put their cups on the table.

"Hello, Jimmy. My name's Angela and this is my partner, Chris," said the woman. There was something in her demeanour that made Jimmy relax a little bit.

"Alright," breathed Officer Chris, "so what happened, exactly?" Jimmy noticed that he had deep bags under his eyes. Chris pulled out a recorder and placed it on the table, and then motioned for Jimmy to speak.

Jimmy didn't know where to start.

"I'm not sure," is all he managed.

"Just go from the beginning. What were you doing, and how did it all happen?" said Chris, with a hint of impatience.

"I was just walking, and then they all came over—"

"Who's they?" Chris interjected.

"Dizz, and all his friends," said Jimmy.

Jimmy watched as Angela began scribbling notes into a little book. Jimmy felt panic begin to set in.

Angela noticed his sudden change, and smiled warmly." You're not in trouble, Jimmy. We just have to know the full story. You've got nothing to worry about."

Jimmy exhaled, trembling a little.

"It all happened so fast. One second, I was walking and the next I was surrounded, and then I panicked…"

"And then?" asked Chris.

"It's all a blur," said Jimmy." I hit Dizz. But I didn't mean to hurt him."

"So Dizz approached you, and then you hit him?" asked Chris.

"It wasn't like that," said Jimmy, taken aback.

"Then what happened? Did Dizz hit you?" asked Chris. Jimmy looked at him uncertainly. It didn't sound as though he wasn't in trouble; it sounded to Jimmy like they hadn't decided yet.

"No…" said Jimmy, a moment later.

"So you hit him first?" asked Chris

"Yes, but…"

"So Dizz approached you, and then you attacked him?"

"No, no!" said Jimmy, "This is all wrong."

Angela was jotting almost furiously into her notebook.

Jimmy leaned forward, in dismay.

"They poured their drinks on me and started filming me, and Dizz kept saying that the first shot was free, and then… I panicked."

Chris looked up at him silently, before leaning back in his seat, satisfied. He took the recorder from the table and pressed the stop button.

"That's all we need, for now. Should we need you for any more questioning, we'll give you a call." He stood, and motioned for Jimmy to do the same.

"I can go?" asked Jimmy.

Chris nodded." Your mum is waiting for you at reception."

"But what about Dizz?" asked Jimmy, in disbelief.

"He's alive, and in a stable condition. We've watched the videos, Jimmy, we know you were only acting in self-defence," said Angela.

"He's lucky," said Chris, "and so are you."

A wave of relief washed over Jimmy. He stood, and felt his legs shake under the weight of his body. Dizz was alive. Jimmy could have cried with joy.

Angela led him out of the room and to reception, where his mother was waiting for him. A new fear came over him at the sight of his mother, uncertain of what she would think of him, and, even worse, what his father would think.

She drove him home without saying anything. He looked down at his feet, ashamed, proud, sad, embarrassed and disgusted with himself all at once.

When they got home, Jimmy climbed up to his room and shut the door carefully. He lay on his bed and looked up at the ceiling.

A little while afterwards he heard a knock on the door. It was his mum. She smiled at him softly. "It's dinnertime."

He struggled out of bed, feeling heavy.

It was quiet at the dinner table, and there was tension between the three of them.

His mum was focusing on her plate, but every now and then she would glance over at him. His father stared right at him the entire time.

Jimmy finished his food and took his plate to the sink, washed it up and placed it on the drying rack.

"He lived, by the way," he said, before going back to his room.

He didn't go to school the next day. He was going to blame it on a bellyache, but was surprised when his mum didn't come to his room to pester him to get ready. When he eventually came downstairs, the whole house was empty. It felt like the entire world was avoiding him. He felt ugly and brutish. He looked at the knuckles on his right hand, they had scabbed over already, but split a little bit when he clenched them.

He wondered how Dizz was doing. He wished the whole situation had never happened, and that he could take it all back, but he couldn't. He had a shift on down at the café that afternoon. For the first time in his life he actually looked forward to it, in the hopes that it would take his mind off of things for a little while.

But when he got there, it felt as though everyone was avoiding him. Henry the barista, who'd normally ask him how school was, looked down at the milk twirling and frothing in his hands. Abbey, the girl on the till who was only a year or two older than him, and who usually flirted with him, looked away when he walked by.

The only person who wanted to talk to him was Simmo, but Jimmy had no desire to listen to him.

Simmo could feel it too. He watched Jimmy wash the dishes unenthusiastically, shoulders slumped and head stooped low.

"I heard what happened, grommet," he said once the final service rush of the day had finished.

Jimmy raised his head a little bit." Yeah?"

"Saw the video, too…"

Jimmy's head drooped back down. He'd forgotten all about the video. No doubt it had done the rounds already. Jenno sent it to him the morning after it happened, and he winced every time he watched Dizz fall backwards and smack his head on the curb. Dizz's friends had even filmed the aftermath. Jimmy watched himself standing there in wide-eyed shock as the older boys raced this way and that in panic. He'd watched the ambulance come and Dizz being hoisted into it, and then he'd seen the patch of dark blood on the pavement where Dizz's head had been.

"Look, man," said Simmo, "it's a heavy situation, and I know you didn't mean to do what you did, but fuck, what could you do? You protected yourself. You gotta be proud of yourself for that."

"I dunno if proud's the word," said Jimmy.

"You're a good kid, Jimmy. But sometimes the world is ugly, and you get forced to do ugly things for the greater good. That could have easily been your head smacking the concrete like that. He woulda done it too – I know that kid Dizz, he's a fuckin 'ballbag. All I'm saying is, don't beat yourself up for defending yourself. You got put in an ugly situation, and got yourself out accordingly. You handled it like a man."

"Yeah, well, if handling something like a man is through violence, I don't know if I wanna be one," said Jimmy.

"It's not about violence, it's not about sex, either. It's about being able to back yourself, and being able to defend yourself and the people you love. A good man doesn't act with violence, he ends it. But sometimes he just has to end it with violence. That's the way of the world, unfortunately. And sex… Meaningless sex is just a bit of fun, grommet. Nothing else."

"Do you feel like a man?" asked Jimmy. It was a question Simmo hadn't expected, and one that he had been asking himself for years.

Simmo thought about it for a while. "I don't think I do, if I'm being honest. I've been doing the same shit since I was young, so I guess not…"

"But why?" asked Jimmy.

"I don't know. I used to think it was because I had no responsibilities. I reckoned I'd feel like a man when I got into a relationship, or if I had a kid. But I know plenty of blokes who have wives and kids and they all feel the same as me. Then I thought maybe it was because I didn't have any money. I dressed like a bum, I wasn't in shape, didn't have nice things. So, I went to the gym and got on the 'roids. I reckoned if people respected and feared me, I'd feel like a man. So, I got fuckin 'jacked. I worked my ass off, made investments, started wearing expensive shit I didn't even like just to try and impress chicks, but eventually that just made me hate myself. I didn't feel like a man at all, I felt like a fuckwit. Like an imposter. I dunno, it just wasn't me. I was bigger than every guy, I dressed better than them all, and I still felt the same. Then I felt as confused as ever, and I dunno… I'm still figuring it out myself, to be honest. But I reckon you'll be a good man, grommet. You've got something about you that you don't see often in kids your age. Don't ask me what it is either, fuck knows… I can just feel it."

Jimmy looked down at his shoes. "Thanks, Simmo."

"Yeah, yeah. Now get back to fuckin 'work!" Simmo winked.

Jimmy walked home slowly after his shift. The sun was setting and the wind had died down in the early afternoon. The air was still and soft, and it felt comforting to be in the stillness and the comparative quiet. He took the long way home, through the park where he, Jenno and Ratty used to ride their skateboards when they were kids.

He walked over the little wooden bridge that arced over the stream and stood by the railing for a while. He watched a family of ducks waddle across the grass in formation, the mother duck leading the march to the water. One by one they waddled in and then floated beneath the bridge and out of view. There were frogs around the lagoon, and fish as well. There was a rumour that there were eels in there also, but Jimmy had never seen any.

It was a beautiful little stream, but the water was brown and dirty from the industrial estate further up course. He felt bad for the family of ducks who lived and fed in the water, and for the fish who swam there on rainy days when all the spilled oil, petrol, rubbish and debris were picked up by the gutters and somehow found themselves floating down the stream towards the ocean. He wondered what it would have looked like before people lived around it. The European settlers at least, who transformed it and took its light away.

The stream finished and became a lagoon at the edge of the beach he and Jenno lived at. On stormy days, when the water was high, the lagoon would break and the water would rush violently into the sea, parting the sand walls further and further apart with its flow until it became just a trickle again. For days afterwards, the sea water would be filthy. Jimmy had paddled past used condoms, Band-Aids, empty chip packets and dead, floating fish.

…

His father finally spoke at the dinner table that evening. Jimmy was just about to put a fork full of roast chicken in his mouth when it fell short.

"It was good what you did," he said. "It showed guts. I didn't think that you had that in you. I'm proud."

Jimmy looked at him, almost in disbelief. His dad had never been proud of him for anything.

"But I attacked him," said Jimmy.

"No, you defended yourself, and you were provoked. And that's right. It's unfortunate what happened to that boy, he's lucky to be alive. But you did what you had to do, and I'm proud of you for that. I bet when that boy recovers, he'll think twice about harassing you."

"I don't know," said Jimmy. He couldn't seem to erase the mental image of Dizz lying unresponsive.

His mum was quiet, although she smiled at him warmly and reassuringly from time to time.

"You did what every man should do. Defend yourself."

Did I? Jimmy wondered to himself later that evening. He thought about the rage he'd felt, about the evening not long before where he looked at himself in the mirror and promised himself that the next time he saw Dizz he would hit him. He had wanted that to happen, and that's why he was disgusted with himself, because deep down, although he would never admit it, he *was* proud.

For the first time in his life he had felt respected.

When he went to school the next day, most people avoided him, with the exception of Jenno. Jimmy didn't mind, though; if anything, it allowed him to focus in class better than he had done in a long time.

After school, he and Jenno walked to the car. Jenno was texting while he walked, but still talking to Jimmy just the same. He was good at social multitasking, but lacked the skill in almost all other aspects of his life.

"I heard Dizz is doing good now. They reckon he'll be out of the hospital in a day or two. Just got a bad concussion. They had to do a bunch of tests on him and scans, but they reckon everything is alright."

Jimmy let out a sigh of relief. He knew that Dizz had survived, but he was still unsure by what means.

"Thank god," he said.

"That was crazy, dude, I've never seen you get that angry! Everyone's been talking about it. You got a bit of a reputation for yourself now," said Jenno.

"Yeah... great," said Jimmy unenthusiastically.

"You reckon he's gonna try and get revenge?" said Jenno.

Jimmy's stomach sank. He hadn't thought about that. The realisation dawned on him that one day he was bound to bump into Dizz again.

"I hope not. I'm not cut out for fighting. I wish this whole thing had never happened."

"Yeah, hopefully. I won't let it happen again, anyways. I talked to all the boys and none of them are angry," said Jenno.

"Yeah?"

"Yeah. Was a clean hit... what can you do? You didn't mean for him to hit his head on the pavement."

"Yeah... I guess so," said Jimmy.

He dropped Jenno home and drove towards the beach.

The news that Dizz would make a full recovery calmed some of the uneasiness that he had felt over the last few days.

But there was one thing that Jimmy couldn't seem to get out of his mind. He wondered if Skye knew, and what she thought about it all.

His question was answered later that afternoon when he left the café after his shift to find her waiting for him just outside of the door. She was next to a telephone pole with her arms folded, but smiled at him softly when she saw him.

"Have you come to take a look at me?" said Jimmy.

"No… I came to see how you are," she replied.

They walked to the headland together and sat down on the patch of grass they always went to.

Jimmy was watching a butterfly flying soft rings around some flowers in front of them. The clouds were soft and golden, and stood painted like mountains on the horizon.

"How did you find out?" asked Jimmy.

"I saw the video, like everyone else," said Skye.

"I'm sorry," said Jimmy.

"What for?" said Skye, looking at him.

"For everything. I never wanted any of this to happen."

"It's ok," she said. "I think I understand a little better now. What could you have done? You're not a monster, Jimmy. And I'm sorry if I made you feel like one."

"Thanks," said Jimmy.

The butterfly was joined by others. They wafted together around the flowers, stopping from time to time to rest on their petals and drink from their pads.

"I love you," said Jimmy, suddenly.

He felt the weight lift off of his shoulders as the words left him.

Surprise flickered across her face. "What?" she said, as if she hadn't heard him.

"I love you," he said again.

She seemed taken aback by the suddenness of it all; she looked at the desperate look on his face and was moved to pity. "I love you too..." she began.

They were the greatest four words Jimmy had ever heard, but they were betrayed by her expression.

"But I don't know. After everything happened between us it made me realise that I don't think I'm ready for something like this. You're amazing, Jimmy. But I just think we should be friends," she finished.

Jimmy's words were caught in his throat; he choked on them for a moment before he gave up and nodded.

"I just came to see if you were ok," she said.

"Yeah, I'm sweet. Don't worry about me," he said.

"I can see that now," she said, smiling. "You've grown a lot, Jimmy. When we first met, you seemed so hesitant about everything. But something's changed for the better in you."

"Thanks. I appreciate it," said Jimmy, feeling a small swell of pride rise within him. He had changed – for better or for worse, he wasn't sure – but he felt as though his life was kicking into motion, and that was all that mattered to him now.

"Well, I guess I'll see you around," she said.

"Yeah, I'll see you around, for sure," said Jimmy.

Skye leaned over and kissed him on the cheek, before she turned and walked away, leaving Jimmy sitting down and trying to make sense of it all.

It felt right to him in the end, and even though he was sad that they wouldn't be together, he was excited for the future and for everything that was to come.

16

The party phase of their lives had finally come, and it seemed like after Letty's, Jimmy and Jenno found themselves invited to more and more. Every weekend there was another birthday, or a gathering, or just a piss-up in the bushes. Jenno prided himself in the amount of beers he could drink, and Jimmy often found himself feeling a sense of isolated observation. He couldn't drink as much as Jenno, and a part of him didn't want to. He had too much on his mind, and alcohol seemed to make him dwell on his thoughts and let them fester.

They were drinking in the overgrowth one night around a fire when some cops showed up and moved them along. Jenno was on the verge of spewing, but had so far managed to keep it at bay.

"Dude, I've had like 10 beers!" he said to Jimmy as he leaned on his shoulder.

"I know… you've told me 10 times. Once after every beer," said Jimmy, moving his shoulder so Jenno would stumble off of him.

"Yeaaaah, whatever, cunt!" said Jenno. "What's doin' now, then?"

"I dunno, I think I might just go home," said Jimmy.

"Go home? What are you, pussy?"

"What else are we gonna do?" said Jimmy. "Everywhere is closed! It's a ghost town around here."

Jenno stopped and squinted, as if taking in the surroundings for the first time.

There was nothing but a bunch of parked cars and some streetlights.

"Yeah, faaark," he said. "I guess you're right."

"Yeah... I got work tomorrow morning anyways," Jimmy said.

They said goodbye and parted ways at the fork in the road that led back to both of their houses.

...

When Jenno got home he stumbled through the door. His dad was sitting on the couch, drinking a beer in silence.

"Where've you been?" he said, quietly.

"I was just skating with Jimmy," Jenno replied, defensively.

"Skatin' with Jimm— Fuck off! Skatin' with Jimmy... You've been out late drinking."

"Yeah, then, so what?"

"So what? You reckon you're so grown now you can do whatever the fuck you want?"

"When did you fuckin' care?"

Jenno's dad shot up from his chair and towered over his son in a rage. He was drunk; Jenno could see it in the wateriness of his eyes and the muffled sound his voice got around the edges.

"Huh? Since when did I fuckin' care? Who the fuck you reckon puts the clothes on your back, sends you to school and makes sure you're fed? Since when did I fuckin'— Fuck you, you ungrateful little shit!"

He pushed Jenno into the wall.

Jenno's mum burst out of the bedroom. "What are you yelling about?" She looked at Jenno, and then to his dad.

"Ah fuck off, both of you! I'm gettin' some fresh air…" he said, and left without looking back through the front door.

Jenno walked past his mum and slammed the door to his room.

She opened the door behind him. "Are you ok?" she asked him.

"Yeah, I'm sweet, Mum…"

She walked across the bedroom and hugged him. He resisted at first but then he gave in.

"I hate him."

"Don't say that. He's your dad."

"Yeah, but I hate him. You see how he treats me? And you, Mum…"

"I know he's hard on you. But he's been through a lot. He cares so much about you…"

"He doesn't care about me… He told me the other day that he never wanted me and that I took everything from him. I remember when I was a kid I wanted to be like him. But fuck that, why would I wanna be like him? Just look at him."

Tears formed in her eyes, and before she could stop herself they rolled down her cheek, but Jenno's face was as hard as stone.

"He doesn't care," he said again.

"He does care…" she whispered into his ear as she hugged him. "Do you know how much he loves you?" she pleaded with him. "It would destroy him if he knew what you thought about him."

And then Jenno knew how to break him.

When his dad finally came home, Jenno was waiting for him in the living room. He came back in a worse mood than he'd been in before, but before he had the chance to say anything Jenno told him what he'd said to his mum. Jenno expected anger. He wanted anger, but the words crushed his dad like a ton of bricks.

"I never want to be like you…" he said. The words shot like poison from his tongue.

It was his greatest regret in life, but also an awakening to the power he possessed.

He watched his dad cry, helplessly and almost sweetly, just as his mum said he would. He stood over his dad, who was crumpled in a heap atop the kitchen table, like a father stands over his young boy, crying over something he didn't understand.

Jenno couldn't stand the sight any longer. Grief washed through his upper body and sat in his stomach, swishing about uneasily. He looked at his dad, and then to his mum, who'd just walked into the living room with a tea in her hand, and felt responsible. He walked out of the living room and into the darkness. He ran silently to the beach.

When he reached the sand he sat on his knees, just like Ratty's mum did. Deep down he felt like a burden, like a curse that had fallen on two unlucky people. His parents were people, just like him. But on the surface, he felt nothing. A giant wall had been built, so big that even he couldn't see over it. The full moon cast a pathway of white light across the ocean so strong that Jenno could follow it all the way into the horizon.

Drenched in light, he peered over the endless expanse of darkness before him, before his eyes were drawn to a small, flickering light at the base of the headland. He wondered what Tahiti was doing.

He passed streets full of houses, all of them lit up brightly from the inside like little flames, symbols of the happy families within. He could see through one of the windows from where he stood on the street. There was a family sitting around the kitchen table laughing about something. He wondered what they were talking about. The TV was on behind them, showing a gameshow that no one was watching, He guessed it just made for good background noise.

The lights were off when he got home. His mum was in bed and his dad's car was gone. When he made it to bed he streamed a gameshow on his phone, and fell asleep listening to the voices in the background.

In the morning, he got up for school to find his dad in the kitchen. He looked tired, as if he'd been up all night. There was silence between them, and then suddenly his dad grabbed him.

Jenno struggled, bracing himself for a throttling, but to his surprise his dad pressed him tightly to himself, and embraced him. Jenno hugged him back. His dad always had the same smell. It hung about on all his jumpers and shirts, even long after they'd been worn and washed. It was his smell, unique to him, and one that Jenno would never forget for as long as he lived.

Nothing was said, then Jenno turned and left for school; his dad sat on his chair in the kitchen and started to draw. The drawing was of a flower wilting, something he'd never drawn before. Jenno saw it when he came home from school. His dad was asleep in the chair with his arms folded over his chest. The drawing lay completed in front of him with different pencils still sprawled across the paper.

Jenno stood over him. He had his face, everyone always told him that. He looked at his dad's arms; they were covered in faded tattoos and a thick coat of hair all the way to his knuckles. He had little scars on his hands, scars on his neck and cheek too, remnants of a time before Jenno, when he had lived a life of his own, much different and wilder, when all the glory of youth was still in his eyes. He grew up fighting and surfing. When he wasn't doing those, he was riding his motorbike or playing guitar. Pictures from his youth were scattered across the house. He looked different back then, happier, more carefree.

…

Jenno's dad awoke not long after his son left, and stared blankly down at the drawing, lost in thought.

Growing up, his biggest dream was to leave and never come back. He had wanted to travel the world and be an artist. There was always something in him, something that he could pull from the ether from time to time. When he was a little boy he would always sing to himself. Sweet little tunes and melodies that he never shared with anyone. He started drawing in secret when he was a teenager. At first, he drew soldiers. Both modern ones and medieval. He was always interested in war. But as he got older his drawings began to change. He started shifting towards faces. It was almost an obsession. He would stay up late every night, drawing in a little exercise book that he was meant to use for school. He was around 17 by then. He drew hundreds of faces. Men, women, children. All of them wore different expressions, and he always managed to place something in their eyes. It would have given someone a strange sense of longing if they had stared into them, like looking at a loved one who had passed away.

When he finished school, he applied to go to an art school in the city. He went to the campus one day to hand his portfolio in. He walked through the corridors and peered into a few of the classes. They were full of people painting, drawing, sculpting and filming. It was an uncomfortable experience for him. He'd never been around so many people making art. It both dignified him and hurt his ego. They didn't look like him, or walk like him or talk like him. He was from a world built by brick and mortar, where self-worth was valued by the amount of work done in a day and the number of beers drunk in the evening. To him, these people seemed like so much more than that. The clothes they wore, their hairstyles and the way they carried themselves were alien to him. He hated them, but he hated himself more.

He left the art school with a feeling of disgust. He hated people who thought they were better than everyone else. Who acted like they were gifted and different. It made him angry, because deep down that was what he thought about himself.

But as the days went by, he couldn't take his mind off of the school. He kept thinking about the studios, the silence and the idea of himself having both of those.

His father was a carpenter and a proud working-class man. When he told his dad he'd applied to go to art school his father turned to him seriously.

"Art school? What, like paintin'? I know a million blokes who tried to do the same thing. Where ya reckon they are? How are ya gonna earn coin? What, you gonna be one of those blokes that sits around all day doin' fuck all cos he reckons he's too good to work? Not my son, nah… Not Reggie's son." He went back to watching his team on the TV.

The next day he came home with a proud look on his face.

"What you smilin' about, Dad?" asked Jenno's dad.

"Got you an apprenticeship! You start on Monday," said Reggie.

"Huh?"

"Yep. A plumbing apprenticeship with an old mate who lives down the road; fuck, I forget his name… Nice bloke, though. His missus is the one who used to volunteer at your school. They had a boy who was around your age, but he died when he was only young."

"What do you mean plumbing apprenticeship? I told you yesterday I'm goin' to art school."

"Alright, how 'bout this…?" Reggie started. "You do the four-year apprenticeship, get your licence and then you can do whatever the fuck you want. How you reckon you're gonna pay for this art school? No way I can afford to pay for the fuckin' thing even if I wanted to. You do this plumbing apprenticeship, then you're your own man."

Jenno's dad nodded. He knew Reggie couldn't pay for it. He never would have expected him to be able to, but he had also never put any thought into paying it himself either.

The following Monday he started his apprenticeship. In his heart, he felt the thud of the first nail in the coffin of his dreams.

At first, he hated the job. He felt useless, and didn't take well to the life of a full-time worker. But he grew to like it, and even to be proud of it. He liked that he was a working-class bloke. It felt good to work with his hands – he even started to think of it like its own form of art. Repetitive motion that slowly breaks down and builds things. The swing of an arm, the push and pulling, observing and solving felt almost poetic to him after a while. The camaraderie and the banter, the sorrows and the regrets that all came to someone in that kind of work.

He'd never felt like he belonged to anything in his life. It gave him an identity and he wore it proudly. He got tattoos and made it a point to never wear nice clothes.

But his art books began to gather dust.

Every afternoon after work he and his boss would roll down to the pub for some beers. They'd end up drinking eight of them and then stumble home afterwards.

On the fourth and last year of his apprenticeship he met his girlfriend, who became Jenno's mum. They were never meant to be together long. They liked each other well enough to sleep with one another and go on a date every now and then, but neither of them were in love. A month before he finished his apprenticeship he got her pregnant.

He heard the next nail thump into the coffin, and it seemed now that his dreams of going to art school were impossible. He signed on as a full-time tradesman and kept working.

He was terrified when Jenno was born. He wasn't ready to have a child. He looked at Jenno's puffy little face. It was the most beautiful thing he'd ever seen. It brought life to an inner instinct that he'd never felt before. When he held Jenno in his hands for the first time he marvelled at how small he was. His little nose and tiny mouth sat perfectly still on his angelic little face. The weight of it all came crashing down on his shoulders. He was a father, even though deep down he felt as though he was still just a boy who hadn't nearly finished growing up.

He worked harder than ever, and drank much more to compensate. And after a few years the toll of that life began to show.

Eight years had passed. Eight years of early mornings and late nights, beers, meat pies, chocolate milk, not seeing sunlight, breathing in dust and grime all day, every day, and covering himself in toxic glue and plastics.

It was as if it had happened all of a sudden. As if he'd somehow changed in a day. He looked at himself in the mirror and realised that he was not the same person anymore.

His face was rounder and rougher, his hair was lighter and thinner, his belly rolled over his belt and his shoulders had rounded. His eyes looked sunken and tired, they had deep bags beneath them, and his facial hair was patchy and unkempt.

It seemed almost laughable to him. The irony. That he had become his father. And despite it all, he still felt like a boy. He wondered if his father felt like a boy too. A world of children raising children.

And suddenly all those years of work felt meaningless to him, because he felt as though he'd taken the wrong turn and never followed his dream. He hadn't drawn anything or painted anything in years. The thought of going to the art school made him laugh. If he didn't feel like he fit in before, he definitely wouldn't fit in now.

He was trapped. He realised all at once that he would never be young again. A currency that had always been so firmly in his grasp was now gone, and he felt as though he was buried in obligation and responsibility. He dreamed of the wide-open world and of adventure. Of watching the sun rise and fall every day, in drawing and painting and falling in love and breaking hearts. He dreamed of everything. But he was stuck. He took every job away from home that he could, and when he was home he grew more distant by the day.

Jenno was just a small boy, and although his dad loved him with all his heart, deep down he blamed him for it all.

Jenno always knew his dad was a drinker, and one of the main memories he had of growing up was of his dad wincing in pain while he talked about what he had planned for his life if he'd never had Jenno.

Jenno took the silent blame and wore it on his shoulders, unaware of the weight that it carried.

17

It was a night just like any other. The boys were sitting on the headland amongst the old weatherworn couches people used to smoke on. The bushes all around them were filled with used plastic bottle bongs, nitrous oxide canisters and deflated balloons.

Jenno'd managed to get his hands on some cigarettes from his dad's jumper when he wasn't home. It was amusing afterwards to watch his dad searching for them frantically.

"They were in my fuckin' pocket… now they're fuckin' gone! Forty bucks out the fuckin' window…" he said, his shoulders slumping disappointedly.

"You haven't seen 'em, have you, Jenno?" he asked. His eyes were watery; if you'd have just walked in on the situation you would have mistaken him for someone looking for a lost child.

Jenno had shaken his head, careful not to let his dad see the bulge in his front pocket where the deck of cigarettes was.

"You want one?" he offered to Jimmy.

Jimmy looked down at the brown and white sticks. They looked harmless enough; aside from the picture of the rotting lung on the front of the packaging, you never would have known they'd be bad for you.

"Alright, why not? They're pretty gross, though. My next-door neighbour smokes. It sticks to all his clothes and his sheets and stuff. I hate it when Mum gets me to go over there and help him. His place reeks of piss and cigarettes."

"Yeah, but that's cus he's been sucking them back for 40-odd years. One cigarette's not gonna do anything."

Jimmy slid one from out of the packet and placed it in his lips.

"Did you bring a lighter?" he asked Jenno.

"Faarrkk…"

"Fuck sakes…" said Jimmy.

They searched the ground around the couches and laughed in relief when Jenno picked one up from the floor.

He sparked it and it worked.

"Alright, let me light yours…" said Jenno.

Jimmy leaned over and let Jenno light his cigarette. He inhaled it but instantly coughed. It tasted awful, but what was worse was the head spin.

Jenno did the same thing, but he seemed to enjoy the head rush.

"This is fucking rank!" said Jimmy.

"I don't mind it," said Jenno. "No wonder my dad loves these things." He looked at his cigarette with a newfound admiration.

Jimmy smelled the fingers that had been holding his cigarette. "Fuck sakes, even my fingers smell. Great… I bet you my mum's gonna know something's up as soon as I get home. Better her than Dad, though."

"Yeah… My dad would kill me if he found out I stole his darts," Jenno agreed.

"My dad would kill me for smoking them. I dunno, seems like he's just angry at me these days."

"What for? You don't even do any bad shit…" said Jenno.

"Yeah, but I don't do anything good either, I guess. I dunno. I've just been confused about it all lately.

He keeps telling me I gotta become a man. But I've got no idea what he's talking about. What man?"

Jimmy put his face in his hands, while Jenno lit another cigarette. He inhaled deeply and blew the smoke out in a thick cloud. He was a natural. Jimmy was in his own world.

"What're you boys doing out here so late?" said a voice suddenly from behind the bushes.

Jimmy and Jenno jumped and tried to hide their cigarettes.

It was Tahiti. He'd been on his way back to his cave with a longneck beer and a blanket when he heard the boys.

"Tahiti!" said Jenno. "We're just chilling, not doing anything."

Tahiti eyed them suspiciously. "Alright. I just never know. Been some kids coming round lately and fuckin' the place up... What's wrong with him?" He nodded at Jimmy, whose face was red and puffy.

"Nothing, just some family stuff. His dad's been riding him real hard lately."

"That's good," said Tahiti. He sat down on a rock next to the boys. He looked out into the horizon for a second. "I wish my dad was harder on me."

Jenno snorted, but the look on Tahiti's face told them that he was being serious.

"Look, mate, I don't know your situation, but whatever your dad's doing, he's doing because he loves you."

"Yeah... I guess so. Doesn't really feel like it..." said Jimmy.

"Yeah, his dad's a shit-cunt to him..." said Jenno.

Tahiti bared his brown and cracked teeth and laughed. "You boys have got no idea!"

"Yeah?" said Jimmy. "Do you have a kid?"

"Yeah, I got one…" Tahiti replied, "so, take it from me. No one really knows how to be a good dad. You know what I mean? When I had my little girl, I couldn't believe it. It was the most surreal feeling in the world. I never knew I could love something so much. I tried to be the best man possible for her. She made me want to try. But I'm just a man. Do you understand? Your dad's just a man too. A better one than me, I'd guess. But a man still."

"Yeah, he acts like he's perfect, though, and he expects me to be too," said Jimmy.

"Fuck him – he's not perfect. Nobody is. And if they reckon they are, then you'd know right away that they're a delusional cunt. You'll understand that when you're older. He's struggling just as much as the rest of us. All I'm sayin' is, you gotta forgive him for being too hard, even if you disagree. He's trying the best way he knows how, and look at the life you've got! It's hard to be a man, is all. I tried to be one. I did it well for a little while. But I cracked."

He looked down at the floor for a moment, as if he was suddenly taken by a memory.

"…I lost everything. That's the tough bit about being a man. People expect you to be there for them. People expect you to work hard, provide, protect, uplift, be compassionate, understanding, stern – all of that. But as soon as you're feelin' low, feelin' down, no one's there for you. Some of us keep all that pain on the inside. I tried to bottle it up, tried to put on a brave face and push through, that's what my old man did. But that's what fucked me in the end. I should have learned how to let it go. That's what I wish I did. I wish I could let it all go."

"Let what go?" asked Jenno.

"Pride. Shame. Anger. Hatred of everything, but mostly the hatred of myself. I dunno. I never stood a chance. My dad was a drunk too. Used to tell me every day how he wished he never had me. Still stuck around, though. So, I gotta respect him for that. But I carried that with me. I made myself feel worthless as a man because of it. All I'm saying is, fuck trying to be a man. That perfect man doesn't exist. He's just some cunt that women made up to make us feel like shit, and insecure men try to be but fail miserably. I tried to be it, my old man tried to be it, from the sounds of it your old man's tryna be it… What you gotta be is yourself. You gotta find what makes you feel like *you*, and fuck what anybody else says about it. Anyone in this world that judges you for trying to be something is an insecure cunt, and they're not worth listening to…"

He was growing more animated, as if he was finally voicing some things that he'd held on to for a long time.

"How old are you, boys?"

"I'm 15, and Jimmy's 16."

"Fuck, you boys are so young! I bet it feels as though you got the world on your shoulders right now… And I bet you're tired of older people telling you this and that, what you gotta be and how you gotta act. But that's just the way it is. One day you'll understand what it was all for. You'll get why your dad is being heavy on you. He's trying to build discipline in you so you can be strong. But he's just a man. That's all I'm sayin'. You gotta forgive him for that."

"My dad's a drinker…" said Jenno.

"Yeah?" Tahiti replied. He looked down at the bottle in his hand and took a swig. "Aren't we all…" He wiped his mouth with the back of his hand. "They reckon weed and all of that is bad for you, but I never seen anyone beat someone's face in after having a joint. I never seen anyone cheat on their partner, or vomit all over themselves and pass out. This shit here is evil. Take it from me…"

"What about your daughter?" asked Jenno.

Tahiti took another sip.

"I imagine she's somewhere happy and free. She's just a little older than you two grommets. But I dunno, I haven't seen her in a couple years. Ex-missus never let me. I dunno what she thinks of me anyways, probably nothing good. She's better off not seeing what I've become, I reckon." He looked around at the trees and the rocks, and then back at the boys.

"Just think… Your old man could be out living in a fuckin' cave with nothing but a longneck and a pack of rollies with some paper and filters for company."

Tahiti laughed, but Jimmy and Jenno were silent.

"But don't worry about me, boys. I'm alright. I'm always alright in the end. I don't need much, never have. Possessions make me uncomfortable. Once you get 'em, what's to stop someone from taking them away? Better to live with nothing to give and nothing to lose, I reckon. But don't listen to me."

He stood up and blew some shit out of his nose, but just as he was about to say goodbye to the boys, Jenno asked him something that made him stop. "Do you reckon if you changed, your ex would let you see your daughter again?"

Tahiti stood in silence for a moment before he answered. "I dunno. Maybe she would. My little girl's an adult now. She can make her own decisions. I dunno if she'd even want anything to do with me anyways."

"Well, you'll never know unless you try," said Jenno.

"Yeah, I reckon so. But I'm fucked now. Look at me," Tahiti said, raising his arms and looking down at himself. His body was gaunt and skinny, his skin was red raw from the sun and his hair was matted and dirty. "No place is ever gonna hire me in the state I'm in…"

"What about labouring on a building site or something? I reckon they'd hire you."

"Fuck that," said Tahiti, spitting on the ground. "My body's fucked, plus I got no practical skills. I couldn't loosen a bolt even if my fuckin' ballsack was stuck in it."

Jenno laughed, but Tahiti was serious.

"Fuck, I dunno, I reckon there's something out there you could do if you wanted to."

"Yeah, maybe you're right. But I dunno. My time's over. I made my mistakes, and now I'm livin' with 'em. Anyways, grommets, I'm off."

With that he turned and continued on towards the caves.

…

Not long after, Tahiti was in his cave, lying on his hammock by the sea. it was more of a shelter than a cave. He was open to all elements except for rain; it was only on windy days when he got wet. It was close enough to the water that he could see the swell lap up against the boulders that were littered across the entire base of the headland, but just far enough away that he didn't have to worry about being swept away by a large swell. It was only very rarely, on stormy days, that he retreated from his shelter to the alleyway behind the lifeguard club, where he could at least hide from the wind and the rain. Before he moved in, the shelter was a local makeout spot. Teenagers would come and carve their names and the date into the rock face and on the ceiling. He liked the carvings, they gave him an odd sense of comfort. He looked out over the horizon and could make out the cargo ships way out in the distance that looked more like stars in the darkness than anything else.

Every now and then he thought of how his life used to be, as he did most evenings. Each time he thought about it he took a big sip, swallowed, and then spat out the aftertaste. Under his hammock was his chest that held all his journals and notes. They were his most prized possessions. No one had ever read them, aside from the boys who had done so a few years before. In a tide of mostly unreadable scribbles were contained all of his love, his fears, his wishes and his deepest regrets. He started writing them the day his wife kicked him out, and had held onto them ever since. They were his only reminders of who he was before. Sometimes he'd open one up and read it, and wonder if it was really him that had written it.

The years had slowly worn him away. He often looked at the face of the headland, which was slowly being reclaimed by the swell, the wind and rain. Slowly but surely, it was crumbling away. And so was he. Against the weight of time, waves of anger and self-pity: the times when he was drenched and pruney in rain and storms that made him feel bare and pure, the moments of clarity where he pieced the puzzle of his life together and was satisfied, only to be taken again by an unexpected alcohol-fuelled rage that brought him right back to where he started. But he was tired now. He could feel that fire in him burning out, and in its place, there was an empty lightness. It was the lightness that made him drift from place to place, never staying anywhere long enough to get comfortable, and never meeting anyone that brought him back down to earth again.

But the thought of seeing his daughter had suddenly sparked an ember. A small ember, but enough of one for him to feel the faint warmth of hope that he hadn't felt in years.

He fell asleep and dropped the bottle from his hands. It rolled from the base of the shelter and shattered against the pile of boulders below.

The sun woke him up in the morning. Its light was white-hot against the sea; he held his hand up to shield his eyes.

"Fuck sakes…" he sighed to himself. He felt fucked, as always. His body was sore, his joints ached and his head pounded from dehydration.

He pulled his clothes off and dove into the sea. He dipped his head underwater and rubbed the oil and grease from the night off his face, and for a moment he opened his eyes and peered around at the dark blue that surrounded him.

Afterwards, he walked up to the local bakery that was run by an old Armenian couple who'd always been generous to him. They gave him most of the deformed goods that were perfectly edible but unsellable to a paying customer. Davit would ask him what he'd been up to when he came by to pick up the food and every time Tahiti would shrug and say, "Fuck all, really."

It became a running joke between the two of them.

Then he'd wander up to the newsagent and grab some tobacco and rolling paper. With a bag of pastries and some tobacco in hand, he'd wander slowly back to the carpark, where he sat on the curb in the sun with his shirt off and spoke to everyone who walked by.

Most people kept walking, but every now and then someone would stop to chat, and he enjoyed their company. He liked asking people where they were from and what they had been up to. Most people said the usual, but every now and then someone would open up to him. He'd listen to their story while he smoked a cigarette he'd rolled up himself with satisfaction, and when they were done he'd shrug and say, "Well, best of luck!"

The bottl-o just down the road opened at 10 in the morning. At 10:30 he'd scoop himself back up from the pavement and wander over to grab a six-pack of the cheapest beer. He wasn't allowed to drink them down at the beach carpark, so he'd climb back around the rocks and sit for a while and watch the ocean.

These were the better parts of his day, when the world was alive around him and there was so much he could watch and get lost in. Come nighttime, his mood changed. People left the beach in herds, and suddenly everything was dark and lonely. That's when he would lose himself in memories, and when he'd turn from beer to something harder to get him to sleep.

He watched the last car reverse and drive away into the darkness, its red taillights getting smaller and smaller, until they were lost in the trees beyond.

The power lines hummed above him, and the waves echoed and crashed in the sea behind the lifeguard club, but all else was quiet. Now he was covered by darkness. The only beacon of light was from the old telephone box at the end of the carpark. The sign was half cracked open, revealing the white fluoro within. This was when he would wander back down to the bottl-o and grab a bottle of spiced rum. He stood up and hobbled down the road, but before he got too far a voice called after him. It was Jenno.

"Tahiti, man!"

Tahiti stopped and turned around. "Aye, grommet! What you doin' around here so late?"

Jenno stopped in front of him, out of breath. "I was lookin' for you, actually. I was thinking about your daughter at school all day…"

Tahiti raised his eyebrows.

A look of shock appeared on Jenno's face as he suddenly realised that what he'd intended to say had come out completely wrong.

He put his hands up defensively. "Nah, nah, not like that! It's just I reckon you should talk to her. I asked Jimmy too, and he reckons he could get you a job at the café he works at doin' dishes and stuff. I dunno if you'd wanna do it, but at least you'd get some cash."

Tahiti felt the little ember of hope reignite in his heart. "Fuck, you reckon they'd let me work?"

"Yeah, dude, for sure!" said Jenno. "They're Christians."

"Fuck me, that's the first time I've ever been glad to hear that," said Tahiti.

"What do you think?" asked Jenno.

"Lemme think about it. Come see me tomorrow?"

Jenno nodded.

…

The next day followed the same as the one before. That evening, Jenno came down to the beach again, looking for Tahiti.

Jimmy had asked the owners of the café that afternoon, and they welcomed the idea of having Tahiti work there a few days a week.

Jenno was excited. The thought of helping Tahiti out made him feel proud of himself. At school he felt like a dropkick, at home he felt like a burden and in the surf he felt like a child. It was the first time in his life where he felt like he could actually be a positive influence on someone's world.

He found Tahiti sitting on Ratty's bench with a bottle of rum in a brown paper bag. He asked him again, and this time, after a few moments of silent consideration, Tahiti nodded.

"Yeah, I reckon I should give it a go anyways – would be nice to get a bit of cashflow."

Jenno skated back home, smiling to himself.

He walked by his dad, stooped over the table drawing. There were empty cans of beer strewn across the table, and the general area had that stunk-out yeasty smell from warm beer left out too long.

"I just got someone a job, Dad," said Jenno.

"Ah yeah, that's awesome, mate," his dad replied without looking up.

"I could probably ask the café if you ever wanted to do some shifts there?" he added, wincing as he said it, but hopeful for his dad's response.

"Don't need to, mate, got some work comin' real soon," he replied.

Jenno peered over at the drawing. It was of a pine tree bent in the wind of a great storm. The colours were dark and violent.

Jenno turned and walked towards his room, but before he got too far his dad stopped him.

"Jenno!"

Jenno stopped and looked around excitedly, thinking that maybe his dad had changed his mind.

"Yeah, Dad?"

"Grab us a beer, mate, would you?

"Oh…" said Jenno, "yeah, no worries." He pulled a beer from the fridge and placed it on the table in front of his dad.

His dad looked up and smiled briefly at Jenno before putting his head back down again.

Jenno went to his room and lay down, listening to music and watching surf clips on his phone.

…

Not too far away, on the other side of the headland, Tahiti was lying in his hammock, listening to the swell crash against the boulders below. With a little battery-powered lantern he balanced on his stomach, he read some of the letters from the bottom of the chest.

They were old now. The paper was browned and flaky. He gently unfolded each one and read, careful not to tear the page.

The oldest was from a week after his ex-wife had kicked him out of the house. He was staying at a hostel then, and was still uncertain of how everything would play out. He never thought that it would end up this way, it was just the way it went. He thought about that time often. He replayed it over and over in his head, dissecting it, changing it and wondering always what his life would have been like if he had never done what he did.

The letter read:

It was a stupid thing to do, what I did. I don't know what I was thinking. I wasn't, I guess. I deserve to be kicked out. Jess deserves a better man than me, and Abbey deserves a better dad, that's for sure. I just hope I can still be there to watch her grow up. I'll have to wait and see. I would have forfeited that, for sure. It's crazy that a moment of lust is all it takes to ruin a life. If I could take it back, I would, but I guess that doesn't change anything really. I don't know what I'm going to do now. I'm staying at some shit hostel out the way. I feel the same way about work as I do about life. I'm sick of it and I need a change.

The future is dark, but that's a choice I made and I guess I'll just have to wait and see where it takes me. All I can hope for is that one day Abbey will forgive me, or at least tolerate me, once she's old enough to understand what I did to her and her mother.

I wonder what Dad would say if he was around to find out what I did. He'd probably never speak to me again either.

One day I hope I read this back and life is different. I hope then I would have figured some things out. Most of all I hope that I'm still in Abbey's life.

Tahiti finished reading the letter. He folded it carefully and placed it in the chest. He took one last swig of his bottle before he closed his eyes and drifted off to sleep.

He dreamed he was back in his old house with his little girl and his wife by his side.

...

Tahiti's first shift at the café started two days later. It was a morning shift on a relatively quiet day.

He woke up earlier than usual that morning and cleaned himself. His stomach was in knots; it was the first time he'd worked in years. He snuck into the toilets at the lifeguard club and looked at himself in the mirror. It was one of the few times where he saw himself properly. He looked at himself, disgusted. He opened the tap and waited for the water to heat up so that he could flatten his hair and tuck it behind his ears. He wanted to look at least half respectable. His heart was racing, and for a few moments he battled with the thought of going back to his hammock and never showing his face around again. But the thought of seeing his daughter won over, and, after checking himself out in the mirror one last time, he walked towards the café.

He showed up 10 minutes early. It was a nice café. The floors were polished concrete and the interior walls were made of old but rustic-looking brown bricks. All about there were little bits of artwork. It had been a long time since he'd heard the sound of coffee being ground.

The owner, Jesse, was a young, kind-looking man with longish blond hair that he slicked back behind his ears with gel. He looked fresh out of university. Tahiti assumed he'd probably come from money, but he was a nice enough guy and made a coffee for Tahiti before his shift started. Tahiti looked down at the mug before he drank. The milk was soft and creamy; it was a treat beyond anything he'd had in years. A happy couple were sitting next to him, talking about things that meant nothing to him, but sounded sweet and hopeful. Although Tahiti didn't know it, it was Fleetwood and Adriaan, talking about their lives before they came to Sydney. Fleetwood looked at Tahiti and gave him a warm smile. She knew who he was, Ratty had mentioned him before, and sometimes she'd see him sitting at the carparks when she walked back from the beach on early mornings. Tahiti looked away when she smiled at him.

When it was time for his shift to start, Jesse led him to the kitchen and showed him the dishwashing station. There was a sink, a hose, a bench for plates and a washer underneath the steel table to the right.

Next to the dishwashing station was the door to the cool room. It was a thick white refrigerator door that slid to the right and made a squeaking noise about halfway open. To the left were the ovens and a salamander and microwave on a shelf that was the perfect height to bump your forehead on if you weren't careful.

It was a simple enough job – just spray and wipe the plates and cutlery before putting them into the washer, and scrub the pots and pans with a soft sponge.

He put his head down and began to work. He didn't say a word the whole morning.

The pace picked up at around eight o'clock, when people started filing in and ordering breakfast.

Simmo, the chef, was constantly swearing and muttering to himself the whole time. Tahiti couldn't tell if Simmo was stressed or enjoying himself. Plates started to stack higher and higher on the bench, quicker than Tahiti could clean them. He started to panic.

Every now and then, Simmo would ask him to run into the cool room and grab him something. Once when he raced into the cool room, searching frantically for a punnet of cherry tomatoes, he had the sudden urge to give up and quit. He stood in the cool room, staring at the fan for a few moments, before he heard Simmo's voice ring out from the kitchen, asking where the tomatoes were. Tahiti found them and raced out again.

He couldn't believe how much food was being wasted. It was as if half the plates weren't even touched at all. Tahiti's stomach rumbled and his mouth watered every time he scraped a perfectly good meal into the bin.

It was torture. He hadn't eaten at all that day, and the scraps he'd had for dinner the night before could hardly have kept him going till the end of the shift.

He spared a glimpse out of the kitchen window at the customers outside; the place was heaving now.

Simmo was growing steadily angrier and his outbursts had become more volatile. Tahiti watched out of the corner of his eye as Simmo cracked an egg and missed the hotplate.

"FOR FUCK SAKES!" yelled Simmo, throwing the shells as hard as he could against the wall. Tahiti looked back down at the sink before Simmo noticed him watching. He had no intention of being Simmo's next target of frustration. An hour or so passed and the morning customers slowly dwindled.

The pace grew slower and slower, and the job felt more enjoyable. It was the first time in a long time where Tahiti had been completely distracted from his thoughts.

When the café was empty, Jesse popped his head into the kitchen and returned a few minutes later with some coffees for Tahiti and Simmo. Tahiti took his coffee and smiled.

"You know Jimmy, yeah?" asked Simmo. He was wiping down the benches and prepping for the lunchtime rush. He seemed a completely different person than he was in the morning. He was cheery, smiley and talkative.

Tahiti nodded. "Yeah, I know Jimmy."

"Good kid," said Simmo.

Tahiti nodded again.

Tahiti's stomach rumbled again, and Simmo saw the look on his face quicker than he could hide it.

"Fuck, mate, you look hungry."

"Yeah, I am a bit," said Tahiti.

"Fuckin'… Why didn't you just say so?" said Simmo.

A moment later the grill was sizzling once again with a chicken breast, bacon, an egg and some onion. Simmo sliced an avocado and stacked all the components together into a burger with some chips on the side. He slid the plate across the bench over to Tahiti, who couldn't believe his eyes.

"Cheers," he said, looking down.

The burger was the most delicious thing he'd ever tasted. He ate it in three bites, and not many more for the chips.

Simmo looked at him with his eyebrows raised.

"Just tell me whenever you're hungry, man. There's no point starving in a café."

Tahiti nodded.

The rest of the shift passed much smoother than the morning. Tahiti finished for the day at four o'clock.

He said goodbye to Simmo, but before he had a chance to say goodbye to Jesse, Jesse stopped him.

"We normally pay on a weekly basis, but I hope you don't mind that Jimmy let me know a little about your situation." In his hand, he held 200 dollars.

Tahiti eyed the money almost distrustfully. "You sure? This looks like a fair bit of money…"

Jesse smiled. "Simmo told me you did well today. We'd love to have you back if you'd like to work here."

Tahiti nodded. "Yeah. I'd love to. Cheers."

He turned and walked towards the door, but Jesse stopped him again. "Tahiti! Here, take a few of the leftover sandwiches from the cabinet. We make them fresh each morning."

Tahiti couldn't believe the generosity. He took the sandwiches and practically bowed to Jesse out of the front door. He left the café feeling happy and excited. He looked at the money in his hand. It was a satisfying feeling to have earned it.

He walked straight to the bottl-o and bought a nicer bottle of spirits, a spiced rum he used to drink years ago, before his life changed. His next shift would be two days from then. He tallied up the money per week in his head. Six hundred dollars cash for three days' work. It seemed an incomprehensible amount to him after years of inconsistent dole paychecks and whatever he could make panhandling in town.

He bought another bottle just for good measure.

Jenno saw him in the carpark that evening. "Tahiti! How'd it go?"

"Pretty fuckin' good, mate. Thanks a bunch," said Tahiti, beaming.

Jenno felt a swell of pride in his chest. "No worries, man. Couple weeks of work and you can get some nice clothes sorted and go and see your daughter! I can help you find her, if you want? It wouldn't be hard to look her up online."

"Yeah?" asked Tahiti.

"Yeah, look." Jenno pulled out his phone. "What's your daughter's full name?"

"Abbey Thomas," said Tahiti, almost hesitantly.

He watched as Jenno searched up her profile. His heart stopped when he saw her little display picture pop up on the search bar.

"That's her!" he said, excitedly.

Jenno clicked on the profile and passed the phone over to Tahiti.

Wide-eyed, Tahiti scrolled through her photos. His hands were shaking. "She's beautiful," he said to himself.

He clicked on a photo of her smiling with a boy who he assumed was her boyfriend. They looked happy together.

The next photo was of her and his ex-wife. They were together standing next to a Christmas tree with an older man Tahiti didn't recognise. The caption of the photo was 'My family.' He looked at the man. He was clean-cut and kind-looking. He held both his arms around the girls.

It was too much for Tahiti. He gave the phone back to Jenno.

Jenno looked at him. "You good?"

He nodded. "Yeah, mate. Looks like she's doin' perfectly fine without me."

"You don't know that…" said Jenno.

"Yeah, nah. Thanks for gettin' me some work, grommet. I dunno how I could thank you."

"Don't worry about it. I just wanna see you doing better, is all. Think of that as my thank you."

They said goodbye to one another. Jenno skated home and Tahiti made his way back around the headland to his hammock.

He thought of his daughter that night. About her life, about her smile and about the clean-cut man who had filled his place as her father figure. Then he drank almost an entire bottle of rum and fell asleep.

…

Tahiti's next two shifts came and went. He was beginning to feel better about himself each day. He had more and more money saved. Although he drank more than he did before, it didn't seem to put a dent into his total earnings.

After two weeks, he had more money than he'd had in over a decade.

He made his way over to the bakery he visited every morning. He hadn't been since he started working at the café.

Davit, the baker, asked him how he'd been, as he did every time he saw him.

"Been workin', actually," said Tahiti, smiling. He pulled out a 20-dollar note and bought a pie, a loaf of bread, some croissants and a lamington.

Davit beamed at him in disbelief. "Good fucking work, my friend!" he said happily. He patted Tahiti on the back.

Tahiti said goodbye and walked away, smiling to himself. He drank and ate all day.

That weekend he went clothes shopping at the mall. The clothes he wore were worse than rags. He hadn't changed them in years. He wore steel-capped boots, but the leather over the toes was shredded back, revealing the steel beneath. His ripped jeans were stiff and stinky from the years living by the ocean. He wore a checkered short-sleeved shirt that was stained with sweat patches, food, drink and whatever else had soaked up over the time he'd worn it. Over the top he wore a black jacket with large pockets big enough for him to carry most of his most valuable possessions with him.

He stopped in front of a department store and looked in through the windows at the perfume stands, watches, handbags and formal clothes. He wanted to look good when he saw Abbey, but he had begun to get second thoughts after looking at the sparkling clean white floors, the sterile white lights and the attendants with smiles stretched across their thin faces, pearly white teeth, and cold, dead eyes. He held his breath and walked in.

He walked right back out two minutes later. He couldn't take the stares. As soon as he walked through the door, security started following him; he could feel eyes all around him burning into the back of his head and his cheeks. It made him feel claustrophobic, scared almost, like an animal that'd accidentally leaped right into the lion's den. That, paired with the cheery department store music, made the whole thing feel like some kind of horror movie. He looked at the attendants for help; their smiles were stretched wider than ever, but their eyes had lit into an almost frenzied fury, hunting him down like some kind of vermin that had slipped its way into the store and had to be removed before any of the paying customers saw. He watched as one of the security guards leaned his head down to the walkie talkie on his chest to say something. Tahiti put his hand into his pocket where his money was and pulled it out almost instinctively. The act brought him a sudden sense of ease. He looked down and checked the price tag of a fancy looking jacket, then started to count the money in his hands.

There was a sudden change in the attendants. Unease had quickly returned to a sort of sickly pleasantness. Tahiti could feel the change almost instantly. But before any of them had the chance to approach him he turned and left the store as quickly as he could.

At the next store he went to, he wasted no time and bought the clothes straight off of one of the manikins. Blue jeans, a white shirt, white shoes and a red cap. The girl on the till eyed him suspiciously when he approached her with the clothes, but relaxed when he pulled out cash from his pocket. He held onto his money as though it were a life raft out in stormy seas. It was the only thing that seemed to bridge the gap between these people and himself. He took the clothes and almost ran to the bathrooms to get changed.

He left his old clothes in the cubicle once he was done. To a stranger walking by, it would have looked as though someone had just up and vanished while taking a shit. The old pants were sprawled over the floor, the old shirt was draped over the toilet and the shoes were left together neatly by the cubicle door.

A new man walked out of that toilet. He looked at himself in the clothes. His hair was unkempt and dirty, and his chin was covered in a thick layer of stubble. He could have been mistaken for one of those new-age startup company CEOs on his day off.

He walked into the barbers and asked for a short back and sides. He barely recognised himself when he walked out. He was the most normal-looking man in the world, and he loved it. Suddenly he had become invisible, but in an entirely different way. Homelessness had made him invisible. People walked right over him as if he wasn't there. He could have screamed his lungs out and it wouldn't have made a difference. That was one of the reasons he migrated to the coast from the city. He couldn't stand the invisibility anymore, the ceaseless flow of people marching back and forth all day long. These clothes made him blend in. They made him feel a part of it all, as if all of a sudden, he had become so uninteresting to look at that he just blended into space. He walked into store after store just because he could. He bought some more clothes, and a nice suitcase to put them in.

"Going on holidays?" said the cashier on the till when he'd come to pay for the suitcase.

"Yeah," he said, "goin' to Tahiti."

"Amazing!" said the cashier. "I hear it's beautiful this time of year."

He caught a bus back to the beach. He climbed across the headland and took one last look at the cave. The hammock swung back and forth gently in the breeze. He looked up at all the names and dates carved into the rock, and placed his hand on the wall. He bent over and picked up his chest, took the notes out carefully and placed them gently into his new suitcase.

He looked out at the horizon, took one deep breath and then left without looking back.

The cave was empty now, except for the hammock, which still swayed back and forth noiselessly.

Tahiti saw Jenno walking up toward the carpark from the beach after a surf.

Jenno nearly walked right past him on the pathway.

"Oi, you little cunt!" Tahiti called affectionately.

Jenno twisted around and stared at Tahiti for a second with a confused look on his face. Tahiti beamed when he saw Jenno's face change into recognition.

"What the fuck!" laughed Jenno. "I didn't even recognise you!"

Tahiti laughed. "Yeah, mate, got a whole new wardrobe and a fresh cut. What'd'ya reckon?"

"Looks good! You gonna see your daughter?"

"Not yet," said Tahiti. "Puttin' myself up at a hostel for a while. Gonna get settled, then go see her."

"Fuck, yeah," said Jenno. "Just let me know, I can message her whenever you want and organise something."

Tahiti nodded.

Later that evening he walked into the private room he'd rented at a local hostel a few beaches down.

He put his suitcase on the floor and took a shower. He turned the heat up until it almost burned and scrubbed himself until he'd almost used up the whole bar of soap. The shower was the start of a new beginning. A new man. He dried himself and put on his new clothes, went down to the bottl-o and bought a bottle of spiced rum. While he was walking the rows at the bottl-o, he passed a woman who looked around the same age. They met eyes and she smiled at him.

He picked out his bottle and paid at the counter, but before he left he glanced at the woman one last time; she watched him leave.

He went back to his hostel room and looked at himself in the mirror, wondering if he was looking at the man he'd meant to become all along if he hadn't let his pride get in the way. Almost. The years in the sun and rain had toughened his skin, his face looked leathery and worn. The only thing he couldn't clean and wash away were the lines in his forehead and around his eyes, the marks of a man who had laughed always, even in the times when he should have cried.

...

Jesse couldn't believe his eyes when Tahiti walked into work the next day.

"What happened to you!" he said, unable to wipe the look of disbelief from his face.

Tahiti laughed. "Yeah, figured it was probably about time for a change. I dunno, your positive attitude must have rubbed off on me."

Jesse smiled. "That means more than anything in the world. Have you considered that maybe there was a greater force than just that at play?"

"Yeah?" asked Tahiti.

"Look, I don't want to ever shove my personal beliefs into anyone's face, but changes like this don't just happen. This is a sign, Tahiti. A sign from God."

"You reckon?" asked Tahiti.

"Yeah, I definitely reckon. I know how it sounds. All I'm saying is that sometimes God shows us signs. He gives us light and guidance. Just consider reading into it all a little bit more."

"Yeah, nah, I will," said Tahiti. He thought about Jenno and all of his guidance and help. "Fuck me dead, that little cunt might be Jesus Christ." He laughed to himself on his way to the kitchen sink. He rolled up his sleeves and got to work.

...

Two more weeks passed the same. Tahiti had saved what was to him a small fortune. His diet had changed significantly, from meat pies and scrapped bakery goods to fresh food and full meals. His face had begun to fill out a little more, and he felt noticeably better in general. The aches and pains of general life had seemed to subside a little bit, and his overall mood had lifted.

His wardrobe had expanded from the clothes he'd taken off the manikin. He now owned a few pairs of shorts, a pair of smart shoes, thongs, board shorts, t-shirts and a jacket he picked out specially to wear for when he saw Abbey.

He was ready.

He went down to the carpark that evening and waited for Jenno to come out of the surf. His heart was racing in anticipation. It felt like the single biggest thing he had ever done in his life.

Jenno smiled when he saw him, he knew why he was there. He grabbed his phone and searched Abbey's profile up.

They wrote the message together. It read:

What's doing, Abbey?

My name's Jenno – we've never met before, but I know your dad. He wants to see you. I know this is probably a weird message to get, but do you reckon you'd meet up with him?

Jenno's thumb hovered over the send button for a few moments, just in case Tahiti had any second thoughts.

"What do you reckon, Tahiti?" he asked. He looked from the phone to Tahiti's face. His eyes were wide with concentration, and a bead of sweat ran down his forehead.

"Yea—" Tahiti cleared his throat nervously. "Yeah, send it."

Jenno pressed his thumb down on the send button.

Tahiti almost gasped as he watched the message bubble suddenly appear in the message bank.

He stared at the phone excitedly, but nothing happened.

"Well?" he asked.

"What?" said Jenno.

"Has she seen it?"

"Nah, not yet. I mean I only just sent it…"

"Fuck sakes…" he said under his breath. "Sorry, mate, I'm just a bit nervous." He ran his hands through his hair.

"Just relax – it'll probably take her some time to respond, I bet. I dunno what she's up to. She might not even go on her phone that much."

"Yeah. Nah, you're right. Guess I'm just gonna have to wait and see."

"I'll come find you as soon as she's replied," said Jenno.

"Cheers, grommet," said Tahiti. He slapped Jenno on the back and then went on his way.

His nerves were shot already. His legs felt like jelly and he almost crawled his way to the bottl-o that night. He bought an extra bottle just in case he needed more to take the edge off.

He passed out on the hostel room bed that night with his clothes on.

...

It was two whole days before she finally responded. Tahiti was washing dishes in the kitchen when Jenno raced in with his phone in his hand.

"She replied!"

"Aye?!" said Tahiti, jerking his head back from the sink. "What'd she say?" he asked, excitedly.

"Haven't read it yet – was gonna let you read it first," said Jenno.

He passed the phone over to Tahiti, who dried his hands on his apron and took it carefully.

Jenno watched his eyes read the text. He could see the light from the phone reflected off of his pupils. They widened as he read.

He passed the phone back to Jenno.

"What did she say?" asked Jenno.

"Says she wants to meet up."

Jenno looked at the forlorn expression that had suddenly befallen Tahiti's face.

"What's the matter? That's good!"

"Yeah, nah, it is," he said, quietly. He was scared of what she would think of him when she saw him, and most of all what she would say.

"When do you wanna see her, then?" asked Jenno.

"Tonight."

"Are you sure?"

"Yeah, I'm sure."

"Alright. I'll tell her now."

Jenno messaged her and arranged a location and a time. The plan was to meet at an Indian restaurant in town at seven o'clock.

Tahiti was deep in thought for the rest of the shift. The remainder of the day seemed to pass in the blink of an eye.

He was terrified.

When he got back to the hostel he had a shower, shaved and got dressed into his new clothes. He didn't look at all like he imagined he would. Suddenly, he was overcome by insecurities. He was all too aware of the lines on his face, the browning of his teeth and the dryness of his skin. He ran down to the bottl-o and grabbed a bottle of spiced rum, downing a few glasses just to take the edge off. It was 5:30. He looked down at the bottle. It was half empty. He was drunk now, but his insecurities were gone. He walked down to the shops and picked up a bouquet of sunflowers. They had been Abbey's favourite flower when she was a little girl.

One of his fondest memories of her was the weekend before her fifth birthday. He had promised her for a long time that they would go inland to his sister's farm to say hello to the cows and the sheep, and finally they had set off. He remembered checking on Abbey from time to time throughout the drive. She was silent the whole time, watching the world go by outside.

He hoisted her atop his shoulders and they walked through an entire field of sunflowers. He cut one down and gave it to her. She pressed her little nose against it and sniffed hard, and then they laughed together when she realised that it had no scent. She held it close to her, and didn't let it go for a second on the way home.

He told her that one day they would all move to a house that was in the middle of a sunflower field so that she could wake up and see them every day.

It was quarter to seven when he walked into the restaurant. There were a few full tables, but for the most part the place was quiet. He found a little table at the back corner and took a seat.

His palms were sweating, and he could feel moist patches forming under his armpits.

At five minutes to seven Abbey walked into the restaurant. Tahiti couldn't believe his eyes when he saw her. She was even more beautiful than in her photos. She was a woman now. Her face crinkled into a warm smile when she met the greeter at the door. Tahiti watched her scan the room until her eyes fell on him, and then her smile faded, replaced by a look of grim determination. He stood up to hug her, but she sat down before he had the chance.

He sat down, painfully aware of his mistake.

There was a tense silence between them. He was suddenly aware of the clatter of cutlery on the surrounding tables, the chatter and laughter. He could suddenly hear the food cooking in the kitchen and the chef giving out orders. He was surrounded by people. And it seemed to him that he was drowning in their happiness.

"Hi," said Tahiti, attempting to silence the world out.

"Hello," said Abbey.

He pulled the bouquet of sunflowers from underneath the table. "I brought you these. I remember they were your favourite."

"Thanks," she said, taking them. "I like roses now."

"Ah yeah, no worries," he said. "You look beautiful," he added, smiling.

"You look different."

"Yeah, nah, I guess I would. I'm a work in progress."

The table across from theirs erupted with laughter. Someone had just reached the punchline of a long joke, but Tahiti couldn't help but feel for some reason that they were laughing at him.

"What are you doing now that you finished school?"

"I just got into medicine," she said. He saw a glimmer of excitement flash through her eyes.

He beamed. "You're jokin'! That's amazing, Abbey."

Her eyes darted down to his browning teeth. He tightened his lips around them so that she couldn't look any longer.

"Thank you. Adam is a surgeon. He helped me a lot with the application and the interview process."

"Is that your mum's boyfriend?" asked Tahiti.

"Husband," she said.

"Ah yeah, well, I'm happy for them. Where are you living now?" he asked.

"In a little flat with my boyfriend."

"That's great. He a good guy?"

"Yep."

"Yeah…" said Tahiti, trailing off.

The silence between them was deafening.

"Hey, you guys ready to order?" said the waiter suddenly. He was standing with a little notepad in his hands.

Tahiti almost jumped.

"Could we have five more minutes? And maybe just some water, thanks," said Abbey, smiling.

"No worries," said the waiter. He turned and left the table.

Tahiti took the chance. "Look, Abbey, I just wanted to say that I'm sorry for everythin'—" He cleared his throat, as if he had just heard himself talk for the first time. "I'm sorry for everything. I don't expect you to forgive me. What I did was horrible, and I never meant for it to hurt you. I just want you to know that you were on my mind always."

"Thanks," she said, coldly.

He didn't know what he expected, but in his heart, he had known that this would always be the outcome. He thought that maybe, just maybe, there would be the same glimmer of hope in her eyes that he had kindled in his. That maybe there was a chance for him to right his wrongs. That it wasn't too late. That all the lonely nights drenched by rain, whipped by wind and parched by heat were all purposeful, and that they all had a lesson for him somewhere.

"For so long I wondered where you went. I cried and cried. I needed you. You have no idea how much I needed you. And then, when I was old enough to know what you did and where you went, I hated you so much I couldn't stand it. I despised everything you were. I didn't know what I would think when I saw you tonight. I was worried I would let my anger get the best of me."

"I understa—" began Tahiti, but she cut him off.

"But now I just pity you. How could I hate someone for not being there for me when they aren't even capable of being there for themselves? I'm just sad now. You look like an empty shell. And I think maybe the man I needed for so long died a long time ago. I know how you've been living. Mum told me when I turned 18. I can smell the alcohol on you. For so long, I dreamed that you would come home. And I never appreciated the man who was really in my life all along. Adam is my father. If not biological, then chosen, and proven by action. And over the last year I've learned to let it all go. And I think that maybe you should too. Let me go. Let us all go. We let you go and moved on a long time ago."

Tahiti looked deep into her eyes, searching desperately for even the smallest flicker of doubt, of uncertainty, of *love*. But they were as cold as steel.

She stood up to leave.

"Thanks for the flowers," she said.

"Wait… please," said Tahiti, desperately. His hands were shaking as he pulled out the stack of letters from his chest that he had written over the years.

He hoped in vain that maybe the letters could explain better than he could. That maybe they could save him. Evidence of everything that he had gone through, and everything he had felt in his exile and his self-pity.

He raised them above his head like an offering. They were the most valuable thing in his possession. They had become a piece of his soul.

"Please. Give these to your mum."

She looked down at the crinkled, browning paper and then to Tahiti. He looked almost pathetic to her. It was too much to take in.

There were tears in her eyes now.

"No," she said, shakily. It was like the knock of a gavel to Tahiti. A life sentence he had so far managed to outrun. To leave behind and forget for a time. But now he was face to face with the truth. And in her he saw himself for what he really was. Her voice quivered. She managed to catch herself, and before he had a chance to say anything else, she turned and rushed out of the restaurant. Tahiti watched her go.

He was suddenly overtaken by that empty lightness he thought he had escaped. He was numb.

The waiter came back with the water.

"We changed our minds," said Tahiti. He stood up and left a tip on the table, and walked out clutching the letters in his hands.

When he walked out of the front door of the restaurant, he broke into a run in hopes of seeing her, but she was gone.

The street was quiet. A kitchen window opened in the apartment above the restaurant. The aircon units hummed in unison, cars screeched and honked far off in the city, and the power lines buzzed above him. These were the sounds of unliving things that had somehow become the sounds of life in the city. The city is an organism unlike any other. An amalgamation of dreams, of desires, of people and of concrete and electricity. The streets are the veins that connects everything to the organism.

The veins of the city led him back to the bottl-o. He bought two bottles of his favourite spiced rum and walked back to his cave beneath the headland. A place beyond, where the sounds of the city and of life could not reach him and remind him of the life he had thrown away.

He clambered down to the edge of the water and bathed in the moonlight. There was a pathway of soft white light that glistened atop the water and into the horizon. Tahiti stood at the foot of it and peered out into the darkness. His shirt was off and he held the bottle of rum in his hand, half-drunk already. In the other hand, he clutched the letters. He lifted them up above his head and winced, as though they weighed as heavy as a bowling ball.

"Yeah…" he said to himself.

"Nah…" he answered himself a moment later. The soft swell lapped against the rocks around him. He could hear the water rushing back and forth through the rock piles, slapping and gurgling as it pushed and pulled, slowly but surely reclaiming the earth that had escaped its depths for a time. He held the letters up to his face and looked at them in the moonlight.

A moment later he made a *pffftt* noise and threw them into the sea. He watched the black water spread through them until they became soggy and indistinguishable. With a grunt, he tossed the bottle at them and watched them sink into the darkness together.

The weightlessness of this act overtook him. Without his letters, it felt as though there was nothing holding him down anymore. In a pillar of moonlight, he floated back to the cave blind drunk and opened the next bottle.

…

Jenno skated down to the café the next afternoon. He was desperate to know how Tahiti's evening went meeting his daughter. He'd been so happy with himself that evening, knowing that he had really helped two people reconnect.

He rounded the corner of the kitchen to where the dishwashing station was, but was surprised to find a younger-looking man, covered in piercings and tattoos.

"Oi, Jenno! What you up to?" asked Simmo from the grill.

"Wasn't Tahiti meant to be workin' today?" Jenno replied.

"Yeah, he was meant to. The dog's gone MIA. We've had a fuckin' cunt of a day in here without the extra help, I'll tell you that much… Actually, you reckon you could stay around and give us a hand packing down?"

"Fuck that!" said Jenno, before he turned and raced out of the café again.

"Little cunt…" Simmo laughed to himself.

Jenno skated down to the carpark, but Tahiti wasn't there either. Before he had a chance to check around the headland, his mum called him and asked him to come and help her move the fridge.

He skated home, wondering where Tahiti was. A part of him hoped that Tahiti had patched things up instantly with Abbey and they'd gone on their way. But deep down, he had a feeling that it wouldn't have been that easy.

Come dinnertime he had put the thought aside. He would go the following day and catch him at work again. He was excited to find out how it all went.

…

Jimmy woke up late the next morning. He walked downstairs still half asleep. His mother and father were in the kitchen drinking their morning coffees. He walked into the kitchen and said good morning. Both of his parents were reading. His mum was reading the local newspaper, whilst his father was reading one of those monthly subscription economic magazines people get mailed to them.

Jimmy shuffled over to the coffee machine and dropped a pod into the top. It was a beautiful day outside. He stuck his head out of the kitchen window and breathed in the fresh air.

"Oh no! How sad…" he heard his mother say.

He looked back from the window. "What's wrong?"

"Nothing…" she said. She looked up from the paper. "You know the homeless man that lives down at the beach?"

"Yeah, Tahiti," said Jimmy. His coffee had just finished pouring. He grabbed the mug and took a sip.

"His body was found yesterday morning around the rocks. Drank himself to death, apparently. Oh, such a shame. He always used to say hello when I walked by…"

Jimmy put the coffee mug down on the marble top. "I gotta go…" he said.

He ran out of the kitchen, grabbed a shirt and his skateboard, and rode as quickly as he could towards the beach.

He clambered around the rocks to where Tahiti's cave was. Jenno was sitting there looking out into the ocean.

The hammock was still there.

Jenno looked down at Jimmy. Jimmy climbed up and sat next to him. Jenno was holding Tahiti's worn-out chest in his hands. It was empty.

Sunlight danced and sparkled off of the water's surface. Little baitfish swam from bigger fish. Crabs scuttled across and under the rocks, claws raised high and on constant alert for predators. The birds glided and dove into the water from above, surfacing again with fish in their beaks. Ants trekked across the cliffside in highways made of thousands. Butterflies wafted in the breeze atop the headland and amongst the trees, and thousands of bugs swarmed in the soil, air and around the rocks. All around were millions of tiny flames of life, all about where one had gone out.

"I just thought I was helping him," said Jenno.

"You can't blame yourself, man. You did help him."

"He's dead."

"He was already dead. But for a little while he was alive again. And you did that," said Jimmy, putting his hand on Jenno's shoulder.

"I dunno. I guess I just saw a bit of me and my dad in that situation. Sometimes I feel like he's heading the same way. It's sad. He just sits there and drinks all day."

"I know," said Jimmy.

Silence fell between them, before Jimmy stood up and held his hand out. Jenno looked at it.

"Come on, Jenno," Jimmy said.

Jenno took his hand, and Jimmy pulled him up and clapped him on the back.

"Let's go home," said Jimmy.

They left the cave for the last time. Jenno never wanted to see it again. The hammock remained for years after, swaying back and forth gently in the breeze until it too was claimed by the elements.

No one claimed Tahiti's body. It was cremated by the local council and the ashes were scattered into the sea, nameless and without ceremony. He had lived and died a thousand times. A thousand lives full of meaning that were meaningless in the end and undistinguishable. In the end, we are all just faces passing by. Going somewhere and nowhere at all. The beauty of life is in the moments when we allow ourselves to melt into crowds full of people just like us. Dissolved into a thousand footsteps, and inhaled and exhaled by the winds of time.

Just like the cliffs that were slowly being swallowed by the tides and time, he was reclaimed by the sea. And in the end he was just another wave passing through the universe, coming and going somewhere we can't begin to comprehend.

…

Days passed slowly and then quickly after Tahiti's death. Jenno couldn't help but look towards the headland whenever he surfed, or to the old telephone box, or the curb where Tahiti used to sit and drink beers. A part of him expected to find Tahiti still sitting there waiting for him.

"You all good?" Jimmy asked him, one afternoon on their way home from school in the car.

Jenno rested his chin on his knee as he sat with his foot on the seat, watching the world pass by outside.

Jimmy cringed as Jenno's dirty school shoes scuffed up the leather seat, but held his tongue.

"Yeah, I'm good…" said Jenno, quietly.

"You've been quiet all week. Your mum's starting to get worried about you," said Jimmy.

"I'll be sweet. I went through this pain with Ratty, I can do it again…"

"That doesn't fill me with any more confidence," said Jimmy.

"Don't worry, Jimmy, I'm good," said Jenno.

Jimmy dropped him home and watched as he walked towards his front door, hoping that he'd turn around and talk. But he didn't.

Jenno grabbed his board and his wetsuit and walked towards the beach, remembering the times when Ratty and Jimmy were by his side. They felt like a lifetime ago to him now. So much had changed in the space of a year. He felt like he'd changed. There were no waves when he got to the beach, save for a few soft lumps of swell that crept unbroken towards the shore until they trickled onto the sand. Jenno put his wetsuit on and walked into the water until he was waist deep, and stood, staring, out into the horizon in silence.

After some time, he paddled further out from shore, and then lay back on his board, thinking of Tahiti and Ratty as he watched the clouds drift slowly by. When the clouds had all passed over and the sky was clear, the light became too strong, so he rolled off of his board and floated.

His breathing slowed and became more calculated, until finally he gulped in one last big breath of air and dove to the bottom. He swam deep, and almost pressed his face to the sand. It was like he was floating above some vast desert, as light and massless as a wisp of cloud. Sunlight broke into pillars against the water and refracted light shimmered against the sand. Jenno stuck his hand into one of the beams of light and stared at it curiously. There was nothing to be heard but the crackling of salt, the distant humming of boats out to sea and the beating of his heart in his ears.

He closed his eyes and let himself float slowly towards the surface.

...

Later, when he was lying on his bed, he pulled out his phone and searched for Abbey's profile.

He could feel something heavy in his throat as he read through their back and forth messages just before Tahiti had met up with her. He exhaled, and typed out a message.

Hey Abbey,

I'm sorry about what happened. I was wondering if you were around to talk about it?

His thumb hovered above the send button for a few moments before he finally pressed down. His messaged bubble popped up in the chat box. He stared at it for a while, waiting for a response. It didn't come until some hours later, when he was midway through the dishes at home. His heart raced when his phone vibrated in his pocket. He dried his hands and pulled it out excitedly. He took a deep breath before he finally opened the response.

The blue light from the phone screen reflected from his eyes as he read:

Hi Jenno,

Thanks for the message. I'm glad I got the chance to speak with him before he died.
I'll be at my mums tomorrow, meet me there if that works for you.

She sent him a time and her address.

The next day, Jenno walked through her front gate and knocked on the door. It was a modest house, single-storey, but with a lovely garden and white pebble path that led to the front steps.

An older man answered. He wore suit pants and a button-up shirt with the sleeves rolled up. He eyed Jenno curiously.

"Hi," began Jenno, "is Abbey there?"

The man smiled; he had a warm, fatherly smile.

"You must be Jenno. Yes, she is. You don't mind waiting a few minutes, do you? I think she's just finishing up a call upstairs. Come in," he said, stepping aside.

Jenno walked through the door and looked around. A grand piano sat in the corner of the front room, and all around it were picture frames hanging from the wall and a few scented candles that reminded him of the beach.

"I'm Adam," said the man, holding out his hand. Jenno took it, and suddenly recognised him as the same man who was in the photo on Abbey's page he and Tahiti saw weeks ago.

"Nice to meet you. You got a sick house," said Jenno, in his greatest attempt at politeness.

Adam laughed." Thank you, Jenno. 'Sick 'was what I had in mind for it when we moved in."

Jenno sat down on the living-room sofa while Adam went to grab him a glass of orange juice.

"I hope you're a fan of pulp, Abbey and I can't get enough of it," he said, as he handed Jenno the glass. Jenno took it, smiling. He sipped it and looked around at the pictures on the wall.

Abbey came down a moment later. Jenno was taken aback by her beauty, but he felt a strange sensation when he recognised some of Tahiti's features in her face.

"Jenno," she smiled, "it's nice to meet you, finally."

Jenno stood up from his seat." Yeah, you too."

"Let's sit out in the garden," she said. "Hey, Dad, could you call Mum? She might want to talk to Jenno too," Abbey called over her shoulder.

Jenno followed her outside. It was a small garden. A veggie patch lined the base of the fence, and in the middle of the grass there was a little wooden bench and table. A soft breeze carried small, withering purple flowers from the neighbour's jacaranda tree. They landed on the table and chairs.

"I'm sorry about your dad," said Jenno, once they'd sat down.

"It's ok. You probably would have guessed that we weren't very close," said Abbey, trying to sound as nonchalant as possible, but Jenno noticed the slightest tremble in her voice.

"Yeah, but still," said Jenno.

A few moments later, Abbey's mum appeared. She was a tall, elegant, but stern-looking woman who wore her hair in a tight bun.

Jenno had a hard time picturing what she and Tahiti would have looked like together; appearance-wise they seemed like complete opposites.

She brought a chair over, wiped the flower petals from the table and sat next to Jenno, smiling.

"It's nice to meet you, Jenno. Abbey's told me about you."

Adam came out outside, holding the bottle of orange juice. Before Jenno had a chance to say anything, he refilled his glass to the top and smiled at him before he went back inside. Out of politeness, Jenno took a sip.

"Yeah, I was friends with Tahiti," said Jenno.

"I didn't know that was his name," said Abbey's mum. "I only knew him as Christopher."

A delicate purple flower landed gently on her shoulder. She studied it for a moment before she blew it off.

"Sorry," said Jenno, "I never knew his real name."

"So, what did you want to talk about?" Abbey asked him.

"I dunno," Jenno started. Suddenly, he felt foolish. He had no idea what he wanted to talk about, only that the answers to whatever he was feeling could be found in Abbey and her mum, but he assumed that they'd come out naturally.

"I just wanted to know more," he said, finally.

Abbey's mum sat back in her seat; her warm smile had turned suddenly into a frown.

"If you're looking for gossip, you won't find it here," she began, defensively. "I've already had enough people come knocking to hear more of the story after he passed. I don't know what happened. I don't know why it happened. I haven't been in contact with Christopher for almost 14 years!" she said.

"Nah! It's not like that," said Jenno, his hands raised in an attempt to ease Abbey's mum's mounting tension. "I don't wanna know any gossip. I wouldn't have anyone to tell it to anyways. Nah, it's something more than that. It's just that—" Jenno paused for a moment, as if trying to push the next words out of his throat. "I feel responsible for everything..." he said, finally. He looked down at his feet, suddenly overcome by some great weight.

A breeze swept by that carried a chill with it. Jenno shivered a little as the hairs on his arms stood up. "If I hadn't got his hopes up and made him contact you, he'd still be alive. It was all because of me..."

Suddenly, the weight of it all became too much. Jenno felt tears well up in his eyes, and before he could stop them they rushed down his cheeks. "I just wanted to say I'm sorry…" said Jenno through tears.

Abbey's mum's expression softened. "It's not your fault, Jenno," she said. She put her hand on his shoulder and squeezed.

Jenno's face was in his hands, he was now sobbing uncontrollably. Abbey stood up from her seat, tears streaming down her face, and held him in her arms. The floodgates had opened, and Jenno could do nothing to stop it.

After a few minutes, Jenno collected himself enough to lift his head up again. His eyes were red and puffy, and his cheeks were still wet with tears.

"Sorry," he said, wiping his nose with the back of his hand and rubbing it into his pants.

"Do you know how he ended up in his situation?" asked Abbey's mum.

Jenno sniffed and shook his head. "He said it was because he always wanted to live his life beautifully, but he never gave me a full answer," replied Jenno.

For a moment, Abbey's mum looked as though she were about to laugh, but then her face turned almost stonelike.

"You're right, he did try to live his life beautifully. But he was never satisfied. For so many years, I tried, but there was nothing I could do. If only you could have seen him for who he was before. When we were young and in love, it didn't matter where we were or what we had, as long as we had each other. When we bought our first apartment, we used to spend entire nights just dancing together and laughing. That was beautiful, but he grew distant. All of a sudden, he'd snap at me, or he'd storm off somewhere. It was like he was always expecting something else, like whatever he had would never be enough. I used to watch him sometimes, I watched him walk from place to place as if he were in some kind of dream. Sometimes, I felt as though he were looking right through me. Do you understand what I mean, Jenno?"

Jenno didn't meet her gaze, but listened on, quietly.

"He could turn from hot to cold in a matter of seconds, and towards the end of it all I had no idea which Christopher I was coming home to. I begged him to go and talk to someone, although I knew he never would. It wasn't in his nature to ask for help. And after it all, after all of my begging, after Abbey was born, after we bought the house, the car, after we planned our lives, he went off and slept with a prostitute, and then abandoned us before I even had a chance to say anything."

Jenno's stomach sank, he shook his head in disbelief. "I'm sorry," he said, quietly, but Abbey's mum didn't seem to hear him.

"At first, I thought something horrible had happened. His phone went straight to voicemail and no one at his office had seen him. When I called the police, they checked the last place he'd used his credit card."

She stopped for a moment and breathed deeply, trying to hold back tears. "The last place he used it was at a brothel. I didn't believe it, but they checked the security cameras, and there he was…"

Jenno bent his head low, taking it all in.

"You have no idea the hurt that he caused us. He destroyed us, and for what? Christopher chose that path. He spiralled into darkness a long time ago, but, for a moment, *you* showed him light. For a moment, *you* brought him home, *you* reminded him of his daughter and all the things that he'd left behind on his search for nothingness. You reminded him of who he used to be. The Christopher I knew died a long time ago. You called him Tahiti – I suppose that's who he became in the end," she said.

Jenno studied her, and saw that in her uprightness, tight bun and strict face, there was a beauty and strength that he didn't notice before. "Yeah, nah, maybe you're right," he began." But I reckon it's wrong to say Christopher died a long time ago. Tahiti always walked around with a bundle of letters. I read them once, accidentally."

Abbey's face grew serious. The vision of Tahiti kneeling before her, holding out the letters in his hand, suddenly flashed through her mind. "He tried to give them to me," said Abbey." I should have taken them."

"Do you remember what they were about, Jenno?" asked Abbey's mum.

Jenno cast his mind back to the day he, Jimmy and Ratty found Tahiti's chest full of letters. He remembered pulling out the yellowing paper from the chest, unfolding it and reading a poem.

I have and will always love you,
Under moon and under stars.
I look towards them and wonder where you are,
Do you miss me, like I miss you?
A thousand days and nights pass so blue,
And if I could take it all back I would,
If only I ever could
Feel the warmth of you...

He repeated it, as clear as if he was holding it in his hands. "That was the only one I read," he said, afterwards.

Abbey and her mum were both crying now. Jenno looked at them curiously, unsure of what to say.

"Thank you, Jenno," said Abbey, finally. She wiped her wet face with the sleeve of her jumper, while her mum dabbed at her cheeks with some tissue she'd pulled from her pocket.

"I said some things to him that night," Abbey began." My entire life, I've been angry at him. Mum never told me what he did until I was older. When I was young, and he disappeared, I didn't know what to do or what to think. I needed him… I always needed him. But, when I saw him that night, all I saw was an empty shell. He looked hollow. I don't know how to explain it. I played out how that scenario would go in my head over and over again for so many years. I wanted to break him, like he broke Mum and I. I knew exactly what I wanted to say to him when I saw him, and I did. I said everything. But it didn't feel at all like how I thought it would. Because the man I wanted to break was already broken. Tahiti didn't deserve the things I said…"

A great gust of wind shook the jacaranda tree and sent dozens of violet flowers spinning and zigzagging slowly down. They fell about the table and into Jenno's orange juice, and caught themselves in their hair. The smell was damp and sweet. Jenno held one of the flowers in his hand, which collapsed gently into itself, unable to support its own weight.

"He's gone now," said Abbey's mum." He's free from everything. I think there's peace in that. And I think that the both of you need to let him go. It's better this way."

Abbey's mum placed her hand on Abbey's, while Jenno sat in quiet reflection.

"Jenno, if there's anything you could take from Christopher's story, it would be to cherish everything that you have, and pay no attention to what you don't. Those unrealistic expectations only lead to destruction," said Abbey's mum.

Jenno walked home not long after, going over everything in his head in silence. It was late in the afternoon, and the sun was falling.

He pictured Tahiti sitting on his hammock watching the sun set, quiet and alone with nothing but his spiced rum and his pile of crinkled letters. He saw the withered lines that ran across Tahiti's face, and his cracked, browning teeth, and wondered if Abbey's mum was right.

18

For as long as Jenno could remember, money had always been a touchy subject in the household. Whenever it was talked about or mentioned, it was with gravity and seriousness, and it was something Jenno was constantly reminded about. Everything in his life cost money. His shirts cost 10 dollars each, his pair of casual shoes cost 20, rent for their place was 650 dollars a week, internet 70 a month; he knew the shopping bill, the gas bill and the water bill. Every dollar and cent was counted and recounted by his mum, and she reminded him daily of what life cost.

Jenno grew to be uneasy around money. It made him feel uncomfortable, and in a way unworthy to have it, because of how serious it seemed to make daily life.

His dad hated everything about it, and Jenno saw the immediate change in him whenever it was brought up, or whenever he had to pay something. It always seemed to be on his dad's mind. Where it would come from, where it would go, how long it would stay and when it was coming again. These were lifelong questions that he hadn't felt like he'd got any closer to figuring out, and ones that Jenno had learned to stress over too, even though there was nothing he could do about it.

"They only want you for money. That's all these fuckin' cunts ever seem to care about. Money, money, money," he said one day after opening up what Jenno thought looked like an overdue fee notice from the mail.

Jenno saw the change in his mood and tried to ease the situation. "It's just money, Dad..."

"Just money?" his dad replied, and Jenno knew instantly that he'd made a mistake. "That money is hours of my life I can't get back. That money is the food that you eat, the clothes you wear and the school you go to. That money's the reason we don't go on holidays and the constant reminder that I've done fuck all with my life and I got fuck all to show for it! Just fuckin' money... You're a kid right now. Money shouldn't mean anything to you. Enjoy it while you can. Just wait till you have a family, Jenno, then you'll see what that money is worth."

Jenno didn't say anything. He put his hand on his dad's shoulder; his dad reached up and patted it.

"Sorry, mate. You shouldn't have to see stuff like this," he said, throwing the overdue notice on the table.

Jenno was silent.

His dad stood up from the table and two coloured pencils rolled off. Jenno went to pick them up but his dad waved his hand. "Ah, just fuckin' leave 'em, mate, I'll pick 'em up when I get back."

"Where're you going, Dad?" asked Jenno.

"Goin' to a mate's for a few beers," he said, then walked out the door without looking back.

Jenno looked down at the table; there were pencils scattered everywhere, along with a few pieces of paper that had been half drawn on, but crossed out before they were completed.

One looked like it would have been the start of a drawing of a windmill; his dad had got as far as drawing the outline and what looked like a little barn house before they were crossed out. The other two looked like they could have been the beginnings of trees with giant roots, but they too were crossed out and strewn across the table.

And then Jenno's eyes stopped on the overdue notice. His heart started racing as he lifted his hand slowly, almost secretively towards it, as if he was expecting it to be hot to the touch. He was afraid of what it might say – as if by reading it, he'd be drowned in an aspect of life he wasn't ready for – but he couldn't stop himself.

His fingers closed around the edge of the letter gently, but before he had a chance to read it, his mum walked through the front door.

"I'm home!" she said.

Jenno let go of the letter and put his hands behind his back in an attempt to look as innocent as possible, but his mum noticed the look of guilt on his face.

"What's wrong? What have you done?" she asked, worriedly.

"Nothing, Mum!" he said, defensively.

She threw her handbag on the sofa and walked over to the table, then stopped when she saw the letter.

She picked it up and looked at Jenno.

"I didn't look at it, I swear," said Jenno, quickly.

He studied her face as she read it. A few emotions were on her face all at once as she read. Initially there was shock, and then anger, sadness and, finally, despair.

"Fuck…" she said quietly. Jenno very rarely heard her swear.

"What is it, Mum? Dad read it just before and didn't seem that phased, I thought it just looked like an overdue notice…"

"I can't say. Not until your dad gets back. Where did he go?"

"I'm not sure… He just left."

She raced over to her handbag and pulled out her phone.

She dialled his number but it rang out.

"What's wrong?" Jenno asked, desperate to know; he felt like a little boy again.

But before he could say anything else, she took the letter into her bedroom and closed the door.

He knocked on the door to her room. "Mum, are you ok?"

It sounded as though she was crying.

He opened the door ajar; the lights were off and the curtains were drawn. He could feel her presence in the darkness somewhere – she was sobbing into her pillow.

"Mum…" he said.

"Please, Jenno… leave me alone for a little while, I just need some time to myself."

"Alright. I love you…" he said weakly as he went to close the door, but he spotted the letter laying on the floor, and picked it up before he left. He looked down at the letter, his heart beating, and read *EVICTION NOTICE* on the front.

A strange sensation came over him. It felt as though whatever had caused this, it was because of him. Suddenly he was overcome with the urge to make things right.

He looked down at the eviction notice and felt a change inside of him. It was a feeling of uncertainty, and a deep existential dread of the future.

The little moments that make the story of our lives are suspended forever in a garden full of memories. Frozen in many little frames like pictures on the wall. Somewhere where we all belong are our youthful souls, surrounded by the ambience of the universe. You see yourself in daydreams, doing what you used to do for eternity, even though we are no longer there in the present. Over time some of those memories fracture, and the weeds of grief grow from the cracks. Not grief for what was, but grief for what could have been, now that everything is so clear. You were too young to understand at the time, as the pieces fell about you, you dealt with them accordingly because you knew nothing else. That is the beauty and sadness of life. To live just on the cusp of knowing, but never really understanding anything at all until its gone and done. Frozen forever there, where all things go in the end, suspended and silent in the sunlight and in the moonlight.

Those memories are lived over again, and again and again, until we've lived them over so many times that they get tampered with and they're no longer what they were before. People stay in our memories forever, even when they're not with us anymore.

Grief. So much grief. Silent grief. In yawning gaps of life when nothing is said at all. When we're alone, thinking of what was that no longer is, and our part in it all. Grief. When our loving words fall upon ears that can't hear them anymore. When things we wanted to tell people are never said. Lives that were never lived together and roads that were once travelled with people are now travelled alone. All in grief.

...

Jenno ran outside to go and find his dad.

His car was gone. Jenno grabbed his skateboard and rode off towards the local Bowlo.

It was a place where his dad spent a lot of time, and his first guess as to where he might have gone.

But when he got there the place was empty. His dad wasn't in the smoking area, the pokies or down at the pool tables.

Jenno rode down to the beach; he knew that his dad liked to sit and watch the waves with the car radio on sometimes. But the only people who were there were Dizz and some of the older boys. They were sitting on a brick wall on the beach side of the carpark with some beers. Dizz was sitting on the floor with his back against the wall. He still had a bandage on his head from when he'd hit the curb.

"What's doin', Jenno?" asked Dizz when Jenno skated past them.

"Just lookin' for my old man, you seen him here?"

Dizz shook his head.

"Yeah, I saw him goin' over the river like half an hour ago," said Slowy, atop the wall above Dizz.

The river was too far away to skate to, but it did tell Jenno that his dad was headed towards the city or down south somewhere.

When he got home his mum was still in her bedroom. He didn't knock. Instead he went to the kitchen and put the kettle on. He looked around the kitchen while he waited for the water to boil. On the fridge were his old school photos and his parents' wedding photos, and a few random birthday cards here and there. Things that he saw every day but never took any notice of. The clock was leant up against the wall above the counter. The sound of its hands ticking was the only noise in the world besides the sound of the water boiling in the kettle. It was the same clock they'd owned forever. The same one he learned to tell the time on, and even on his loneliest, quietest days the clock was always ticking. It had its own noise, and one that Jenno had never appreciated until that moment when the water started to boil. Suddenly he felt protective of it all, as if at any moment it could all be lost. The littlest things had somehow created the foundation of all his memories, like some tiny orchestra that had made the soundtrack of his life. The ticking of the kitchen clock, the humming of the fridge, the sound of the toilet flushing from the lady who lived upstairs. The sound of waves crashing in the distance. A feeling in his stomach was telling him that it was all about to change.

He grabbed a mug and made a tea, and sat up on the kitchen bench while he drank.

Half an hour passed before the door to his mum's room opened and she slowly walked out.

Her hair was up and she was trying to keep composed, as if nothing had happened at all. But she was given away by the redness in her eyes and cheeks.

"Are you ok?" asked Jenno.

She smiled; it was a tender smile, almost apologetic.

"I'm ok. Sometimes I just need to cry," she said. She was holding the letter in her hand.

"What's happening?"

"You would have found out soon enough anyway," she said, handing him the letter.

Jenno took the letter and straightened out the creases. When he finished reading it, he looked up at his mum. "Where are we going to go?"

"I don't know. But I don't think we can afford to live near the beach anymore."

Jenno's stomach sank. "What do you mean? We lived here and did fine until now…"

"Only because Mike is an old friend of your grandmother's. I knew this day would come eventually. I just ignored all the signs."

"I can work more and pay towards the rent!" said Jenno, suddenly inspired by the idea of washing dishes with Jimmy down at the café.

She laughed at this. "We're going to need a lot more than 200 dollars a week…" A forlorn expression fell across Jenno's face. "But thank you. And don't worry, Jenno. Save your money for yourself. I don't want you to stress about this. This is my stress, I'll figure something out," Jenno's mum added, after seeing the look on his face.

"Where's Dad gone?" said Jenno.

"I don't know," she replied. Her face suddenly hardened.

"Is he gonna come back?"

She didn't reply. She walked into the kitchen and poured herself a tea from the kettle, walked into the back garden and sat on a little wooden stool outside.

…

Jenno rode to Jimmy's place, unsure of how to feel about it all.

He didn't feel anything yet. About the house, about his mum or even his dad. He was almost angry at himself that he felt emotionless, and deep down he wondered if there was something wrong with him. He felt like he should have taken it worse, or acted like his whole world had come down around him, but he felt nothing.

Jimmy was sitting playing computer games when Jenno looked into his bedroom window. Jenno stared at him for a few seconds before he glanced up quickly, back down and then back up again in shock. "OH, FUCK!"

Jenno laughed to himself as Jimmy came over and opened the window. "Fuck you! You scared the shit out of me," he said, laughing.

"What's doin'?" asked Jenno.

Jimmy looked back over his shoulder at his laptop and then back to Jenno. "Nothing…"

Ten minutes later they were skating down the street, crisscrossing one another as they rode.

The sky was purple and violet over the horizon, but inland it was blazed in golden flames. In the middle, where both night and day met for a short time, there was a turquoise that tapered off into a soft pink.

Cars passing on the street were beginning to turn on their headlights, and street by street rows of lights lit up all at once, as if some theme park had suddenly come to life.

They rode to the beach and then walked up the top of the headland.

They followed the dirt path up to the main lookout, but halfway up they took a sharp right turn and bush-bashed for a couple of metres before finding an overgrown path that led up to the local smoke spot. At the top of the path there sat an old sofa and a weathered wooden table low enough to rest your feet on.

They leaned their skateboards against the side of the sofa and sat down. All around their feet were used nitrogen cartridges, old balloons and various makeshift bongs, left there by the local grubs and feral children. But the view of the ocean was beautiful. Night had won over day, and now the moon was in the sky. As it rose, it cast a pathway of white light across the steadily darkening sea.

Jenno told Jimmy all that had happened that afternoon. About his dad leaving, about his mum crying and about the eviction notice. Jimmy looked down as Jenno talked, listening to everything.

"So, where are you gonna move?" he asked after Jenno had finished.

"I dunno. You know as much as I do now. Hopefully we don't move far, but Mum reckons we will."

Jimmy was quiet.

They watched a cloud of bats fly over; they could just make out the curvature of their wings against the deep purple sky.

...

Across the headland, in their own spot, were Fleetwood, Adriaan and Milly.

Fleetwood was holding Milly's hand while she smelled all the different coloured flowers that grew around the headland. Adriaan was sitting on a picnic blanket a few metres away, a smile on his face while he watched Milly and Fleetwood laughing together. It was a strange feeling to him, and one he suspected was too big to understand fully at that moment.

Watching Fleetwood and Milly, instead of his wife and Milly, was a feeling of bittersweet understanding, of a universal irony, a deep grief, but beyond all of it a sensation of thankfulness he had never thought possible after losing the love of his life. He couldn't tell if he was happy or sad, and figured in moments like these they were one and the same. A rare moment in life where we see it for what it is, just a moment in time, with a beginning and end, a beautiful blast and flourish into a slow fade, or sometimes a sudden collapse.

Back at Adriaan's house they put Milly to bed and then watched a movie. Fleetwood fell asleep midway through, so they went to bed themselves.

Adriaan awoke the next morning to find that Fleetwood had already left, as she had done every time she stayed over.

It was still dark outside. Adriaan got out of bed and went to check on Milly. He opened her door quietly and stuck his head in; she was fast asleep.

He grabbed a jumper and walked to the beach.

The crown of the sun was just rising from beneath the sea when he got to the beach carpark. He looked over to the base of the sand dunes and saw Fleetwood in the distance, sitting on her knees with her hands resting on her legs.

"I had a feeling you'd be here," he said, smiling.

She looked up and smiled.

"I hope you don't mind me intruding, I just wanted to give you some company…"

Fleetwood looked at the open spot next to her, and Adriaan sat down.

The world was slowly coming back to life. One by one, the clouds turned from dark morning grey to deep, fiery red, and in the waking of the day the birds called out to one another.

"This is where I come to be with my son," said Fleetwood, after some time. "You must think I'm crazy coming here every morning and talking to him. I know a lot of people do."

"I don't think you're crazy."

Fleetwood didn't reply.

It was quiet for a time. The light from the sun radiated off of the water as it rose higher into the sky, bathing them both in golden light.

Fleetwood closed her eyes. Her lips were moving silently.

Everything fell into place the moment the sun had fully risen.

Adriaan looked at Fleetwood and realised that he was in love.

Fleetwood, as if sensing his gaze, opened her eyes and smiled at him. "What are you smiling for?" she asked.

"Nothing, I'm just happy," he said.

"I'm happy too. I've loved spending all this time with Milly. You're very lucky."

"We're lucky to have been able to spend it with you. Milly loves you; in fact, she never shuts up about you, it's getting annoying now…" He laughed.

Fleetwood's expression changed. "But whenever I go back home, I remember that my boy is gone… and that I'm alone. It's been a confusing couple of months."

"I couldn't start to imagine what you've gone through. It was strange watching you and Milly together last night. I was happy and sad at the same time," he said, but then added, "in a good way…"

"It was the same for me too. It felt right, and wrong…"

"Yeah… But please don't feel alone… Milly and I are always here."

"I know…" said Fleetwood. She smiled and rested her head against his shoulder.

He kissed her on the cheek and put his arm around her waist.

Not long after, he left Fleetwood at the beach and walked home to check on Milly. He opened her door quietly and stuck his head through. She was still fast asleep.

He put the kettle on and prepared breakfast. Pancakes with fruit and yogurt on the side.

When she was up, Milly asked where Fleetwood had gone. Adriaan lifted her up onto his lap while she ate breakfast, and he sipped his coffee and read an article from the local newspaper. Some story about a gang of youths that had been going around pushing over letterboxes and spray-painting people's front fences. It was an entertaining read.

...

Fleetwood had realised that she was in love too. When Adriaan had gone home, she stayed at the beach for longer than usual, thinking about it all.

She was in love and she was terrified. She couldn't go through it all again. Loving and then losing. It seemed as though that was the cycle of her life. She was tired now, and empty. She felt like there was nothing left for life to take from her besides life itself.

She thought about going back to London to be around her family, or even back to Trinidad to stay with her granny. At least there she would be surrounded by music and food and family.

But she couldn't leave Ratty.

19

The Garden of Eden of early childhood is one that has never felt the pain of loss, or of failure and shortcoming, because everything that is has always been. It's only when we get older that we realise that there were things astray, and our parents, who we looked up to as unbreakable beings of strength and guidance, were fighting every day just to keep afloat financially and emotionally. The wonder and thankfulness comes when we realise that, in the face of that responsibility, we were none the wiser to their pain.

It was the end of term at Oceanside High School, and that meant two things. One was that school would be out for two weeks, and the other was that the boys would have to bring home their report cards. Jenno was never stressed, his mum just hoped he didn't fail too many subjects that he'd have to repeat. But it was a time that Jimmy dreaded. He was a smart kid, and usually did well when he applied himself. But after Ratty's passing, and his introduction to girls, his marks had plummeted significantly. His mother was reluctant to scold him for it. She watched him always with a worried expression, as any mother would have done if their child had gone through something like that. But his father was relentless. He would come home from work late most days, and Jimmy rarely saw him during the week. But when he was around he was always distant. There was nothing Jimmy wanted more in life than to make his father proud. He'd never told Jimmy he was proud of him once. In his mind, he was strengthening him and driving him to succeed. But it was what strained the relationship the most and made it one based on results, not acceptance. It was the one thing he was jealous of Jenno for. His dad was no angel, and had a mountain of issues himself, but he loved Jenno for who he was, and was accepting of who he was. And to Jimmy, it felt like his father would never be satisfied until Jimmy was the best at something.

The bell rang for the end of term and everyone rushed out of the classrooms. Jimmy got out before Jenno and waited for him at the front gate. He was fingering his report card nervously; it was still in the envelope, ready to be opened.

"Yeeeeww! School's out, let's get out of this shithole!" said Jenno as he skipped out of the front gate.

"How'd you go on your report card?" asked Jimmy.

"I got like three Cs, two Ds, an E and an A!"

"An A?" Jimmy repeated.

"Yeah, dude, I got an A." Jenno laughed.

"What for?"

"Music."

"Huh? I didn't know you played music…"

"Yeah, I play piano, it's fuckin' easy," said Jenno. "What marks did you get?"

Jimmy looked down at the envelope. "I haven't checked yet."

"What? Why?"

"I dunno, just nervous I guess."

Jenno started laughing. "Nervous? What do you mean, they're school marks…"

"Yeah, I know, but my dad wants me to do three-unit maths next year."

"Fuck that cunt," said Jenno.

"Don't say that about my dad…" said Jimmy.

"Nah, yeah, you're right, sorry. But still, fuck him. Do you wanna do three-unit maths?"

"I dunno what I wanna do…"

"Fuck, well, I can't help you then. Just open it, at least, I wanna see how you went," said Jenno, looking down curiously at the large brown envelope clutched in Jimmy's hands.

Jimmy eyed it fearfully before he tore the seal and pulled the cards out.

Jenno watched his eyes widen as he studied the pages intently. He looked up and down, left to right and back again.

"All good?" asked Jenno, watching the look of distress ripple across Jimmy's face.

"Dude, I'm fucked…" said Jimmy, helplessly.

Jenno grabbed the cards and looked at them. "What do you mean… you got all Cs? That's heaps good!"

"Nah, dude, I don't reckon I'll get into three-unit maths…"

"Fuck yeah! That's what you wanted, wasn't it?" said Jenno.

"No, dude, I said I didn't know! But now I can't do it anyways even if I did… Fuck sakes, my dad's gonna go skitz."

Jenno paused for a moment, weighing up what Jimmy had said, and then came to a sudden understanding, which he followed with a faint, "Yeah, faarrk."

They walked passed the school carpark, and Jenno looked at Jimmy confused, "We not driving?"

"Nah," Jimmy began, "Mum's got the car."

Jimmy didn't say much else on the walk home, and what would have usually been an excited rush to get back and get out of his school uniform now felt like a hopeless march towards his inevitable doom.

The fork in the road came, and they said goodbye to one another. Jenno raced home to grab his surfboard, while Jimmy walked reluctantly back to his place.

He opened the front door; no one was home yet.

He placed his bag onto his bed when he got into his room and closed the door gently. For the rest of the afternoon before his father came home from work, he cleaned the house in a vain attempt to soften the blow that he was sure would come.

At six o'clock he heard the front door open. His father walked through and placed his coat on the hanger by the door. His work shoes clopped against the marble floor as he walked, the sound echoing down the hallway and into Jimmy's room.

His stomach sank as he walked down the stairs.

"Jimmy, how was your day?" said his father as he undid his tie and walked towards the wine cupboard in the kitchen.

"Yeah, good," said Jimmy, hoping a short response would avert attention from him.

"Did you get your report card today?"

Jimmy's stomach sank.

"Yeah…"

"And?"

Jimmy pulled out the report card from his bag and handed it over.

His father took it and inspected it.

His face grew serious as his eyes scanned across the paper.

"All Cs," he said, calmly.

"Uhh, yeah," said Jimmy, hesitantly.

"Are you happy with yourself?" His dad placed the report card down on the living room table.

"No..." said Jimmy, stooping his head low so he wouldn't have to look at his father's face.

"Then why did you do so badly?"

"I'm sorry..."

"Sorry? Don't apologise to me, apologise to yourself. How do you think your life is going to go if you just get by? All Cs... You think you have any chance of being successful with all Cs?"

"No," said Jimmy.

"Do you understand the privilege you have? Going to school every day, living by the beach, having a roof over your head. Do you understand how the rest of the world lives?"

Jimmy didn't look up.

"You disrespect all of them by not living to your full potential. Do you know how many people would kill to be in your position? They would KILL, Jimmy, and all you seem to do is mope around all day and do fuck all. You've disappointed me."

"I'm sorry, Dad," said Jimmy.

"Bah!" His father threw up his hand and walked to the kitchen. The conversation was over.

Jimmy went up to his room and looked at himself in the mirror. He hated what he saw. The scrawny boy in the reflection looked weak and pathetic.

But a flame had risen in him, and a thirst to prove himself.

...

The next morning, he woke up early and caught the bus to the city. He wanted to feel what it was like to be a part of it all. The hustle and bustle. All the people coming and going from meetings, lunches, calls and drinks. When he got off the bus he looked at all the faces walking by, and very few of them looked happy.

He hoped that being surrounded by people would make him feel some sense of belonging, but the effect was the opposite.

He wondered how he could find himself in a city swarming with people, stuffing themselves into subway trains and buses and somehow feel lonelier than he did before. People stepped and weaved and dodged one another on busy walkways, they rubbed shoulders with him all day long, but he may as well have not been there at all, it wouldn't have made any difference. It was a city full of noise, full of people talking. People on their phones, people selling things, people preaching their beliefs and people pushing for political agendas. There were people everywhere he looked. He could stick out his arm and touch one. Yet, he felt alone.

He wondered if all those people felt just as lonely as him. There were too many faces, too many bodies, too many voices and sounds. Too many stories. So many that they all cancelled one another, or muddled each other up, and at the end they all seemed like blurs. Faces undefined and conversations just out of ear's reach. The people preaching couldn't be heard over the people selling things, and at the end of the day it all began to sound like the same thing anyways.

After a while, he hopped back on the bus and watched the world go by out of the window on the way home.

...

The two weeks of holidays came and went quicker than the ones before. They were uneventful, but Jimmy had found a new drive within himself to do well at school.

Jenno, on the other hand, was the opposite. The idea of going to school filled him with an existential dread, and he was finding more and more excuses to skip it and surf all day instead. His love for surfing grew every day. And in the face of the turmoil at home, he turned to the ocean for quiet and understanding.

There is an energy in the ocean much greater than what we can comprehend. A perfect wave is almost like a miracle. It takes every element of nature to be in tune with one another for a perfect wave to form. The wind, the tide, the swell and also the sandbanks. All four of them need to line up in order for the perfect wave to take place. It didn't happen often, and when it did it was usually packed with people to the point where there may as well have not been any waves at all. Too many times had the boys watched in dismay as perfect waves rolled by in front of them, ridden by two or three people at once, all of whom were shouting at one another. But every now and then there would be a perfect wave with no one else out, and those were special days. It had happened maybe once or twice over the years, when the boys had wagged school for the day and found the lineup empty. Most of the time there were people surfing during the weekdays, older versions of themselves who had checked the swell forecast and had pulled a sickie from work.

Early one morning, a freak storm had happened out to sea, and in the wake an unexpected surge of swell had risen from the east.

Jimmy and Jenno were on their way to school when Jenno checked the beach livestream on his phone.

"Get fucked…" he said, stopping in his tracks.

"What?" said Jimmy curiously.

"Have a look at the fuckin' swell! It's double overhead and barrelling!"

Jimmy took the phone and covered the screen with his hand to block the glare of the morning sun.

"Holy shit… I thought it was meant to be flat today."

Jenno grabbed the phone back off of him and looked at it once more.

"Fuck this shit, dude, there's no way I'm going to school…"

"It looks pretty good. But I can't skip a day, my dad will kill me…"

Jenno looked at Jimmy almost desperately, as if Jimmy saying no was the one thing stopping him from surfing the session of a lifetime.

Jimmy looked at Jenno's face, and then over to the front gate of the school down the road.

"Fuck sakes…" he said to himself, knowing deep down that there would be repercussions. "Fine, I'll go. But for two hours max. We'll have to say we had an emergency or something…"

"YES!" screamed Jenno, jumping in the air with excitement.

They took the backroads towards Jenno's place. His mum started work at 8:30AM down at the medical centre. He knew she left the house at around quarter-past. It was 10 past as they walked down Jenno's street.

"I'm gonna take the big board today, I reckon I might need the extra speed. What you gonna take?"

Jimmy thought for a second. "I dunno, maybe I'll just watch…"

"Come on, man…" said Jenno, "this might be the best surf of your life!"

"Yeah, I know… I just dunno if I'm ready to surf again."

"If you're not ready now you're never gonna be…" said Jenno. "Just bring a board at least. I still got one of yours in my garage anyways…"

"One of mine?"

"Yeah… That big wave board you found in—" Jenno stopped suddenly, peering down the road at his mum's little bubble car making its way towards them.

"Fuck, dude, hide!"

Jenno leapt behind a car and Jimmy, who was a few paces back and caught off guard, didn't think quick enough and was left standing.

The car slowed to a stop and the window lowered.

"Good morning, Jimmy," Jenno's mum said.

"Good morning," he replied, flustered.

She eyed him closely, suspecting something. "Where's Jenno? I thought you two walked to school together…"

"Yeah, nah, ah yeah— We did, I just dropped my earphones and came back for them."

"What, and Jenno didn't come back to help you find them?" she asked.

Jimmy shook his head. "Nah, he didn't…"

"He's a little shit, isn't he?" she said. Jimmy feigned a laugh and nodded enthusiastically.

"Alright, well, good luck searching and have a good day!" she said.

"You too," said Jimmy; his legs felt heavy.

When she turned the corner at the end of the road Jenno pulled himself back up.

"Fuck, that was close!" he said.

"Yeah…" said Jimmy. "Dude, I dunno if I wanna surf anymore, I got a bad feeling about it."

"What do you mean? You'll be sweet, man," said Jenno.

"Yeah, I dunno, it's just a gut feeling."

"Well, tell your gut to stop being pussy…"

"What if we get caught?"

"Fuck it, dude, I'm gonna be a chippy anyways."

Jenno had worked out that being a chippy – a carpenter – might suit him best. It was an honest job, but more importantly it was one with a knockoff time of three o'clock, which meant that Jenno could still surf every day.

They got to Jenno's place and grabbed their boards. Then they ran to the beach and were amazed to find the carpark empty. Everyone was at work.

"This is crazy!" said Jenno, excitedly.

"Yeah…" said Jimmy.

He looked out across the beach. There were no people on the sand. The water looked calm and blue, and in the path of the sunlight the water glared white-hot. No waves had formed yet, but even in the stillness the water had an energy to it. A minute later the first set of waves formed. They were even bigger than the boys had thought. Walls of crystal blue water rolled in from the horizon, pitched and then raced across the sandbank towards the shore, where they finally exploded into white water. They were beautiful. Both of the boys pictured themselves riding them, and knew that they could do it. They were big waves, bigger than either of them had ever surfed, but they were perfect.

The two of them ran towards the water, laughing with excitement.

Jimmy had forgotten about his gut feeling; it felt good to be holding a board under his arm again. It was a feeling he hadn't realised he'd missed so much.

The water was warm and the breeze was slight.

When they paddled out the back Jenno looked over at Jimmy. "How're you feeling?"

"Good," he said. He was still making sense of it all. It felt as though he'd never stopped surfing.

It all felt natural. The push and the pull of the water, the currents and gentle bobbing. Jimmy couldn't help but smile to himself; it was as though some dark cloud had been washed away by the water, and he'd just felt the warmth of the sun again for the first time in a long while.

The first set of waves rolled through. They were enormous, but Jimmy was able to paddle around them easily. Jenno, on the other hand, turned around and paddled for them.

Jimmy watched in amazement as Jenno stood up and free fell down the face of the wave, landing at the bottom and scooping up to the centre again. It had been a long time since Jimmy had seen Jenno surf. He was starting to surf like the older boys.

"How was that?" Jimmy asked when Jenno paddled back past him.

"Was good, I want one of the bigger ones now," he said determinedly.

A bird flew past; Jimmy looked up at its underside as it glided over them.

The sky was clear, the only clouds he could see were far off into the horizon, and looked more like colossal snow-covered mountains than anything else.

The headland stood bold and jagged against the backdrop of the sea and the beach was yellow and clean. It was one of those days.

Jenno had near enough surfed himself out by the time he sat next to Jimmy, out of breath but smiling.

"Dude, this is fuckin' crazy! Did you see my last wave?" he asked.

"Nah, but I saw your others. It's so beautiful out here," said Jimmy.

Jenno gave him a funny look. "Have you caught anything?" he asked.

Jimmy paused for a moment before he shook his head. "Nah, not yet… I dunno If I can."

"You just gotta go for it! They look way heavier than they are. I ate it on one but it barely held me down," said Jenno, seriously.

"Yeah…" Jimmy trailed off.

"Next wave that comes, you gotta go it. Otherwise, I get a free shot," said Jenno.

"No way… A free shot where?"

"Wherever I want," laughed Jenno.

Jimmy didn't say anything. He lay on his board and watched the horizon closely, waiting for any sign of a wave.

A few minutes of stillness passed, Jimmy peered at his submerged hand, made pruney and pale by the water. He took a breath and dunked his head in the water, listening to the salt crackling for a few moments before opening his eyes and peering into the empty darkness below. Suddenly, Jenno whooped. Jimmy looked up to see a set of dark, heavy-looking waves rising just ahead.

"Go it, Jimmy!" Jenno screamed, way off in his periphery.

Without thinking, Jimmy turned and paddled as hard as he could. He could feel the wave picking him up, and he watched in a mixture of fear and excitement as he climbed higher and higher above the water bed. In that moment, it felt as though there was nothing else in the world besides himself and the wave. He stood up as fast as he could and felt his stomach flutter as he plummeted down the face of the wave. He wobbled at the bottom, but managed to steady himself. He could hear Jenno cheering him on somewhere in the distance, but he could have been a world away for what it mattered. Jimmy held on, and managed to climb the wall of the wave. He could feel its full power beneath him as his board skimmed across the water, and buckled his knees with every bump. Before him was eternity; he steadied himself and danced with its energy. Life pumped through his heart and shot through his fingers and his toes, and before he could stop himself he roared with excitement.

When the wave was over he pulled off and sat on his board, grinning to himself with delight.

"You sick cunt!" said Jenno, when Jimmy finally made it back out.

"Did you see that!" said Jimmy, laughing.

"See, I told you they weren't that heavy," said Jenno, smiling. But, before he could say anything else another set of waves rolled towards them.

They surfed for a few hours before they finally got out and headed back to school.

It was a once-in-a-few-years kind of morning, and neither of them cared if they got in trouble over it.

They did get in trouble. When they finally arrived to class, word was given to the headteacher, Mr. Pollard. He was a tall, slender man with a small pointy face that was permanently fixed with a look of annoyance. He was cruel, impatient, spiteful and just an absolute ballsack of a human being in general. He hated his job and his life, and took it out on his students.

He had already taken an instant disliking to both Jimmy and Jenno, and nothing they ever did got past him. Jenno despised him; Jimmy was indifferent.

He pulled both of them out of their classes at once when he'd heard they'd finally arrived at school.

"Now," he said to them at his office. He made them sit down and began pacing around the room with his hands behind his back. Jenno thought it was a little theatrical, like he'd practiced it a bunch before they'd come. "Tell me this once, and be honest. Where have you been?"

He eyed Jimmy and Jenno seriously, assessing which one he thought he could crack first.

Jimmy's mouth twitched and Mr. Pollard swooped down on him like an owl.

"Someone had a crash and we stayed and helped out until the tow truck came..." said Jimmy.

"Oh yeah, how nice of you both!" Mr. Pollard replied. "But it does seem strange... I could have sworn I saw what looked like exactly you two surfing down at the beach?"

"What do you mean?" asked Jenno, innocently.

Mr. Pollard twisted his desktop screen around. There was a screenshot from the online surf camera; it was of Jimmy and Jenno running across the sand.

"Looks an awful lot like you two. When neither of you showed up to class this morning I had a feeling I knew where I'd find you both. And here it was... I could recognise your slouch from anywhere, Jimmy."

Jimmy straightened his back in his seat, suddenly aware of his slumped posture.

Mr. Pollard hit the space bar on the keyboard and another screenshot showed Jenno on a wave. It was one of the biggest waves of the day; Jenno's body looked tiny in comparison.

"Fark... could you send me that, sir?" asked Jenno.

"You think this is a joke, mate?" Mr. Pollard began. "You were on your last warning already… And you, Jimmy – you used to be a half-decent student. What happened, mate? You're about to be going into your HSC…"

"I'm sorry, sir, I know…" said Jimmy, looking down and feeling disappointed in himself.

Jenno looked at him, trying not to laugh at the look on his face.

"I suppose you think none of that matters with your old man's money? Well, we can't all be as fortunate as you, Jimmy. Oh! If only I could live in a mansion, date a model and go surfing every day!"

"A model?" asked Jenno.

"His mum, mate…"

"That's fucked, sir… that's his mum!" said Jenno indignantly.

"I don't think I remember asking you to speak," said Mr. Pollard. "You're suspended, Jimmy. Get your bag and go home. I've called your mum already. As for you, Jenno, I've already called your mum. She'll be here at lunchtime and we can have a meeting."

Jimmy and Jenno left the room. Jenno wasn't allowed to go back to class; instead, he had to sit outside the staffroom until his mum got there.

"Fark, suspended! That's heavy…" said Jenno.

"Yeah… I wonder what's going to happen to you," said Jimmy, standing near the doorway that led to the grounds.

"Dunno," Jenno began, "probably gonna expel me, I reckon."

"You think so?"

"Yeah! Didn't you hear what he said? I was on my last warning…"

"Yeah... I didn't realise you were on such thin ice..."

"It was bound to happen. The first warning was when I made Champo cry in class, and then the second warning was when I locked Mr. Garret in the toilets. I was lucky to make it this far, to be honest." Jenno laughed.

"Yeah... Well, good luck, anyways. I guess I'll see you later," said Jimmy, and then he left the room and went home.

...

Jimmy got home and took his uniform off. His parents wouldn't be home until later. He considered for a second. Something was running through him that he hadn't felt for the longest time. It was yearning and an excitement. It was as if his whole body was being drawn back to the ocean. He put on his board shorts, grabbed his surfboard and ran back down to the beach.

The waves were slightly smaller, but still perfect. There wasn't a soul about, and he laughed out loud, whooped and screamed with delight.

He was out all day without any sunscreen on. When he got home he looked like a bomb had just gone off in his hands. His face was bright red and his hair was stuck up stiff by saltwater and wind. He tried to clean his hair up before his parents came home, but even after showering it was still thick.

When his parents got back, his mother walked right by him without looking. She went to the kitchen and put the kettle on for some tea. His father followed a moment later. He stood at the door and looked at Jimmy in cold silence.

Jimmy was quiet; he knew what was about to come.

His father nodded to the living room, and Jimmy walked in and sat down on the sofa.

His father pulled his coat off, walked over to the kitchen and poured himself a glass of wine. His business shoes clip-clopped against the cold floor tiles and echoed across the large room.

When he had finished pouring the glass, he walked over and sat opposite Jimmy.

Jimmy readied himself for the lecture that would come.

"You're a disgrace," he said. That was it.

Jimmy looked at him, confused for a moment, before the meaning of what he'd said came crashing down.

A *disgrace*.

His father stood up and placed his empty glass upon the table, then left the room, went upstairs to his bedroom and closed the door. Jimmy's mother was standing by the living-room table in silence.

She looked conflicted, divided between being a parent and being a mother. The parent side of her knew that Jimmy needed to be disciplined, but the mother side of her wanted only to comfort him. The result of the internal battle within herself was a twisted expression on her face. Jimmy looked up at her, tears swelling up in his eyes.

She turned away and left the room.

Jimmy sat in silence for a while, then went to his room as well.

He was lying on his bed looking up at the ceiling when Jenno called him.

"Sup, brah," said Jenno.

"Hey, how'd you go?" Jimmy asked.

"Yeah… they expelled me," said Jenno.

"What are you going to do?"

"I dunno, I reckon I'll work at the café for a bit then just get an apprenticeship, I'm not even that phased, to be honest. Mum doesn't really care that much either."

"Really?"

"Well, she's kinda disappointed, for sure. But she knew I was just gonna end up doin' a trade anyways. So, in a way I'm getting a head start from all the other fuckwits who are gonna finish school and do a trade."

"Yeah, I guess so…" said Jimmy.

"Fuckin'…" Jenno began, "I'll be fully qualified at like 20 years old, cunt, earning like 40 bucks an hour while you're at uni on the dole and eating people's leftovers right off their plates."

"No way you're gonna earn 40 bucks an hour!"

"One hundred percent I will. My uncle's a sparky and he reckons he earns like 300K a year in the mines."

"Yeah, but would you really want to work in the mines?"

"Fuckin' oath I would!"

"What about surfing? Can't do that in the mines…"

"Yeah, but miners work two weeks on, two weeks off. My uncle reckons a lot of them live in Bali and just fly over every two weeks. So while you're surfing here with 300 other sweaters getting in your way, I'll be surfing empty waves in Indonesia."

"That does sound pretty good."

"Yeah, I reckon I'll be sweet. How'd your parents take it?" Jenno asked.

"Not good."

Jimmy told Jenno about the afternoon, and what his father had said to him.

"Damn, that's heavy. I dunno, man, what do you think?"

"I'm not sure. I'm disappointed in myself a little bit. But I feel happy also, in a weird way. I haven't felt that alive in a long time – after we surfed, I mean. I don't care about what my dad thinks anymore. He's miserable all the time. I look at him, and all the money he's got, but all he does is work and drink, and I think to myself, is that who I wanna be?"

"Yeah…" Jenno began, "my dad does that too, but he lives in a shithole. I dunno if it's the money that's the cause of it all."

"Yeah. I think maybe it's the expectation. My dad's never satisfied. Honestly, I haven't seen him laugh properly in years."

"My dad's the same. He always wanted to be an artist. He told me not that long ago that he never wanted me. That I was an accident that trapped him into the life he has now."

"That's awful."

"Yeah… but also fuck it, what was he expecting from life? Everyone always reckons they're destined to be shit, but the only thing we're probably destined to be is parents, and somehow most people fuck it up. My mum's a good parent at least…" added Jenno. "My dad is as well, I guess. He's paid for everything, but he hates me for it. My mum just loves me."

"Yeah, my mum as well. Have you heard from your dad?"

"Nah…" Jenno replied.

Jimmy didn't know what to say. He could tell by Jenno's response that he didn't want to talk about it.

"You wanna surf tomorrow?" asked Jenno.

"No way! My dad will murder me if he finds out…"

"Yeah, true. Well, if you change your mind I'm gonna be out there mid morning."

"Yeah, sweet," said Jimmy, and then he hung up.

He lay back down on his bed and thought about his   father.

"Happiness is the most important thing in the world," he said to himself, as if the thought had suddenly dawned on him. "I don't care what I do anymore. Like Jenno said: Rich or poor, both of our dads are miserable. It's   all   about   being   happy…"

The world suddenly seemed clear to him. He picked apart his father's character, he twisted it and turned it around in his head until it was unrecognisable. And afterwards he felt more knowledgeable, wiser and mature than his father was.

Why should he be punished for being happy? Surfing was the only thing that seemed to bring him that sense of joy, and his father told him he was a disgrace because of it. Suddenly he grew angry and resentful. Why should he feel shamed and embarrassed for what he loved?

The next day, once his mother and father had left for work, Jimmy snuck out of the house and rode down to the beach with his board. Jenno was already there, sitting on Ratty's bench.

"Fuckin'… Look who decided to show up!" said Jenno.

"Shut up." Jimmy laughed and sat down next to him.

"Your parents still angry?" asked Jenno.

"Yeah, I think so."

"Damn, you sure you wanna surf, then? I dunno, man, my mum's chill, but I don't wanna pressure you to surf if it's gonna get you into more trouble…"

"Nah, it's sweet. Surfing makes me happy, and that's all I wanna be at the minute."

…

They surfed for most of the day, and for a brief time, Jimmy forgot about everything that was going on.

He got home just before his parents returned from work. The school had given him work to complete while he was home. He filled out the sheets as quickly as he could in pencil, and made it look like he'd been working on them all day.

They sat around the dinner table in silence. His mother had made a lasagne.

The tense atmosphere was broken from time to time by the sound of cutlery hitting plates too hard, the odd shuffle of a chair or clearing of a throat.

Finally, his mum gave in. "How was your day?" she asked Jimmy's father.

"Good. We've got a new client and it looks like an easy case," he replied shortly.

"How about you, Jimmy?" she asked him.

"Yeah, good," said Jimmy. He didn't look up from his plate.

"Well, I'm almost finished painting the naked lady piece I've been working on," she said, trying to lift the mood. "Just a few more touches and then it'll be done. There's an art show coming up next month. I think I'm going to enlist it!"

"That's awesome, Mum…" said Jimmy, giving her a weak smile.

Then there was silence again.

Jimmy finished his plate and stood up to put it in the sink.

Before he had the chance, his father said, "Sit down. I want to speak to you once I'm finished."

Jimmy sat back down.

Once his mother was finished, she stood up and left the room.

His father poured himself a glass of wine from the bottle that was on the table. "This is what's going to happen now," he began. "On weekdays you're to go to school and come home. I'm enrolling you into night-study classes down at the youth centre. You'll do them every Tuesday, Wednesday and Thursday. Mondays and Fridays, you will work after school. Saturdays you can surf in the morning, but in the afternoons, you'll start working on the house with me. On Sundays, I want you volunteering."

Jimmy looked at him in shock. "What?"

"Don't question it. I've let things get out of hand. The way you're going you'll be lucky to even finish school, let alone do anything worthwhile with your life. I'm going to start what I should have a long time ago, and teach you discipline, respect and hard work."

"So, what – you have to finish school to be anything worthwhile in life?" said Jimmy.

"You have to finish school if you ever want to be a man who provides some kind of life for his family."

"Yeah, but at what cost?"

"What do you mean, at what cost?"

"Happiness…" said Jimmy, trying as best he could to stand strong against his father's gaze.

"Happiness?"

"Yeah," said Jimmy boldly, "I'm happy about who I am."

It was the most powerful thing he'd ever said in his whole life, but he didn't get the reaction he was looking for.

His father laughed to himself. It was a cold laugh, and every chuckle sliced into Jimmy bit by bit, exposing him for what he really felt like behind his feigned boldness: a scared boy.

"You're happy now. What do you have to be unhappy about? You're 17, living by the beach. In fact, you being unhappy is an insult to the rest of the world. Wait till you have a wife and a child. Wait till you have a mortgage, bills, food money, school fees, holiday money, money for your little toys and surfboards, money to keep her happy, money to keep me happy, money! Money! Money!… How are you going to be happy when you have no money because you were a dropkick at school and aren't hireable in the slightest?"

"Yeah. You have lots of money, are you happy?" said Jimmy, standing up in anger.

"Of course I'm happy," his father said.

"How come you never smile, or laugh?"

"You think that's what happiness is?" his dad said, suddenly growing serious. He lowered his voice, and Jimmy sat back down.

"What is it, then?"

His father put the wine glass to his lips and tilted his head back until all of it was gone.

Jimmy watched the wine slip quickly down his throat. His dad winced and put the glass back down on the table.

"I work like a dog, and my life isn't the least bit fun," he said, calmly and calculated, as if he'd been saying it in his head for years. "You think I like being stuck in an office all day? You think I like leaving to work in darkness and coming home in darkness? You think I like dealing with accountants, with bills and bills and more bills? You think I'd be happier if I just let all that go, sold everything and moved us all to the country?"

He unscrewed the bottle again and filled his glass until it was a quarter full. Jimmy could feel that he had more to say.

"I hate it all. I die a little more inside every time I put that fucking suit on and walk into that fucking office full of absolute fucks. You think I like that? I don't. But I'm happy because all of that means I can send you to a good school; I'm happy because you can surf, because you live near the ocean and I see how much joy that brings you. I'm happy because you have a roof over your head, because you have food to eat every meal, because you have every opportunity in the world. Even if my life isn't fun, and that is *my* sacrifice. That is the sacrifice of a *man*," he said, suddenly working himself up. "And even after all that – you may as well have spat it all back in my face! What? All because you want to surf a little bit more? That's all my sacrifice is worth to you? *Your* pleasure? *Your* happiness? Fuck you, then. You want to be like your mate Jenno and grow up to be a bum, then by all means do so. But not under my house, not with *my* money! And not after all of *my* sacrifice."

Jimmy was silent for a time while his father's words sank in.

"I'm sorry…" was all Jimmy managed.

Where before there had been vindictive confidence, now there was an equal mixture of shame, of anger and of sadness for himself and his youthful ignorance. In the face of all his father's anger there was love, and in that love Jimmy both hated and adored himself.

His father remained silent. Satisfied, he stood up, put his wine glass in the dishwasher and left the room.

Jimmy sat there alone for a time before he washed the dishes and went to bed.

Fleetwood woke up to her alarm. It was still dark outside, but the sun would be coming up in half an hour. It gave her enough time to silently get dressed, make herself a coffee and walk down to the beach.

She lifted Adriaan's arm from her shoulder, but before she had a chance to roll out he touched her back softly.

"Where are you going?" he said.

"You know where I'm going…"

"I know…" he said. "Sometimes I just wish you would stay."

She didn't respond, and rolled out of the bed.

Just before she left, she kissed Adriaan on the forehead. He rolled over and went back to sleep.

She got to the beach and sat in her usual spot. A minute or two after, the embers of the morning sun started to glow low in the horizon. She closed her eyes and breathed. She thought of Ratty. She focused her love towards the horizon and listened to the world around her – the crashing of the waves, the sounds of the birds calling out to one another – and in their noises, she tried to find Ratty within them. She opened her eyes. The reddish crown of the sun was materialising before her in waves of light that were bent and distorted by the sea. Her face glowed in the soft light.

Within a few minutes the sun had fully risen. The glory of its awakening golden light radiated and shimmered across the water and the sky, giving birth to a new day.

"I love you, my boy," she whispered solemnly.

She sat there in silence for almost an hour before she left and got a coffee, just as she did every morning.

Adriaan was waiting for her at the café.

"Good morning," he said, holding two coffees. There was something in his tone that she'd never heard before.

Scrunch was wagging her tail excitedly, and Fleetwood bent to scratch the underside of her chin before she took one of the coffees from Adriaan's outstretched hand.

"Thank you," she said, almost inquisitively at his tone.

"How was the sunrise?" he asked her.

"It was beautiful this morning. It looks like it's going to be a hot one today."

"Yeah, it does," he said.

There was a strange tension between them; Fleetwood could tell that Adriaan had something he wanted to say.

"Is everything ok?" she asked him.

"Yeah, everything's fine," he started, but a moment later he added, "we can talk about it later."

"Alright," said Fleetwood. She kissed him on the cheek and walked to the school.

At work, she wondered what the problem could be.

She walked Milly back home after school. Milly was walking on the curb with her arms outstretched for balance; Fleetwood held on to her hand in case she fell.

"How was your day, Milly?" asked Fleetwood.

"Good! We painted our houses this morning. I got it in my folder to give to Daddy," said Milly.

"I'm sure he'll love it! Can I see it?" Fleetwood asked her.

Milly stopped and took it out of her bag.

The painting was of a basic house, the outlines done in green and red. Out front of the house were four people, including a woman Fleetwood assumed could only have been Milly's mother, and also a woman painted dark brown but with green hair.

"Who is this?" laughed Fleetwood.

"That's you! We had to paint our families outside of our house!"

Something caught in Fleetwood's throat when she looked back at the little painting. *Our Family.*

All four of them were holding hands, and there were love hearts floating around them all.

"I love it, Milly!" she said, trying her best to stop her voice from shaking.

Milly beamed a gap-toothed smile at her and put the painting back in her bag.

Adriaan was just getting home from work when they reached his place.

Milly ran towards him and he lifted her up and hugged her.

"She's got something to show you in her bag!" said Fleetwood.

"Does she?" he said.

Milly showed him the painting. He looked at it, and then up at Fleetwood. His eyes were glazed and watery.

"That's really beautiful, Milly," he said, shakily.

He kissed Milly on the forehead before she ran inside and into the back garden to play on the trampoline.

Fleetwood could still feel tension between them.

"Thanks for dropping her home," said Adriaan, breaking the silence.

"No problem at all, I like doing it."

He smiled.

"Is everything ok?" asked Fleetwood.

"Yeah. It's fine. It's just—" He paused for a moment, collecting himself and carefully piecing together what he was trying to say. "I feel like you're blocking me out. I think you're amazing, and I want to be with you, and Milly loves you, I don't need to tell you that. But I always feel like I'm just someone who's there. I wake up alone every morning you stay over, and sometimes I wish we could connect deeper."

"You know why I can't be there in the morning," she said, defensively.

"I know. And I understand why. I'd never want to take something like that from you. But I think it's something that's keeping us from growing together. I hope you can forgive me for thinking so far ahead, but what if one day we want to go away on holiday? What if one day we decided to do something spontaneous and move countries, or pack everything up and drive around the country. I'm not asking you to let that go. But I just think in order for us to connect better you need to be willing to forgive yourself."

"Forgive myself?" said Fleetwood. Her heart was racing and blood was rushing to her head.

"Yes! Forgive yourself!" said Adriaan, suddenly invigorated to express what he'd been feeling for what felt like a long time. "What happened wasn't your fault! You can't live the rest of your life trapped here because of it. You have to let it go!"

"Let it go? How dare you!" she said.

Adriaan put his hands up defensively, and she realised that she was yelling.

"I'm not asking you to let your son go. I'm not asking you to move on. I would never ask something like that, nor would I ever expect you to agree. I'm just asking you, for me, and for Milly, to free yourself."

Fleetwood couldn't look at him any longer. She turned around and reached for the front gate.

"Please, Fleetwood! Don't go..." he said.

She didn't reply.

"Please! Don't go, Fleetwood. I love you..." he said. The words were so heavy they fell from his mouth. "I love you," he said again, more firmly this time.

Fleetwood stopped in her tracks, with her back facing towards him still.

It was the first time either of them had said it.

For just a moment, he thought she'd turn around, but she kept walking without looking back.

Adriaan watched her go, until she rounded the corner and disappeared.

...

Later that evening she was sitting in her living room listening to music.

She had shed a few tears, but not many, before she grew angry at herself for crying.

She walked to Ratty's room, opened the door and looked around. Everything was left just the way it had been that morning. One of the last bits of evidence left behind to her that he had really been alive.

The bed was left in a mess, and all around the room there were surf posters ripped straight from various surf magazines and stuck all around the walls unevenly with blue tack. Every now and then she pushed one up against the wall again, but most of them were stuck well.

A few of his old notebooks were left open on his table. She picked one up and read through it. They were all his old notes from his maths class. There was a drawing of a barrelling wave, a sword, a skateboard or something of that nature on every second or third page. His handwriting was shaky and messy. It was just like his father's.

She wondered if his father had heard the news. He must have; a few days after it had happened, she had phoned his sister to let her know.

"I'm sorry," was all his sister had been able to manage to say over the phone.

She had offered to take Fleetwood out for breakfast, but Fleetwood declined. She had needed space, but after weeks and months of cancelling breakfasts and not showing up to events, she had found herself alone. Until Adriaan.

She lay on Ratty's bed, and then all at once burst into tears. There was a knock on the front door. She stopped crying and wiped her eyes.

Wondering who it could be, she walked over to the door with her robe on and opened it.

It was Adriaan.

She looked at him for a moment in surprise.

"Fleetwood, I'm so sorry," he said, before she had a chance to say anything. His face was ghostly white. "I should never have said what I said. I couldn't imagine the pain of losing Milly. And I'd never want to stand in the way. I just wanted to say that I'm sorry."

"Come in," said Fleetwood, "Where's Milly?"

"The neighbours have her tonight, they have a little boy around her age and they sleep over every now and then," he replied.

He shuffled past her and she closed the door behind him.

The two of them sat in silence at the kitchen counter while the kettle boiled.

"I've only got herbal," said Fleetwood once the kettle clicked.

"I'll take anything," Adriaan replied.

Fleetwood grabbed two mugs and two bags of peppermint tea, and poured water into both.

She handed Adriaan's his carefully and he smiled.

Wind rustled through the trees outside and made the windows rattle; the first breaths of the storm that would come.

"What you said to me before – did you mean it?" Fleetwood asked.

"Yes, I meant it," he replied.

She took a sip from her mug.

"I love you, Fleetwood. The last year and a bit I've walked around so empty. If it wasn't for Milly I don't know where I would be. Since I met you it's like I suddenly feel alive again. After we met the first time, I was so excited. I haven't felt like that in so long. I counted down the hours before I got to bump into you at the café again, and every morning you didn't show I was scared at how disappointed I was. You make me want to live, Fleetwood. Of course I meant it." He looked at her desperately.

"I feel the same," she said, after what felt like an eternity.

He smiled, but her face didn't change expression.

"I'm sorry," she said.

He took her hand and held it between both of his. "There is nothing you have to be sorry for. I love you for being you. Every part of you."

"But you're right," she said. "It wasn't my fault. But mine is the guilt of a mother. My boy will never come back. And I have to accept that."

Adriaan was quiet.

Before she could fight them back, tears welled up in her eyes and trickled down her cheeks. Adriaan stood from his seat and held her. She sobbed into his chest, and before he could help himself he was tearing up too.

"I'm sorry, I'm so sorry," was all he could say.

The storm had finally arrived. The windows shook violently with every gust of wind, and in the darkness the silhouettes of trees stood bent and twisted by the elements.

Heavy rain fell, and thunder rumbled in the distance.

Fleetwood's living-room window looked like a small beacon of warm light from the darkness outside. A small refuge within the raging storm.

By morning the storm had come and gone. The air was sweet with moisture, and a layer of frost had coated the grass and the leaves.

Adriaan woke up to find Fleetwood sitting on the edge of the bed. He looked at his phone; the sun had risen already.

"You didn't go?" he said.

She turned around and smiled at him softly. "No."

He didn't know what to say; there was nothing he could have. He took her hand instead and kissed it softly.

21

It was Thursday afternoon when Jenno's dad walked through the door, almost two weeks after he'd left.

Jenno was sitting on the sofa. He stood up when he saw him. He looked at him for a moment, almost as though he was still trying to figure out whether what he saw was real or not.

"Where the fuck have you been, Dad?" asked Jenno.

"Whaddya mean?" he said angrily. "I been workin' and earnin' money for you and your mum, that's where I've fuckin' been!" He said it defensively, but then he saw the look on Jenno's face; it was one of desperation, not anger.

Suddenly he felt ashamed of himself. He walked over to the sofa and sat down next to where Jenno stood. "I had to go away after I saw that letter. I got a mate who needed some work done, so I left and did what I had to do."

"What, you couldn't have said bye or anything? You had mum crying, and I was worried for you..." said Jenno, sitting down next to him, but looking down at the floor.

"Gah..." his dad said, "don't worry 'bout your mum, I got a lot more on her than she's got on me. And don't worry about me, mate, I'll be right."

"What do you mean?"

He paused for a moment, but then thought better. "I'll tell you when you're older, mate."

He saw the worried look on Jenno's face.

"Look, Jenno, I just wanna tell you that I love you. And that I'm sorry. I just wanna see you do good in life. Better than your old man, that's for sure. I'm sorry I'm a fuckup of a father, and I'm sorry we gotta move away from the beach."

"You're not a fuckup of a father," said Jenno.

"Don't say that too soon…" his dad said, then winked.

"Where're we gonna move?" asked Jenno.

"Dunno yet. Might have to live with Auntie Marylyn for a bit on her farm."

"But that's out in the bush…"

"Yeah, mate. I know it's not ideal, but that's the only option we got at the minute…"

"But what am I gonna do for work? I was gonna do an apprenticeship with Jesse Costa's dad as a chippy."

"A chippy? What about school?"

"I got expelled…"

"What for?"

"The surf was pumping and no one was out, so Jimmy and I skipped the first class of the day and went out…"

"What? And they expelled you for that?"

"Yeah, pretty much."

"Fuckin' cunts… That's one thing you gotta learn about life real quick, Jenno. Nobody gives a fuck about you. So, if you wanna do something, then do it. Don't let anyone get in the way, cos they'll end up fuckin' you over anyway."

"Even you?" asked Jenno.

"Even me? What? You don't think I care about you?" he asked.

Jenno didn't reply.

"Of course I care about you! I couldn't imagine a world without you in it. You know, I never wanted a kid. Honestly, I would have been better off if I'd have just stayed single my whole life. But I wouldn't take it back. Having you gave me a meaning to my life. I'm sorry we gotta leave here, Jenno, I really am. But it's just temporary. And what? You and I can work on the farm for a bit. Just you and your old man. Your auntie's got a lot of work for us to do, could be a good bonding experience..."

"What does Mum think?" said Jenno.

"What do you reckon she thinks? Doesn't have a choice either way, unless she finally leaves me."

"When are we going, then?" asked Jenno.

"Monday week... Got it all sorted. With the money I made the last few weeks we can hire a van and move all our shit out on the weekend. Might take a few trips."

Jenno didn't say anything.

...

Later that afternoon he rode around the neighbourhood on his skateboard. He rode past the lagoon where he, Jimmy and Ratty used to play when they were little kids. Past the oval and over the little wooden bridge that he used to go to with his parents to feed the ducks. A melancholy feeling took hold of him, but within it was a deep sense of gratitude for everything that he had called home his entire life. It felt as though he was only looking at it all properly for the first time, like he'd never realised how beautiful it all was.

There was a feeling of fear inside him also, a fear that he'd change for the worse when they left. He imagined himself coming back and being different, and none of the boys liking him anymore. He was scared to be alone, and for everyone he'd grown up with to change together and leave him behind.

He had never been forced to change in his entire life. He'd lived in the same house, in the same bedroom, with the same neighbours in the same place for as long as he could remember.

He thought of Ratty too.

As the sun set he rode up the little pathway that followed the edge of the little stream towards the beach.

He rode to Ratty's bench and sat down.

The bench's dark green paint was beginning to peel and flake off, and the bronze plaque that had Ratty's name and life dates on it had lost its shine.

When Jenno got home later on, his dad was drawing at the kitchen table while his mum was cooking dinner; it was as though nothing had happened.

Without saying anything, he slipped past them and went to his room. He lay on his bed and looked up at the ceiling. The paint was peeling from there too. His carpet was covered in little stains; he could recollect the accidents that had caused most of them. All the spilled food, drink, paint, crayon, crushed debris, hair, skin, blood, sweat and tears over all the years that he had lived in the house. It was as though his entire body had been soaked into the carpets.

All throughout the house were little parts of his history, scraped, chipped and stained into the walls and the floors. But they never belonged to him in the first place. The walls, the floors and the ceilings were all borrowed. Rented from someone else who lived somewhere much nicer. And as soon as they left, the carpet would be ripped up and replaced, the walls would be fixed and repainted, and it would have been like they had never been there at all.

He thought of Jimmy's house. His family owned every inch of it. It was theirs to call home. But it was bare and perfect, almost as though no one lived there. The tiled floors repelled any stains, and they were cleaned up almost instantaneously anyway. There were rules in that house that did not permit anything to happen to the walls, or the ceilings and floors.

The deck next to the pool in Jimmy's backyard was stripped and lacquered every six months, and the walls were given fresh licks of paint every now and then. Everything was in a constant pristine condition. That wasn't so great either, Jenno reckoned, before he sat up on his bed, lost in thought.

...

Jimmy was in his room doing homework that his school had assigned him for his suspension.

His father sat in the living room reading with a glass of wine, while his mum was in the garden looking after her tomatoes. The tension had steadily eased as each day passed, and Jimmy looked forward to going back to school and getting on with things.

When Jenno called him and told him the news that they were leaving the following week, Jimmy was gutted.

"But what about your apprenticeship?" he asked.

"Dad reckons I should hold off on it for now. He said I can be a farmhand and help him out around the property for a while. I dunno, man, it's not permanent. As soon as I turn 18, I'm outta there."

"And surfing?"

Jenno was quiet for a moment on the other end of the line. Jimmy could picture him leaning his forehead against his bedroom wall. "Yeah… I guess not for a bit."

"Fuck, dude, why don't you stay at our place? We've got a few spare rooms you can have, and Mum and Dad will let you stay for sure." As he said it, he imagined his parents would have thought otherwise. Jimmy's parents had never taken a liking to either Jenno or Ratty, and the prospect of having him live under their roof rent-free wouldn't have sat well with them.

Jenno knew it as well, and declined.

"Nah, dude, it's sweet. I'm kinda looking forward to the change," he said, trying to convince himself just as much as Jimmy.

Jimmy knew he didn't mean it.

The idea of not having Jenno around was awful to him; it was as if all at once he'd realised how prominent a role Jenno played in his everyday life. A fear sat in his stomach; it was of being alone once Jenno had left.

...

A little over a week later, the final moving box was lifted into the back of the van Jenno's dad had rented.

Jimmy was there helping them, and while they moved the last few boxes out, he tried to soak in as much of the place as possible before he left for the last time. There was uncertainty, and the entire situation felt wrong to everyone, but Jenno and his family were left with little choice.

"Fuck, that's it!" said Jenno's dad once the last box had been moved.

The three of them took one last look around the house. It was empty now, back to its basic form. Soon the painters would be in, and it would look as though nobody had been there.

Jenno stood in the middle of his room and closed his eyes, soaking it in one last time.

"Are you sure you don't want to stay at mine?" said Jimmy when they were back out front of the house.

Jenno's dad was waiting in the van; he started it up and the whole thing rattled.

"Thanks man, but I'm good. Will be good to help my dad for a bit. I'm gonna get my driving licence soon anyways, so I'll start coming on weekends to surf. It won't be long…"

Jimmy smiled. "Sweet. I just can't believe you're going. It happened so quick."

"Yeah," Jenno replied. But before he had a chance to say anything more his dad leaned out of the truck window and yelled over the rattling, "Alright, wrap it up, boys! I gotta get this cunt of a truck on the highway before all the after-work traffic starts."

"Alright, I'll see you soon then," said Jimmy. They hugged goodbye briefly before Jenno jogged towards the truck and hopped in.

Jimmy stood and watched the truck drive down the road, until it disappeared around a corner.

He grabbed his skateboard and rode home. It felt like the end of something great. They said goodbye to one another just like they did every other day, neither of them fully realising it was the end to everything that had been.

With Jenno gone, the last ties of Jimmy's childhood were severed. Something felt different within him.

School was different; he drove to and from it alone. His weekends were different. He spent them mostly working, studying and surfing. He spoke less and listened more. He never appreciated just how big a part Jenno was in his life. He was more than a friend; it felt as though he were an extension of himself.

...

Jenno felt the same as Jimmy after he left. He and his dad worked the land at his auntie's place from dawn till dusk most days.

Digging, lifting, dragging, pulling, carrying, dropping; these are the motions that define life, and the ones that Jenno grappled with each day.

Two weeks had passed by of backbreaking labour. In the years after her husband's passing, Jenno's auntie had let the property go. It had been mostly reclaimed by weeds and vines, and Jenno and his dad had a hell of a time removing them all.

They'd been at it all day. The sun was starting to set over the distant hills and all the birds were flying home.

Jenno was panting. He was covered in dirt and grime, but he felt satisfied with the day's work. He sat down against the edge of the barn door and caught his breath. His dad sat down next to him, wiping the sweat from his brow.

The wind that had come down through the valley and whipped at their backs all day had finally eased into a light breeze that caressed their saturated bodies.

"You know, I never planned on this happening, Jenno," he said.

"I know," said Jenno.

"I'm sorry that it all happened like this, that you've gotta be away from the water. I dunno, I was never good at puttin' my emotions into words, I reckon that's

why I gotta draw. All I'm trying to say is that I'm sorry –
none of this was part of the plan."

He put his hand on Jenno's shoulder and squeezed
it.

"I understand," said Jenno, looking up.

A flock of birds flew over them in formation,
crying out to one another amongst the final plumes of
golden light from the sunset.

"I'm sorry for everything too," began Jenno.

His dad raised an eyebrow.

"I'm sorry for you, that your life didn't go how
you planned it, and I'm sorry for my part in it all," said
Jenno.

"What are you talkin' about? You got nothin' to
say sorry for, Jenno!" Jenno's dad began, but Jenno
wasn't finished.

"I know. But If I had never come into your life
you would have been free. All I'm trying to say is that I
understand in a way. It mustn't be easy to have to throw
everything you imagined for yourself away."

His dad was silent for a moment, taken aback.

"I forgive you, Dad, and I'm thankful for
everything you've done for me despite it all," said Jenno.

Bats took to the sky in the final moments of a
waning sunset.

Nothing else was said between them. When night
had fallen, they stood up and got clean before they went
inside for dinner.

It was one of the last proper moments they were
to share with one another for many years.

22

Months went by on the farm, and it seemed crazy to Jenno that he hadn't seen the ocean in so long. His hair was no longer its usual shade of sun-bleached blond, but a dark brown that looked as though the light had been sucked out of it. He'd taken to farm work. He learned to love the wide open countryside, the rolling hills and chilly winds, the ceaseless sounds of wildlife and the smell of dirt and vegetation. His old surf brand clothes had become too filthy to wear, so now he dressed in flannels and thick jeans. He'd almost forgotten what surfing felt like. The floating, the rush, the spray and the deep, rolling drum of crashing waves. Every time the wind sliced through the valley, or a deep, rolling thunderstorm passed through, he closed his eyes and imagined he that he was standing on the shore, listening to the waves crash out to sea. Sometimes, when he was finished with work for the day, he'd sit next to the creek and watch the water bubble and spit against the stones, and imagine what it would be like if he were the size of an ant, so that maybe then he could surf the little bit of white water that gurgled and folded against the creek bed.

On cold nights, he sat by the fire in the backyard and watched the flames dance and lick at the wood. When the stars were out, he'd lie on his back and count them in silence, and wonder if, somewhere out in the vastness of the universe, there was another life form that had experienced the pure joy of surfing.

...

It was an exciting day, because it was the day that Jenno and his mum were making the long drive back to town to go and visit his grandparents for a week. When Jenno and his parents had left, Jenno had begged his grandad to make some room in his workshop for his surfboard and wetsuit, so that he could use them when he came to visit.

It was a 12-hour car ride to the coast, across endless expanses of wheatfields, salt planes and river passings, until they finally made it to the outskirts of town. They were atop the hill that bordered the area, and now, for the first time in what felt like forever, Jenno was looking out across the ocean in the distance. The sliver of it he could see from the hill looked like a thin, turquoise line on the horizon – if it were just a few shades lighter it would have been lost within the sky.

Jenno almost pressed his cheek against the glass to look at it, before his mum lowered the window, smiling. All at once, the thick and salty smell of sea breeze flooded the car, which made Jenno almost salivate.

"We're home, Jenno!" she said, squeezing his shoulder.

Jenno felt light, as if he were already floating in water.

They were home, but some changes were apparent already in the relatively short time he'd been away. When they drove through the main strip of the town, the first thing he noticed was that the local chip shop had shut down. Stuck against the windows were advertisements for the new pilates studio that would take its place.

"Farrk… I never got to have one last deep-fried Mars bar!" said Jenno in dismay as they drove slowly by.

After they'd arrived, and Jenno's grandmother had finally tired herself out kissing him, he found the first excuse possible to grab his board and run to the beach.

He found Jimmy waiting on Ratty's bench for him when he got there. Jimmy was watching the waves quietly, with his arms folded and his legs stuck out. He looked the same as he always had, except for the pathetic excuse for a moustache that was resting on his upper lip. His surfboard was lying face down on the grass behind the bench.

He looked up when Jenno's shadow lay in front of him, and grinned widely.

"What happened to your hair?" he laughed.

"Been fuckin 'workin', that's what happened. Unlike you," said Jenno.

He sat down next to Jimmy, and stared out over the water. The waves were small, but fun-looking, and not many people were out. Jenno didn't care, it was already surreal enough to finally be sitting on Ratty's bench again. He peered out and searched the horizon. Every now and then his eyes would rest momentarily on a sailboat, or a cargo ship far out in the distance. A set of waves crashed loudly; he let the sound wash over him for the first time in what felt like an eternity.

"What's been doing?" he asked Jimmy, after some time.

"Not that much. Dad's been making me study loads, it's been alright though."

"Yeah? Did you get into maths?"

"Sorta. I didn't get in initially, but then Dad had a meeting with Mr. Pollard and Principal Rose to tell them I'd had a hard time ever since Ratty passed away, and to give me another chance," said Jimmy.

"Mr. Pollard?" began Jenno, "That ballsack of a human being. What did he say?"

"He said no, but Principal Rose convinced him to change his mind."

"Fuck yeah." Jenno laughed.

"You should have seen his face, he looked like he was about to explode." Jimmy laughed too.

"I bet it would have killed him inside to let you go through…" said Jenno.

"Did you come back with your mum and dad?" asked Jimmy.

"Mum's back at my grandparents' place, I dunno where Dad is. He disappeared a few months back, kept talking about submitting all his art into this competition in Sydney and I haven't seen him since. I reckon that's the last we'll hear from him for a long time."

"I'm sorry," said Jimmy. He put his hand on Jenno's shoulder.

"Nah, it's alright. He did what he did, I can't blame him. Mum and I are doing good, that's all I care about. We're gonna stay on the farm for a little while longer and save some money."

"You reckon you'll ever be able to move back here?" Jimmy asked.

"I hope so, but I dunno. Mum reckons the rent is too high now. I reckon she's right too, look at it all. Everything's gone. We drove past the chip shop on the way here and even that's shut down…"

"Yeah," began Jimmy, "pretty heavy, that closed down the other month. I saw them on the last day and they told me that the landlord upped the price way too high for them to justify holding on to the place. They figured he wanted them out of there anyways. He owns that whole row of shops. Look at what the others became – they're all designer clothes places, or salons, besides the bakery, but I reckon even that'll go soon too."

"It's sad, dude. All those memories gone. In a few years' time it'll be like we were never here at all."

"Don't talk like that, Jenno. You're making me depressed," said Jimmy.

"Sorry," said Jenno." It's more than all of that, anyways. All those things will go, just like my old house. You reckon the people who live there now care that it was the place I grew up in? I don't reckon so. Nah, it's more than that, it's the beach and the ocean I think about when I'm away, and they can't set up a yoga studio on that."

"I guess you're right," said Jimmy.

A moment later, Fleetwood, Adriaan and Milly walked by. Fleetwood stopped and smiled when she saw them.

"My boys, together as always," she said.

"Fleetwood," said Jenno, "What are you guys up to?"

Fleetwood pointed to a campervan parked a few spaces up from the bench." We're about to set off."

Jimmy and Jenno looked over their shoulders in unison.

"Where are you off to?" asked Jimmy.

"We're going to Byron for a week. This is just a little test trip for what's to come – eventually we're going to drive across the whole of Australia," said Adriaan.

"That's sick," said Jenno, "I'm glad to hear that."

"Talk to Ratty for me," Fleetwood said, "while I'm gone…"

She looked at Jenno, who met her gaze momentarily before bowing his head.

They climbed into the campervan and honked as they drove away, and Jimmy and Jenno waved after them. Fleetwood waved back, but she was looking past them.

"I'm happy for her," said Jenno. "Must have taken her a lot to wanna leave. I don't reckon she's missed a sunrise yet."

"Yeah, must have been a big decision for her. The beach isn't going anywhere, I guess," said Jimmy.

"Yeah, and speaking of," said Jenno, pointing towards a little wave that'd just started barrelling.

They grabbed their boards and ran down towards the water, laughing as they went. Ratty's bench stood under the high sun, and the tarnished plaque shone dully in the light.

Each one of them, in their own ways, found themselves back sitting on Ratty's bench periodically throughout their lives. It was the only remainder of who they were before. Of what was lost, and gained along the way. Of their pain and joy and bittersweet memories. Of grief and sadness, of insecurity and anger, of quietness, understanding and the sweet tears that make life beautiful and worth living.

The End

Thank you for reading.

YOUTH

E.S. Higgins